"A WILD RIDE …

It draws you in …

the suspense builds and builds …

until you scream for more …

AN INCREDIBLE FIRST NOVEL, AND HOPEFULLY NOT THE LAST!"

- Don Piccoli

Published by Hogg Valley Press
www.roszell.ca
email: *hoggvalleypress@roszell.ca*

This book is a work of fiction. Names, characters, places and incidents are either products of the author's imagination or are used fictitiously. Any resemblance to actual events, locales or persons, living or dead, is entirely coincidental.

Printed in the United States of America

ISBN   0986749605

The
Golden Reckoning

Reckoning:
1. *the act or an instance of reckoning; as an account or bill*
2. *a settling of accounts*
3. *a summing up*
4. *to take into account or deal with*

Dexter Snell inherits a fortune and squanders it on an extravagant, obscene lifestyle in Key West. When he attempts to rebuild his life in a simpler, gentler fashion in a primitive stone cottage on the Caribbean island of Cayman Brac he is swept up in a vendetta that began 67 years ago.

The Golden Reckoning is the gripping story of Dexter's search for love, truth and the secret that will clear his father's name and avenge his horrible death. It rolls through the Caribbean like a hurricane, from the dark world of the Colombian cocaine cartels back to Key West, and changes Dexter Snell forever.

Dedicated to Sylvia, sweet Sylvia,

and Chris and John

THE

GOLDEN

RECKONING

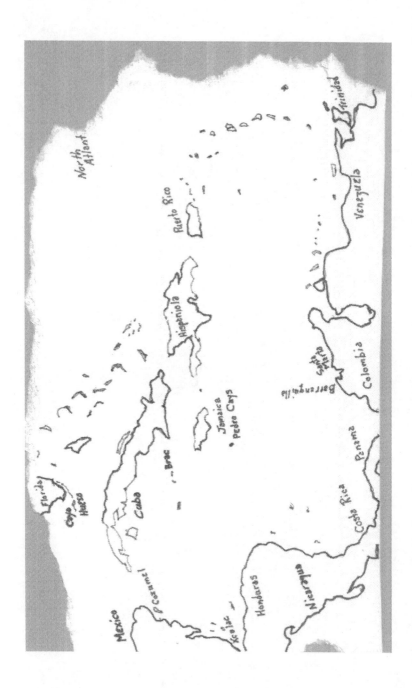

1 Key West: 2004. October 30

He was small and wiry, and dressed like a street bum. He could have been any of those who eke out a living in Key West by scrubbing the boats of the idle rich or working at other odd jobs around the harbor.

"Got a light?" he asked.

"Sure," I answered, taking a good look at him.

"Got a cigarette, too?"

I pulled the smokes from my pocket and shook one out. He dropped his bag to the ground beside mine and leaning forward, put the cigarette in his mouth and cupped his hands around the end of it. His weather-beaten face showed more clearly in the flickering light of the match.

"Is everything there?" I asked.

"Mister," he said, "I'm doing this for a friend. A close friend. I already got paid and whatever's in that bag was in it when I took the money. I didn't look, and I don't want to know."

He picked up my seabag and headed toward the harbor. I turned back to the Gulf, waiting a few minutes before flicking my cigarette into the water and picking up the bag he'd left behind. I casually wandered up Duvall Street toward the hotel.

I was counting on the darkness and the nature of the annual Fantasy Fest as much as on the change in my appearance over the last year to avoid being recognized. The loss of fifteen pounds had little effect compared to the change in my physique due to the new layer of hard-earned muscle. Gone were the long hair and beard and the wasted look in my eyes and face. My hair was quite short now, not much more than stubble, and the sun had stolen most of the color; the same sun that had darkened my skin. It was a darkness that couldn't be confused with the tan that spells long hours on a golf course or lying by a pool, but the deep, underlying hue that comes only from day after day of hard labor in ocean-reflected sunlight. It was a darkness that contrasted sharply with the still-pink scar over my right eye. And it was a darkness that matched the malice I held for the man I'd come to kill.

The party flowed out of the bars and fully onto the street, the typical mix of Fantasy Fest participants roughly grouped into those in costumes and those who were there to watch those in costumes. Most were high on something; alcohol, drugs or both. Mood altering substances were in plentiful supply; inhibitions were not. A year ago I was the host with the most and what amused me then served as little more than cover for me now.

I wouldn't have noticed them if the blond hadn't run right into me. She and the brunette were laughing, chased by a big guy in a biker costume. They were young, nineteen or early twenties, and he looked to be about forty. The blond stopped laughing as he grabbed her by the arm, and I realized his biker outfit wasn't a costume.

Twelve months ago I would have walked on.

"Let her go." I slung my bag over my shoulder, behind my back where it was safe.

"Fuck off," he spat.

If appearances alone could intimidate, the biker would have been the clear winner but he saw something in me that perhaps even I didn't recognize; killing two men will do that. He stared at me eye to eye and then moved on, cursing me under his foul-smelling breath.

The girls withered a little under my stare and their defiant looks took on a trace of doubt. Just a trace, and momentary at that. I shook my head and walked on but didn't get far when the blond darted around in front of me.

"Wait," she said. "Thanks, but we were okay."

"Right little girl. Don't tease big bad men. They bite."

"We're not little girls, mister," chimed in the brunette, "and if anybody bites, we do."

These weren't innocents out to play on the edge. Attractive in a blatant, animalistic way, both had wide, sensuous mouths and a knowing look about them that guaranteed they'd be as hard as nails in a few more years. Curiously, their chains, bracelets and earrings weren't costume pieces; they were real. Wanton little rich girls. Tough, wanton little rich girls. Their eyes glittered with the effect of whatever chemical was de rigueur now. I stepped on past them without saying any more and made my way around to the service entrance at the back of the hotel.

The staff was far too busy to pay any attention as I went through to the service elevator and none of them would have recognized me anyway. I used to own this hotel, but I'd never spent any time in it. I stepped into the elevator and punched the button for the top floor, checking inside the bag on the way up and taking out the key to the suite.

It must have been close to 3:00 a.m. when the tension and stress of the last weeks – hell, months – gave way to exhaustion and I collapsed into a troubled sleep.

II

The droning sound flirted with the edges of my subconscious until it gained a foothold, insinuating itself into the background of my dream. As irritating as the sound was, the dream was still foremost in my mind, a cacophony of screams, cries and pleadings stronger than the droning. Then the shrill ring of the telephone accomplished what the droning of the alarm clock alone couldn't. I jolted fully awake.

Silencing the alarm was easy. A sweep of my right arm knocked the clock to the floor as I jumped up and started across the suite to the phone. The phone scared me.

It was well past noon. I grabbed the handset, shoved the French doors open and stepped out onto the balcony. My stark nakedness didn't even cross my mind. This was, after all, Key West.

I punched the answer button as I looked down on Duvall Street. The evidence of the previous night's drunken debauchery was gone, the street made ready for the next onslaught of transient, moneyed people. And money, more than anything, is what Key West has always been about. Scratch the skin of Key West and the city bleeds money. Scratch deep enough and you'll find the dirty money. It motivates some and contributes to the ruin of others.

"Yeah" I said into the telephone, still looking down at the street and trying to quell the anxiety that threatened to overwhelm me.

"You're here," came the slow reply.

It was a man's voice, one I recognized immediately. One long year since I'd heard that voice over anything but long distance, and the fact it was a local call unsettled me. The fact there was any call at all unsettled me. I was supposed to be dead, and this man knew it.

"Yes, I'm here. I came in last night."

A deep throated, menacing, controlled rumble that passed as a laugh came over the phone. I used to find it amusing when other people heard it for the first time and mistook it for something else. It didn't sound like a laugh to me anymore either.

"I didn't fall for that death thing and nobody sneaks into Key West without me findin' out. Last night made sense - nice touch."

"The room is registered under another name. How did you find me?"

"You kiddin'? Fact is I knew you were here before you even went to the hotel. That's one reason we got along so well, remember?"

Remember? How could I forget? Well over six feet tall and blacker than the ace of spades, Shando was many things. But forgotten was not one of them. He knew, or knew somebody who knew, everything that went on from Miami to Key West. And the closer you got to Key West, the more personally knowledgeable he became. Drugs, sex, gambling, smuggling, payoffs and bribes – the underside of Key West – were an open book to Shando. I kicked myself for believing I could surprise him.

"Yes, I remember," I said, hoping I sounded more confident than I felt, "and I knew you'd find me, but not this quickly. I need to see you later tonight."

There was no hesitation, and no change in his voice.

"11:30 – use the back stairs," and then he hung up. I knew where, without being told.

I took another quick look down Duvall toward the pier, and as I turned to go back into the suite I saw the couple on the balcony next door. They were watching me in that sly way people do when they don't want you to know they're watching. Pretending they're looking at something past you, something off in the distance. I turned fully toward them, smiled and said 'hi' while I casually scratched my balls with the telephone handset. I heard the woman's shocked intake of breath and the sharp crack of her coffee cup smashing on the concrete of the balcony floor as I turned back and went inside.

2.   Dexter Snell: 1975

I read somewhere that of the five senses, the sense of smell is most closely related to memory. For me, it's the combined smells of the sea of my childhood. Diesel fumes and fresh, raw shrimp.

My earliest memories are of being aboard the *Estrela de Marques*, balanced on the hip of either my father or my Uncle Patricio and held by one strong arm while they steered the *Estrela* with the other. The smell of the shrimp in the hold, the diesel fumes in a following wind and the ever-present overlay of the tang of salt water fade into the background after weeks at sea, but the first whiff of that combination after any prolonged period ashore evokes immediate, powerful memories and feelings. The strongest is the sense of the security I felt while being held by one of them.

The *Estrela*, along with the little stone cottage on Cayman Brac, was my first home. The first six years of my life alternated between time spent aboard her, always in the company of my father and frequently with my uncle, and with sojourns on Brac. *Estrela* was not only my home, but my school, too.

"Take over, Dex, and hold her steady on," ordered Uncle Patricio, kicking the battered wooden crate over to the helm so that I could step up and see the compass and beyond through the windows of the curved wheelhouse. I was only six years old, but knew what to do. It was in my blood. A quick look at the compass fixed the bearing in my mind as I took the smooth, sweat-stained spokes of the oak wheel in my small hands. Patricio stood behind, watching me while he pulled the battered old tin from his pocket and rolled a cigarette. The shrimp net was out, and school was in.

"Forty-five minutes, Dex. Check the clock." I glanced at the old wind-up clock screwed to the ledge that ran around the base of the windows in front of the helm, and marked the time.

"Why forty-five minutes, Dex?"

I knew the answer by rote. "Because our mother of the sea provides us with what we need, uncle, and she doesn't like waste. We seek only the shrimp and the crabs. The turtles that get caught along with them will drown unless we pull the net every forty-five minutes and set them free." His silence was pleasing to me; it was, as a rule, all the praise that he gave.

"Today we'll keep the eels and rays as well, Dex. There is a market for them in Cayo Hueso. Where are we right now?"

I looked again at the clock and the compass, and did a quick calculation. "I think we're about sixty-five miles west of Key West." I used the modern name of the westernmost key, originally christened Cayo Hueso by its discoverer Ponce de Leon. The correct, literal translation was Bone Key, but the name had been bastardized in the transition from Spanish territory to American in the early 1800's.

"Do you think, Dex, or do you know? You must always *know* where you are at sea. If a storm comes up you must know not only where you are, but where the reefs lie. And what direction to steer for the nearest harbor."

I looked at the barometer fastened to the bulkhead behind me. It was holding steady at 29.24 inches; there were no signs of a storm on the horizon.

"Yes, uncle, Key West is sixty-two miles east, northeast. I would steer 82 on the compass."

Forty-five minutes had passed, and Uncle Patricio went out the port side door and made his way back to the work deck where my father and the other striker were preparing to winch the net aboard. I throttled the *Estrela* back to a crawl, and held her steady while I waited for my father to come forward.

Father and uncle took turns in the wheelhouse with me. Normally, there is one skipper and two strikers, or deckhands, aboard a shrimp boat the size of the *Estrela*. It was a treat to have Uncle Patricio with us. Our time together was less frequent as my father and uncle continuously added to their fleet of shrimp boats while relentlessly growing and improving their processing and distribution business. They had over fifty boats now spread all over the Caribbean and Gulf of Mexico, all identified with the name Marques. Uncle Patricio, the rare times when he fished now, was usually aboard the *Sol de Marques,* one of three sister ships identical to the *Estrela*. The other boats, mostly larger and more modern than the sixty-foot *Estrela* and *Sol*, were skippered and crewed only by trusted Portuguese and Cayman Islanders.

II

Uncle Patricio wasn't really my uncle, but he and my father were all the family I had. My mother died, stolen from me even as she gave me life, and it wasn't until my father returned to Cayman Brac the week after my birth that I was first held in the arms of a blood relative.

Despite the fact that my father had lovingly rebuilt the ancient stone cottage with his own two hands and improved it every year according to my mother's wishes, it and I were not enough to hold him ashore. He stayed only three weeks before the irresistible urge pulled him back to the sea. I was left in the care of a wet nurse, a solid Cayman woman who had given birth to her own son only the week before my father returned to his first love. For the next seven years I would alternate between five months at sea with my father and Uncle Patricio and six months on Cayman Brac with my adopted family. Those six months were punctuated with periodic visits from my father; visits that were always too short, spent in the little stone cottage listening spellbound the entire time to his tales of the sea – fishing and the history of the Caribbean. To father, history was centered around the time of the Spanish plate fleets and the famous pirates who preyed on them. I never questioned any of his tales, and it wasn't until years later that I realized how much he knew.

The other four weeks a year I spent in Brunswick, Georgia, in the midst of the dwindling Portuguese fishing community where Patricio Marques was an important man.

The Portuguese had immigrated to the Brunswick area in the early 1900's. From a seafaring nation, the Portuguese knew a good thing when they saw it and the first immigrants sent word back to their families that they had discovered a fisherman's paradise. Consequently, Uncle Patricio arrived in 1923 and immediately found work as a seventeen year-old striker. His single-minded determination and good luck as a fisherman ensured he was never without work.

I'm not sure how or why, but my father, Jebediah Snell, met up with Patricio in 1934. Twenty-eight at the time, twice my father's age, Patricio took an immediate liking to him. Neither dreamed that it was the beginning of an improbable partnership that would last for over fifty years, and make both of them rich men.

For the four weeks a year I spent with Uncle Patricio's family in Brunswick, I was in the care of Aunt Izabel. I spent my days down at the docks around the fish house watching for the return of the *Estrela* or the *Sol*, and then begging to be taken with them when they returned to sea. Some unspoken agreement between the men and Aunt Izabel precluded this; she had me in her grasp for those four weeks every year. I suppose she was trying to civilize me, or at least counter the forces that had made my father a captive of the sea.

III

"Where are you, Dex?" asked my father as he entered the wheelhouse, breaking my reverie.

"Sixty-two miles west, southwest of Key West, father," I answered instantly.

"No, silly one. I know where we are. Where were you?" he asked, laughing. "Dreaming of girls, I suppose." He tousled the long curls at the back of my head and lifted me down from the box. "I'll take the wheel. Go back and see what we've caught. But stay out of the way."

I ran out of the wheelhouse and scooted back to the work deck. Uncle Patricio had engaged the winch, and the shrimp doors and the mouth of the net were already aboard. The shrimp doors always fascinated me. They didn't really look like doors. They looked more like wooden slabs, heavy and with a leading edge of steel. They were awkward out of the water, and I was still unsure how the whole apparatus worked.

"See the doors, Dex?" asked Patricio, "do you understand how they keep the mouth of the net open when we are dragging for shrimp?"

Although I was far more certain how to navigate and steer the boat, I didn't want to appear stupid. Such is the power of learning by rote that I could spiel off an explanation without truly understanding it.

"The doors are fastened to the opening of the net, Uncle. And then they are hooked to the harness that is attached to the tow line." I looked to Uncle Patricio for his approval, and taking his silence for positive encouragement, I plunged on. "The doors sink the net to the bottom, and when the boat pulls forward on the harness the doors are dragged flat along the bottom of the sea. The top of the net has floats on it to hold it open, from top to bottom." Still hearing nothing from Patricio, I continued. "The doors themselves are fastened to the harness so that when they are pulled, they move away from each other as far as the chain connecting them together will let them. This opens the net from side to side, and the chain keeps the doors from pulling the net apart?"

Uncle Patricio must have heard the question in my voice, indicating that I wasn't sure, and he either ignored it or decided to give me the benefit of the doubt. Either way, I was pleased with myself. I added one further comment, again parroting what my father and uncle had told me many times. "The net and rigging is the most important part of the boat, uncle. Without it, the boat is just a boat."

The net is long, and not all of it gets hauled in. Once the doors are aboard, the line called the purse string is pulled tight, pinching the net closed toward the far end where the catch is, and the resulting 'bag' is hauled aboard, still using the purse string. The long middle section of the net stays in the water. The end of the 'bag' is then opened, letting the catch spill out onto the deck for sorting. Before sorting starts, the end of the net is closed again, the purse string released and the whole contraption including the doors is lowered to start another drag.

I was itching to help sort the catch. "Can I help now, uncle?"

"In a minute, Dex. Stay here until I call you. It wouldn't do to have you bitten by a shark now, would it?" Patricio always said the same thing, although I could see that there were no sharks in this catch.

The seagulls were screaming and swooping just over the deck of the *Estrela*. They would fight over the trash fish discarded overboard, and I cursed them in the same way I heard the strikers on the other boats curse them. It felt good to know that I was using this language with impunity out of the reach of Aunt Izabel.

"Come, Dex," called my uncle, "and tell me what you see."

I ran back on the deck, careful to avoid slipping on the wet surface and falling into the hold which was almost full with the previous catches and the ice which kept it all fresh until we made port.

It was the turtles I always looked for first, and Patricio and the striker were easing one into a sling attached to a boom to lower it back over the side. It was much bigger and heavier than me, about two hundred and fifty pounds I would guess. The turtles don't have the right muscles to allow them to maneuver easily out of the water, and simply dropping them over the side would kill them. I will never forget the gentle way Patricio and my father handled the turtles unfortunate – or I suppose fortunate – enough to be caught in the net of the *Estrela*. Other fishermen, and particularly those on the much larger, modern shrimp boats, dragged their nets for longer than forty-five minutes, and any turtles trapped in them drowned before they could be released alive.

I watched the turtle being lowered to the water and swim away.

"Always give back to the mother of the sea what you can't eat or sell, Dex, and she will be kind to you in return."

I helped sort the catch, putting the shrimp into the baskets and the crabs in a drum. Then we packed the baskets and drums full of ice and lowered them into the hold with a few minutes to spare before we pulled the net again.

We made one more haul before pulling the net aboard for the last time, inspecting it for holes and stowing it carefully. I was asleep in the cabin behind the wheelhouse before Uncle Patricio swung the bow toward Key West.

IV

The Portuguese fleets used to fish all the way from Brunswick, Georgia down and around Florida, then along the coasts of Alabama and Louisiana to Texas. Shrimp boats were becoming less migratory, but father and Uncle Patricio still made the annual expedition aboard the *Estrela*, inspecting their other boats and processing facilities along the way. I loved this trip, but I would never make it aboard the *Estrela* again. Aunt Izabel was waiting for us in Key West, and she took me back to Brunswick to start school. It was 1975. It would be another fourteen years before I next set foot in Cayo Hueso, and I would arrive not on a shrimp boat, but aboard my own jet.

3 Key West: 2003. October 29

We were running down the Hawk Channel from Miami to Key West. It was rough, and the fact that we were behind schedule due to my dalliance with a model I'd met in a club the night before did little to assuage my annoyance. The constant satellite calls to *Party Girl* from my ancient Uncle Patricio didn't help either. I ignored the calls.

Uncle Patricio knew I would come to see him in the next week or so, as I did every year. And once again I'd sit through his low-keyed, soft-spoken lecture on my spending habits, drawing veiled allusions to how hard my father had worked to accumulate the assets that financed what he called my 'extravagant, obscene' lifestyle. The odd part this time was the repetitiveness of his calls. He usually called only once, and then waited for me to come to him.

The *Party Girl* was my floating castle. At a hundred and fifty-two feet she was considered a megayacht; not the largest private yacht in Florida, but she certainly attracted attention. *Party Girl* was an ocean-going event with a reputation that fit her name. I usually kept her in Miami and used her as my base there. It was a short hop from Key West on the Bell 206 helicopter, and I probably should have just taken the chopper back this time and had the captain and crew bring *Party Girl* down.

We were less than an hour out of Key West, and as soon as the captain secured an anchorage the launch would take my guests ashore. I still hadn't decided whether or not to go to my house on Caroline Street, but I knew that I wanted everyone except the crew off of the *Party Girl.*

Although I didn't recognize it as such, I had an unfamiliar sense of foreboding. With enough money to do as I wanted, when I wanted, I really didn't have a care in the world. Maybe it was the repeated calls from Patricio. I tried to put those out of my mind, unsuccessfully.

I showered and dressed in the master cabin, which was in fact more like a luxury suite at the Four Seasons. Crossing the darkened salon on my way up to the bridge I was still deep in thought about Uncle Patricio's calls when she spoke.

"How long until we dock?"

I was caught by surprise, and spun around. "We'll make anchorage in about forty-five minutes. I'm heading up to the bridge now."

"Forty-five minutes," she said. "Everyone's in their cabins getting ready to hit the town. We have time for some fun. You won't regret it," she smiled, moving across the salon toward me. She was opening her blouse, exposing her tanned breasts and small but swollen nipples. "Assuming that you're man enough."

She was older than me, late thirties I'd guessed when she'd come aboard last night with the hangers-on from South Beach. She differed from the others in the group; not just in her age but in the way she dressed and the way she carried herself. She was confident in the way that money breeds confidence. And she was alone, which was odd. All I really knew about her was that her name was Mirtha Cardeli, which meant nothing to me.

"I'm man enough," I said, as she pressed herself against me and rubbed my cock through my chinos. "The question is, are you woman enough? You're a few years past the girl stage."

She took one step back and slapped me, hard. I hadn't seen it coming. My eyes watered as she stood glaring at me, her hands on her hips, legs apart and those hard nipples pointing straight at me. I slapped her back, harder, with enough force to drop her to her knees.

She had real fire in her eyes now, and came back at me quickly. But instead of hitting me, she grabbed me by the back of my head and pulled my face down to hers. She moaned deep in her throat as she crushed her lips to mine, forcing my mouth open with her thrusting tongue.

I shoved my hand up under her skirt and found that she was soaked. Her hips thrust involuntarily against my fingers; I could tell she was already close to orgasm. I grabbed her hair with my other hand and jerked her head back, only causing her to groan louder.

Some women are turned on by money. I have no trouble finding those; they find me. Others are turned on by speed, heights, fear, drugs, danger – even scents and sounds. The list seems endless, and if anything consumed huge amounts of my time and attention, it was discovering and exploring the perverse things that excite certain females sexually. I'd even heard that some women are turned on by love. I hadn't experienced that yet. But then, I hadn't spent much time looking.

And some women crave pain – the skillfully applied sting of a slap, spanking or even a whip.

"So you like it rough, do you?"

"Shut up and hit me again. Then fuck me," she panted.

I forgot about Uncle Patricio.

4   Patricio and Jebediah

The morning of July 1, 1934 was a watershed not only for Key West, which declared bankruptcy and threw itself on the mercy of the state of Florida, but for a fourteen year-old boy who was thrown to the mercy of the sea.

The yelling and cursing from the decrepit, soot-stained package steamer departing from the Mallory docks attracted the attention of all those within earshot, and particularly that of the captain of the shrimper *Flor de Marques*.

Two members of the steamer's crew were wrestling with a struggling boy, who was the source of the noise. They had him by the arms and legs and were hauling him across the deck to the port rail. Despite being outnumbered and grossly mismatched in terms of size, the boy was putting up a hell of a fight. He managed to break free for an instant, but was quickly recaptured with the assistance of a third crewmember. The three men wrestled him back to the rail, hoisted him up and unceremoniously dumped him, still cursing, over the side. The cursing abruptly ceased with the sound of the splash, and he sank below the surface of the water. He reappeared, coughing and sputtering, just in time to see his satchel hit the water ten feet away. He swam over to retrieve it and then struck out for the docks. He was a strong swimmer and since there would not be the excitement of witnessing a drowning, everyone returned to whatever they had been doing; everyone except the captain of the *Flor de Marques*.

The boy headed directly toward the *Flor*, that being the boat docked closest to the end of the pier. The captain made his way to the lowest point at the stern of his boat and hooked him by the collar as he swam by, swinging him up and onto the deck. The boy clutched his satchel to his chest and stared at the captain with cold, steel-blue eyes.

"You aren't going to thank me?" asked the captain.

"For what?" he answered defiantly. "I was almost at the dock. I could have gotten up by myself."

The captain laughed. "I saw that you required assistance getting into the water, so I thought you might need a hand getting back out."

"I don't need help from anybody, particularly to get aboard a stinking shrimper. I just need a job, and I'll get one on a real boat."

The captain looked at him more closely. He guessed he was about fourteen or fifteen, but tall for his age. His skinny body belied the courage and strength he had shown struggling with the three larger men minutes before. The captain only thought about it for a second, and later couldn't figure out why he said what he said next.

"This stinking shrimper is short a striker. Ever worked a fishing boat?"

"No, but it can't be that hard to drag a net around and then empty it."

The captain laughed again. "There is a little more to it than that," he said, looking at him speculatively. "Not a thief, are you?"

The boy glared back at him. "No, I'm not a thief. I'm a man. You aren't a buggerer, are you?" he sneered.

So that was it. The boy had been tossed from the steamer for resisting the advances of a more senior member of the crew.

"I'm a man, too. Nothing like that happens aboard any boat I captain. If you work hard, you will earn a share of the spoils. If you do not work hard, you will be gone." The captain stuck out his hand. "My name is Patricio, Patricio Marques."

The boy hesitated only briefly, and then took Patricio's hand in a firm grip that belied his age and his skinny body. "I'm Jebediah Snell."

They shook hands, there by the dock in Key West in 1934, and thus began a lifelong partnership.

II

Patricio soon recognized the boy had potential. He worked as hard or harder than anyone he had ever employed, and he had employed quite a few. Patricio began to teach him more about shrimping, and how to navigate and run a boat.

Jebediah was like a sponge. He soaked up and retained every drop of knowledge that Patricio patiently shared. He had a natural sense of exactly where they were at any point in time and quickly grasped the rudimentary elements of dead reckoning, basically the same navigation technique used for centuries until other means became available and then affordable.

The sea is a featureless expanse, and there were no electronic navigation devices as we know them today aboard the *Flor*. Between the times when position could be ascertained accurately in relation to a visible landmark or ascertained approximately in relation to the stars, the only means available was extrapolating from the last known position using the compass, clock and an estimate of speed to determine the distance and direction traveled. Jebediah never erred.

The first year they were together was a good one, and Patricio was true to his word to share the spoils.

III

Patricio watched the boy stride into the cabin, although he could hardly be called a boy anymore. The hard work and plentiful Portuguese food aboard the *Flor* must have agreed with him. He'd sprouted three inches and added fifty pounds in the last year. He was becoming an imposing figure.

"Take a seat, Jebediah," said Patricio, nodding to the bench opposite him at the galley table. "We will leave Brunswick next week and head south again, but before we leave we must settle accounts for your time aboard."

Jebediah nodded as he sat down, his eyes narrowing. Patricio had provided him small advances against his share of the profits every time they made port; advances that Jebediah squirreled away. He had no interests ashore other than finding the spots in every port where seamen congregate, and listening to their tales of the sea. The only money he parted with he used to buy essential clothing, or to buy the occasional drink to keep the tongue of a particularly interesting seaman loose. He took all of his meals aboard the *Flor de Marques*, and slept aboard every night.

"Your share is considerable, Jebediah, since you have taken no more than your draw. The other crew members who come and go squander all of theirs and more as soon as they get their hands on it." Patricio paused, waiting for Jebediah to give some indication of curiosity as to how much he had coming. Jebediah sat, silent.

"Before I tell you how much your share is, I have a proposition for you."

Jebediah still showed no sign of curiosity to learn how much he had earned.

"I am buying a second boat, which will be named the *Coroa de Marques*. In return for your share of the last year's profits I will make you captain of the *Coroa* and give you one share of ten." Still, Jebediah said nothing. The silence and lack of response would have unnerved most, and even Patricio must have wondered if he was making a mistake. "I can assure you that this interest in the *Coroa* is worth more money than you have coming, but I understand that you will need to think about it."

Patricio pushed a tattered, dirty envelope across the table to Jebediah and waited for him to open it. Instead, Jebediah went to his berth and returned quickly with his own envelope. He pushed both back in front of Patricio.

"Here is my share, plus what I've saved from the advances you gave me. You can have both, but I want two shares of ten in the *Coroa*."

Patricio knew this was folly. Jebediah had no idea how much was in the first, fatter envelop, and had never seen the *Coroa*. If Jebediah opened the envelope, counted out his share and then took the time to measure it against an even cursory inspection of the *Coroa*, he would realize what a great debt he owed to Patricio.

Then Patricio realized what Jebediah was doing. Jebediah would owe no man for more than he earned. And he would ask for no more than he was worth.

Patricio smiled, and extended his hand.

"Done."

The *Flor* and the *Coroa* left Brunswick two days later, on August 15, 1935, and headed south toward the Keys. Patricio and Jebediah didn't know it, but they were on a collision course with history.

IV

It began to form, virtually unnoticed, northeast of the Turks Islands. The first real record of the storm was made in the Bahamas, Long Island to be exact, and the depression deepened and reached hurricane force by the time it reached Andros, 250 miles east of the Keys.

The *Flor* and *Coroa* were running in tandem, fishing just outside Molasses Reef, and the seas were building. The fishing was poor, and Patricio reached a decision.

"*Coroa*, this is *Flor*, come in" he spoke into the mike. The unreliable, tube-type radios had been giving them trouble since leaving Brunswick two weeks earlier, and they intended to have them repaired or replaced once they reached Key West. He waited 15 seconds before repeating the call. This time, the answer crackled back.

"Go ahead, *Flor*."

"This is a waste of time, Jebediah. Pull the nets and head for Tavernier. The barometer is dropping, and those low clouds on the horizon worry me, over." The radio crackled static, and then came to life again.

"Ok, we'll pull in ten minutes, over."

Patricio watched the horizon intently for the next ten minutes then throttled back and sent his strikers to pull the nets. He checked the barometer and saw that it had dropped again. It was falling faster than he had ever seen it fall, and he looked out the port side windows to check on Jebediah. The *Coroa* was not where it should be; it was well back of the *Flor* and turned sideways to the waves, rolling wildly. The *Coroa* was being blown back toward the reef, possibly fouled in its own net.

Patricio lashed the wheel in position and ran back to the work deck.

"Quickly, pull the net and release the catch. Then prepare the hawser. The *Coroa* is in trouble." Patricio ran back to the wheelhouse, and grabbed the mike.

"*Coroa, Coroa, Coroa*. This is *Flor*, over." The radio only crackled. "*Coroa, Coroa, Coroa*. This is *Flor*, over," he repeated. "Damn this radio," he cursed aloud.

The strikers were pulling the nets as quickly as they could in the rolling seas and having difficulty maintaining their footing. Patricio held the bow directly into the rapidly building waves even as the *Coroa* fell further and further behind.

"*Coroa, Coroa, Coroa*. This is *Flor*, over." At last the radio crackled into life.

"Patricio, we .... problem .... the engine .... out .... can't pull the net without .... winch. .... fouled .... over."

"Hold on, Jebediah. We're pulling our net, and preparing the hawser to put you under tow, over."

".... no good, Patricio .... going over the side to cut the net loose ...."

"No, no, no. You'll be killed in this sea," screamed Patricio, but the radio had gone dead again. He shot another glance at the barometer. It now read 28.4 inches, and was still falling. It seemed like forever before the wheelhouse door burst open and both strikers tumbled in.

"The net's in and the hawser's on the winch," the first man gasped. "It's hell out there."

Patricio didn't answer. The waves were building at an impossible rate and he was too busy watching them, judging when he would be able to swing the *Flor* about without capsizing. He thrust the mike at the striker, "Keep trying to raise the *Coroa*."

Jebediah had stripped off his shirt, shoes and socks, and was struggling to maintain footing on the pitching deck. The *Coroa* was sideways to the waves, and he knew that his chances of freeing her from the net were slim. But Patricio would never reach him in time, and there would still be the problem of catching and securing the hawser. The *Coroa* would be on the reef before that could be accomplished, and probably the *Flor*, too. He would be damned if he was about to lose the *Coroa*. His two shares in ten were all he had in the world. That, and his friendship with Patricio.

Jebediah whirled around to shout at his strikers. "One of you go to the wheelhouse and try to get the *Flor* on the radio. Tell them to stay away. One of you get the small hand net and secure it here. I'll need to climb up it to get back aboard."

The strikers looked at each other in horror. Surely this Jebediah boy/man was crazy. Before they could protest, they watched him clench his knife between his teeth and dive over the side.

Patricio judged the wave, and swung the *Flor's* wheel as hard and fast as he could. There was a sickening moment as the boat hung up, its propeller and rudder clear of the water and therefore useless. Then they finally bit into the churning sea and the *Flor* swung about. Patricio strained to catch sight of the *Coroa* as he tried to hold the *Flor* on the back of one of the massive waves. If he misjudged his power and crested the wave, he would be in danger of broaching as he slid down the front. Similarly, if he slid down the back of the wave he was riding, he could be broached as the following wave crashed against his stern and swung him around. The *Flor* would be capsized in an instant. He risked a quick glance at the barometer – 27.85 inches – and turned whiter.

The radio static cleared. "*Flor*, this .... *Coroa*, over."

Patricio grabbed the mike and shouted into it. "*Coroa*, this is *Flor*. Stand by, we're on our way, over."

"Hurry .... captain .... over the side .... blown toward .... reef, over."

Patricio threw the mike down and took the wheel with both hands to wrench the *Flor* back on line. He didn't know how he would get the hawser to the *Coroa* in this sea.

Jebediah was in trouble. He could easily become entangled in the net and the rolling of the boat threatened to crush him. He flailed backwards, away from the pitching hull, and then waited for it to roll away again. As it did, he could see the net caught in the prop and rudder and made a quick decision. He knew he would have only one chance. The boat heeled back toward him, and when he judged that it had reached the limit he struck out toward it before it started to rise again. Then, as the bottom of the hull rose, he managed to get close enough to grasp the propeller shaft, and was hoisted up with it. If he could hang on tight enough, he would be slammed back into the water but be able to at least wedge himself against the hull clear of the prop and rudder. He had seconds to fill his lungs before being plunged underwater with the next roll, and as he submerged he began sawing frantically at the net with one hand, desperately clinging to the shaft with his other arm and both legs.

It was impossible to see clearly but he began to saw at the netting, trying to cut it against the steel propeller shaft. He could feel the strands parting but couldn't tell whether he was making progress or simply cutting through random strands. The roll of the boat slowed, and he knew that it would start back the other way and that he would break surface shortly. His lungs were aching due to the exertion and fear. He was still sawing at the netting when he burst up into the air again, gasping and taking in almost as much water from the spray as he was air. He could see that the netting itself was working free but that the problem was with the much heavier purse string. The middle of it was wound around the shaft close to the propeller, and the rotation of the shaft had pulled it tight. Unless he could cut through the heavier line and free one end, cutting the net was useless. Jebediah took another spray-filled gulp of air before being plunged under again. He knew this would be his one and only chance.

He let go of the shaft and seized the purse string. He was being flung about against the rough bottom of the boat as he sawed and he could feel the skin being flayed from his back. His strength almost exhausted, the roll slowed and then started back in the other direction. There was no way he would be able to hang on through another cycle and he redoubled his efforts. Just as he cleared the surface he sliced through, losing his grip on the purse string at the same time as he dropped the knife. He desperately clawed backwards away from the hull that was rising above him again. As it rose, he could see that the net had fallen free but was still connected to the purse string, the one end of which was still wrapped around the shaft. At least the net was being dragged clear as the boat was blown faster than the heavy doors dragging along the sea bottom. Jebediah was just beyond the hull as it crashed back down, and he screamed for the striker to lower the hand net over the side. He barely had enough time to swim back and grab the section of net before the boat began to rise again. He was jerked from the water with enough force that he almost lost his grip, but he got his feet in the mesh and scrambled up and over the side, sprawling exhausted on the deck.

The striker was staring at him as if he had returned from the dead, and in a way, he had. He yelled for the man to help him to the wheelhouse.

Patricio was still scanning the tortured seas in front of the *Flor*, frantically looking for some sign of the *Coroa* when the radio came alive again.

"*Flor*, this … *Coroa* ….. lost net … clear …. try to …. engine, over."

"*Coroa*, where are you, over." Again, the crackle of static. "*Coroa*, where are you, over." Patricio looked at the barometer again – 27.45 inches! The lowest recorded reading ever was 27 and the barometer was still falling.

Jebediah was hanging on to the wheel of the *Coroa*, his weakened legs braced against the wild roll of the boat. The Molasses Reef, and certain death, was only minutes away. There was no time to try to set the anchor and it wasn't worth the risk of sending a man forward, as he knew there was little chance of it holding or even slowing their drift. The look of terror on the strikers' faces clearly showed that they, too, were useless now anyway. He checked the transmission lever to make sure it was out of gear. His only chance was to get the engine started, slip the boat into reverse for a few seconds and hope that the purse line would unwind cleanly before engaging the forward gears.

Jebediah was not a Catholic, but he offered a silent prayer to the small statue of the Lady of Fatima fastened to the starboard window frame and pushed the starter button. The engine coughed, started, sputtered, and then stopped again. The crashing of the waves against the reef was clearly visible now, only a hundred feet away. Jebediah hit the button again, and this time the engine caught and continued to run. He slipped the engine into reverse, counted to five, and then disengaged the transmission again. He was committed now; there was no time for any alternate course of action. He closed his eyes and prayed before pushing the lever forward.

Jebediah gave the engine full throttle and wrestled the wheel counterclockwise to turn the bow of the *Coroa* south, into the waves. He had no time to judge the moment and prayed to Fatima that they wouldn't broach. The *Coroa* responded to the rudder and the power of the engine, and within seconds Jebediah knew that the purse line must have cleared the propeller. He held his course south, directly into the waves and away from the clutches of the Molasses Reef. Jebediah grabbed the microphone.

Patricio was desperate now. He knew that the *Coroa* must be on the reef or, if by some miracle she had missed Molasses, she would soon wreck on one of the other reefs that lay beyond, separating the Florida Straights from the Hawk Channel. He was still fighting to control *Flor* when the radio came alive again.

"*Flor*, this …. underway, heading south …. south …."

"*Coroa*, this is *Flor*, turning south now too, repeat, turning south, over."

Patricio gritted his teeth and prepared to make the dangerous turn once again.

VI

Ten and a half miles to the southeast, at the Alligator Reef light, the glass shattered from the windows one hundred and thirty-five feet above the level of the churning sea. One section of lens was blown seven miles away and found, intact, on the beach a week after the storm had passed. The Weather Bureau in Washington later confirmed that at the height of the storm the lowest barometer reading was 26.35 inches, making it the strongest hurricane to ever hit the United States. Four hundred and twenty-three people were confirmed dead; Patricio and Jebediah were not among them.

VII

"I lost the net, Patricio. I can't afford to replace it, and I am unfit to captain the *Coroa*." Jebediah was disconsolate. His entire body ached and his back was a mass of scabs and open wounds from the battering he had taken beneath the *Coroa* the previous day.

"No, it is I who owe you, Jebediah. You saved my eight shares of the *Coroa*, and that is worth more than the net. I doubt that anyone else could have saved her."

Jebediah sat silent. He had done nothing more than needed to be done. He continued to look out the wheelhouse windows at the devastation of Tavernier. Such was the power of the hurricane that there was nothing ashore left standing.

"I have a new proposition for you, Jebediah. I will retain my ownership of the *Flor,* plus nine shares of ten in the *Coroa*. I will replace the net, and we will complete our fishing together for the year."

Sullen and still brooding over the loss of the net, Jebediah looked at Patricio. "I don't know what to say, I don't deserve … " he started, but Patricio cut him short.

"Wait until you hear me out. I am convinced that the future lies not just in fishing, but also in processing and marketing the catch. That will require someone to manage the operation ashore, and someone to look after the boats and the fishing. I want to buy boats, lots of boats, and I want to buy land in every natural harbor, developed or not, between Miami and Key West. I want to base the boats out of those harbors instead of moving from port to port. The government will replace the railroad that was destroyed in the storm, or maybe even build a road, and Key West will continue to grow as the gateway to the Caribbean …"

Jebediah was stunned by what he was hearing. Until now, his vision had been limited to what he could see from the deck of a boat. "But that will require more money than I think you have, Patricio," he said, "and you know that I have none."

"Listen, Jebediah. I have seen what you are capable of, and I know that I, too, am capable of more, in other ways perhaps. I am proposing a gamble; a risk based on what we can do together. The land between Miami and Key West was cheap before the storm, and will be even cheaper now. I am proposing that we risk everything and borrow as much as possible to secure that land, and more boats, starting now. I will borrow from everyone I can find for five years, and then we will concentrate on paying them off. Ten years from now, everything should be paid for, and there will never be any more borrowing. Only profits from that point on will be used to finance growth." Patricio's eyes narrowed and he leaned forward as he continued, knowing that he had Jebediah's attention.

"This cannot be done without two partners, one at sea, and one ashore. And the partners cannot waste time worrying about what the other is doing. I propose that I keep ownership of the *Flor*, and nine of ten shares in the *Coroa*. You will run both, and whatever other boats I can buy. But the boats and land that are purchased from now on will be owned by Marques Snell, and we will each own five shares of ten in that company."

Patricio sat back now, watching. Then he stuck out his hand to Jebediah for the third time in a little over a year. Jebediah didn't hesitate this time, and they sealed their pact.

VIII

The partnership worked much as Patricio had predicted, and Marques Snell grew quickly.

Jebediah concentrated on fishing and finding skippers and crew for the boats that seemed to arrive every month. The boats were never new, and Jebediah fell into a pattern of assuming command of the latest boat while he fished it and brought it up to the level of mechanical fitness that satisfied him. He found that in addition to his natural aptitude for navigation and finding shrimp he was adept at repairing the running gear, in many cases improving the original design if not inventing totally new systems.

He also found that he was a shrewd judge of other men, most of whom were older than he. In agreement with Patricio they only took on Portuguese and Cayman Islanders. New crewmembers always started on the latest boat that Jebediah was working on and if they were not up to his standards and incapable of learning quickly, he cut them loose and replaced them. Word spread quickly that Marques Snell was the best company to work for. They were fair, and shared each boat's profits with the crew. The best men became captains, each taking over the latest boat that Jebediah prepared.

Patricio was also busy, and in addition to acquiring boats whenever one became available at a bargain price he was quietly acquiring land. Much of the land was undeveloped, but always on a natural harbor or bay. Although Jebediah and Patricio went out of their way to maintain a low profile, concentrating on their own business, they were not immune to the jealousies of other operators as word of their success spread. The competition and jealousy was particularly intense in Key West, and Patricio and Jebediah frequently found themselves there together looking at various opportunities, be they boats or more land.

"So what do you think of the *Catherine the Great*, Jebediah?" asked Patricio as they climbed up from the engine compartment.

Jebediah considered the question carefully before he answered, knowing that it would be his responsibility to make the boat not only seaworthy, but also profitable. "It needs a lot, Patricio. The engine has been neglected, as has the winch. The net must be replaced, too, and all of this has to be done quickly so that the boat can generate profits to pay for itself."

"Yes, I understand that. And I know that you can do it. I suppose, as always, that it comes down to what we pay for it," Patricio said, looking off toward the horizon. "And it is becoming more difficult to find lenders for our purchases."

"Why is that, Patricio? We have always made our payments. I would think that lenders know that."

"True, but there are a limited number of lenders who are willing to loan money for the purchase of boats, and I have extended our credit with them as far as I can. They worry about what would happen if we had a major disaster like another hurricane, and although our boats are spread out and are not likely to be hit all at once, they still worry. It is the nature of lenders."

"So perhaps we must slow down for a while, Patricio, and give me a chance to just fish. We are finding fewer and fewer boats available at low prices, anyway."

Jebediah was not uncomfortable with that thought, but he knew that Patricio wanted to stick to his original plan for two more years. He also suspected that Patricio had another idea that he was holding back for the right moment. Jebediah was right, and Patricio turned to face him.

"You have judged the situation correctly. There are fewer boats available at the prices we have become used to paying, and coupled with the fact that lenders are becoming scarce at the same time, we are at a stalemate. The only answer is to pay more for the boats than our competition is willing to pay, and at the same time find new lenders who are willing to give us better terms and take some of the risk," he said, watching Jebediah carefully.

"Sure, Patricio. That sounds easy," Jebediah laughed. "and if I can at the same time convince the shrimp to jump directly into the hold, we will have it made." Patricio, however, was not laughing. Jebediah became serious. "Tell me what you are thinking."

Patricio hesitated a second, then laid out his plan. "The owner of the *Catherine the Great* died and his widow wants to sell it at the highest price she can get. We and at least two others want to buy, at the lowest price possible. Suppose that we offer more money for the boat than the others," Patricio's eyes narrowed, "but that instead of paying up front, we pay the owner a percentage of the proceeds from the catch until the boat is paid off. We can guarantee her a certain amount every month, a low amount, and in good months, she will get more. She can retain ownership of the boat until it is paid for in full, and in the end she will have been paid a higher price. Our reputation – your reputation – for making more money with a boat than anyone else will make the decision easier for her."

Jebediah looked at Patricio. "Let's try it," he said.

The deal with the widow was struck much as Patricio had suggested it could be done, and he hurried back to the wharf to tell Jebediah. "We have another boat," he called out as he approached Jebediah. "There is only one condition that I didn't foresee."

Jebediah froze, afraid of what Patricio might have agreed to in order to continue the purchase of boats. "What is it?" he asked nervously. "You know that I can do only so much to make a profit."

"Relax, Jebediah. This is only a minor inconvenience, well, perhaps two inconveniences. And you will just have to figure out how to deal with them," he said. He crossed his arms in front of his chest and stood looking at his partner.

Jebediah finally broke the silence. "Damn you, Patricio. What are these two inconveniences?"

"First, she wants the boat renamed *Catherine the Great de Marques*, immediately and for always. It is a long name, and rather awkward."

Jebediah breathed a sigh of relief. That wasn't too bad. Then he saw that Patricio was grinning at him. There was more.

"And what is the second thing?" he asked cautiously.

Patricio leaned forward. "It seems that she spends a lot of time down here on the wharf, and that she misses little that goes on. She is familiar with our operations, and ..." Patricio stood back and opened his arms wide, pausing for effect, "she insists that you must have dinner with her every month until the full amount is paid off."

Jebediah cursed loudly and profanely, but Patricio was laughing too hard to hear him.

"Come, partner. It's late, and I would like to treat you to a drink and something to eat ashore tonight."

Patricio led Jebediah, still protesting, to the nearest saloon.

IX

The drinking establishments in Key West catered to a rough crowd, and the noise level was already high when Patricio and Jebediah came through the door and selected a table in the corner. The evening started out well enough but was ruined shortly after their meal was served.

Jebediah saw the two men enter and make their way directly to the bar, which was already crowded. They must have been regulars as a space cleared for them immediately. They stepped up to the rail and someone shouted down the bar.

"Well, did you buy her?"

"Shut up and drink your whiskey," answered the bigger and older of the two.

The man would not be quieted, however, and made his way over. "What's the matter, Card?" he asked the younger man, "your Pa not in a good mood?"

The older man tossed back the whiskey that had appeared before him, and ordered another. "No, I'm not. That stinking Portuguese bastard Marques and his trained puppy stole the *Catherine*," he spit out, immediately draining the second glass of whiskey. "Somebody ought to teach those bastards a lesson."

Jebediah started to get up, but Patricio grabbed him by the arm and sat him back down. "Let it go, Jebediah. It is the whiskey talking. I will pay for this, and we can go back to the boat." Patricio laid some money on the table, and rose to leave.

"Hey Pa," said the younger man they called Card, "there's the bastards right over there."

The big man whirled around and spotted Patricio and Jebediah. He pushed his way over, followed by his son.

"You think you're pretty damned smart, don't you, you Portugoose son of a bitch," he spat.

Patricio raised his open hands in front of his chest in a conciliatory gesture and stepped out from behind the table. "No offense sir, but we purchased the *Catherine the Great* fair and square. We do not want any trouble, and we will leave quietly."

The big man stepped sideways to block Patricio's path to the door. "You already caused trouble, Portugoose, unless you want to pack up and leave Key West."

The younger man, Card, was grinning excitedly. He had a narrow, long face and his eyes were open wide and sparkling dangerously. His tongue darted back and forth, licking his thin lips like a snake about to strike. "Teach him a lesson, Pa," he shouted.

"We do not want trouble, mister," Patricio repeated. As he turned to motion to Jebediah to follow the big man grabbed him.

Patricio whirled back around immediately. Slipping from the big man's grasp and neatly stepping behind him, he forced his right arm up and behind his back between his shoulder blades. It happened so quickly that the younger man was still grinning for a second before he realized that his Pa was helpless in Patricio's grasp.

"Card", the big man yelled, "get him off me!"

Card grabbed and smashed a bottle from the table beside him and lunged at Patricio's exposed back. He never made it. Jebediah was quicker.

He was behind Card before he could react, and had both of Cards arms locked behind his back, Jebediah's left arm linked through the crook of Card's elbows and bending him backwards. A knife had appeared in Jebediah's right hand, and was at Card's throat. It had happened so fast that until the blood started to flow, no one even realized that Jebediah had sliced Card's face open from just under his left eye to the left corner of his mouth before putting the knife to his throat. It took a few more seconds before Card, too, realized that he had been cut.

"Tell him to let me go, Pa," he screamed, tears mingling with the blood running down his face and onto his chest.

Patricio wrenched the big man around so that he could see his son, and he sagged visibly in defeat.

"Did anyone see who started this?" yelled Patricio to the excited crowd gathered around in a circle.

"I did," called a large black man who stepped forward into the ring. "They started it. And not only that, the widow Smithers told me not an hour ago that you paid more – a lot more – than anybody else offered her for the *Catherine*. And that she's beholden to you."

The crowd rumbled at this news and started to break up, heading back to the bar. Patricio pushed the big man out through the doors and into the street. Card followed, running and crying after his Pa as soon as Jebediah released him. To Patricio and Jebediah's relief, the pair left Key West that night in shame. And although it would be many years before either of them actually returned, their paths would cross again.

5   Dexter and Jebediah: 1984

I was nervous. Scared in fact. It was the last week of school, and I'd just about made it through the last two months without an incident. Without a major incident, anyway. Until a few days ago.

There was a knock at the door, and it swung open. "Report to the dean's office. Your fathers are here." The proctor didn't say anything more. He didn't need to.

We made our way across the quad, and Ben started again. "Let's just tell them, Dex. This isn't worth it," he whined.

"Ben, we've talked about this. Just keep your mouth shut. Don't volunteer anything, and if you have to answer any questions, remember what I told you. Nothing more than 'we didn't take it'. It's the truth, isn't it?"

"Well, yes, but it's not the whole truth, and my Dad will be furious. This was his school, and my grandfather and great grandfather both went here, too. And none of them ever got into as much trouble as I have with you."

"I'm telling you, just stick to 'we didn't take it'. I know what to say, and when to say it." I could tell by the way that Ben stared at the ground as we walked that he wasn't convinced, but I knew that he would do as I said.

Ben's dad, Colonel Jamieson, was waiting in the outer office with my father. Colonel Jamieson stood with his back to the room, looking out the leaded glass windows at the ancient oak trees that lined the main drive into the walled grounds of the military school. Even from behind he was imposing in his uniform.

Father sat in one of the chairs beside an empty table. He would have looked fine at the helm of the *Estrela*, but looked out of place here in his faded jeans and windbreaker, particularly in contrast to the uniformed and beribboned Colonel. He was fiddling with a medallion attached to a leather thong.

Colonel Jamieson whirled when he heard the door open and immediately strode across to Ben, taking him by the shoulder and purposefully moving him away from me as if by doing so he could distance him from a distasteful influence. "Come on, son, let's get this cleared up." He shot a withering look at my father, who simply came over and put his arm around me.

"How are you, Dex?"

"Fine, father. I'm glad you're here." Father was always happy to see me, no matter what the circumstances, and I loved him for it. He tried to keep a stern look, as if not to offend Colonel Jamieson, but then he grinned and hugged me to him before turning back again. It was those hugs from my father that made my life bearable.

"Tell General Smith that Ben is here now and we're ready to see him," Colonel Jamieson ordered the assistant sitting behind the reception desk. The assistant rose and went to the double doors of the inner office. She went in and closed the doors quietly behind her.

While she was gone I looked over at the table by the wall. It was a fair sized table, draped in a black, velvet cover, and looked silly with the ceiling-mounted spotlights shining directly on its empty surface. The covering material was slightly faded, made all the more obvious by the darker, depressed rectangular spot in the middle where something heavy had obviously sat, protecting the velvet from the light.

Both doors swung open and the assistant beckoned us inside. Colonel Jamieson strode through first, followed by Ben and then me and father.

"General," Colonel Jamieson said, snapping off a quick salute.

"Relax, Colonel. I'm retired," said the dean from behind his desk. "Have a seat, gentlemen. The boys can stand." Father and the Colonel sat in the two old walnut chairs placed squarely in front of the dean's desk.

"Do you know why I asked you to come here?" said the dean, getting right to the heart of the matter.

"Something to do with a missing statue, I think," said my father.

The Colonel whirled quickly, leaning toward him. "It's not just a statue, Mr. Snell. It's a Remington, one of the early castings, and it's sat on that table out there for as long as I can remember. This is a disgrace, and I'm sure it's all your son's fault." Colonel Jamieson turned back to the dean. "I told you something like this would happen once you lowered the standards of this school by granting admission to the likes of these people." The Colonel was livid, and continued, "It's a damned disgrace --"

The dean cut him off. "Thank you, Colonel. Let's just get to the bottom of this please, without the comments on our admission policies. You've made your position clear before. Now, gentlemen, let's look at the facts.

"Two nights ago, the boys were here for discipline in regards to another matter." Colonel Jamieson's face grew even more flushed, and a vein started to pulse in his neck. The dean continued, unfazed by the Colonel's simmering rage. "After my assistant showed them in I sent her home, as it was late. We dealt with the other matter fairly quickly, didn't we boys?" He continued as we nodded. "And then I sent them back to the dormitory and took a telephone call from the Governor. The boys closed the door to my office on the way out, and when I left about forty-five minutes later I saw that the Remington was gone. I've questioned the boys several times, and they insist they didn't take it." The dean leaned back in his chair. "And that's why you're both here."

The Colonel leapt from his chair and turned on Ben. "Did you take that statue, Ben?" The Colonel was intimidating in his uniform, even without the withering look in his eyes.

Ben hesitated, glancing at me.

"Don't look at that troublemaker, Ben. Answer me. Did you take that statue?"

"No Sir, I didn't take it," Ben whispered, looking at the floor.

"There, he says he didn't take it, and he didn't. That's the end of it, General. The Snell brat must have done it."

The dean was not intimidated by the Colonel, and he stared at him for him fully half a minute before the Colonel sat back in his chair, ramrod straight.

"Colonel, the statue weighs two hundred and fifty pounds. Dexter couldn't possibly have made off with it alone."

At that point, my father spoke up. "I think that maybe I can get to the bottom of this, sir," he said in a calm voice that served to point out how close the Colonel was to losing control. "May I ask a few questions?" He continued without waiting for a response. "Dex – did you take the statue?"

"No, father, I didn't," I answered confidently, looking straight into my father's eyes.

"Did Ben take it?"

"That's ridiculous," the Colonel shouted at the dean, " I object to that question. This old bastard is trying to pin this on my son, and I won't have it."

"Hold it right there," my father said. There was a steely edge to his voice now and danger flashed in his eyes. "I may be almost sixty-five years old, Colonel, but I could rip that uniform off your back and then break your neck without raising a sweat. If you insult me or my son again, I'll prove it to you." He turned to the dean. "May I continue, sir?"

"In a moment, Mr. Snell." The dean turned to Ben's dad. "Colonel Jamieson, in the three years that I've known you as Ben's father, you've done nothing to demonstrate to me that you are a gentleman. In fact, you've been a pain in the ass. You may object to the way I run this school but please remember that you are an officer. You do no honor to yourself or your uniform by casting disparaging remarks. Please continue, Mr. Snell."

The Colonel compressed his lips together in a thin, straight line and stared at the dean as father resumed his questioning.

"Dex, did you and Ben take the statue together?"

"No father, we didn't take the statue."

Father's eyes narrowed and he rubbed his chin with his right hand as he looked at me and thought for a minute.

"Why were you here in the dean's office two nights ago?"

"We were here because the instructor said we were not paying attention in our strategy and tactics lecture, father. The instructor felt we were being disruptive, and he said that trying to teach us anything was hopeless."

"And were you being disruptive, Dexter?"

"Not really, father. I was telling Ben about Sir Henry Morgan. How he made a superior Spanish force at Maracaibo believe he had more men than he really did, and that sometimes tactics include making someone believe in something that isn't really there. It wasn't Ben's fault, father."

The Colonel interjected again, "See? Even this punk admits it's his fault, not Ben's! And I object to the idea of a god-damned pirate as suitable --"

"Shut up and listen, Colonel Jamieson," shouted the dean, slapping his hand on his desk and narrowing his eyes in thought, "I have a feeling you are about to learn something. Continue, Mr. Snell."

"Dex, do you know where the statue is?" asked my father.

"Yes, father, I do."

"That's it, case closed," Colonel Jamieson seethed, "like father like son. The little bastard took it."

My father was behind the Colonel in a flash. His hands were at either side of the Colonel's throat, pulling back on the leather thong of the medallion he had been examining in the reception room. The Colonel clutched and grabbed at my father's hands, desperately trying to relieve the pressure on his throat, but it was futile. Father stood looking at the dean, holding the struggling Colonel in an iron grip. Then, as suddenly as he had seized the Colonel he let him go, returning the medallion and thong to his pocket. It was over in an instant, quick enough that the Colonel hadn't even missed a breath. Even so, the Colonel was too shocked to speak. Fear was written all over him.

The dean was unperturbed. "Mr. Snell, I thank you for putting that away. Your restraint under the circumstances is admirable. And

Colonel, if you don't want word to get out that you were disabled and almost garroted by a sixty-five year old 'bastard', then I suggest you keep quiet."

Father turned back to me quickly while the Colonel slumped, beaten, in his chair.

"Explain, Dexter."

"Well, father, it seemed to me that if Henry Morgan could make something appear to be there that wasn't, then I could make something that was there appear not to be. The statue is under the table, hidden behind the cloth cover."

There was a second of incredulous silence before the dean burst out laughing. "So, Dexter, you were in fact telling the truth. You never took the statue."

"No, Sir. I never took it. And neither did Ben. You didn't ask if we knew where it was, Sir."

"No, Dexter, I didn't. And I certainly didn't consider that you were," he cleared his throat, "practicing diversionary tactics." He then spoke to my father. "Mr. Snell, I'm not certain there is anything more that we can teach Dexter this term. But over the course of the summer, I would appreciate it if you could see that he gathers some of his thoughts about tactics used," he looked at the Colonel briefly, "by the god-damned pirates. I'd like him to lead a class discussion at the start of the fall term. That's a class, by the way, that I'll make a point of attending.

"And Colonel," the dean continued, "I suggest this matter, and what happened here this afternoon, remain between us. Mr. Snell?"

"Yes sir. I've forgotten it already," my father answered.

"Colonel, I want to see Ben back here next year, too. It wouldn't do to have to explain his absence, would it?"

The Colonel glared at the dean. "We'll see," he said, taking Ben by the shoulder and pushing him out the door.

I never saw Ben again.

II

That summer was glorious. We drove directly from the boarding school across Georgia to Uncle Patricio's modest house in Brunswick. Aunt Izabel was waiting for us, and the house was rich with the delicious smells of a polvo guisado that had simmered all day. I missed her Portuguese cooking. There was nothing like it at the military school.

"Dexter," she squealed, crushing me to her ample bosom, then stepping back and holding me by the shoulders. "Let me take a look at you. You're becoming a man!" She hugged me again, and we kissed each other on both cheeks.

Patricio, hearing the commotion, appeared from the parlor. He extended his hand as he strode toward us.

"Let me see him, Izabel. Welcome to your Brunswick home, Dexter."

As I shook hands with Uncle Patricio, I could see that he had changed little. He never did. He wore his seventy-eight years well and the only signs of his age were the deeper wrinkles around his eyes and mouth as he smiled.

"Thank you, uncle," I said as I took his hand.

"And how was school this year?" It was obvious that he knew about the trouble I'd caused, in the same way he always seemed to know what I'd been up to.

"Fine, uncle. It was fine." I quickly changed the subject. "But I'm looking forward to spending the summer with father aboard the *Estrela*. We're going to Cayman Brac first, then to Jamaica and the Turks, then down along the Antilles to South America. We're chasing the path of the pirates. I wish you would come with us."

"Yes, I know all about it, Dexter. It should be quite an adventure, but I must stay here and take care of business." He turned to father. "Jebediah, let us leave Dexter with his aunt, I'm sure she has things to talk to him about. I would like to finalize the details of our new arrangement in my office." With that, father and Uncle Patricio left us in the kitchen.

Aunt Izabel went to the hallway and called up the stairs. "Catalina. Come down – your cousin is here."

Like Uncle Patricio and Aunt Izabel, Catalina wasn't really related to me. She had arrived from Portugal three years earlier as a shy five year-old who spoke no English. A distant relative of Aunt Izabel's, she was sent to live with her relatives in America when she was orphaned. For a time Aunt Izabel must have thought that in Catalina and me she had the children she had always wanted. But my troublesome ways had proved too much for her, and I'd been shipped off to military school two years ago.

Catalina came into the kitchen. She was a little taller than when I'd seen her last year, but beyond that she hadn't changed much. Aunt Izabel had tied her dark hair up and back, and she was wearing a long plain dress that complemented her hair and pale blue eyes. She was still skinny and awkward, and looked at the floor as she walked over and stood beside Aunt Izabel.

"Give Dexter a welcome home kiss, Catalina. See how big he is getting." Aunt Izabel pushed her toward me, and she shyly turned her cheek for a quick peck. I performed my duty, and then turned and ran for the back door.

"I'll be back in time for dinner," I shouted as I bolted out and ran down the steps toward the wharf.

I heard the screen door slam and my aunt calling out, "Don't get dirty, Dexter, and don't be late."

I made my way to the wharf, and was overcome by the scents, my scents. They were all there. The shrimp, the sea and the diesel fumes from the boats maneuvering around the harbor. The *Estrela* was there, too. My heart leapt. I felt secure.

I half-walked, half-ran along the wharf to the *Estrela*. She wore a new coat of paint; primarily white topside – decks, cabin and wheelhouse - and a blue outer hull. The roof of the wheelhouse and cabin were trimmed in the same blue as the hull and the rigging was all white. She was beautiful sitting there with the water lapping gently at her sides. I clambered aboard at the stern, eager to check out the new equipment father had described to me. I didn't understand how it all worked, but I had to see it. I headed forward to the wheelhouse, and went inside. It had been painted, too. White, just like the outside of the boat, that emphasized the natural warmth of the oak paneling, trim and the big, spoked wheel.

The ledge in front of the helm was crowded with the wondrous new devices. There was what I guessed was the location finder, which father said worked by picking up radio signals. Beside that was a unit I recognized instantly as radar, and another box with a screen I supposed was the machine father said could detect schools of fish as well as give a good fix on the bottom. The radio was new, too. It was far more complicated-looking than the old one, and father said it had a greater range, although he also explained that the range of a marine radio is as dependent on the height of the antenna as anything else.

I was most interested in what father called the autopilot, but I wasn't sure just which one that was. Apparently, he could set that in a way that would allow the boat to hold a course and steer itself.

I heard a noise behind me and spun around to see Catalina coming into the wheelhouse.

"You probably shouldn't be aboard the boat," I said, "especially in the wheelhouse."

"I've been aboard the *Estrela* lots of times in the last while," she said, giving me immediate pangs of jealousy. "I even helped paint in here." Her English had improved, but was still heavily accented. "Do you know what all these things are?" she asked, innocently.

"Of course I do. Do you?" I shot back.

"Yes, Uncle Jebediah explained them all to me," she said as she made her way tentatively forward.

"This is the radio, and this is the, the," she hesitated, then continued "the radar."

I managed to hide the fact that I had misidentified the radar.

"And this is a, a, uhm, sonar."

I wasn't sure what sonar was, but by the process of elimination I concluded that it was the fish and bottom-finding unit.

"And this box is the one that can steer the boat." Catalina turned toward me, still pointing at the autopilot.

"That's pretty good," I bluffed, "but you had better get off here before Aunt Izabel finds out where you are."

"You won't tell, will you?" she asked. "You used to try to get me to come down to the wharf all the time, and get me into trouble. I thought you'd be happy I came here on my own. Uncle Jebediah and Uncle Patricio even let me steer the boat when they were checking out all of this new stuff."

That was all I needed to hear. I turned and ran from the wheelhouse, scrambled onto the wharf and ran back to Uncle Patricio's. My emotions were in turmoil, and I was hurting from jealousy. I crawled in behind the bushes at the side of the house where I used to hide when Aunt Izabel was angry with me. I wanted to be alone to sort out my feelings.

I had always felt that the *Estrela* was a special place that was just for father, Uncle Patricio and me, and to find they had been aboard with Catalina was too much for me to handle. I felt abandoned, even more than I had felt when I had been shipped off to school.

It was only to get worse, quickly. My hiding spot was directly below Uncle Patricio's office window, and I could hear he and father arguing.

III

"Damn it, Jebediah, none of this makes any sense. Why now – why do you want out of Marques Snell?" The use of even such a minor expletive by Uncle Patricio shocked me, and I didn't understand the actual implications of what he'd said.

"It's not Marques Snell in total, Patricio. It's just the fishing. Keep the handling and processing if you want, but the boats have to go. And it's not just me – you should get out, too."

That I understood. Sell the boats? I knew this was more than just a business conversation, the kind that father and Uncle always had in front of me. I couldn't breathe, as if somehow by holding my breath this would all go away. I screwed my eyes shut and listened, hoping this was all a dream. A bad dream.

"I cannot believe you are saying this. We built this company – you and I – with those boats. You, more than anyone, must realize that. It is our roots you talk about."

"Patricio, we have enough. I'm telling you, get out of the boats. Get out now."

"But you have worked so hard. You have established bases all through the Caribbean, Venezuela, Colombia, Panama, Guatemala, and Nicaragua. What about all of those people? Those captains and crews? What about them, Jebediah?"

"It's not the same as it was years ago – I keep telling you that. I'm not as close to these people anymore – there are too many of them, and I just can't be everywhere at once. And it's not like when we only hired Portuguese and Caymanians. These people are different. Why can't you understand that?"

"That is it, is it not, Jebediah? You did not like it when I insisted we hire more locals, particularly further south. It was the only way – we could not operate in those countries without them. You resented it, did you not?"

"Patricio, please. Let's just say that I'm tired. I'm done – I can't do it anymore. Leave it like that, damn it." Father was upset and his voice was getting louder. "Sell them, Patricio," he yelled, "for the love of god, listen to me."

Uncle Patricio didn't answer. I was confused. This couldn't be happening. In my mind, behind my closed eyes, I could see Uncle Patricio leaning back in his chair, his hands clenched behind his head while he sat silently staring at my father. Waiting. It was his most powerful weapon, the long delay. Waiting until whoever he was talking to felt that they had to break the silence, had to say more. I knew what he was doing because he had done it so many times to me. With every additional second of silence, I had to struggle harder and harder to resist revealing myself by jumping up and shouting "No!"

Finally, Patricio himself broke the silence. It was a clear sign of just how strongly father felt.

"Make this trip with Dexter, Jebediah. You know how much I think that taking him south in hurricane season is a bad idea, but make the trip. Be careful, and take the time to think this through. If you still think we should sell when you return, we will sell."

There was a brief silence. "Thank you, Patricio," father said simply.

"Wait, Jebediah. There is one condition. If you tell me to sell, I will. But first, you must tell me why. And you must tell me the truth."

That was it. I didn't understand it all, and I was confused.

I heard the scrape of the chairs as father and uncle got up and then I heard the door to the office open. I ran around to the back door and into the kitchen where Aunt Izabel was ladling the steaming polvo guisado into bowls. She turned away from me, but before she did I saw she had tears in her eyes.

"Wash your hands, Dexter, and take your seat in the dining room."

Father and I left aboard the *Estrela* before dawn the next morning. Uncle Patricio did not see us off.

IV

It is 550 miles by sea from Brunswick to Key West, and it took us just over two days. They were intense days because father drilled me constantly on the operation of the new equipment, particularly the radar and the navigation gear, called a Loran. He taught me how to use the autopilot as well, and how to calculate fuel consumption and range.

The *Estrela* was fully fueled and with the new tanks held 8,000 gallons – 3,000 in the original main tank below the floor of the engine compartment straddling the keel and 2,500 gallons each in the new saddle tanks along the port and starboard sides of the engine room. At her cruise speed of 10.35 miles per hour and fuel consumption of 8 gallons an hour, she had a theoretical range of over ten thousand miles. With the 15-kilowatt generator and 3,400 gallons of water, we could stay at sea for a long time.

I was excited about seeing Key West again, the first time since 1975, and when father relieved me at midnight the night before we were to arrive I had trouble getting to sleep. I tossed and turned, my mind reeling alternately with thoughts of Key West, all the things I was trying to learn and the disconcerting memories of the conversation I had eavesdropped on between father and Uncle Patricio. It seemed I had just fallen asleep when, before dawn, father woke me and announced a change in plans. He had decided we would skip Key West and head directly to Cayman Brac.

'Directly' is a relative term. Cayman Brac lies south, southeast of Key West, about 350 miles as the crow flies. But between Key West and Cayman Brac lies Cuba – and father explained that we had to stay outside of Cuban waters.

"The charts are on the table there, Dex," he said. "I've already marked our present position. Plot a course for us around the western end of Cuba, and then on to Cayman Brac. I want you to mark the waypoints and estimate times and distances while I radio through to the Marques Snell office in Key West and tell them we're going straight through to Brac."

I worked through the calculations as I had been taught and by skirting well outside Cuban waters made the course to be a total of 782 miles. I laid out the legs in pencil on the charts and marked the waypoints, course changes, distances and time estimates. I was too busy double-checking everything to pay any attention to the radio exchange. When I finished, I nervously asked father to take a look.

"I'm letting you take responsibility for the navigation to Brac, Dex. Just answer a few questions. First, what heading should I take from here?"

"South west, father, 225 degrees on the compass. I allowed for the deviation."

"Have you allowed for the Gulf Stream?"

"Yes, father, I have."

"Very good. How long at our cruising speed until we change course?"

"Seven hours and twenty minutes, father."

"Good. Set the alarm clock for seven hours and fifteen minutes," father said, "and then make coffee."

I was pleased, but a little nervous as I went to the galley and fixed two big mugs of black coffee. The task of plotting the course had taken my mind off of the argument between father and Uncle Patricio, and I hurried back to the wheelhouse.

"Thanks, Dex. Now, I want you to set the autopilot and then put the cover on the Loran. We won't check it again until the alarm goes off, and we'll see how close we are to where you've calculated. As soon as I've finished my coffee I'm going to sleep. It's your watch and you need to make sure the autopilot is doing what you want it to do. Make any corrections you think are necessary. Understand?"

"Yes, father," I replied, confident but still excited.

"And to keep you from getting bored I've brought along my books on the early explorers of the Caribbean, the Spanish treasure fleets and, of course, the pirates. There is a folder in there, too," he pointed at the canvas satchel in the corner, "that has some information on the Spanish fleet of 1715. The exact location of the wrecks hasn't yet been discovered, but there is an excellent chance that we cruised right over top of them about thirty hours ago as we came down the Florida coast below Vero."

That was much the way the trip to Brac went, with father and me taking turns on watch, making course corrections and checking our estimated position against the Loran periodically.

A little over eighty hours later, we sighted Cayman Brac.

V

Cayman Brac is small. Fourteen miles long and just over a mile across at its widest point it is the smallest of the three Cayman Islands. Father told me that it was the 'brac', or bluff, that runs through the center and rises to its highest point at the east end at about a hundred and forty feet that Christopher Columbus first saw in 1503. As we neared according to my calculations I watched for the peak to appear on the horizon, and so it did. It was difficult to spot at first, then difficult to decide if it was really the Brac or just my imagination. But it rose steadily from the surface of the ocean until there was no more doubt.

Father told me how the first regular visitors were pirates and the first permanent settlers were deserters from the British naval base in Jamaica. It was probably one of the deserters who had built the cottage, using ballast stones salvaged from an early wreck. I liked to imagine it was the wreck of a pirate ship, and I suspect father did, too.

As we drew closer I could see the cottage silhouetted by the spine of the brac. It was as I remembered it from our brief visit the year before, although that time we had arrived on a small plane chartered from Grand Cayman. When we were about a hundred yards from shore father sounded the foghorn three times, swung the *Estrela* about and dropped the anchor. He backed the *Estrela* until he had the correct scope, then bent the anchor rode to the post and with a final thrust of reverse set the anchor to his satisfaction. When he shut down the engine I could hear shouting from shore.

"Dex! Dex!" I ran to the stern and saw a boy my age wading into the surf and waving frantically.

"Felix!" I yelled back, just as my father, naked, dove past me and into the sea. He sliced into the water cleanly, and when he surfaced he turned back toward the boat and yelled at me to try to beat him to the beach. I stripped off my clothes, leaving them in a pile on the deck, and dove in after him. He was waiting, treading water until I surfaced beside him, and then he set out with powerful strokes that belied his age. I was the best swimmer among all of my friends but I couldn't catch him. He made it to the shallows a good thirty feet ahead of me and ran whooping and hollering toward Felix, scooping him up in his arms and then throwing him, laughing and screaming and fully clothed, back into the surf toward me. Felix landed with a big splash, and I hugged him as we danced around in a circle yelling.

Our celebration was interrupted by a female voice calling from the beach. I looked back over my shoulder and saw Bibi standing barefoot on the sand, her long sack dress billowing gently in the breeze, right arm waving and towels draped over her left.

"Welcome home, Dex!" she called.

We ran toward shore and I slowed as we emerged from the water, embarrassed at my nakedness. Father showed no such inhibitions, and was toweling himself dry and listening to an endless stream of chatter from Bibi as I walked up, covering myself modestly with my hands.

"Master Dex," she laughed, handing me a towel even as she crushed me in a powerful hug, "such modesty from one who suckled at my breast as a babe."

Father was laughing as he wrapped his towel around his waist. "I'm guessing he'll get past that modesty someday, Bibi. He just needs a little more exposure to girls his own age."

I could feel the color rising in my face, and wrapped the towel more fully around myself as soon as Bibi released me from her clutches.

"Come on you three pirates," Bibi ordered, "I have fresh fruit and lobster ready for the pot. I've cleaned your cottage, Jebediah, and everything is ready for you." She took Felix under one strong arm and me under the other and marched us toward the path that lead to the cottage. Father followed us, unable to get a word in as Bibi prattled on about anything and everything. Her monologue was peppered with questions that remained unanswered as she would follow them immediately with another string of sentences about the weather, the exorbitant prices at the general store, the growing number of tourists and the unreliability of males in general.

"Bibi," father finally shouted, "slow down and let us get a word in."

Bibi just laughed, and then picked up right where she'd left off. It felt good to be home on Brac, and it was as if nothing had ever changed.

Bibi was the closest to a mother I had. She was different from Aunt Izabel not only in her color, which was coal black, but also in the easy way she had with people in general. She was outgoing and generous to a fault and those characteristics were even stronger with Felix and me. Felix was only weeks younger than me, and when father returned to the sea shortly after I was born Bibi took us both through our infancy.

Felix had never met his father, who, to the best I could figure, had been a brief visitor to Brac. He had availed himself of Bibi's hospitality and bed before moving on, not knowing he had planted the seed that became Felix. The only thing he left behind was Felix and his lighter colored skin. I suppose the strong bond Felix and I shared was partially due to his never knowing his father, as I had never known my mother and in some primal way the fact that we had suckled together at Bibi's breasts. We finally made it to the cottage which, true to form, Bibi had decorated with fresh flowers anticipating our arrival.

"Go and get dressed, you two," Bibi ordered father and me, "and Felix, run back to the house and get into some dry clothes. I'll throw the lobsters into the pot. Hurry now, don't make me wait."

It was hours after we had eaten before Bibi finally wound down enough to allow anyone else to get more than a few words in. She had been giving father a run-down on the repairs needed to the cottage.

"... and the well still needs attending to. How long has it been since I told you about that, Jebediah?"

Father was leaning back in his chair, looking out over the porch rail and watching the *Estrela* swing on her anchor. He seemed surprised when the silence continued more than a few seconds, and he turned to Bibi. "Pardon me?"

"Jebediah, you never listen to anything I say," Bibi chattered. "You men are all the same."

Father laughed and ventured a reply, expecting to be cut short again, but he wasn't. "Bibi, I listened to every word for the first hour or so trying to remember everything you said and asked so that I could answer when it was my turn."

Bibi feigned annoyance, and then laughed herself. "The well, Jebediah. It hasn't fixed itself in the last two years. The stones have tumbled in at the bottom, and it needs to be dug out and relined."

"Yes, Bibi. I'll get to it, but not this trip."

Bibi looked at him, her face taking on a stern look. "And just how short is this visit to be, Jebediah? Are you planning on just dropping Dex here and then taking off again?"

"Not exactly, Bibi," he answered.

"Well, what then?"

"Dexter and I are here for a few days. I want to pick up some things, including the dinghy, and then we're heading for Jamaica and on down to South America."

As excited as I was about the trip I was disappointed we would be on Brac only a short while. I hadn't really thought about it, but assumed

Felix and I would have time to visit all of our secret hiding places in our continuing search for buried treasure.

"Jebediah, that's unfair. Felix has been looking forward to spending time with Dexter for months now."

"Well, Bibi, I need to talk to you about that. I hoped we could take Felix with us …"

Felix and I stared at each other, our mouths open in surprise. We both started to holler at the same time, jumping out of our chairs and imploring Bibi. "Please, can we both go? Please?"

Bibi stared at father, and then at Felix and me, then back at father.

"Jebediah, you're the very devil himself. I knew this would happen sooner or later. It's not enough you've taken one of my babies away, but now you've come back for the other." There were tears forming in the corners of her eyes as she looked at us. "I suppose it had to happen, didn't it," she said, not really asking a question. "If I agree, Jebediah, you have to promise you won't let these two break the hearts of any island girls, and you have to promise to bring them both back here, safe and sound."

We left Cayman Brac two days later, Bibi standing in the surf fighting back her tears as we rowed out to the *Estrela*, the well untouched.

VI

Felix turned out to be as good a sailor and as quick a student as I was. Father and I both coached Felix on all of the things I had learned and the healthy competition between us to outdo each other reinforced our skills. There was, however, something new for both of us to learn, and father surprised us with it on the morning we anchored off an uninhabited little island near Montserrat.

Felix and I were fishing over the stern of the *Estrela* when father came out of the cabin. He was carrying a duffel bag, and laid it down on the deck behind us.

"Boys, we're going to try something new today," he announced, opening the bag. He took out four packages wrapped in oilcloths, two long ones and two smaller ones. He placed them on the deck and unwrapped them.

Felix and I looked at each other, and back at father. There was a rifle, shotgun and two pistols plus boxes of ammunition.

"Dex, I know you had rifle training at school. Have you fired a pistol or a shotgun?"

"No, father, I haven't. And we just practice with older rifles, not anything like these."

"Felix?" father asked.

"No, I've never fired a gun. I don't think that there are any on Brac."

"No, not legal ones anyway, Felix," father answered.

We spent two days at anchor there, diving, exploring and learning how to strip, clean, reassemble and fire the weapons. Father showed us where he kept them aboard the *Estrela*, hidden in the bulkhead that separated the wheelhouse from the cabin, and accessible from both areas of the boat. It was all quite exciting and we felt like grown ups. We didn't attribute much to it other than learning a new skill until we got closer to Trinidad, when it became clear the weapons were for more than simply target practice. It was there, during our first night at anchor in the harbor, that father explained.

"I want you to listen carefully to what I have to say," he started. "The Caribbean has become a dangerous place over the last ten years." He had our attention. "This part of our trip is not a game, and although I want us to enjoy ourselves, it's important to realize just how dangerous it is. Are you paying close attention?"

"Yes, father," I answered.

"Felix?" he asked.

"Yes, Mr. Snell."

Father continued. "The drug trade between South America and the United States runs right up through the Caribbean. Most of it is flown into Norman's Cay in the Bahamas and then on into the States, but some of it is being shipped by boat. And it's boats like the *Estrela*, with lots of cargo capacity and a long range, that are being used."

Felix and I looked at each other, not quite understanding what that had to do with us specifically.

"The boats are being hijacked, or pirated, by drug runners. They kill the people aboard, repaint and rename the boat and make one run before they sink it. Do you understand?"

The seriousness on father's face was enough in itself to make us understand.

"So from now until I say otherwise there will never be a point where we are all asleep, and there will never be a time where we leave the *Estrela* unattended. We will keep a close watch on all boats within sight and particularly any boats that approach us. There will be no exceptions – do you understand?" he asked, making sure we were fully aware of how serious he was. We both nodded.

"In particular, when we are at anchor day or night, I want you to be watching for small boats that look like fishing boats. If we're approached from one direction, keep your eyes peeled all around. It's a common ploy to distract you one way while you are being boarded elsewhere, understand?"

We looked at each other, and then back at father.

"Yes, sir."

"And don't assume anything. If you are on watch and even suspect that something isn't as it should be, let me know immediately. There will be no chances taken."

VII

The days faded into one long blur of swimming, exploring, honing our navigation skills and dragging for shrimp using the small rig father called a 'try' net. The objective wasn't to fill the hold – we didn't keep more than we wanted to eat ourselves – but rather to satisfy father's undying curiosity about where shrimp might be found. When Felix or I weren't actually running the boat we took turns reading from the books father had brought along and then told each other about the history of the waters we were in. The entire coast along the north of South America – Venezuela and Colombia – was rich in the Spanish and pirate history we loved, and there wasn't anything Felix or I read that father didn't already know or couldn't add to. Days would go by when we wouldn't see any other boats along the coast, then we'd run into clusters of them and father would reinforce his warnings about keeping a close watch. The strangest events were when father would raise one of the Marques Snell boats on the radio and arrange to meet with it.

Every time this happened father would remove the guns from their hiding place and station one of us in the cabin with the shotgun. He kept a pistol tucked in the back of his waistband and placed the other in the wheelhouse, under a pile of charts. The other boats were never allowed to come alongside. Instead, he would hoist the dinghy into the water, row over to the other boat and take the captain off. Then he would row back to a point midway between the *Estrela* and the other boat and just sit there talking to the captain out of earshot of both boats before taking the captain back and then returning to the *Estrela*. He never told us what they talked about and we never asked, intimidated by the serious manner he adopted whenever one of these meetings took place. We were always left with the instructions to keep the *Estrela's* engine running and to leave immediately, abandoning him should there be any signs of struggle, should he actually go aboard the other boat whether it looked to be voluntary or not, and finally, if he approached the *Estrela* closer than two hundred feet with anyone at all aboard the dinghy other than himself. These situations scared Felix and me enough that we didn't even discuss what might be happening. We were just relieved each time father dropped the captain off and rowed back to the *Estrela*, alone. Father downplayed each event after it was over to the same extent that he cautioned us before it took place. It was strange, but I never thought about it much until years later.

The weather was predictable most days, sunny and hot with a gentle, daily rain mid afternoon, like clockwork. We were, as father explained, below the imaginary hurricane line at twelve degrees forty minutes north latitude and therefore theoretically safe from that threat. The only storm we encountered blew up suddenly when we were between Santa Marta, Colombia and Barranquilla, on our way to Cartagena.

We were making our way slowly, with the try net in the water, when we jerked to a stop. Father quickly slipped the boat out of gear and after some instructions to us tried reversing while we took up the slack on the winch. When that didn't work he brought the Estrela around and we tried to free the rig by heading back in the other direction. All the time that we were working to release the rig from the snag the wind was picking up with storm clouds forming to the east and moving toward us.

Father casually told us what had happened in 1935 when he was captain of the *Coroa*, and reassured us that if he had had as good a crew then as he had in Felix and me that he would have had a much easier time of it. The story was not reassuring, and I eyed the oncoming storm nervously.

"I'm going to dive down and try to free the rig," father finally announced. I was against it, and said so.

"Father, let's just cut the rig. It's only a try net."

Father wheeled on me immediately. "A boat is only a boat without its net, Dexter. Don't ever forget that."

"Why don't we leave a float marker then and come back after the storm passes," I said, eyeing the clouds to the east once again.

"That's a last resort. I'm going down to try to release it first," father said as he stripped down. "Get the diving mask from the storage box, Felix."

By the time Felix retrieved the mask father had removed his clothes and shown me how to disconnect the rig should it be necessary. I didn't want to ask why it might be necessary to do this without him here to do it with us, but I paid close attention. Felix and I kept exchanging nervous looks as father jumped over the side, pulled his mask on and with a quick wave to us was gone.

I couldn't believe how long he was under. It must have been at least two minutes, and the rain was driving at us by the time he resurfaced and scrambled up the rope ladder we had slung over the side.

"Can you free it Mr. Snell?" asked Felix.

Father seemed particularly agitated and he headed for the cabin without answering. He emerged seconds later with a pair of heavy canvas work pants that he struggled into on the pitching deck, tying a short piece of rope through the loops and then slashing the legs off above the knees before fastening the stout knife and its scabbard to the rope belt he'd fashioned. He issued orders to us as he donned his gear.

"Dexter, do you know where we are? Felix?"

I answered first. "I think so."

"It's not enough to *think* you know, Dexter. You must *know*."

I nodded, ashamed.

"I'm going back over the side, and I want you two to go into the cabin and write down on paper where you believe we are. Don't think about the storm, or about me. Write it down. Then go to the wheelhouse and check what you wrote against the fix on the Loran. I want you here on the deck when I come back up. Now go!" he yelled as he jumped back in the water.

Felix and I scrambled for the cabin and wrote down our best guesses as to our position, then ran into the wheelhouse to check them against the Loran. We weren't even close, at least by father's standards, and we ran back to the work deck expecting to see him by that time. He wasn't there.

"Father!" I yelled, looking around frantically in the driving rain. "Father!"

I looked at Felix, who was horror-stricken. "What do we do now?" he cried.

"Get ready to help me release the cable," I shouted.

"Father!" I screamed again.

And then I saw him. He was astern of us, and slightly to the port side. And he was swimming strongly toward the *Estrela*. He made the side and hoisted himself up the ladder, sprawling on the deck. "Release the rig, Dex," he yelled.

I spun around to Felix. "Get a float and attach it," I yelled.

"No!" shouted father, "just let it go."

I was shocked. The net was the most important thing. Without it, the *Estrela* was just a boat.

"Release the rig, damn it!" father yelled once again.

I jumped to it, and with Felix' help I soon watched the cable slip into the water and sink. Father was already in the wheelhouse and we ran forward to join him. He had stripped off the canvas pants and was standing at the wheel of the *Estrela*, laughing.

"Done, boys?"

"Yes, Mr. Snell," Felix answered, looking at me as if to ask whether the dive had stolen my father's sanity.

"And did you write down what you thought was our position?" he asked, swinging the *Estrela* about and into the oncoming waves.

"Yes, sir," we chorused together.

"Good. Tell me what you thought our position was and what the Loran showed," he ordered, holding the *Estrela* in position.

We told him. He had us repeat the Loran position twice and then told us to look at the chart and describe to him from that what landmarks would be visible if they weren't being obliterated by the storm.

We did so, and then checked the chart again for any reefs or other dangers that might be in immediate proximity. When father was satisfied with all of our answers he throttled up and spun us around toward Cartagena. He broke out in a pirate ditty and we joined in, laughing and singing our lungs out. We were still singing fifteen minutes later when the storm abated as quickly as it had blown up.

With the excitement of the singing, the anticipation of arriving in the ancient stronghold of Cartagena the next day and father's tales of how Sir Henry Morgan had terrorized the entire Spanish Main, I forgot about going back to retrieve the net until much later.

In fact, for many years there was only one other thing about that entire trip I was able to remember. And as father swore us to secrecy, Felix and I never told anyone about our visit to the whorehouse in Panama.

6 Key West: 2003 morning, October 30

Mirtha stirred beside me, stretched lazily then rolled over onto her back. She cocked her right arm up over her face, hiding her eyes in the crook of her elbow and sinking back into a deep sleep.

We were in the master cabin of the *Party Girl*, and the clock beside the king sized bed showed 11:34 a.m. I adjusted the slide control on the console that brought the indirect lighting up just enough so that I could see.

Mirtha's body was lush but by no means fat, subtly rounded in that erotic way that no young girl can be. I once again judged her age as late thirties, at her sexual peak. There are no games at that age; she clearly knew what she wanted and had no qualms about getting it.

The lingering smell of sex hung in the air and the sweat-stained sheets were piled at the end of the bed where they had ended up sometime during the night. She shifted again as I watched her, bending her left leg slightly and exposing the smoothly shaved, generously padded mound at the juncture of her well-toned thighs. The lips were still swollen from the previous night's exertions.

Mirtha's hot button was clearly pain, and I had pushed it repeatedly. All it had taken to bring her back to her peak after each orgasm was a slap or a hard, twisting pinch of her permanently erect nipples, and positioning her over my knee for a brisk spanking was all it took to drive her, screaming, over the edge. I had been careful to leave no marks where they would show the next day but I wondered if the cheeks of her tight ass were bruised. The faint chirping of the telephone broke my thoughts. I got up and padded across the thick pile carpet to take the call in the outer part of the cabin.

"Yes?"

"Sir, Mr. Shando is aboard. He's been shown to the open dining area on the upper deck and is having coffee."

"Tell him I'll be there in ten minutes." I hung up the phone and jumped into the shower.

II

Shando was leaning against the rail looking at the waterfront when I arrived.

"It's a different view from out here, isn't it," I said.

Shando turned and nodded. "Yep. Looks mostly peaceful." He walked over and sat down in a deck chair, one of his long, powerful legs stretched out casually in front of him. The mid-day sun had raised a light sheen of moisture on his smooth, black scalp, but his loose tropical shirt was dry. I wondered what size shirt it took to appear loose on that massive body. Shando could easily be mistaken for a professional football player, and much to my amusement, sometimes was.

"Anything new in the last few days?" I asked.

"Nope. Same old same old," he answered casually. "Except for the hot little number Shando met last night. She was askin' about the *Party Girl*, and I suppose she's heard the rumors. Pretty cagey little thing, but I got the feelin' she's done her homework," he said, looking at me from behind his oversized sunglasses. I couldn't see his eyes, but I suspected that if I could there would be that familiar glint of amusement lurking there.

"Nice try, Shando. I can find my own women," I replied, pouring a coffee from the urn the steward had set up on the table along with a selection of fresh fruit slices and pitchers of freshly squeezed juices. "Was she any good?"

"Shando didn't get to first base, and Shando didn't try. This one's different, not my type," he said, sliding his sunglasses up to rest on the front of his scalp. "But Shando's thinkin' you should meet her. Invited her to your pre-party function here this evenin'. You can decide if you want to extend the invite to include the main event at the house later, but Shando thinks that scene would paralyze her," he smiled speculatively.

"Morning," announced Mirtha coming up the stairway and stepping onto the deck. "Am I interrupting anything?" The short bathrobe with the *Party Girl* emblem emblazoned on the back did little to hide what was underneath, and Shando didn't miss a thing.

His eyebrows shot up causing his sunglasses to shift at the same time as a lascivious smile exposed his perfectly straight, gleaming white teeth. If a shark ever smiled, he'd look just like Shando.

"Well, hello," he said, glancing back at me with a knowing look. "You're not interruptin'. Fact is, Shando was just leavin'," he said, unfolding himself from the chair and rising to his full height.

"Don't let me chase you away," she answered, looking up at him. Her wide mouth was slightly open, and the brief image of two sharks circling each other flashed across my mind.

"Lady, you couldn't chase Shando away," he laughed, striding over to the companionway and down to the launch that would take him back to the pier.

Mirtha stood at the rail and watched him silently for a few minutes before turning back and walking over to me. She showed no signs of wear and tear from the night before, and if possible actually looked refreshed and ready for another round. She hiked the already short bathrobe up, perched her bare ass on my knee and put her arms around my neck, leaning close enough to brush those hard nipples against my chest.

"He always call hisself Shando?" she asked, laughing.

"Yes, he does," I answered. "Except on the telephone. You get used to it after a while."

"I can think of something else I'd like to get used to," she whispered, crushing her nipples against my chest.

"I suggest you get into town and buy something to wear to the party," I said. "A cocktail dress for the party here, and something racier for the party at the house later."

"Any suggestions for the 'later'?" she asked.

I didn't have to think about it. "Black leather skirt, short, with a matching leather vest that can be opened easily. Black stockings and garters, matching heels. And a feather trimmed mask that just covers your eyes. You won't need a bra or panties; I don't want you overdressed."

She leaned into me again as she whispered in my ear. "I think I'm going to like this lifestyle."

I pushed her back just far enough to look into her eyes.

"You think so, do you?"

"Baby, I know so," she purred.

I made to stand up and she got the message, rising slowly and turning her body half away so that she was looking at me over her shoulder. The robe was hiked up over her ass and I could see it was still red, but unbruised. Her face took on that now-familiar look, and she reached back with both hands to grasp her cheeks.

"I'm a little cold. Do you think you could help me?"

The unsettling image of sharks flashed through my mind again.

7 Dexter Snell: 1986

It had been two long years since father, Felix and I had taken the *Estrela* through the Caribbean. I was more or less behaving myself at military school and I was in my final year, preparing for college. I didn't really know what I wanted to study; there were no courses in the subjects that interested me most. History and mathematics were perhaps the closest.

The argument I'd overheard between father and Uncle Patricio had been settled as they had left it. Father was fixed in his decision that the boats should be sold, and Uncle Patricio complied. Father kept the *Estrela* but all the others went. The fish processing and distribution business remained and Uncle Patricio busied himself with those.

Father seemed to disappear after the final boats were sold at the end of 1985. The only contact I had with him aside from rare, brief visits, were telephone calls and letters from Colombia and Brac. I wrote him more often than he wrote me, and I had a difficult time expressing exactly how much I loved him, missed him and needed him. The frequent visits by Uncle Patricio were welcome but only served to accentuate father's absence. I suppose that to put it into terms father would understand, I was rudderless and adrift, but I never found the words to tell him.

II

"Dexter – your Uncle is here."

The proctor left the door to my dorm room open and I struggled up out of bed. It was just after midnight and for a second I thought I was dreaming. Uncle Patricio had been here only two days before. I threw my clothes on and made my way down to the common area.

Uncle Patricio was waiting there, alone. I immediately knew something was wrong. Seriously wrong. He walked toward me, and then stopped.

"Is it father?" I asked, suddenly knowing.

"Yes, Dexter." I saw the tears in his eyes.

"Is it bad?" I stammered, turning away.

"I'm sorry, Dexter. Your father is dead."

I walked across to the window, smashed my hand through it and then just stood there looking out. Uncle Patricio came up behind me and enfolded me in his arms. I turned to him and buried my face against his chest, sobbing and trying to hold back the tears at the same time.

So many thoughts ran through my head all at once. The unfairness of it. The fact that I hadn't seen him in months followed immediately by anger at him, at myself, then the whole world. The flash of the memory of father, Felix and me singing pirate songs in the storm on the way to Cartagena. The *Estrela*. Cayman Brac, Felix and Bibi. And finally, that it just couldn't be true. Father was invincible, and he had been stolen from me at a time when I needed him the most.

"How did it happen, uncle?" I asked.

"I do not know everything yet, Dexter. It happened on Brac, two days ago while I was here with you. They just found him a few hours ago and Bibi called right away."

I stepped back from his arms and looked at him through my tears. "I have to go to Brac."

"Yes, Dexter. We must both go. The plane is waiting for us."

III

It was a blur, and I can't remember much about it now.

There was the twin-engine plane, the interminable flight to Brac and then Bibi and Felix meeting us at the small landing strip. I broke down again at the sight of them as Uncle Patricio went to talk to the constable.

"Dexter," sobbed Bibi, taking me in her strong arms, "I'm so sorry." Felix stood a few steps away not knowing what to say, and then he started to cry, too.

IV

Uncle Patricio made the arrangements between visits to the constabulary to speak with the police officials. As he had been found on a secluded stretch of beach and Uncle Patricio said that the crabs had gotten to him, it was a closed coffin. So I didn't even get to see him one last time. We buried him beside my mother on the bluff for which Cayman Brac was named, facing southeast toward his beloved Caribbean. It was over quickly and we left two days after we'd arrived. Bibi promised to take care of the cottage and Felix promised to be my friend forever. I was numb, still in shock and denial. Uncle Patricio was unable to console me, although he tried again even as he bundled me aboard the plane for the return flight to Brunswick.

The flight back, like the flight over, was a blur. The plane was noisy enough that I didn't have to talk to Uncle Patricio and I closed my eyes and feigned sleep. We went straight from the airport to the house in Brunswick, where Aunt Izabel waited for us. This was the first time that I ever went into that house and didn't immediately smell something cooking. It was a small thing, but just seemed to call attention to the fact that nothing in my life would ever be the same again.

She looked frail and old, and she was sitting in a wicker chair on the front porch, wrapped in a blanket. The doctor was with her and he tried to stop her from getting up, but she threw off the blanket anyway and stood on weakened legs holding her arms out to me. I went to her immediately, and I'm sure that she attributed the shocked look on my face to my grief rather than my realization that she was really sick and that she would be stolen from me, too. It was the first time that my hug was stronger than hers, and I started to cry again. She felt like a bag of sticks in my arms.

We sat on the porch until well past midnight, and the long, awkward silences gradually turned to patches of conversation punctuated with shorter and shorter pauses as the three of us recalled memories of father. Uncle Patricio told us of how he and father had met, how he had seen him flung from the steamer and fished him from the harbor at Key West. He told us about the hurricane in 1935, and how strong and certain father was whenever the situation demanded it. And he told of how father went every month to have dinner with the widow Catherine Smithers in Key West, and that it was at her house in 1960 that he met my mother, Otillia Cruz, married her and took her to Cayman Brac where she was so happy that she never left.

The shared remembrances were the tonic I needed. I was calmer now, and the tears had stopped hours earlier. I told of our trip with Felix two years ago, and how father taught us how to run the *Estrela*. I tried to describe the excitement, the sense of adventure and danger we felt when father taught us how to shoot the weapons and how grownup we felt when we met with the Marques Snell boats. I was in the middle of that story, staring out at the moonlit harbor when Uncle Patricio interrupted me abruptly.

"Dexter, I'm sorry, but your aunt needs her rest. Please help me put her to bed."

I looked over and saw she was asleep in the chair, wrapped in her blanket. Uncle Patricio and I bundled her up and he carried her inside to the bed that had been set up in the front parlor. When he was satisfied she was comfortable, propped up with pillows and in a deep sleep, he apologized and sent me off to my room upstairs saying he needed to talk to me alone in his office tomorrow. I slept soundly for the first time in four days.

V

"Come in, Dexter. Did you sleep well?"

"Yes, uncle, I did, thank you."

He motioned to a chair in front of his desk, and I sat. The folder he had been reading was in front of him, and he closed it and moved it to the center of the desk. He tapped it with his fingers. "Dexter, your father left his affairs in good order. I want you to know you are well provided for."

"Thank you, uncle."

"Your father named me as his executor and your legal guardian until you are nineteen, which is a little over eighteen months. I expect you will want to continue with school, and that you will go on to college as planned." He said it not so much as a confirmation, but more as a given. I nodded.

"The size of your father's estate is considerable, and I will not go into all the details but just give you an idea. First, there is the property on Cayman Brac. The cottage is small, but there is a lot of land that goes with it. Bibi has agreed to take care of it.

"When your father and I sold the boats we split Marques Snell apart as well. I did not want to do that, but it was your father's wish. I took only the properties and buildings that are directly needed for the fish processing and distribution, including those in South and Central America, and your father took the rest of the land and some commercial buildings and other types of property, all in the Keys." Uncle Patricio paused to make sure I was listening. I was, but not fully comprehending.

"The holdings are significant in size, but with the exception of a few of the properties, largely undeveloped. The value of your father's share being more than mine and based on his assertion that he had few immediate needs, the greater portion of the cash proceeds from the sale of the boats went to me to balance the transaction.

"Your father set off to, shall we say, pursue other interests, and I agreed to manage the properties for him with an annual accounting. The commercial properties have been leased and otherwise contracted to specific corporations on extremely lucrative terms and the proceeds from those arrangements are being used to further develop the sizable land holdings. Many of these were acquired well before real estate development drove prices up and what were once considered marginal lands are now prime properties. As I said at the outset, you are well taken care of."

The impact of what he was saying was completely lost on me, and I think Uncle Patricio realized it. He stood and came around the desk and put his arm on my shoulder.

"Dexter, I owe your father a debt that extends beyond partnership. It has been difficult for me the last few years, breaking Marques Snell apart, but through it all I have done my best for him. I will do the same for you, for as long as you wish."

Uncle Patricio stuck his hand out, and I took it.

Aunt Izabel died a month later, unknown to me because I ran away the day after meeting with Uncle Patricio. I didn't return until my nineteenth birthday, but in reality I have been running ever since.

8   Key West: 2003 evening, October 30

The launch began to ferry my guests to the *Party Girl* just after sunset, and the party was well underway as I fastened my cummerbund and slipped on the jacket to my tuxedo. "Come on Mirtha, let's go," I called.

Mirtha strode out of the bedroom, pausing briefly to ensure that she had my attention before walking over to me.

"Is this okay?" she asked, twirling coquettishly so that I got the full effect.

My look must have said it all. She was wearing a gold lamé dress that concealed as much as it revealed. The dress stopped halfway to her knees and the neckline was cut deeply enough to frame the entire cleavage between her lightly freckled, luscious mounds, revealing their ripe firmness. If that wasn't enough to draw attention, a gold pendant dangled there to serve as a focal point for any eyes that hadn't already found her breasts. The scooped back revealed her smooth, tanned skin and the outline of her spine. Gold, high-heeled pumps lengthened and tightened her shapely legs and dangling gold earrings completed the outfit. Her hair was done up, leaving her neck bare and inviting.

She walked over, staring at me the entire time, took my right hand and pulled it up and under her dress. She was wore nothing under the dress and she was already wet, or maybe still wet.

"Feel how much I like you, Dexter?" she teased, pushing my fingers into her and holding my hand there.

"I like you, Mirtha," I answered.

"And I like you. You made me come at least a dozen times last night, but you didn't come at all. Is there something wrong?" she asked, entwining her fingers with mine so that she could show me exactly where she wanted to be touched.

"No, Mirtha, how could there be anything wrong?" I answered, laughing. "You just said that you came a dozen times, and I was hard all night wasn't I?"

She pouted briefly and then brightened again. "Yes, you were. I just might keep you around," she said, dropping my hand and readjusting her dress as she swept past me and out the door to join the party.

I followed, briefly irritated at the suggestion that *she* might keep *me* around.

II

The party was in full swing and the deck was crowded. There were eighty guests invited, and they were spread out everywhere. Some were dancing to the soft music of the three piece combo playing on the upper deck while others were strolling the other decks or gathered in groups in the salon and elsewhere, discussing whatever it is that people discuss at cocktail parties. White-jacketed waiters made the rounds with trays of canapés and glasses of champagne. The harder drinkers congregated closer to the three bars.

The irony of this annual function was intertwined with the date and the event that followed later at my big house on Caroline Street. This was a black-tie affair aboard the *Party Girl*, and it was a definite counterpoint to the drunken climax of Fantasy Fest gearing up just a short distance across the water in the streets of Key West. The guest list too was designed purposefully. It included not only rich socialites from New York and other power-centers who owned get-aways in Key West, but politicians like the senator and his wife, plus judges, surgeons and other hoi polloi thrown together with people from more pedestrian walks of life that I had found interesting at some point or another. For added measure, there was the usual Key West mix of people with varying sexual proclivities, persuasions and inclinations. The undercurrent to all this were the activities every year at the house, later. The thirty or so people who also had an invitation to the house knew what was to come, most having been there before, and the rest held titillating suspicions. Regardless, invitations to both functions were among the most sought-after of any October event in a four-state area.

I was engaged in a polite conversation with a lawyer and his new wife when I realized something was attracting attention behind me. I looked casually over my shoulder and was amused to see that it was the arrival of Shando, replete in a white, four-button tux with a powder blue vest and blue, four-in-hand tie. He was making his way toward me when Mirtha, causing a stir of her own, neatly intercepted him. Shando turned and extended his hand to someone behind him, and when I saw her my heart stopped.

III

She was in her late twenties, I guessed. Just under six feet tall, impossibly slim and wearing the requisite little black dress. Where Mirtha's dress was revealing and obviously provocative, hers was conservative. The hemline ended just above her knees, and there was no hint of cleavage. She didn't need it. Her long dark hair reflected the light from the deck above, and even from that distance I could see that her eyes were the same light blue as my father's eyes had been. She was wearing black pumps with shorter heels, and even without them would be taller than most men. I politely disengaged myself from the lawyer and his wife, and made my way over.

Mirtha was sizing up the competition and I could tell from the smile pasted on her face that she was not pleased. Shando was enjoying the stir his entrance caused. Even standing motionless he was still drawing stares.

"Dex, Shando was just introducin' Cat to Mirtha," he grinned, "Cat, this is Dexter Snell, owner of the *Party Girl*."

She extended her hand, and I took it. "Nice to meet you," I managed to say. Up close, she was even more striking. She was everything that Mirtha was, but in a more conservative, natural way. There wasn't anything contrived or calculating in her appearance and her smile was genuine, if somewhat uncertain.

"Nice to meet you, too," she answered, withdrawing her hand. "I've of course heard about you, and was curious."

"Not too curious, I hope," Mirtha interjected before I could reply.

Shando took control of the situation, and Mirtha.

"Shando's rememberin' somethin' about you scarin' him off," he said, placing his huge black hand low on Mirtha's bare back and then sliding it lower. He steered her away, grinning. "A drink on the upper deck'd be nice while you tell Shando how you would do that."

Mirtha shot me a dirty look even as she turned all her charms on Shando. "Yes, let's go. I certainly don't want to keep Dexter from his guests," she said, turning her back to me and letting Shando lead the way.

"I hope I haven't caused any trouble, Mr. Snell."

"No, Cat, you haven't. Mirtha is someone I met only two days ago, and she's already laying claim. It's nothing," I answered, waving over a waiter with a tray of champagne. I took two glasses and handed one to Cat.

"And is that something that happens often, Mr. Snell?" she asked. "Women laying claim to you, I mean?"

I laughed. "It happens sometimes. It's nothing, I assure you," I answered again, captivated by her eyes. They were in fact lighter than I had first thought, almost pale, and seemed to change shades even as I talked to her. "And where are you from, what do you do, and what brings you to Key West?" I asked, "and before you start, call me Dex, please. Mr. Snell was my father." I raised my glass to her, and then took a sip.

She strolled over to the rail of the boat as she answered. Even the way she walked projected an unconscious, unspoken challenge.

"I'm from Georgia, and I studied economics at Harvard, Mr. – Dex," she corrected herself. That explained the intriguing accent, which I hadn't been able to place. "I'm working in my family's business."

"And what brings you to Key West during Fantasy Fest?"

"Don't you know, Dex?" she asked, turning those impossibly blue eyes back on me again.

"No, but I can guess." I smiled at her.

She turned fully toward me now; the smile disappeared from her face. "It's you. It's because of you that I'm here."

I was puzzled. She didn't look like the type who sought me out, and even if she was, it wasn't something that was readily admitted let alone announced up front. I was thinking I'd misjudged her, and was somehow disappointed. For a few minutes I had been swept up in unfamiliar but pleasurable emotions and I was deflated before I had even figured out what they were.

"You don't know who I am, do you Dex." It was a statement, not a question, and I shrugged my shoulders.

"No, I honestly don't. And I know I would remember you if we'd met before."

She stared at me for quite a while and when it was apparent I didn't know who she was, she spoke again.

"I'm Catalina, Dexter. Catalina Marques."

I dropped my glass and it smashed on the deck, splashing champagne on her shoes. A waiter ran over quickly to clean up the broken glass and wipe up the champagne. Before I could answer, she continued.

"Patricio asked me to find you. He has been calling and you've been ignoring him. He needs to see you."

It hit me like I'd been punched in the stomach by Shando, and a feeling of dread overcame me. "Is he okay?" I asked.

"Dexter, he's ninety-seven years old, and frail. He's been in decline for the last few months and the fact that you haven't returned his calls is killing him as surely as if you were holding a knife to his throat." Catalina was angry now, and the more she said, the angrier she became.

"Your life and the disgusting way you choose to lead it is entirely your business, but for God's sake, Dexter, don't do this to Patricio."

I turned from her and made my way toward the stairs to the upper deck, calling back to her as I went. "Wait for me by the gangway – I'll be right back."

I took the steps three at a time and emerged at the top, looking around for Shando. He was standing at the starboard rail with Mirtha. I strode over to him, ignoring the people who spoke to me as I passed by.

Mirtha was holding one massive arm in her hands and pressing her breasts against him.

"Shando – I need you to take care of some things for me."

Mirtha smiled at me wickedly. "You haven't abandoned your new little plaything already, have you?" she said, sneering. Shando ignored her.

"What d'you need? You know Shando'll take care of it."

"Have the captain find the pilot. I need the Lear ready to go when I get to the airport. Have him file a flight plan for Brunswick, Georgia, and to have a car and driver waiting there for me. Then take care of things until I get back, including the party tonight."

"Where in the hell do you think you're going you bastard?" Mirtha demanded, "running off with that stuck-up little bitch?"

"Shut up, Mirtha. She's my cousin," I answered, looking back up to Shando.

"Shando'll take care of things, Dex," Shando growled.

"I know you will, and thanks."

I was turning to leave when Mirtha grabbed me by the arm and leaned close to hiss at me. "See what happens when you come crawling back here, you son of a bitch. I would have kept you around, but not now. Cousin. Bullshit."

Her words made no sense, but I had no time to think about them.

"You can take care of her too if you want, Shando. She likes it rough," I spat as I turned away.

I could hear Mirtha cursing and Shando laughing as I ran down the companionway to find Catalina.

IV

The jet was warming up when we drove onto the runway and I hurried Catalina up the stairs and aboard. The attendant closed the door behind us and as we were buckling in the pilot ran up the engines and started down the runway. I didn't know it at the time, but I was leaving Key West the same way I'd arrived fifteen years ago, aboard my own jet, and it would be another year, less a day, before I returned. But instead of swaggering off my own jet, I would be sneaking ashore at night.

V

The flight from Key West to Brunswick takes an hour and twenty minutes from wheels up to wheels down, and the brevity of the flight only made me feel guiltier as I thought back on how rarely I found the time to visit Patricio. How simple it would have been to fly up once a month, have dinner with him, and come back the same night.

But I was kidding myself. It wasn't the time involved. It was the inner guilt that I had buried somewhere deep inside about the way I lived my life, and I was surprised I hadn't realized it before. My mind skipped back to the flight home after burying my father, and I prayed for the first time that I could remember. I prayed Patricio would be all right.

I shot a guilty glance across at Catalina, comparing her to all the women I'd known and finding that the comparison wasn't fair. And I don't mean fair to them, I meant that it wasn't fair to Catalina to lump her in the same category. She sat and stared out the window, deep in her own thoughts.

As we sped along I could see the outline of the coast marked by the darkness at the edge of the lighted urban sprawl that was Florida. I thought back to all the times I'd traveled that coast with Uncle Patricio aboard the *Estrela* and the *Sol*, and how I had been happy then, happier than I'd ever been aboard my helicopter, jet or even the *Party Girl*. In fact, I suddenly understood, there wasn't anything I owned that really meant anything to me. They were all just possessions that insulated me from the people I really cared about.

I was wondering if it was too late to make amends and perhaps even start anew. I glanced across at Catalina again and realized I didn't even know how to behave around someone like her. And then another revelation hit me; that I desperately wanted her. I wanted her in all the ways that I'd never wanted a woman before, and at the same time all the ways that I'd had women before. I needed someone in my life besides just me. Someone who loved me as a person, and not for what I owned. And someone who was at the same time a match for my ravenous libido, perhaps even challenging me and taking me further.

I brought myself up short, realizing I was fantasizing. I must be. Still
…

The attendant came back to tell us we were beginning our descent, and to buckle up. She was nervous since I'd snapped at her shortly after takeoff, and I apologized. Her reaction showed that my apology made her even more nervous, and I made a mental note to send her flowers and to change the attendants' uniforms from the Hooters knock-offs to something more conservative.

VI

Patricio was waiting for me in his office, asleep in an overstuffed chair and bundled up in a blanket much as Aunt Izabel had been that night we returned from Brac. He looked old and tired and I realized that at ninety-seven he had every right to. Catalina went to him and woke him gently.

"Uncle, uncle," she said as she stroked his wizened cheek.

He woke slowly, as if he wasn't sure where he was.

"Catalina, did you bring Dexter?" he asked.

"Yes Uncle Patricio, he's here. I'll leave you with him." Then she left without looking at me, closing the door softly behind her.

I walked over to him, and then bent down and hugged him.

"Are you okay, uncle? You had me worried," I said, realizing too late just how stupid a thing that was to say to someone whose calls I had been ignoring.

"I am better than I have a right be, Dexter, but you should be worried more about yourself."

For a brief instant I thought I was about to receive the same lecture I received every year, but as I looked deeper into his tired eyes I saw there was something else.

"Pour yourself a brandy from the sideboard, Dexter and then take a seat here where I can see you."

I turned to the sideboard, and poured two fingers of brandy into a snifter.

"You had best make it a bigger drink than that, Dexter. The doctor has cut me off and you will be drinking for both of us. And I am afraid you will need it."

I filled the snifter to the halfway point, recapped the decanter and sat in the chair he'd indicated.

"Just listen to me Dexter, and you can ask questions when I am through," he said. He shifted in his chair trying to get more comfortable, and then he started.

"As I have explained to you for the last few years, your expenditures have exceeded not only the income but the cash flow from your properties. When this began, you instructed me to borrow against them to make up for the shortfall, and I reluctantly followed your instructions.

"In the first twenty-four months after what they now call 9/11 the economy deteriorated sharply, particularly in travel-related businesses. The revenues at your hotels – those you own and operate outright, as well as the ones under management contract to the big-name chains – collapsed. And that caused the underlying values to fall." He was watching me as he spoke, his eyes locked on mine. "Take another drink, Dexter – this one is for me."

I drank, while Uncle Patricio readjusted himself in the chair.

"The properties under development required continuing cash injections, and the hole became just too deep. There is no more cash."

I nodded. "So you're telling me I have to cut back," I said. "I can do that."

"No, Dexter. This is difficult. Please hear me out."

I settled back in the chair. I'd already decided on the flight down that my free-spending days were over.

"As you are well aware, I have been asking you to cut back for over three years. It is too late for that." Uncle Patricio paused again. "Take another drink, Dexter. This one is for you. I am sorry to tell you this, but you are broke."

I looked at him in disbelief. "Well then, I'll just have to sell some of the property, maybe one or two of the hotels." I felt a little better having finally voiced myself what he was trying to say, and began to reassure him that I could live with that when he interrupted me by holding up his hand.

"No, Dexter. The properties were already heavily mortgaged before 9/11. Since then, as I said, their values dropped and the interest bill still exceeds the somewhat recovering revenues. They are worth less than what you owe on them." Uncle Patricio paused again to let that sink in.

"But these properties have been good for years, uncle. Surely the banks know that. They'll just have to wait until things turn around completely," I said. "Let's go and talk to them tomorrow."

Uncle Patricio sat silently, looking at me with those tired eyes. He sat for a long while before speaking again.

"The banks no longer hold the paper, Dexter. It has all been bought up. They were happy to sell and get out from under the risk. Virtually everything is gone. The properties, your house in Key West, the jet, helicopter, your boat – almost everything."

"Well then, we'll go and talk to whoever holds the paper. Do you know who that is?"

"Yes, Dexter, I do." He sighed deeply and closed his eyes. I almost thought he'd gone to sleep when he opened them again and stared at me. "Forget it. There will be no relief there. The only thing of value that you have left is the cottage on Brac. I never told you, but I never allowed that to be encumbered. And there is one hundred and twenty thousand dollars sitting safely in an account on Grand Cayman. That too is safe thanks to the banking laws there." I let that sink in. I couldn't laugh at the fact that Uncle Patricio had set some money aside for me, but it was barely enough to cover what I currently spent in a week.

"Who holds that paper, uncle?" I asked again.

He closed his eyes again as if it was too painful to look at me and speak at the same time.

"There is a man in Miami, Dexter. An evil man. He has held a grudge against your father since 1935. Your father cut his face open with a knife protecting me, and he vowed to never return to Key West until he had broken your father and whatever children your father ever had. Since your father died, it appears he has bided his time to take it out on you, and that he has succeeded."

"What's his name?" I asked quietly, in deference to Uncle Patricio's closed eyes.

"We did not know his name at the time. All we knew was that his nickname was Card. After your father sliced him from the corner of his eye to his mouth, he has been called Scard behind his back and that has only served to further fan the flames of his hatred."

I started to grow cold, and my chest felt constricted. "What is his real name?"

"Niccolo. Niccolo Cardeli."

Now it was my turn to close my eyes. I wished that I could hide behind them forever.

"Does he have a daughter named Mirtha?"

"You know her?" Uncle Patricio asked, the surprise apparent in his voice.

"Yes, I regret to say I do. I know nothing about her. I only met her three days ago."

"She is not his daughter, she is his wife," he said.

I sat forward and opened my eyes. Uncle Patricio was staring at me again.

"But he must be what, eighty or so? The Mirtha I met is in her late thirties, maybe early forties. It can't be the same one," I said, stupidly relieved somehow.

"Yes, Dexter. That is her. He found her in Colombia when she was nineteen. It was 1981, and he was sixty-three. It is rumored that she is the daughter of a drug lord and that she was given to Cardeli in order to seal a pact. She bore him two daughters soon after he brought her back to Miami, and it is said that she is even more ruthless than he. She stays with him for his money. There is little else between them. Other than the evil they wreak together he takes no interest in her or his daughters, and she finds her pleasures elsewhere. How is it that you know her, Dexter?"

I felt empty and cold inside. I got up, draining the rest of the brandy.

"It's of no consequence, uncle," I said, moving to kneel before him. I put my hands on his knees, and rested my head sideways on them.

"I know you will not believe this now, Dexter," he said softly, stroking my hair with one hand, "but you still have what your father wanted you to have the most. Go home to Brac, Dexter. Go home to your mother and your father. I predict your life is about to start anew, in a fresh direction."

I left the next morning, on commercial flights. It was the first time in fifteen years I had flown on a commercial airline, and people must have wondered at the sight of a man in a tuxedo with no luggage. I had nothing to take with me.

Uncle Patricio was right about my life starting anew. But he couldn't have known where that new life would soon lead, and what I would discover that set my direction squarely on the path of vengeance. And not vengeance for what I'd lost monetarily. I could have lived with that.

9 Cayman Brac: 2003

Except for the brief flurry of rumors and speculation my financial crash would cause in Key West, I was now a nonevent. My arrival on Brac was a nonevent as well, except on a personal basis. I had a lot to learn.

I realized suddenly there was no car waiting to meet me. First lesson learned. Then it dawned on me my credit cards were now worthless. I scrounged through my wallet, found a twenty and walked out to the front of the small terminal. There were a few cars available for hire, and after determining the twenty would in fact get me to where I wanted to go, we set off. The driver was amused by my tuxedo and lack of luggage. I simply explained my luggage was lost, as in fact it was – along with everything else I owned.

I actually began to feel better during the drive. The best of the thoughts and feelings of the last twenty-four hours returned and I realized that in the end I had gotten exactly what I'd so fervently prayed for. Uncle Patricio was still alive and although he was frail, he was amazingly sharp and lucid at ninety-seven. I had a chance to start over, and I actually had something to dream about that I couldn't simply go out and buy. Strange it would be Catalina, and I hungered to learn more about her.

The car pulled up at a weed-choked, broken gate and I was briefly disoriented. I knew my arrival would be a surprise to Bibi and Felix but I'd expected the property would be in a better state of repair. I gave the driver the entire twenty and later chided myself for the foolish extravagance.

I made my way around the gate, down the overgrown pathway, and found the cottage too was in a state of disrepair. It had been boarded up and there was a padlock on the front door. I cleared the trash out of the way and sat on the porch to look out over the sea. With the cottage behind me and outside my range of vision, the view of the sea was exactly as I remembered it. For a brief moment I was able to trick myself into believing father, Bibi and Felix were sitting behind me. I closed my eyes and tried to conjure up a vision of what they would look like, but it just wouldn't come. I stood up and removed the tuxedo jacket, tie and vest, tossed them on the porch and headed up the ridge to where my father and mother were buried. To my surprise, their graves were well tended. Flowers had been planted at the foot of each grave, and the stones were straight.

I sat between them, resting my arms and head on my knees and closed my eyes. I thanked my mother for giving me life and thanked my father for the wonderful gift of the cottage. I realized everything else I'd lost was meaningless, with the exception of the loss of the time I could have spent with Uncle Patricio. I was strangely calm and at peace.

I don't know how long I sat, but when I opened my eyes I saw a fishing boat was pulling in to the anchorage, evoking memories of the *Estrela*. My heart ached immediately and my eyes teared over. I wept for a moment and when I rubbed my tears away to look at the boat again I felt a shock go through me. It couldn't be. This boat even looked like the *Estrela*. I jumped to my feet – it *was* the *Estrela*!

I ran down the path to the shore, tripping once and ripping the knees out of my trousers. I hit the beach and tore off my shirt, shoes and socks and plunged into the sea, making for the *Estrela* with choppy, out-of-practice overhand strokes. Soon winded by the unaccustomed exertion, I paused and tread water to regain my breath and stare at the *Estrela*. There were three people aboard, a man and two boys. The boys were coal black, but the man was lighter and he was showing them how he wanted the anchor released. I yelled as he made his way to the wheelhouse to back the boat down and set the hook, but he couldn't hear me over the rumble of the diesel. I struck out again for the boat.

I made it only another hundred feet or so when I had to stop and tread water again. The engine had been shut down, so I yelled once more.

"Ahoy *Estrela*!" I shouted. The three of them stopped stowing gear and turned to look. I waved my arms and called again before resuming my swim, a crawl this time. I finally made it to the side of the boat and tread water as I looked up and saw the three of them staring at me.

"Felix?" I panted.

"Yes," said the man. "Who are you?"

"It's me, Dex, damn it. Help me aboard before I drown."

He stood there like a statue for a second, peering at me. Then he gave a whoop and tossed a rope ladder over the side and hauled me up. I collapsed on the deck, wheezing and sputtering and laughing. Felix was perched on the rail, grinning and watching me. Finally he stepped over and reached down to pull me to my feet. He threw his arms around me and squeezed me so hard I started to cough. He let me go and slapped me on the back.

"God Dex, you look like a beached whale. And a sick one at that," he laughed. "You obviously don't get much sun or exercise in Key West."

"No, I guess I haven't for a while." I laughed and stepped back. "Let me get a good look at you."

Felix stood there like a rock with his legs shoulder width apart and his hands on his hips, grinning. He had grown a little taller in the seventeen years since father's funeral, but not much. He was only about five foot eight but he had filled out. Not a hint of fat, and well muscled. Not the defined, ropey muscles of a body builder, but the solid muscles that come from hard work.

"What brings you here after all this time, Dex?" he asked, the smile fading a little.

"Well, it's a long story. Let's go ashore and find Bibi and we can talk about it," I said.

His smile disappeared completely. "You don't know, Dex?" he asked, and then answered his own question. "No, I suppose you wouldn't. You haven't returned a single call in fifteen years." The smile was not just gone; he was struggling hard to hide the contempt. "She died four years ago, Dex."

I just stood there, not knowing what to say.

"And I suppose you expect to fly in on your fancy jet – yes, I've heard the stories and saw the pictures in the magazines. The fancy yacht, the big house, the beautiful people I think they're called – fly in on your jet and show off a little and then leave again." The open contempt was there on his face now, and I deserved it.

We stood there looking at each other for what seemed like forever.

"Felix, I'm sorry."

"Sure, thanks a lot. You're not half the man your father was," he said. Then, turning to the boys, "stow the gear and wash down the decks. When you're done, bring the dinghy ashore." He turned back, looked at me a second and then dove over the side and started to swim for the beach. I hesitated only a second, and dove after him.

There was no way I could keep up with him let alone catch him, and I was gasping by the time I reached land. I walked up the path, and saw he was waiting for me on the porch.

"Where's your luggage and stuff? And why are you wearing this monkey suit?" he asked, glancing at the jacket and vest lying amid the trash.

"Felix, this monkey suit is all I have. Along with the cottage." He looked at me with a blank expression, uncomprehending. "I'm broke."

"Bullshit. You can't be broke, Dex. No way."

"It's true. I didn't believe it at first either. Uncle Patricio told me last night. Believe me, I was so stupid I had no clue."

Felix' blank look was replaced with a frown, and then he looked at the *Estrela* riding at anchor. He seemed to arrive at a decision. "It's seventeen years since I saw you last time, and fifteen since we spoke on the phone. Maybe we better sit down and cut some bait."

II

Felix didn't know where to find the key to the padlock on the front door of the cottage so we smashed it loose and then tore the boards from the windows to let in some light. Most of the windows were intact, but the inside of the cottage was a disaster. Felix explained that after Bibi died, and because no one had heard from me for so long, it was easier and safer to just board it up to keep the vandals at bay.

I found one of my father's sea chests Felix had kept at his house until he boarded up the cottage and broke into that as well. It was cedar-lined and contained a good assortment of musty-smelling but sturdy, serviceable clothing and a canvas hammock. Like every child who has lost a parent, my memories pictured him as having been bigger and I was surprised, and pleased, that the clothing fit me. Even the shoes. It felt good to be wearing father's shoes.

We grabbed an old cast-iron pot and sent the boys, who had come ashore with the dinghy and a pail of fresh shrimp, to wash and fill it with seawater and gather up some firewood. Then Felix dispatched them to his house to fetch a bottle of rum and sent them on their way. We settled down on the stone steps after lighting the fire on the ground in front of the porch and setting the pot on to boil. We hadn't had more than a perfunctory exchange of words since coming ashore, and before saying anything Felix uncorked the rum, took a swig and handed it to me.

"I missed you, Dex. It hurt you never called in all those years."

I took a deep drink and wiped my mouth with the back of my hand before answering. "I won't lie to you, Felix. I've been so self absorbed for the last fifteen years I rarely thought about anyone but myself." I let that hang in the air, and he just kept looking out at the sea. "I did think about you, Bibi and Brac from time to time, but I just never did anything about it. I'm sorry."

"Sorry now that you've lost everything else," he said in a voice so quiet I had to strain to hear him.

"Almost, but not quite, Felix. For what it's worth, when I was flying to Brunswick to see Patricio – before I knew or even suspected I was broke – I thought he was dying. I had enough time to realize what a fuck-up I've made of my life, and how I've hurt the people who matter most to me. I'd already decided the way I was living had to change and that little of what I owned meant anything to me. As it turns out, I have no choice in the matter. But that doesn't change the fact I'd already made up my mind, and although that decision made my crash no less of a shock, in the end it made it easier to take." I looked at him. "Does that make any sense to you?"

He was still staring out to sea, and he seemed to be considering what I'd said, weighing it in his mind. He turned his head slowly, and stared into my eyes.

"Did you ever tell anyone about the whorehouse in Panama?"

"No, I haven't, Felix. Father, you and I swore one another to secrecy and I've never betrayed that oath. Have you?"

"No, I haven't either," he said.

We sat there for a while, and I took another drink before handing the bottle back to him. He started to raise the bottle, then stopped.

"You may be a bastard, but you never lied to me." He kept his eyes on mine as he took a drink and passed the bottle back. "We can start with that, and see where it goes. Okay?"

I was so choked up I couldn't answer him in words. I just hugged him close, and he hugged me back with those powerful fisherman's arms.

We didn't talk a lot more that first night. We enjoyed the shrimp and he helped me rig the hammock between two of the pillars on the porch before he went home. I fell into a deep sleep and didn't awaken until the sun came up.

III

The next few weeks passed in a blur. After an initial, emotional exploration of the *Estrela,* I set about cleaning and repairing the cottage while Felix continued his fishing. We would meet every time he returned and share more and more of the last fifteen years as we rekindled our old bonds.

The cottage was a mess, to put it mildly. After Bibi died Felix had tried to keep it up, but his absences made it an impossible task and the periodic vandalism just made it easier to board it up. He had, however, lovingly maintained my parents' graves along with Bibi's, and for that I'll always be grateful. It was so much more than I'd ever done for anybody.

I settled into a surprisingly satisfying daily routine that consisted of a pre-dawn swim followed by a breakfast of fresh fruit and a long day of work. There were hand tools strewn about that I figured out how to use by trial and error, and it took a full week to clean out the cottage and repair the windows and front door. At last the inside of the cottage began to take shape.

The tougher physical labor began after that, consisting of repairs to the stonework and clearing the weeds and debris from the property. The work would have been hard on someone who was fit but it was brutal on me. I threw myself into it, straining and sweating in the tropical sun. I carefully disassembled crumbled portions of fence, porch and walls, piling the big, heavy stones in a way that I could mortar them back in their original positions. I hauled and mixed the materials by hand, and as the cottage began to take shape, so did I.

I hadn't been considered fat or even overweight in Key West, but I noticed from the first day that in comparison to Felix fitness is a relative term. As the softness disappeared from my body and was gradually replaced by muscle I took increasing pleasure from my exertions and the discovery I had an aptitude for working with my hands.

It was four weeks before I had my first visitors other than Felix and his helpers, and I hadn't given a thought to Key West or anything else connected to my former life in the last three of those.

IV

I was taking a mid-day swim when the twin-engine plane swooped low along the shore and then climbed sharply, swinging back toward the airport. Private aircraft weren't uncommon so I never gave it much thought.

While cutting fresh fruit for my lunch I heard them coming down the path. They made a fair amount of noise and I put my knife down, went out onto the front porch and then around to the back of the cottage to take a look. Through the trees and shrubs I could see what appeared to be two people pushing something. When they made the turn at the bottom of the path I froze for a second, turned, and ran back to the porch before they could see me.

I stood on the porch looking out at the sea, my heart hammering in my chest. I didn't want to be found like this. I wasn't ready. And then, as suddenly as the first reaction had overwhelmed me I felt a calmness replacing it. I smiled, then grinned and ran back around the corner, whooping like a little child.

"Uncle Patricio! Catalina!"

They stayed for two days and a part of the third, and Uncle Patricio took as much pleasure in seeing what I'd done with my own two hands as I had taken in discovering my own capabilities. We spent our days together, sitting on the porch watching the sea and talking about anything and everything. I prepared our meals, fresh fruit and fish, and my initial embarrassment over my old, second-hand clothes faded quickly.

I realized just how spartan the cottage was with no running water and few other amenities. I hadn't even started rebuilding the well father had left unfinished before his death years ago. It was the same well I remembered Bibi complaining about, but I was content hauling water up from the sea by the bucketful and walking to Felix' for drinking water. There were no adequate sleeping accommodations because of the vandalism, and Uncle Patricio's male nurse returned every evening to wheel him back up the path and take him and Catalina to the hotel at the other end of Brac. As much as I felt alone when Uncle Patricio left each evening, it was Catalina who consumed my thoughts.

She was quiet and aloof and I found myself stealing glances in her direction whenever I thought I was unobserved. My feelings about her were, if possible, more intense now than they were when I first saw her aboard the *Party Girl* a month ago.

Her pale blue eyes drew me in with alternating flashes and depth that complemented her facial expressions. The way she sat and walked, even stood, caused a constriction in my chest. She was as tall as I'd first thought but she wasn't as skinny as I remembered. Slim, yes, but definitely not skinny. I could see she was self-conscious about her body, her breasts in particular. She concealed them in a modest bra that was at least one size too small, presumably in an attempt to flatten them against her chest, but it was a futile effort. Her ripe nipples rebelled against her modesty and whenever she moved, the loose blouses she favored came into contact with her bra and those nipples dimpled the material noticeably. Her loose-fitting clothing couldn't hide the promise her body projected unconsciously. If anything, her physical desirability was enhanced by her attempt to conceal it.

On the afternoon of the second day Uncle Patricio wanted to rest on the porch, alone. He had brought two small shrubs he said were from Portugal and as the path was impossible to negotiate with a wheel chair, he asked that Catalina and I plant them for him at my parents' graves. Catalina tried to excuse herself but Uncle Patricio would not hear of it.

Catalina led the way up the narrow path while I carried the plants and a shovel behind her. We weren't too far along when she must have realized what a tantalizing sight her backside, in her loose shorts, presented climbing the steep path ahead of me. Her neck went a deep red.

"Oh," she exclaimed when we reached the top and emerged into the clearing, "what a beautiful spot." Any mortification she felt from the climb fled as she looked out over the sea. "Dexter, there couldn't be a more perfect place for Uncle Jebediah."

"Yes, he chose it for my mother. He said that from here she would always be able to see him coming home, and I know he believed that."

She turned toward the markers, and read them aloud. "Otillia (Cruz) Snell. Beloved Wife of Jebediah Snell, and Loving Mother of Dexter Snell. 1934 – 1969." She paused. "Dex, she was so young." Another pause, then she continued. "Jebediah Snell. Beloved Husband of Otillia and Loving Father of Dexter. 1920 – 1986."

We stood there for a while watching the sparkle of the sunlight dancing on the waves and I finally began the task of digging the holes for Uncle Patricio's plants. Catalina got down on her knees, removed the plants from the pots and placed them gently in place, patting the soil down around them. When she was finished she turned around, still sitting, wrapped her arms around her legs and looked out at the sea again. I sat down beside her.

"Dex," she finally said, "I want to tell you something I've never told anyone else. I have a secret mantra I made up years ago. I call it my 'so' prayer." She looked at me shyly, and then back at the sea. "It changes from time to time as I get older, and it's kind of silly, but it goes something like this.

"When I was a little girl and was sent to America to live with Patricio and Izabel after my parents died, I was so afraid. Everything was so different, and I didn't even speak English. They were so kind to me, and I needed that so much. As I grew older, I tried so hard to make them happy with me. And I think that I have done so.

"The world is not a fair place; it is what it is. But we can always choose to make it a better place. No matter what happens to me, I can decide whether to let it knock me down, or whether to get up and carry on. So …

"And that's it, Dex. I always choose to end it with 'So … I choose to carry on'."

I didn't know what to say.

She turned to me again. "You've hurt so many people, Dex. You've hurt them badly."

"I'm sorry for that, Catalina. Truly sorry. I realized it for the first time the night you came to get me, during the flight to Brunswick. And that realization came before I knew I'd lost everything."

"Is that true, Dex?" she asked, and I almost melted as I looked at those blue eyes.

"Yes, Catalina, but I don't really expect you to believe it. Not yet. Please give me the chance and the time to prove it. Perhaps I need to prove it to myself."

We sat in silence for a long time. Then she spoke again, softly.

"Dex, I don't know how to say this, so I'm just going to say it." The silence that followed was long enough that I thought she changed her mind. "You scare me," she whispered.

I didn't know how to answer. Then she continued again, looking out at the sea once more.

"I fully realize we're not cousins, but I feel drawn to you. I always have. In ways I can't explain, because I don't understand it myself. There is something in you that I see in myself and perhaps that is what scares me. I'm afraid that if I let those things out, even acknowledge them, somehow I'll end up like you. And I can't stand that thought. Do you understand what I'm saying?"

I was watching her, and she looked at me again with those eyes; those eyes that were now a darker blue.

"I'm not sure I do, Catalina. I'm sorry."

"Dex, I hope you're right about changing and there's more to you than what you've shown in the past. Because the part of me that's like you is screaming to come out. And I'm afraid once that part is out, it will take over everything. I want to know it doesn't have to."

Then she jumped up and ran down the path back to the cottage. I couldn't catch her.

V

Catalina wouldn't look at me at all the last day they were on Brac, and she carefully avoided being alone with me even for a minute. No matter what I tried, she outwitted me.

At noon Uncle Patricio, apologizing to me, asked Catalina to go and see if the car was at the top of the path and if it was, to fetch his briefcase and the notary. When she returned with the case, the notary in tow, he withdrew a handful of file folders and put them in his lap.

"I am sorry, Dexter, but there are papers you must sign and have notarized in the course of straightening out your affairs."

"That's fine, uncle. I expected it," I answered, getting up and clearing the fruit from a small table and moving it over beside him.

"These have been reviewed by my own lawyer, Dexter, and I have vetted them too. By signing them you will be relinquishing all title to the three hotels as well as the resorts in Key West itself, and in return you will be absolved from any further debts relating to them or for any shortfall in their value as measured against the loans they secure. Do you understand?"

"Yes, I understand. Show me where to sign," I said.

"Dexter, you should read them over. Catalina and I can come back tomorrow for them if you wish," he suggested.

"No, I took little interest in my own affairs before, and certainly never took your advice. I am quite prepared to take it now."

Uncle Patricio briefly explained what each document was and I quickly signed them in the multiple places required and passed them to the notary for his signature and seal. There must have been fifty or more signatures required, but we finally finished.

"There will be more in the weeks and months to come, Dexter. There are the house, the yacht, the helicopter and jet, and the hotels, resorts and developments in Marathon, Islamorada, and Key Largo. They are all intertwined, but separate, and it will take some time."

A thought crossed my mind. A thought that was devious perhaps in terms of its implication, but entirely grounded in my genuine concern for Uncle Patricio. I felt a brief stab of remorse at using him as an unwitting accomplice because ten years ago he would have seen through my ploy instantly. I plunged on anyway.

"Perhaps I should come to Brunswick to sign the rest of the papers as they are ready, uncle. It can't be easy for you to travel like this, even using the King Air," I said, looking to Catalina for support. "Don't you agree Catalina?"

She nodded her head and replied immediately, "Yes, uncle, that makes a lot of sense. You know how worried I was about this trip, as much as you wanted to come here and see Dexter."

I leaned back, secretly elated. She had fallen neatly for the first part of my ploy.

"No, Dexter, that will not work," he said.

I knew what he was about to say, but leaned forward in feigned puzzlement. "Why is that, uncle?"

"You cannot come back to the U.S. until this is all finalized and cleared up. If you do, you could open yourself up to further problems, possibly even the loss of this property," he explained.

"Then just send the papers with a courier, and I'll sign them," I said, "although I must admit I feel better having you here in person just in case I have questions." I held my breath. This was going so well it was as if I had scripted it. The remorse at using my uncle this way stabbed me briefly again.

Uncle Patricio nodded. "I know. I always felt better dealing face to face. I never felt comfortable doing things like this by telephone, even with someone I could trust." He closed his eyes and leaned back in his wheelchair. I decided to count to ten, slowly, before I delivered the coup de grace, but I was too slow.

He opened his eyes and leaned forward before I could speak. "I know," he said, "I have the perfect solution that should also satisfy dear Catalina's heartfelt concerns for an old man." He paused only a second, "I will send Catalina by herself. She knows as much about this as I do."

It was exactly what I'd intended to suggest, and my surprise was exceeded only by Catalina's. She turned and stared at me red-faced in wide-eyed shock, and in doing 'so' … my remorse evaporated. For in that brief instant when she was looking at me instead of Uncle Patricio he gave me a big, exaggerated wink.

10 Cayman Brac: 2004 March

During the times Felix was ashore we continued to renew our bonds by sharing stories from the missing years. I had little of consequence to share since most of what I could tell him now seemed trivial, if not embarrassing, so I recounted the tales that Patricio had shared with me about he and father and the early years they spent together building Marques Snell. I glossed over any mention of Catalina and fielded the few specific questions he asked about her with perfunctory answers and then neatly changed the subject.

The repairs to the cottage continued apace, and the first week in March I began to turn an eye to making it more livable. I had grown accustomed to sleeping in the hammock, but that arrangement precluded accommodating visitors of any kind. I straightened up the two bedrooms and repaired the old wooden bed frames. I'd burned the ruined mattresses shortly after I first arrived so I took measurements and had new ones delivered along with pillows, bedding and other linens that a home should have and then turned my attentions to sorting out the small library where I had simply dumped everything in my initial cleanup.

The books had been pulled from the shelves and were strewn about when I arrived, and I had piled them haphazardly here and there. Since the library windows were intact there was no water damage but they were a mess from mould and mildew plus the physical damage they suffered in being pulled from the shelves.

I set the library table upright after repairing a broken leg and set about examining the books, charts and other papers one pile at a time. I was not surprised that they consisted almost exclusively of books about the Caribbean; the Spanish plate fleets, pirates, buccaneers and privateers and assorted charts, maps and correspondence on the same subjects. Some of the books were the same ones that father had brought on the trip with Felix and me in 1984 and I felt a twinge of sadness whenever I came across and recognized one of those.

Due to the sheer mass of materials I decided to simplify the task by assigning specific shelves and drawers to general topics and then storing everything accordingly until I had the time to go through them in detail. I resisted the urge to spend more time on some of the items that caught my interest and made a mental note to come back to them later. It took a full day to get everything on the correct shelves and in the right drawers, and as I was nearing the end I realized that father's leather-bound journals were missing. I assumed that they were still aboard the *Estrela* and put it out of my mind, deciding to look for them there later.

II

I knew I had to tackle the well sooner or later, but perhaps due to some quirk of genetic engineering I, like my father, found ways to avoid actually starting that major project. Nevertheless, I did take a look at it to determine what had to be done.

The well was up the path and behind the cottage. It was a dug well which had originally required a tremendous amount of effort. The well, as Bibi had said, was caved in at the bottom. The original construction consisted of a stone lining and it was apparent from the weed-choked pile of rubble beside it that father had started the necessary repairs before he died. The hand pump and piping that led down to the cottage had been completely disassembled and buried in the pile of rubble with bits and pieces sticking out here and there.

I sat down and looked at the remains and decided that instead of completing what father had started I would restore the cistern by the back of the cottage and rig a series of catchments on the roof to collect and fill it with rainwater. I was pleased with that solution and started to examine the pile of materials to see what I could salvage when I heard Felix hailing me from the cottage. I happily abandoned my chores and made my way back, looking forward to preparing dinner from whatever Felix had returned with this time.

III

"Good fishing?" I asked Felix as I rounded the corner.

"Very good, and I sold everything at the pier. The kitchens at the hotels seem to swallow up whatever I can catch," he grinned. "I kept some shrimp for us and found some lobster in the trap."

We set about our normal routine of lighting the fire, filling the pot with seawater and setting it to boil before settling down on the porch to pass the bottle of rum back and forth while we watched the sun set.

One of the nicest things I'd discovered about friendship is the ability to simply sit together for long stretches of time without feeling the need to talk. It was a new experience for me, and I looked forward to sitting quietly with Felix as much as I did to sharing our stories.

The silences also served to pace the rate at which we moved toward dealing with some emotional and touchy subjects that we had avoided so far – Bibi's death, the discovery of my father's body and the circumstances surrounding his death, and the strange events that Felix and I had been exposed to with the guns and clandestine meetings with the Marques Snell boats in 1984. There were a lot of questions forming in my mind, but I instinctively knew that Felix was still feeling me out and I decided to let him take his time.

"Did I tell you that I met my father?" Felix asked, finally breaking the after dinner silence and passing the rum bottle.

"No, you didn't. I'd like to hear about it."

Felix chuckled. "It's actually a pretty funny story. It happened the year before my mother died," he started. "I was at the main dock aboard *Estrela* and unloading the last of the catch. Bibi had walked into town and was coming down to the dock to ride back with me aboard the *Estrela* when I heard her yelling. She was standing at the end of the dock, and there was a little man jumping around in front of her.

"You should have seen it, Dex," he grinned, "there's Bibi, standing with her big arms on her hips and her dress blowing in the breeze, yelling in that loud voice of hers. A crowd gathered around the two of them, this little guy jumping around like a banty rooster.

"All of a sudden, she reached out with that big right arm and picked him right up. She tucked him under her left arm and started down the dock. She was still yelling at him while he was kicking and struggling and the crowd moved out of the way, and then followed her, cheering her on."

I laughed at the image he was painting. I could almost see and hear Bibi. I passed the bottle back to Felix and he took a swig before continuing.

"She stopped when she got to the *Estrela* and held him up in both hands so he could see me and yelled 'here's the only good thing that's ever been squeezed out of you, you good-for-nothing' and then threw him into the sea." Felix was laughing so hard now that tears were rolling down his face and he was in danger of losing his grip on the rum bottle. I reached over, laughing just as hard, and rescued it.

"He swam around the dock looking for a safe place to climb up, but she kept following him wherever he swam, still yelling at him. The crowd was calling for him to climb out so they could watch her throw him back in again."

We were both rolling on the porch now, laughing through our tears. Then Felix' laughter faded and he got up and walked over to the edge of the porch. He stopped and turned toward me.

"I've never regretted that brief meeting with my father, and never wanted any more to do with him. I saw him, and that's enough." He looked out toward the sea.

"But it was terrible watching Bibi die. The cancer just ate her up."

Then he turned and went home.

IV

I finally went to work on the cistern and the roof catchments after digging the pipes and other bits and pieces from the pile up by the old well.

The cistern itself was an interesting relic. Like most of the other structures on the property, it had been constructed from ballast stones recovered from some long-forgotten shipwreck and then lined with mortar. Where the mortar had fallen away, I saw there were a number of stones of the type that had always made the walls of the cottage so interesting to me. These were more or less rounded or at least oval-shaped, which I'd learned in my geology class so long ago indicated they had been tumbled along the bottom of a stream or river somewhere for thousands of years.

Many had a lighter colored stringer of quartz through them. Depending on where the stones were used in constructing the cottage so long ago, some of them had been split to present a flatter face and the quartz stringers were exposed as stripes that appeared in the finished wall at random angles. Felix and I, in our explorations of Brac, had never found any like them, reinforcing father's belief that they were ballast stones from some long-forgotten wreck.

The mortar was pretty well crumbled so I made a list of what I would need to complete the catchments, the rudimentary plumbing and the new cistern lining, and put them on order. That done, I turned back to the library.

I'd forgotten to ask Felix about father's journals, and made a note to do that when he returned in the next day or so. In the meantime I started with the most interesting of the collection, the charts.

The charts were a mess. Many of them had been ripped, some into pieces. There must have been two hundred of them or more - many of them hand drawn - and father had constructed special drawers at the bottom of the bookcases to hold them. The drawers were large but shallow, and could hold open charts of a size up to three feet by four feet. I first decided on a filing system for those that were more or less intact. I was about halfway through when I heard the roar of a low-flying plane and hurried to the window to see the King Air making a low pass before making a swooping turn and heading toward the airport.

I abandoned the charts and the library and hurriedly set about fussing with the main part of the cottage. Although the cottage, with the exception of the library, was pretty well sorted out and completely clean I suddenly saw it in a different light in the hope that Catalina was aboard the plane. I noticed the lack of curtains and the general absence of colors although I had made the most of what I'd salvaged, repairing the old furniture and cleaning and polishing the brass nautical pieces father had collected. I'd replaced the hurricanes on the oil lamps and carefully positioned the additional ones Felix gave me so the cottage was warm and inviting after sunset, and arranged the furniture to make the view of the sea the focal point. In my excitement at seeing Catalina again, I found myself rearranging some of the pieces one more time and then after a few minutes putting them all back again. It seemed like hours passed before I heard a car at the top of the path and hurried outside. I waited at the corner of the porch anxiously watching and preparing to be disappointed, when she appeared.

"Catalina," I called to her, resisting the urge to run over and sweep her up into my arms.

"Hello, Dex," she said just before I noticed the notary following her. She was carrying a leather briefcase and not dressed for the tropics. Long, baggy slacks, a loose blouse buttoned to the top and brown loafers completed her modest outfit. "I was hoping you'd be here so we can go over the latest papers and get them signed quickly." She smiled politely, and offered her hand.

"Well," I answered, "come and sit for a bit at least. I'll get some drinks and you can tell me about Patricio. How is he doing?"

She made her way past me and around to the porch, answering over her shoulder as she walked. "He's fine, Dex. He's improved since telling you about your financial collapse, but you have to remember his age. How are you?"

"I'm okay. I'm making progress on the repairs to the cottage, and doing better than I have a right to. But I find I miss Uncle Patricio." She started to say something in reply and I raised my hand and continued. "I know what you're about to say, Catalina, and there is nothing I can do to make up for the years of neglect. That doesn't keep me from wanting to fill in for those years while I can."

I went to fetch glasses and a pitcher of juice from the icebox. When I turned around, she was standing behind me. I looked at her, waiting for her to say something.

"I'm sorry, Dex. I'm still angry about the way you treated Patricio for so long. He's so much happier now believing you've changed, and I don't want to see you hurt him again."

I let that sink in before answering, and then decided to leave it for later. She made it clear on her first visit how she felt, and her doubts about me were understandable. Protesting would not erase those concerns.

"Come on, Dex. The notary is waiting for us on the porch."

We went through the papers more slowly this time, not due to my interest in the details but because I was trying to draw out the time I could spend with Catalina in any way possible. I was secretly pleased to find there was nothing I could ask, no detail too small, that she didn't have an explanation and an answer for.

The interminable signing and notarizing completed she rose to leave, extending her hand. "Thanks, Dexter. I'll be going now."

"Wait, Catalina. Why not stay over and fly back in the morning?" I asked, trying not to sound too desperate. "You're the only link I have with Patricio, and I want to talk to you about him." I saw that was unconvincing so I continued immediately, "and you know he will ask about me. What will you tell him – that you just got the papers signed and left?"

I held my breath and watched her face as she considered that. She looked out over the sea and although she wasn't smiling, she wasn't completely frowning either. She seemed to reach a decision.

"You're right, Dex, although I question your motives. I'll go up and tell the driver to take the notary back to town and to make a reservation for me at the same place Patricio and I stayed last time. He can come back and get me later."

It wasn't exactly what I had in mind, but the prospect of spending any more time at all with Catalina was preferable to having her leave immediately. As she went up the path, I made plans for dinner.

V

We caught two lobsters from a rocky point up the beach, or I should say I caught them as I couldn't even coax Catalina into removing her loafers and rolling up her slacks. Her mood lightened, however, as I made a show of clowning around in the water while finding the 'right' lobsters and then walking back to the cottage holding them by their carapaces.

While the water boiled I showed her what I'd accomplished in the months that I'd been there. She was full of questions about the well, the cistern and the stones that I explained were from someplace other than Brac. Her smiles came more often, and she was more relaxed.

After we ate we walked back up to my parents' graves to check on Patricio's plants and then sat down to watch the sunset where we'd sat two months earlier. There was a long silence, much like those that I'd grown accustomed to with Felix, and I left it alone waiting for her to say whatever it was that was on her mind. I felt strangely content just sitting there beside her, and was wondering about that feeling when she spoke.

"I know that Patricio manipulated this arrangement, Dex. Did you put him up to it?"

I considered her question carefully before answering.

"No, I didn't Catalina. But if he hadn't, I would have." I continued looking out at the sea and let my answer hang there in the air between us.

"Dex, I told you more when we were up here than I've ever told anyone. As much as I loved Izabel, and as much as I love Patricio, I have always held part of myself back. Perhaps it's a result of losing my parents at such a young age. I don't know. But I've thought about it a lot."

I looked at her now, and with an indescribable effort resisted taking her in my arms. She was expressing emotions that I had ignored, or perhaps buried, and by talking about them she opened the floodgates of my own feelings. That, too, was completely new to me. I realized how I'd repressed, but not resolved those feelings through my headlong pursuit of instant gratification and the acquisition of material possessions. And I'd further avoided confronting them by minimizing contact with Uncle Patricio for years. I was wondering what was in Catalina's makeup that allowed her to deal with things that I obviously couldn't, when she spoke again.

"I know you've been hurt too. And when your father died, although I was only ten years old and you were seventeen, I felt I could somehow comfort you." She turned to look at me and I felt like I would drown in the depth of those blue eyes. Her mouth was open slightly and her lips quivered as she continued. "But you ran away before I had the chance. You stole that from me, and I'd almost purged it from my memory when Patricio sent me to find you."

I looked at her and started to speak but she interrupted me by holding up a hand. "Don't say anything, Dex. Please, just sit here for ten minutes," and she stood up and walked back down the path, alone.

I sat, disconsolate, and watched the final flashing of colors as the sea swallowed the sun. I waited as she'd asked and then made my way slowly down the path. As I got closer, I saw that she'd lit the oil lamps, bathing the inside of the cottage in a soft light that spilled out the windows and the open doors onto the porch. She was standing near the edge of the porch looking out at the sea. I came up behind her and touched her shoulder, and she spun around and stepped close, wrapping her arms around my neck and staring at me with those blue eyes for only a second before she crushed herself against me and pressed her lips to mine.

I can still summon up the intensity of the emotions that washed over me in that instant. And the sensations. The softness of her lips and tongue against mine, the instant heat that infused our bodies, the fullness of her breasts and the hardness of her nipples pressed against my chest, the smell of her; what I came to think of as the Catalina scent, full of desire, promise and raw sexuality.

And then as quickly as it had happened she broke away, ran around the corner of the cottage and up the path to the waiting car.

VI

It was a long night. Perhaps the longest I've ever experienced.

I sat on the porch for hours trying to sort out my emotions, replaying all of those feelings and sensations so I could burn them permanently into my memory. I found that I could close my eyes and summon the image of her face in the instant before she kissed me, and feel again the incredible passions burning so deeply inside her. I ached to hold her again, as if it was something I'd known all my life that had been torn from me instead of something that had occurred in the flash of a few brief seconds. I realized with a start that I still knew so little about her, and even with the short, infrequent visits I'd shared with Uncle Patricio that I'd never asked about her, and that he had never mentioned her.

All of these thoughts and emotions were colliding with the physical desire that had first hit me when I'd seen her step out from behind Shando that night aboard *Party Girl*. Perhaps colliding isn't the right word, because the all-too-familiar physical desires were now amplified by my emotions into an unrecognizable caldron of overwhelming, burning passion. Those first feelings were nothing as compared to what I was experiencing now, and the comparison embarrassed me. It was a slap in the face from a past where the only emotions I'd felt were the physical ones - the desire to possess, discard and move on in search of the next conquest. This was unfamiliar territory for me, and it infused my entire being. I finally realized with a shock that this might be love.

I crawled into my hammock, exhausted but still unable to subdue the unfamiliar emotions that were rattling through me, keeping me awake. Sometime just before dawn I fell deeply asleep.

VII

My dreams were a jumbled mass of events and people, mostly people. They ranged from father and the *Estrela* to Uncle Patricio, Aunt Izabel and Bibi, but they had a recurring theme. Each time the person in the dream tried to talk to me they would fade away, as if they were being taken from me somehow and unable to tell me what it was they wanted to convey. Their faces would became more animated even as they faded, and no matter how quickly I ran after them or tried to listen harder, they would eventually disappear as if in a wisp of smoke. And each time that happened Catalina would appear behind me, calling to me to 'come back, come back, come back'. She appeared as I now knew her, fully grown, but her voice was the small-girl voice I remembered with a strong Portuguese accent. I would turn to go back, and she would withdraw as if afraid of me. The cycle repeated itself over and over and although I knew it was a dream, I couldn't seem to break out of it. Finally, her 'come back, come back', switched to 'wake up, wake up', and I was jolted awake to find her there, shaking me.

"Dexter, are you all right?" she asked, clearly upset.

It took me a few seconds to realize I was no longer dreaming, and she was in fact standing there beside me.

"What time is it?" I asked stupidly.

"It's past two o'clock," she answered, and then looked away as if she was embarrassed.

I mustn't have yet been fully awake, because it took me a few more seconds to process everything.

"But you were to leave this morning ..."

She turned back to me and took my face in her hands. "I sent the pilot and plane back to Uncle Patricio with the documents, Dexter," she said, staring at me wide-eyed. I could read the doubt and nervousness in her expression as she searched my face with those blue eyes. Then it hit me.

"You're staying on Brac?" I asked stupidly, and as the full realization sank in I jumped out of the hammock and tried to put my arms around her. She held me off and looked at me shyly.

"Dex, I have a confession to make. I was hoping that somehow, something would happen between us, and at the same time, I was afraid. I never intended to fly back yesterday and I spent the entire night lying awake, trying to sort out my feelings." She turned away and then continued. "It was the pleasure and pride I saw in you as you showed me what you have accomplished here with your own two hands that finally did it. I truly believe you are happy, Dexter. I want to take a chance and get to know you." She looked at me again, and blushed. "And I have another confession."

"Yes?" I asked, afraid to say more.

She looked at me with those incredibly big, shining eyes, and whispered, "I checked out of the hotel."

As my face revealed that I understood what she'd just said, she rushed into my arms and picked up immediately where she'd left off the night before.

Tears ran down her face at the same time she was kissing me, and all of the feelings came roaring back. I lifted her in my arms, her mouth still locked to mine, and carried her inside.

VIII

The rest of the day was a blur as I look back on it now. We made love – and I truly believe it was the first time I'd ever actually made love – repeatedly, breaking only to swim naked in the sea, share secret thoughts or to simply lay still, cradling each other silently as we rested. Every time I thought I was sated and couldn't possibly make love again, she would do something to arouse me once more. Her appetite matched mine step for step, and it was another revelation on my new journey of discovery.

It was sometime around midnight as we lay together, her head resting on my chest, that she asked about the death of my father.

"What happened to you after that, Dex? Where did you go, and why?"

I'd never talked to anyone about the eighteen months following father's death when I'd run away. It was the beginning of the wall I built around myself to shield me from the pain of losing the people I loved, and my initial reaction now was to somehow avoid telling Catalina about it. But even as I was contemplating how to change the subject the mortar began to crumble in that secret wall and the first brick fell with a thud that reverberated in my chest.

"I was in pain, Catalina, and I had to run," I started. "Deep inside I knew Aunt Izabel would be next, and then it would be Uncle Patricio. I never really confronted or even acknowledged that until the night we flew from Key West to Brunswick and I thought Patricio was dying." I paused to gather my thoughts before continuing and Catalina just lay there with her head on my chest, listening while I wrestled with my inner demons.

"I ran as far away from the sea and fishing boats as I could go. I hitched my way to Texas, working at odd jobs along the way. I stayed for about six months in El Paso." I took a deep breath and continued.

"In El Paso I found I could make easy money smuggling marijuana across the border from Juarez. It was small time at first, and I made enough to get a single room in a grubby motel where no one bothered me." I paused to let the repressed memories refresh. "I spent my money on books. Books of all kinds. And I lost myself for days just reading, trying to fill my mind with anything but thoughts of father, Patricio, Izabel or my mother, who I'd never known." I paused again for a long while and then Catalina moved her hand to stroke my hair, indicating she was still listening.

"The smuggling escalated to where I was running marijuana in larger amounts for others, and once I started I couldn't stop. It wasn't as if I had a choice; I mean I couldn't stop because the group I was smuggling for wouldn't let me stop. I tried.

"They must have known I was preparing to leave and they set me up. I was sacrificed as a diversion for a much larger shipment but in the confusion of the bust I managed to escape into the darkness and made my way to California. I ended up south of San Diego, again close to the Mexican border, and finally ended up in Tijuana." I stopped now, struggling with whether to continue or to simply skip through to my return to Brunswick twelve months later. Catalina made the choice for me.

"What happened in Tijuana, Dex?" she asked in a whisper.

I gathered my thoughts once again, and plunged on.

"I had a little money now, but not much. I was determined to stay out of smuggling although it would have been easy to pick up from where I'd left off in El Paso but staying small this time.

"I wandered around the harbor in San Diego thinking I could get work on a boat, and I did for a while but the memories were just too painful. On my eighteenth birthday I went to Tijuana and rented a room in a house. I had some notion I could hide in Mexico, not far from the States, and work at something there.

"I ended up in a nightclub as a waiter, and then a bartender. It was an upscale nightclub by Tijuana standards and it catered to a monied American crowd who were looking for the kinds of excitement they couldn't find easily and anonymously at home." I stopped again and wound my fingers loosely into Catalina's hair.

"What kinds of excitement, Dex?"

I let the question hang in the air for a while, and then plunged on.

"Drugs and sex, mostly," I answered, taking a deep breath. "It wasn't long before I realized certain women, generous women, found me attractive. At first I catered to women who just wanted to fulfill the fantasy of being with a younger man, and they spread the word among their similarly inclined friends back home. It was easy and lucrative. But it soon went beyond that." I closed my eyes and Catalina stroked the side of my face.

"Please go on, Dex."

I struggled for the words, and then continued again. "I suppose it sounds fatuous, but I'm a quick learner. I found an even more lucrative clientele that wanted something beyond dinner, dancing and a night of straight sex with a younger man. They wanted an edgier experience, something they couldn't get or were afraid to ask for from their husbands. And it didn't take me long to learn how to draw those fantasies out and satisfy them. Fantasies and desires of every kind." I stopped again, realizing Catalina had stopped stroking my face, but at least she was still there. I waited, dreading another question, and when it didn't come, I continued.

"I learned something about people through that. I became friends with a twenty-two year old girl from Los Angeles – it seems strange to call her a girl now, since she was older than me and I thought of her as a woman then. We became friends and we sometimes worked together when one of my clients wanted that, and she told me we would never be able to make a living if husbands and wives just shared their innermost desires and fantasies with each other instead of bottling them up until they boiled over in other ways." I paused again trying to decide how much more to say when Catalina made the decision for me.

"What made you decide to come back to Brunswick?"

I began immediately, relieved to shift away from my time in Tijuana. "You know it was my nineteenth birthday, and I fooled myself into believing I was coming back for my inheritance, but it wasn't. I came back because I thought I'd learned enough about people to finally face my own fears, and I missed Uncle Patricio and Aunt Izabel. But when I got back and found Izabel was gone, the same fears returned and I ran away again. Differently this time if only because I was now wealthy, but I ran away again. This time I ran to Key West and hid behind all of the trappings of material possessions and the false sense of protection they afforded me. And I hid behind that wall until you came to Key West and got me."

Catalina lay still for a long while and then shifted so she was lying alongside me, her face turned toward me. One hand was still against the side of my face and her other arm was across my chest, and she began to whisper to me.

"Dex, I've been deluding myself, too." Now it was her turn, and I closed my eyes and gave thanks she hadn't run after hearing about my past.

"I told you how I felt about you after your father died, and how hurt I was when you left. I threw myself into trying to replace you for Patricio and Izabel, but no matter how hard I tried it wouldn't work. It wasn't that they didn't love me, but that they loved you, too. It was like there was a big hole in their lives, and therefore in mine as well.

"I did my best to be the perfect daughter, excelled at school and even learned to cook like Aunt Izabel. But it wasn't enough. Not just for them, but for me, either. I studied economics and business so I could help Uncle Patricio in his work, but all the time, there was something missing." It was Catalina's turn to hesitate, and I gave her the time to gather her thoughts as she had given me.

"On the surface, I was everything a dutiful daughter should be but I was always looking for more. I have had a long string of relationships, Dex, but I never allowed any of them to get close to me, and I particularly kept them from Patricio and Izabel.

"I was attracted to some men because they reminded me of you. And when they didn't measure up to my fantasies of you I discarded them. Then I would find someone who was as different from you as possible, and I would quickly cast him aside for the same reason – he wasn't you. There were a lot of them, Dex," she whispered, and then fell silent.

I started to say something but she cut me off.

"Wait, Dex, there's more." She gathered her thoughts and started again.

"I was obsessed with you. I read everything I could find about you in the newspapers and magazines, and there was a lot. When reading about you no longer satisfied me I began to spend time in Key West, and in Miami when you were there. I manipulated whichever man I was with at the time to take me to clubs and restaurants where I could see you, and every time I tried to convince myself that your behavior and that of the people you were with was disgusting. But that didn't work, either. Somehow I knew there was more to you – and I don't say this to hurt you – I thought there was more to you even though any sensible person would have discarded that notion.

"And all the while I was working my way through man after man and finding them lacking I was petrified that Izabel and Patricio would hear of my behavior, but I couldn't help myself." She was quiet for a long time now, while all kinds of confused thoughts, questions and emotions swirled through my feverish mind.

She finally whispered again, so softly I could barely hear her. "Dex, that's all I can share with you right now. I'm still afraid, but I want to keep seeing you."

We finally fell asleep in the wee hours of the morning, our bodies entwined, and slept through to dawn when her gentle kisses woke me and we made love again.

11 Cayman Brac: 2004 June

Catalina's visits became more frequent and her stays became longer. And although we both enjoyed Felix' company he tended to stay away for all but a day or so when she was on Brac, allowing us to spend long periods of uninterrupted time together.

It was after she left midway through the third week in June I started thinking again about my father's death and other loose ends like the trip in 1984. In addition, I was now certain there were journals missing from the library.

I wrestled with how to broach the subject with Felix and decided to simply start with father's death. The opportunity came the first night after Catalina left and Felix arrived with fresh fish for dinner. We cleared away the pots and sat down on the porch with our rum to watch the sun set. I decided to ask directly.

"Felix," I started, "I need to know about my father's death."

He sat for the longest time, and finally, without turning to me asked, "What is it you want to know?"

"Who found him?"

He turned to me now, and I could see the tormented look in his eyes. "I did. Are you sure you want to talk about this?"

"Yes, Felix. I'm certain. We've been avoiding the subject, and it's time."

He nodded, and then started. "I found him by accident. He had been gone for a day and a half, which wasn't strange except that the *Estrela* was at anchor." He stopped and looked at me again. "This is hard."

I nodded, and then he continued.

"He was on the beach around the point, and …" He got up and walked down to the end of the porch, stood there for a minute and then walked back. "Dex, he'd been staked out by his wrists and ankles in the sand at low tide and left there to drown. The crabs had been at him, and though they chewed him up pretty good it was nothing compared to what they did to him with a knife before they left him." Felix couldn't look at me.

I knew there was more to my father's death than a simple drowning, but I wasn't prepared for this. I felt my chest constrict and I stopped breathing, as if that could somehow get me through. My head began to pound and I squeezed my eyes closed until little bright points of light began to pulse behind my eyelids. My hands cramped as I clenched them into fists and crossed my arms tightly across my stomach, leaning forward. It was as if I was trying to shut my body down in an attempt to make time stand still so I could deal with what I'd just heard.

Subconsciously I had known there was more, and perhaps that explained why I'd never called or visited Brac in all those years. Those years, however, didn't dull or ease the pain I was feeling now. All I could see was my father being tormented, tortured, and the tremendous struggle he would have put up. This wasn't something one person could do to my father; it would have taken more of them to escape unscathed. And I could picture him, his indomitable will power intact until the end, resisting them right up to the point his body failed him.

I felt a momentary surge of anger at Uncle Patricio but it faded just as quickly as I realized I had never given him the opportunity to tell me the truth. I'd run away and continued running for all these years. It was as though he knew I was unprepared to handle it. Well, I was ready to handle it now, and if I hadn't already stopped running, this settled it.

I slowly unclenched my fists, sat up and uncrossed my arms. I took a few deep breaths and looked at Felix. "There's more, isn't there. Give it to me. I want to hear all of it, Felix."

"Yes, there's more. Whoever did it wasn't finished. They came back a few more times over the years and tore the cottage apart each time. They were looking for something that they didn't get out of Jebediah before he died. The damage wasn't from vandals, not here on Brac. It was them, searching." Felix sat back down on the porch.

"What do you think they were looking for, Felix?" I asked.

Another long silence, then "You remember the trip in 1984?"

"Yes, I remember – it has to do with the rendezvous with the Marques Snell boats, doesn't it."

"I think so, Dex. I don't know what they were looking for, but it has to do with that. It's the only thing that makes sense to me."

We sat there for a long time, both looking out at the moonlight sparkling on the sea before he spoke again.

"Dex, this is going to hurt me as much as it's going to hurt you, and I hope you'll forgive me for saying it. But I've had years to think about this. It's the only answer I can come up with."

"Go ahead and say it, Felix. I think I'm ready."

"Jebediah was gone a lot that last year. He'd leave in the middle of the night, and he'd come back at night, weeks later. He wouldn't tell me where he'd been – not that I came right out and asked – I was only seventeen, but he was almost sneaky about it.

"He spent a lot of time with me. We fished, swam, ate our meals together - much like you and I do now – we even sat here and drank rum in the evening while he told me all of his stories about the Caribbean. But there was always that mystery about where he'd been when he disappeared every now and then. It was something we just didn't discuss."

He looked at me and finally said it straight out. "Dex, this had to have something to do with the cocaine smuggling he told us about. I think he was running coke up from Colombia."

There. He'd said it. And although the same suspicion had been lingering in my mind, it was as though in hearing someone else verbalize it I could now categorically reject the possibility.

"It may have something to do with the cocaine smuggling, Felix, but father was not running drugs. He wouldn't have done that," I said flatly. "He didn't need the money. In fact, I know he had more than he needed. His whole life was fishing and exploring and after the breakup of Marques Snell in 1985 he had more money than he knew what to do with. He just left it with Patricio."

Felix was silent for a long time. "I'm sorry, Dex. I've had this bottled up inside me for all these years. I've had nobody to talk to about it. Patricio came back here a few times to meet with the constables, but nothing came of it. He asked me to board up the cottage and to take care of the *Estrela* – he told me to fish with it, as that is what Jebediah would have wanted. I just didn't know what else to think."

"I know, Felix. It's okay." My mind was slowly focusing again, recovering from the shock of hearing about the horrible way my father died. "Were there any charts or journals aboard the *Estrela*, Felix?" I asked.

Felix thought before answering. "No journals. And the only charts were for the waters immediately around the Caymans – Grand Cayman, Little Cayman and Brac. But the *Estrela* had been searched too, like the cottage. It wasn't as obvious, but the secret bulkhead cabinet was open and the guns were gone."

We sat there for a long time, each deep in our own thoughts. I finally broke the silence.

"I want you to help me go over the *Estrela* tomorrow. I want to go over every inch of it. And after we've done that, I want to use the phone at your house to make some calls."

Felix nodded and I could see that he was relieved to finally have someone to talk to about this. I just hoped I was right about father, and that he hadn't died as a cocaine smuggler.

But proving my father wasn't a smuggler was secondary to me; I knew who killed him. And as long as the blood of Jebediah Snell ran in my veins, nothing would stop me from avenging his death.

II

Felix and I rowed out to the *Estrela* the next morning even though I wasn't certain what I was looking for. The journals and any hidden charts were an obvious target, so Felix and I talked about all the possible places these could be hidden before we began. We decided to start at opposite ends of the boat and work our way toward the middle, pass each other and then continue on so that the entire boat would be thoroughly explored twice. We each took a handful of tools – screwdrivers, wrenches, pliers and a flashlight – and started our search. I started at the bow and Felix took the stern.

The anchor locker was simple, but time consuming. I had to pull all of the chain up onto the forward deck in order to empty the locker and make certain there weren't any hidden compartments, and then feed it all back in through the hawse pipe. My arms ached by the time I was finished but I was confident there was nothing hidden in that locker.

Next, I went into the cabin and down into the gear storage area. This was located forward, below deck, and contained a jumble of assorted bits and pieces, tools and spare components like alternators, water pumps and parts for the generator. I was surprised to see that a large air compressor had been fitted amidships against the rear bulkhead and made a mental note to ask Felix about it. It took two hours to look through the gear storage area, paying particular attention to removing the few panels that were bolted or screwed into place and checking the cavities carefully using the flashlight and a metal probe. I left the panels off to make it easier for Felix and chided myself for not leaving the anchor chain piled on the forward deck for the same reason. I also inspected all of the welds and seams looking for any signs of tampering, and found none.

I made my way out of the gear storage compartment and went aft to see how Felix was doing.

"Find anything?" I asked, and then broke into laughter at the sight of Felix' face, covered with grease. "You look like a Zulu warrior preparing for battle."

"Not yet," he grinned, "unless you call finding out that the area around the rudder post is cramped and needs a good steam cleaning. How are you doing?"

"I found nothing, but I'm curious about the compressor in the gear compartment. Did you add it?"

"No, Jebediah had it installed right after we got back from that trip in '84. He bought scuba gear – enough for him and me – and spare tanks. I took the gear off the boat years ago, and it's all back at my house. I haven't used it since he died."

I thought about that for a while. "Did you dive with him often?"

"Only three or four times, enough to learn how. He just bought all the stuff somewhere and never got certified. He bought some books on diving and I remember reading to him the parts about how dangerous it could be unless you knew what you were doing, but he scoffed and said we wouldn't dive deep enough to hurt ourselves. I never used the gear after he died, mostly because I didn't have anyone to dive with."

That raised another question in my mind. "Did he dive by himself?"

"Yes, a lot. I warned him about it but you know what he was like. I knew he was diving alone because all of the tanks were new when he got them and every time he came back after one of his trips they'd have more scratches and marks."

I wondered exactly what it was he was diving for, alone, and went back to search the wheelhouse.

It took the best part of the day before Felix and I met up amidships, and we rowed back to shore after discussing what we'd found – nothing. We started again at dawn the next morning, this time switching places so we would cover the boat twice.

The second search went more quickly since both Felix and I had left all the panels open. We were sitting in the wheelhouse, discouraged, and talking more about the scuba diving when a thought hit me. I was surprised I hadn't thought of it sooner, given my experience smuggling marijuana across the border from Juarez almost twenty years ago.

"I checked all of the welds around the fuel tanks, but I didn't check the inside. Where's the dip stick?"

"I don't have one," Felix said sheepishly. "I just fuel up whenever I'm in Grand Cayman, and keep track of fuel consumption by calculating running hours."

I retrieved a metal rod from the gear locker, and made my way to the rear deck. There were two saddle tanks aboard the *Estrela*, one starboard and one port, in addition to the main tank below the floor of the engine compartment. I removed the deck fill plates for the saddle tanks and inserted the rod.

"I'm just making sure that there isn't a false bottom in one or both of the tanks," I explained. Felix watched with interest as I measured the length of the rod inserted into the tank. It matched my estimate of what it should be and I sat down again, discouraged.

"Felix, you really should know better than running without a dipstick. You need to physically check the fuel levels every once in a while and compare to your calculations," I scolded him. I was probably harsher than I should have been because I was disappointed at not finding anything aboard the *Estrela*. I was certain she held a clue, and was still mulling over the diving.

"I know I should Dex. You always did it when we were aboard together and I guess I just never got into the habit. I know I can run about five hundred hours without refueling and I just go by the hour meter on the engine."

I was about to apologize when it hit me.

"How long, Felix?" I asked excitedly.

"About five hundred hours. Don't get worked up, Dex. I never run more than four hundred without tanking up, just to be safe."

I jumped to my feet and ran back to the engine compartment, Felix trailing behind me.

"What is it, Dex?"

"We've found it, Felix," I almost shouted, "the *Estrela's* tanks held eight thousand gallons in 1984, enough for a thousand hours of running time. Let's go."

We climbed down into the engine compartment again and again inspected the two saddle tanks father had installed in 1984. They were each about twelve feet long and five feet high. They were wider at the top than at the bottom, allowing for the angle of the sides of the hull, but about four and a half feet wide in the middle. I found a pencil and paper in the wheelhouse and did some quick calculations.

I remembered the original, main tank below the engine room floor held three thousand gallons, and my volume calculations using the measurements of the saddle tanks showed that they were each approximately two thousand five hundred gallons, which matched the total fuel capacity I remembered – eight thousand. Felix watched me scribbling the calculations and followed me back down into the engine compartment.

"The fuel fills go into the front of each saddle tank, Felix, and the depth of the tanks is correct according to the dipstick," I said, looking more closely at the tanks. "They must be compartmented vertically – the rear three quarters or more of each tank has been isolated."

The *Estrela's* tanks were welded into the boat, but I now noticed there were also three metal straps securing each – one at the forward edge, one in the middle, and one at the back edge of the tank. The straps went around the front and top of each tank and were bolted securely to studs where they met the floor and rear bulkhead.

"Hand me the wrenches," I said, still looking at the straps.

Felix retrieved the wrenches and I went to work on the rear end strap on the starboard tank, which is where I would have made the seams, if there were any. I worked the nut at the inboard, bottom end of the strap first and as soon as it loosened and popped free the end plate of the tank shifted.

"Bingo!" I yelled, "Help me move this, Felix." We shifted the plate, and it came all the way loose. "Had me the flashlight."

I shone the light inside the tank and saw that it was compartmented as I had thought it would be. The workmanship itself was flawless; the edges of the seam had been cut with a torch and then carefully ground for a tight fit that wouldn't shift easily unless the straps themselves were removed. The strap hid the seam.

"Jebediah went to a lot of trouble to do this, Dex. He must have been hiding something valuable in here."

I left the implication hanging and climbed into the tank to look for any clues as to what it might have contained. The hidden compartment was big, about twelve feet long, five feet high and tapering from over five feet wide at the top to about three feet wide at the bottom. I examined the inner seams carefully, half hoping to find some clue, perhaps some type of residue, anything that might offer a hint as to what had been transported inside. There was nothing other than scratches and scrapes.

"Pull the other plate while I keep looking in here, Felix."

Once I could hear Felix working on the other tank I wet my finger and carefully ran it along the inside bottom seam, trying to pick up any residual powder. There wasn't anything I could see, and I licked my finger occasionally trying to detect any hint of cocaine. Nothing.

"I've got it open, Dex," Felix called.

I exited the starboard tank and went over to the port side. Felix was already in the tank and I could see it was the same as the other, right down to the scratches and scrapes on the inside. I knew I wouldn't find anything in there, either. We refitted the end plates and straps carefully, ensuring we left no telltale marks on the nuts. When we were satisfied everything was as we had found it we went back topside.

Felix didn't say anything, leaving me with my thoughts. When I was ready, I broke the silence.

"I know this looks bad, Felix, but I still don't believe father was involved with cocaine smuggling."

"I don't want to believe it either, Dex, but I just don't see any other answer. Everything points to that."

I didn't reply, simply moving aft and climbing into the dinghy with Felix for the row to shore.

III

The calls to the States didn't go well, either. Felix left me alone inside his house to place them, making the excuse that he had to go and see his two helpers.

I made the call to Patricio first. Catalina answered and although I was pleased to hear her voice I didn't speak to her long before I asked for Patricio. Her disappointment was obvious, but she went to tell him to pick up the phone in his office.

"Hello Dexter, this is a nice surprise," he said as he came on the line. I waited to hear the click of the other phone disconnecting before I got down to business.

"Felix told me how father died, uncle, and I need to talk to you about it." There was a long silence.

"Just a minute, Dex," he finally said, and he cupped his hand over the mouthpiece but I could hear him asking Catalina to leave him and close the door. I heard Catalina protesting and a brief exchange of quiet words, then Patricio came back on the line.

"Dexter, I wanted to talk to you about this a long time ago but I never had the chance."

"We don't have to go into that, uncle. It doesn't matter. I'm not blaming you; I just need to understand everything. I've got a lot of questions."

"Yes, Dexter. I am sure you do. And I do not wish to do over the phone what should have been done long ago face to face. I will come and see you," he said. I could hear the sadness in his voice.

"That's not necessary, uncle," I answered.

"Yes, it is, Dex. Today is what, Sunday? Yes – I will be there on Thursday," and before I could say anything, he'd hung up the phone.

I sat for a while thinking, and decided it was worthless to try to read anything more into the conversation. I knew whatever it was had to be serious, and that in itself wasn't a surprise.

I picked up the phone again and dialed Shando's cell number. He answered on the second ring.

"Yeah."

"Shando, it's me, Dex." Before I could say more, he interrupted.

"Okay, it's arranged for 9:30," and he hung up.

He obviously couldn't talk to me now and I checked my watch. It was just after eight, so I had about an hour and a half before I was to call him again. I settled back and waited. I wasn't sure exactly what I was going to say, so I thought about it carefully.

I called promptly at 9:30, and he answered on the first ring.

"No names," he ordered.

"Okay. I got it. I need some information, though."

"What d'you need?"

"That package I left with you, the one in the gold lamé wrapper – do you still have it?"

"Sure do. Have to say it was interestin' once it was unwrapped," he chuckled. "Damned near unwrapped itself."

I had to think about how to work this without using names. "I mean, do you have it somewhere close by?"

"It doesn't get too far away, if that's what you mean. It needs a lot of attention." Shando's answers came quickly. It was obvious he was used to talking like this.

"What do you know about it?" I asked.

"A bit. It's an interestin' package, but dangerous in the wrong hands. I know who the owner is, and he doesn't seem to care too much about it except where it concerns the person who had the package before it was left in my care."

I stopped and thought about that for a while. He meant me.

"Have you met the owner?"

"Not face to face. He never comes here, somethin' to do with unfinished business. Business that goes back a long time. And his bodyguards are always around him, somethin' to do with another piece of unfinished business that has somethin' to do with an import export deal that went sour almost twenty years ago. Seems he and the type of people he associates with have long memories."

I pondered that before continuing. "Anything else you can tell me?"

"Not much. Other than be careful and stay where you are. Not plannin' on any travel, are you?"

I felt an alarm go off in my head. It might be that Shando was just telling me not to come back to the States, but it nagged at me. "Not for the next week or so, anyway. Then I might wander a little further south, but it depends on a few other things."

Shando's pattern of quick responses changed. He didn't answer immediately and I got the impression he was thinking about something.

"Lemme know if you're leavin' in case I need to get in touch with you," he finally said.

I hung up without replying, but before I did I heard Mirtha calling to him in the background. I walked home and spent a restless, sleepless night as my mind worked overtime.

IV

The next day, Monday, I borrowed Felix' battered old truck and made a futile trip to the police headquarters. There was nobody there from 1986 and the files on my father's death were gone. The chief constable suggested they might have been moved to Grand Cayman, and after asking if he'd check and getting a non-committal answer I went back home.

The sense of outrage I'd felt at hearing the details of father's death had settled, but not diminished, somewhere inside me. It was complicated by the realization that the very resources that would have made exacting revenge easier were now in the possession of my target, and that I had made that possible by my profligate lifestyle.

I also realized the evidence was mounting against my father's reputation. That evening, while sitting by my father's grave, I made a silent pact to him to clear his name.

I sat up there until after midnight, and mentally and physically exhausted finally walked down to the cottage and stretched out on the bed. I don't know how long I'd been asleep when the front door crashed in.

V

I barely had time to jump out of my bed when I was seized and my arms were pinioned behind me. Struggling and twisting in an attempt to get free, I kicked out and made solid contact with someone who shouted in pain. I remember being struck in the head with something solid, the dull thud reverberating from the back of my skull to the front before I sagged to the floor.

Regaining consciousness is a slow process. Unlike waking from sleep, even a deep sleep, it is a sluggish jumble of events as the mind tries to sort out external stimuli from other more physical sensations. My mind was trying to deal with all of these at once and the confusion was compounded with each passing second as my senses came back online. I was first aware that I was in pain, but couldn't remember why or how it had happened. There was a sensation of paralysis, my body unable to react to the simple commands it was being given by my brain. My hands refused to respond to the need to touch my throbbing head and my feet were numb and incapable of movement. I became aware of voices and other sounds that further confused and complicated the return to consciousness, as at some underlying level my brain realized that they didn't belong there. The shock of a bucket of seawater thrown in my face instantly cast all of the competing stimuli into the background, probably only for a second or two, but just long enough that my brain could then sort each of them in turn and at least bring some semblance of order to the cacophony that had existed before.

I was sitting in a chair, hands and feet tied securely to the arms and legs. That accounted for the paralysis and the numbness. I had no idea how long I was out but because of the dim light it seemed it might be near morning. I realized I was in the middle of the main room in my cottage. My head still throbbed and it took some time for my eyes to begin to focus. I was now aware it was still dark but that the lamps had been lit, accounting for my first impression of the pre-dawn gloaming. I was aware of people talking, but I couldn't yet make out what they were saying. Then with a sudden stab of lucidity I remembered being seized and the blow to the back of my head. A slap to my face cleared most of the remaining cobwebs from my mind, and as I blinked away the tears I saw there were six or seven men standing around me. The man in the middle spoke first.

"So, you have decided to rejoin us. You may regret that."

He was old, but younger than Uncle Patricio. About five eleven, and dressed in casual but expensive clothes. His full head of white hair was slicked straight back and he had a long, narrow face dominated by dark, glinting eyes. Not the kind of eyes you would describe as sparkling, but rather the kind that shoot sparks like those that fly from a flint striking hard steel. They were like the uncontrolled sparks that could ignite a flash fire or an explosion. The eyes were riveting, but they were not the most dominant aspect of his face. That feature was the scar. The angry, white line that stretched in a curve from just under his flickering left eye to the corner of his cruel, thin-lipped mouth.

"Have you enjoyed your exile, Dexter Snell?" he spat, sneering.

"What do you want?" I managed to say, although it didn't come as much more than a whisper.

"Ah, right down to business. I appreciate that." He looked at me speculatively before continuing. "Do you know who I am?" He said, looking at his henchmen. Most of them smiled obediently, shuffling their feet or shrugging their shoulders as if the question was rhetorical. I suppose in their world the question was, in fact, unnecessary.

"No, I don't know you," was all I could think to say.

The answer pleased him. He shifted his gaze from right to left, making sure everyone was listening. I got the impression that not listening to him could be a grievous offense.

"I'm an old friend of your father's Dexter. Jebediah and I went back a long way," he said, reflexively tracing the line of the scar on his face with the fingers of his right hand. His bushy white eyebrows shot up as he asked "Did he ever mention his old friend Niccolo Cardeli to you?" He dropped his hand from his face as if he suddenly realized what he was doing.

"No, he didn't."

"Then perhaps you remember my wife. She certainly remembers you, Dexter Snell. She sends her best regards, and asked me to remind you that she offered to let you stay in Key West and continue to enjoy your playthings." His eyes and menacing smile revealed no more than they had before, and I realized that whatever this was about, it wasn't that I had been with his wife. "Mirtha is taking good care of your playthings, Dexter Snell. She is making as good a use of them as you ever did. Perhaps better."

"What do you want here?" I asked again, my voice now a little stronger.

"Back to business? That surprises me. The Dexter Snell I watched for years never had much time for business. But of course why should you have concerned yourself with such mundane activities when you had so many other things to distract you. You're not like Jebediah at all," he said, sneering. "Now there was a man who could focus."

I refused to answer him, afraid that the rage building inside me would spill out and somehow provide him with more satisfaction.

"No, you're not like Jebediah. You prefer to run rather than stand and fight," he said. His eyes narrowed speculatively and he seemed to be considering what to say next.

He turned away and walked over to the door, standing with his back to the room.

I looked at the others and was not comforted by what I saw. Despite the fact they clearly deferred to their boss, they were all dangerous-looking. They were, to a man, Hispanic. I guessed Cuban or Colombian, and they had that aura of men who put no value on lives – the lives of others, that is. I had no doubt that they would do whatever they were told to do with no compunction, probably with pleasure.

Cardeli turned and walked back to stand in front of me. He seemed to have reached some type of decision.

"Your father cost me a lot of business, and he didn't have to. He not only wrecked my cocaine transportation network, but he also destroyed my connections in Colombia. It's only fitting that you will get those back for me."

"What makes you think I would do that?" I asked, secretly relieved that my belief in father was confirmed.

"Like I said, Dexter Snell, you are not Jebediah. He was like the oak tree - he would not bend no matter what type of pressure was put on him. I admit I lost my temper and went too far, but I still don't believe he would have come around. No, you are not Jebediah. You are soft." The sparks were flying from his eyes now, and he turned to his men. "Diego, Nestor – give this pup a small taste of pain. I am going for a walk down to the sea, and I want him still alive and conscious when I return." With that, he left the cottage with the others.

The ones called Diego and Nestor didn't say anything, simply removing their jackets and rolling up their sleeves. Diego opened a duffel bag and dumped its contents on the floor. I knew it would be useless to try to talk to them and steeled myself for what was to come. I prayed to my father for strength.

Diego chose a bat from the pile and hefted it in one hand, smacking it into the open palm of the other while staring at me. I stared back, knowing any other reaction would be useless anyway.

He stood squarely in front of me and wound up like a right-handed major league batter preparing to face a pitch from a twenty game winner. I readied myself for the blow that would surely break my left arm, and as he swung the bat I twisted to my right as far as the ropes would allow. The movement exposed the side of my chest, and I felt ribs crack. The pain was incredible and I almost passed out. The air had been driven from my lungs in a whoosh and every gasp brought a new surge of pain. I couldn't even scream. I broke out in a sweat, and tried to calm myself so I could breathe.

"Nice stroke, Diego," Nestor commented as if complimenting a golfing buddy on a particularly long and accurate drive. He pulled a pack of cigarettes from his shirt pocket and offered one to his partner. They took their time lighting up while they watched me. "I don't think there's any rush. Let him savor this."

"You bastards," I managed to spit out.

Nestor handed his cigarette to Diego. "My turn," he said, picking up the bat and moving around to my right side. I closed my eyes.

The blow was different than the first one. I was steeling myself for the smash on my right arm but it again caught me in the ribs, this time on the right side. Nestor must have jabbed me with the bat, but the impact had the same result as I again felt ribs crack. It was worse this time, as the pain of expelling air and then trying to gasp it back in now came from both sides of my ribcage. I was in agony, and the knowledge that they were just starting compounded it.

I was again left alone while they finished their cigarettes and talked about different ways they had inflicted pain on different people as if they were discussing the weather. I tried to take short breaths, but it didn't help much. I was now drenched in sweat. I closed my eyes again to hide the terror I was certain was written in them. The thought crossed my mind that father had undergone similar treatment so many years ago, here in the cottage he loved. I took what strength I could from my memories of him.

I heard Diego and Nestor rummaging around again, and then felt someone seize my left hand. I reflexively clenched my fingers into a fist, and opened my eyes to find Nestor at my side. Diego was brandishing bolt cutters. My mind went numb even through the pain.

I couldn't resist as he twisted my little finger loose, and stared in horror as Diego positioned the jaws of the bolt cutters over the joint at the end of my finger and squeezed the handles. I felt the bone crush as the joint gave way between the hardened steel jaws, severing the end of my finger. The scream that was torn from my lungs echoed inside my head even as the pain from my hand combined with the grating of the pressure on my broken ribs to drive me over the edge and into unconsciousness.

I'm sure the respite wasn't long, as I was once again doused with a pail of seawater. Through the pain I could feel blood dripping from my hand onto my left leg and running down onto my foot.

"Are you enjoying this Mr. Snell?" Nestor smirked. "Remember, as painful as this is, it is only a taste," he laughed.

"Think of it as an appetizer for a main course that you don't want," laughed Diego, nudging me in the ribs with the bat. The pain was overwhelming, and I couldn't imagine worse although I was certain they were capable of inflicting it.

Cardeli came back into the cottage with the rest of his entourage, and stood surveying the damage.

"Just a sampler, Dexter Snell. I hope you enjoyed it," he laughed. "Now, some more business."

I couldn't even answer him. Whenever I thought I might be able to control the pain, Diego would tap my ribs with the bat.

"Bring my briefcase, Miguel."

The man he called Miguel handed Cardeli a black leather case, and Cardeli put it on the table and opened it. "Bring him over here," he said as he took out a large manila folder.

Diego and Nestor picked up the chair with me in it and carried me over to the table. Cardeli pulled up a chair and sat across from me with the folder.

"Leave us now," he ordered, "and wait for me to call you. Move away from the cottage. I want to speak privately." He picked up the folder and examined its contents while he gave his men enough time to comply with his instructions.

"Now, Dexter Snell, you have had a flavor of what is possible. You must know you have no choice but to do as I ask, and if you foolishly consider running away as you have in the past, please be assured I will find you."

The thought of running had not crossed my mind. All I could think about apart from the pain was how long it would take me to kill this man.

Cardeli opened the folder and I saw it contained pictures. He took the first from the top of the pile and slid it across the table in front of me. I tore my eyes from his to look down and saw with a shock it was a picture of Catalina. It was her graduation picture.

"Leave her out of this, Cardeli," I spat.

He leaned back in his chair, and smiled. "No, Dexter. That would not be fair. To you or to her. You must know that if you do not do as I ask, when I ask, that she will suffer as you have. This is not an option, so it is only reasonable that I warn you." He took the next picture and slid it across.

I tried to resist looking at it, but I couldn't help myself. It was another picture of Catalina, but this time she was running, naked, from the sea in front of the cottage. It had been taken only weeks earlier, and I was behind her, chasing her. The realization that we had been watched and even photographed diverted my mind from the pain. Cardeli smiled as he slowly placed picture after picture in front of me. Each was worse than the one before, including photos of her in intimate situations with an assortment of men. Most of the images were grainy, as though taken through a telephoto or night lens, but Catalina was unmistakable in all of them. She had told me of her past, but being told was different than being confronted with pictures. Pictures that had been taken by strangers; pictures that Cardeli had probably gloated over.

I realized he had been spying on Catalina for years and wondered why when the next pictures offered a clue. They were photos of Uncle Patricio, many taken with Catalina. They showed the joy and pride he felt toward her, and following the previous pictures seemed obscene being in the same folder.

Cardeli closed the manila folder and, sitting back, stared at me.

"Just in case your imagination has been impaired, Dexter Snell, let me complete this for you. First, you can appreciate the pain I can inflict. You cannot run – I will find you. And if by some remote chance I do not, I can find your precious Catalina and inflict that pain on her. Or Patricio. Or I can send Patricio these pictures, perhaps with new ones showing what I have inflicted on Catalina, how I have tortured her. Or perhaps I can even disfigure her in terrible ways, and let her live."

I couldn't speak, but Cardeli misinterpreted my silence for fear, terror and resignation. If he even suspected the conflagration he had unleashed within me, he would have had to kill me on the spot. It was the blood of Jebediah Snell roaring through my veins now, and dripping onto floor even as he looked at me.

"There is something else, Dexter Snell," he said, his eyes narrowing. "In the last year before I killed Jebediah, he was up to something, after something. At first I thought he was smuggling cocaine, perhaps taking over my business, but that was not the case. He could not have done that without me finding out, and I tried. No, it was something else he was after. I mean to know what that was, and I want it.

"Have I made myself clear Dexter Snell? You will reestablish my cocaine supply from Colombia and find out what Jebediah was up to, if you don't already know. If you comply within the next five months, I will leave Catalina and Patricio alone."

What was clear to me was that any resistance before I killed him would result in terrible consequences for the people I loved the most. Even through the pain and anguish I was focused on that knowledge. Somehow, I would kill this man.

"Yes, everything is clear. Crystal clear," I rasped, trying not to move my ribs.

"Good," he said, standing up. "Nestor, Diego," he yelled.

Cardeli instructed them to put me back in the middle of the room as he replaced the pictures in the folder and then put them back in his briefcase. When he was finished, he came and stood in front of me, his left hand in his pocket. He was looking at me, fingering his scar with his other hand when he moved. It happened so fast that I almost missed it. As he withdrew his hand from his pocket I caught a flash, and then felt something like a slap hit me above my right eye. Blood ran from the slice that had been opened in my scalp, blinding me. The next blow broke my jaw and I slipped mercifully back into nothingness.

VI

Felix found me later that morning, and I must have been quite a sight. The blood from the slice over my right eye had run down my face, congealing in the hair on my chest and soaking my shorts. My jaw was swollen to twice its normal size and skewed to the left. The severed finger joint had also bled copiously, dripping down my left leg and forming a pool on the planked wood floor.

I was unaware of Felix cutting my wrists and ankles free from the chair but I screamed into consciousness when he tried to lift me. I swear I could hear the cracks in my ribs grinding, and slipped away again.

My next memory is of the doctor bending over me, flashing a light in my eyes. He straightened up and turned toward Felix.

"Well, it's not as bad as it looks Felix, if you call a concussion, sliced scalp, broken jaw, cracked ribs and severed finger tip not bad. He's been brutalized, but should be more or less mended in six weeks or so barring complications."

I tried to speak, but couldn't manage more than mumbles. The doctor turned back to me.

"Relax, Dexter. Your jaw is wired shut. Come over here Felix, and I'll go over this for both of you." The doctor went and wrote in a notebook for a few minutes, giving me time to look around and get oriented.

I was in my bed, and had been cleaned up. I was dressed in fresh shorts and saw a bucket filled with blood-soaked towels by the door. I raised my hands to gingerly explore my forehead and swollen jaw and tried to shift onto my side. The movement sent lightning bolts of pain shooting through my ribcage and the full memory of what had been done to me flooded back. I closed my eyes again. It was almost too much to take.

The raw beating was just that – an assault from which my body would recover over time – but I could already feel the effects of the emotional trauma. I've heard people whose homes have been robbed describe the feeling that they have been personally violated, and I never understood it; probably because I didn't have anything I really valued until recently. But I understood it now, and it was overwhelming.

Storm-driven waves were crashing against the seawall of my mind, a seawall that could only resist for so long. A maelstrom of furious, foam-flecked waves were attacking my psyche from all angles, threatening to overwhelm me with the relentless nature of their power. I slowly realized I was in danger of being smashed into irreparable pieces and swept away, leaving the people I loved the most exposed to the next inevitable onslaught. With this realization came a growing sense of calmness I initially misinterpreted as resignation, but soon comprehended was the only course of action open to me. I had to allow Cardeli to set the course for the immediate future, lulling him into a false sense of security while I patiently and meticulously created the opportunity for vengeance. And then complete calmness enveloped me, as I understood that vengeance wasn't enough. No, it wouldn't be the heat of vengeance; it would be the cold, hard fury of a reckoning.

I opened my eyes, and saw that Felix was standing at the side of the bed with a pitiful look on his face, as if he was afraid to say anything.

I spoke through immobilized jaws and began laying the groundwork for the illusion of resignation. "Sorry you weren't at the party last night Felix. It got a little out of hand." I tried to smile, but I'm sure it was more of a grimace.

"I thought you were dead when I found you, Dex. It was just like ..." he stopped, and I knew he was thinking back to when he'd found my father on the beach. I also knew in that instant that I would not be able to carry this out alone. I would need the help of someone I could trust, and Felix was the obvious choice. Just how much I could tell him, and when, was up in the air. But I had to get us both past the next day or so with some semblance of normalcy, allowing for the circumstances, until I was ready to offer more than what I was feeling right now.

The doctor put his notebook aside and filled the silence. "I'm Doctor Spock, Dexter. No relation to either Benjamin or the Starship Enterprise, and I'd appreciate it if you resist the urge to either laugh or crack a joke. I've heard them all, thanks. You can call me Bones." He said it with a straight face and his eyes challenged me to ignore the context. I liked him immediately and silently thanked him for temporarily pushing aside the talk Felix and I would need to have before Patricio arrived on Thursday. I focused my attention on him in order to further quell my emotions.

He was short, about five foot four, and fat. There's no other way to describe a man who is that short and carrying something in the neighborhood of two hundred pounds. His long, red, unkempt hair was pulled back and tied into a ponytail that hung well below his shoulders. Striking, green eyes were set in a round mug whose nose and cheeks displayed the red splotches of a serious tippler. Plain, steel-rimmed circular glasses that seemed too small were jammed on his face, the arms splayed out and then bent to hook behind his ears. A single gold ring through a piercing in his left earlobe completed the improbable picture. I made him out to be in his mid sixties.

"We've met before, Dexter, although I'll excuse you for not remembering. I attended your birth and assisted Bibi, who delivered more babies than I ever will. And I'm sorry we lost your mother. I agonized over that for years, but I don't believe there's anything that could have been done to save her, even in a proper hospital."

I thanked him through clenched teeth, now completely distracted from my other circumstances.

"As I was saying to Felix, your injuries are painful but not life threatening. I saw many similar traumas in Vietnam so I'm not unfamiliar with them.

"I've stitched your scalp and closed the wound on your finger. Both were relatively clean cuts, but I've administered a tetanus shot as a normal precaution. There will be scars, of course, but the one on your forehead is mostly above your hairline. Any questions so far?" he asked, immediately continuing before I could speak. Maybe it was his military training.

"You have a concussion, but as far as concussions go, it's not all that serious either. Your mandible – that's your jaw – is broken on the left side, and I've wired your mouth shut. The wires are attached to your upper and lower teeth and fastened together to immobilize your jaw while it heals. About six weeks." He held up what looked like a small pair of pliers. "These are cutters. If you begin to vomit, cut the wires, or have someone cut them." He looked at Felix, then back at me. "One of Felix' helpers has gone to get ice. Wrap it in a plastic bag and a towel, and apply it to your jaw for about ten minutes every hour or so for the next couple of days.

"The jaw will set reasonably well, but there's a chance it might be crooked. In that event, it's a simple matter of consulting a maxillofacial surgeon who will rebreak and reset it. There isn't such a surgeon here or on Grand Cayman, but arrangements can be made for a visiting specialist through Georgetown Hospital.

"Quite frankly, it's been my experience that the prospect of having a jaw rebroken and reset makes some misalignment and slight, continuing discomfort quite acceptable," he laughed as if he'd made a joke.

"The cracked ribs could conceivably offer a complication, but only if you fail to follow instructions. It will hurt to breathe deeply, but you must in order to keep your lungs clear. It will help if you hold a pillow against your chest with your arms while you take those deep breaths. Any questions?" This time, apparently finished with his report, he actually waited.

"I don't have any," I mumbled.

"Felix?" he asked.

"Well, yes. How does he eat?"

"He doesn't," the doctor laughed, "I intend to eat all the food that he can't swallow in liquid form, and I'll protect him from any possible temptation by drinking anything and everything of an alcoholic nature that might be laying around here. I'd appreciate your assistance in that particular endeavor, Felix. I'll visit every night at dinnertime to check on him until he is completely healed or until the food and rum run out, whichever comes first. I'll send over some high-protein supplements for him that you can add to milk. Eggs and soy are good. Thanks to the low-carb fad, there are other mixtures available in lots of flavors. I'll find some.

"Now, I'll have to file a report on this with the chief constable. I expect he'll pay you a visit.

"No police, Bones" I murmured.

Both he and Felix started to protest, but I cut them off with a wave of my hand. "No police."

"But I have to report this, by law. Any medical care given in response to a suspected illegal act must be reported."

"There was no illegal act," I stated flatly. "I fell while installing catchments on the roof."

He considered this bold lie for a minute, and then spoke. "Dexter, your father and I were good friends, particularly in the last years before his untimely death. We spent many hours on the porch here and I found him to be by far the most interesting, well-read person on the island. Few people know how much he gave. A sizable, anonymous endowment that I administer on behalf of Faith Hospital is only one of the many good things he did. In consideration of that friendship, I'll do as you wish. Jebediah never asked more than a few things of me, and I'll consider this to be a request directly from him. I hope you know what you're doing."

With that, he gathered up his things and left, promising to come back later that night.

"Help me up, Felix, I need to see if I can walk."

"Dex, why don't you just lay here for a bit?" he pleaded.

"You want me to wet the bed?" I asked, and he hurried to help me.

It hurt my ribs and my head spun for a bit, but at least I found that I could walk.

VII

I feigned exhaustion in order to avoid Felix' questions and despite my pleas for him to go home until later, he insisted on staying close by. He used my wired jaw as an excuse, but I know he was afraid that whomever did this to me would return.

I propped myself up slightly and lay on my back trying to think things through. Felix' constant peering in through my bedroom door unsettled me so I closed my eyes. All I saw was a bright, pulsing red. As much as I tried to calm myself, I felt the rage coming back. It was simmering inside me and I couldn't quell it. Hell, I didn't even try to quell it.

I struggled back out of bed and made my way out of the cottage and up the path to my parents' graves, Felix protesting all the way. I finally turned and snapped at him to leave me alone.

Sitting between the gravestones, my emotions back under control, I reached some decisions. First, I would have to tell Felix sooner rather than later. I would have to decide just how much to disclose even while I opened up to him and I hoped he would understand. I needed him if I was to have any chance at all – he was the only one I could turn to. Trusting Shando was out of the question at this point, but I knew he would be useful in other ways that didn't necessitate trust.

Other than trying to find out what father was up to the last year of his life, I would have to push Patricio away. I needed to show Cardeli that Patricio meant little to me, and in a final, painful moment I faced the fact that I would have to push Catalina away as well. My only chance to save them would depend on convincing Cardeli that his assessment of me was completely accurate – that I was a selfish coward who cared more for the opportunity to regain some of the material trappings he'd taken from me than I cared for Catalina and Patricio. I ruefully contemplated the irony in now being forced back into the self-serving persona that I had willingly embraced for years. But the only way I could see to save the ones I loved the most depended on hurting them terribly by once again convincingly readopting that selfish role.

I stood and looked at father's grave, wondering if he would understand or even approve of what I was about to do. And then it came to me. It crept through my body like a stealthy, forceful band of reinforcements shoring up a beleaguered but determined platoon in the middle of the night. I realized that I was about to do what father had done so long ago when he removed himself from both Patricio and me during the last year of his life. The only difference was that this time, somehow, we were doing it together; and together, we would have the reckoning that we sorely needed.

VIII

Bones showed up at 7:30 p.m. carrying a box of protein supplements as he had promised. He mixed up a large pitcher of banana-flavored slop and examined me again while Felix prepared shrimp and lobster.

"Pain?" he asked, probing my ribs.

I jumped in response, and glared at him as he stuck a stethoscope in his ears and slapped the silver end on my chest. "Breathe," he ordered.

I took a few shallow breaths.

"Deeper, dammit."

I braced myself and humored him with two deeper, but still relatively shallow breaths. It hurt.

"Good. Enough of that" he grunted, heading for the icebox. "Now for some proper libation."

He filled a glass with ice cubes and then poured in enough dark rum to nearly overflow it. "Cheers," he toasted, "to wives and sweethearts. May they never meet." He downed the glass in one go and filled it again. "Rum and water. Great drink. The trick, though, is to finish it before the ice has a chance to melt and dilute the rum," he laughed. I tried to laugh as well, but quickly stopped as the pain shot through my ribcage.

"Did you know there are only two ways to drink rum, Dexter?" he asked. "One is with ice," he said before downing the glass again and then throwing the ice cubes out the door and past the porch. As he refilled the glass with straight rum this time, he added, grinning "and the other is without ice. Come on, let's see how Felix is doing."

We went out to the porch and sat, he on the step while I settled into a chair. Felix had the big cast iron pot on the fire, and glancing at Bones' glass went in to fix himself a drink.

"Yep, I spent many hours on this porch with Jebediah, Dexter. Fascinating man."

"Thank you," I lisped. "It's nice to meet someone who knew my father. What did you talk about?"

"Different things, Dex. A lot about the history of the Caribbean, and a lot about fishing. I don't think there were too many places that Jebediah hadn't been in the Caribbean."

I thought about my father's life and how rich it must have been. "Did he ever show you his charts or journals?"

"Many times. He'd get started on a story and the next thing I knew he'd be spreading charts out or retrieving a book from the library. He had an amazing memory, and it was as if he used the charts so that I could understand more clearly what it was he was describing. And he'd always send a book or two home with me so that I could read more about whatever it was he was talking about. No journals, though. I never saw any journals." Bones took a deep drink of his rum and then called out to Felix to bring the bottle.

"And what about you, Dexter, did you ever accomplish anything other than spending money?" he asked.

I was taken back by the boldness of the question and it obviously showed on my face. I wasn't sure how to reply when Felix chipped in as he emerged from the cottage with his glass in one hand and the rum bottle in the other. "Dex has changed, Doc. I've watched him change while he's been here."

"Perhaps. Perhaps. But squandering a fortune might create the illusion of change, Felix," he said. "What do you think, Dexter?"

"I think that you are rather bold, Bones. I can see why my father liked you," I answered calmly. "But to answer your question, yes. Undeniably. Losing a fortune the way I did – actually, not losing it but squandering it as you more accurately put it – could create the illusion of change in a person."

Bones narrowed his eyes and looked at me as he thought about my answer. "And a royal beating to boot. Was that related to your financial collapse or to the murder of your father?"

Felix took a step forward, a storm of emotions playing across his face. I held my hand up to stop him. "Wait, Felix. Bones is just asking a question. I think he has a purpose in mind." Turning back to the doctor I answered him, but not completely.

"It was related to my financial collapse, Bones. My biggest creditor ordered the beating. To the extent that I could have avoided the collapse the beating was avoidable, too. At least to the extent I might have chosen not to squander my inheritance, that is. And by the way, squander is more accurate than financial collapse."

Bones hoisted himself up and held out his empty glass to Felix. "I'm not sure I buy that, but fill this up for me please, Felix." As Felix poured, Bones pursed his lips and exhaled in a manner that reminded me of the snort of a horse. Well, maybe a pony. A fat pony.

"Come on, Dex. Show me what you've accomplished around here in the last few months." He smiled at me and led the way down the steps from the porch. "Excuse us Felix, but do you think dinner will be ready in twenty minutes or so?" He didn't wait for an answer, simply setting off around the corner of the cottage.

I turned to Felix and winked as I left to follow Bones. Moving was painful, and I tried different ways of holding my upper body in relation to the motion of my legs, but nothing worked.

I gave Bones the same tour that I'd given Catalina, only in slow motion. It seemed like a lifetime ago I'd walked Catalina around the same route, and I felt pangs of remorse at what I was going to have to do in order to insulate her and Patricio from Cardeli. Bones seemed to sense something was troubling me.

"I'm afraid I'm rather blunt, Dexter. My third wife called me tactless, but when I pointed out to her that if I was tactless I wouldn't be able to so successfully conceal from her the fact that I considered her mother to be a spiteful, meddling, two-faced, social climbing, back biting, gossiping bitch. She must have agreed, because she didn't argue with me. She just left."

Bones continued talking as he huffed and puffed his way up the path toward the well. "There's something more than the beating bothering, you Dex. I can feel it exactly the same way I could feel it with Jebediah. And it's not regret at losing everything. It's something else." He got to the well, took a look around and shook his head. "Digging is such a waste of time," and then turned and headed back down the path again, taking a big gulp from his glass. I just followed him, amused as much by his ability to carry on a one-sided conversation as by his insight.

"I see Jebediah in you, Dexter. You're not what people say you are – or were."

He reached the cottage and strolled inside, surveying the meal laid out on the table with obvious approval. "Well, Felix, you've done a fine job while Dexter bent my ear about all the work he's done. How about a pre-dinner drink to whet the appetite?" And, true to form, he proceeded to pour another without waiting for an answer.

Dinner was excellent, along with the monologue Bones considered conversation. I was surprised he could still talk by the end of the evening, let alone walk back up the path to his car after demolishing my supply of rum. But that was nothing compared to the surprise he would deliver two months later.

IX

Sleeping was a challenge. Anyone who has had cracked ribs or a broken jaw can attest to that, and those few who have had both at the same time know exactly what I mean. As if that wasn't enough I had a burning sensation at the end of a fingertip that was no longer attached to me.

Felix would not leave me alone in the cottage, insisting on sleeping in the second bedroom so that he could respond quickly with the cutters should I have a fit of vomiting. I lay awake, racked with dull, throbbing pains and the insistent burning of my missing fingertip. I was no longer tortured by what I had to do, simply because it had to be done, although it continued to cause an ache deep inside me. I eventually drifted in and out of sleep while trying to decide on how to go about it. I needed to talk to someone and decided to begin with Felix first thing in the morning.

My restless sleep was filled with dreams. Like the one I had the night Catalina first kissed me and then ran away to the inn at the other end of Brac. The dream was populated with Uncle Patricio, Aunt Izabel, Bibi, Catalina and father. But this time, instead of Catalina calling me back she was with the others, calling to me and then fading away with the rest of them. Except for my father. He was standing beside me, his hand on my shoulder. And every time my other loved ones faded away they would be replaced by a huge image of Niccolo Cardeli's face, sneering and fingering the scar that ran in a curve from his eye to the corner of his mouth. And then father would lean toward me and whisper "Patience, son. Be patient."

X

I finally fell into a deeper sleep because when I awoke it was full daylight. I struggled out of bed after first rolling onto my side while holding a pillow tight against my chest. It still hurt to move, even with the pillow.

Felix was sitting in the main room and he immediately stood up. "Are you okay, Dex? I checked on you every hour or so since dawn."

"I'm fine. What time is it?"

"Just after two. Let me get you some of Bones' magic potion."

As he got the banana mix from the icebox I went out onto the porch and sat down in my chair. I was just settled when he came out with a glass and pitcher and put them on the table beside me.

"We have to talk, Felix. And it can't wait until dinner time."

Felix looked at me, realized it was serious, and pulled up a chair. "Let's get started then."

"The men who beat me – and the man who is the ringleader – killed my father." I paused to gather my thoughts.

"I knew that, Dex. I knew it as soon as I found you tied to the chair. Will they be back?"

"Yes, they will. One way or another. I won't be able to run or hide and I don't want to. I'm finished with that." There was no resignation in my voice. I stated it as a cold, hard fact and Felix didn't blink an eye. His face was like stone; there was no trace of the easy-going, amiable visage he inherited from Bibi. The intensity in his chocolate-brown eyes was frightening as he stared at me, leaning forward to rest his elbows on widespread knees and locking his fingers together while he flexed those massive fisherman's shoulders.

"I'm going to kill him," I said, leaving the statement hanging there between us.

We looked at each other for a long time. Something was flowing between us, a throwback to the days when we explored Brac together as children and instinctively knew that something we were about to do was dangerous or forbidden but that we were going to do it anyway - we were in it together. In that instant we both recognized that whatever barriers had arisen between us during my years in Key West were gone, swept away as if they'd never existed.

"Jebediah was the father I never had, Dex. I've been waiting for this. I never understood it, but somehow I knew this day would come. I want a piece of that son-of-a-bitch."

I breathed a sigh of relief. "This makes it easier for me, but I need to tell you there's a good chance we'll be killed. And if we are we'll probably be written off as cocaine smugglers. You have to consider that."

He didn't hesitate. "If I'm dead, it doesn't much matter. I can't live without doing something about this, and I won't let you do it alone. So lay it out."

I didn't waste any time. "Uncle Patricio told me of a fight in Key West many years ago, a fight that he and father did not start and tried to avoid. Father cut a man's face open, and that man has carried out a vendetta ever since. His name is Niccolo Cardeli, and he lives in Miami surrounded by bodyguards." I went on to describe him so that Felix would recognize him if he ever met him, and explained how he had taken over the properties I'd inherited.

"But this isn't about the properties, Felix. I don't give a damn about them. If he'd stopped there I wouldn't care except for the fact that he tortured and killed my father. And now he has threatened to do the same to Catalina and Patricio if I don't do as he wishes. I have every reason to believe he can and will do that."

"That's good enough for me, Dex. Do you have an idea of how we'll go about killing him?" he asked almost as a matter of fact. The intensity in Felix' face was frightening, and I'd never seen that side of him or even suspected it existed. I knew I'd made the right decision to include him.

"Yes, I do. We'll have to bide our time, doing as he wishes until we can either manipulate him into dropping his guard or until an opportunity presents itself by chance. Doing what he wants will be dangerous in and of itself, and that is where we face the risk of being killed and dying as drug runners."

"Was Jebediah running drugs, Dex?" he asked, "Not that it matters to me. Whatever he did, he didn't deserve to die like that."

"No, my father wasn't running drugs." A momentary hint of relief flashed across Felix' face. "But he was involved with it to the extent that he destroyed Cardeli's cocaine operation. I don't know how he did that, but Cardeli said he did and that he wants me to reestablish it. That's the first condition of leaving Catalina and Patricio alone."

Felix' eyes narrowed as he contemplated that, and what it would entail. "I can help there, Dex. Smuggling is a national pastime throughout the Caribbean and everybody does it or knows someone who does. I suppose it's a throwback to the buccaneers and pirates. It was the first business in the islands. You know the history as well as I do, thanks to Jebediah." He flexed those powerful shoulders again, and thought for a second as he looked at me. "There's more, Dex, I can see it in your eyes. What else is there?"

I wasn't sure how to answer that one, since I didn't know myself.

"That's the mystery, Felix, and I suppose it's what you and I have been looking for. My father was up to something, but I'll be damned if I can figure out what. The easy answer and explanation for his clandestine comings and goings and the hidden compartments in the *Estrela* is that he was running coke, but we know that isn't it."

I had been unconsciously leaning forward in my chair as if moving closer to Felix, and the position started to cause an ache in my ribcage. I straightened up and that created another pain. My jaw ached as much from being broken as it did from trying to talk through clenched teeth. I took a few sips of the banana mix through a straw, and continued.

"Cardeli knows that he was up to something, too. And he wants whatever that was."

Felix considered this. "That explains the searches of the cottage for the first year or so after they killed Jebediah. If they have the journals, then they must know."

I nodded. "Yes, or maybe he didn't write anything in his journals that would give it away. In either case we need to keep looking to try to find out what it was. I suspect it was that secret that father guarded well enough to cause his death. And whatever it was he felt so strongly about, I want. I'll die before I let Cardeli get his hands on it."

"So we search the *Estrela* again?"

"No," I answered, "there's nothing there. I'm convinced of that. And Cardeli searched the cottage thoroughly, so it's reasonable to assume it's not here either. Maybe father left a clue that would only mean something to a certain person. That would have to be me, Patricio or you."

Felix thought about that while looking around speculatively. "Jebediah was a pirate, Dex. He was just born too late to give Henry Morgan a run for his money. Maybe he buried something somewhere." Felix' eyes narrowed. "Maybe it's in the well."

"I thought of that, Felix. It's not there."

"How do you know?" he asked.

"Because the ground at the well is sandy. In order to dig a well in that type of ground you have to line it with stones as you go or it will cave in on you. I started to dig at the bottom of the well, and I soon got past the stones that form the top of the lining and hit a huge rock, one that is too big to have been put there by father. Water was seeping in slowly – there must be an underground stream or aquifer – and I stopped. Besides, it's too obvious. Father wouldn't have hidden anything valuable in a place like that. It's somewhere else."

I finished the banana mix. I hoped there were more flavors in Bones' box. The prospect of six weeks of banana left me cold.

I started again. "Felix, someone has been watching me here on Brac."

"Watching you? How do you mean?"

"Cardeli had pictures with him. Ugly pictures. Some of them were of Catalina and me, taken here on Brac with a telephoto lens." I let that sink in.

"Where were they taken from?" he asked.

"The best I could tell is that it must have been from the east. They were taken when Catalina and I were on the beach and in swimming, and the perspective indicated someone was either on the shore to the east, or perhaps inland on a high point."

Felix thought about it for a while, and then said that he'd see if he could find any signs of an intruder.

The talking combined with the relief and comfort I felt at sharing everything with Felix had exhausted me. I stood up and told him I needed to rest again. Felix helped me into bed and left the cutters by my side. It wasn't long before I fell back into a deep sleep.

XI

Bones came to check on me that night, Wednesday, and continued apace with his endless monologue liberally fueled with rum. I was in awe at his capacity and said so, momentarily interrupting his explanation of how amputees often have sensations from a lost limb. It stopped him only long enough to notice his glass was empty and he resumed his explanation of the nervous system as he refueled.

I was up early on Thursday, nervously awaiting Patricio's arrival. I wasn't sure how I was going to find out what I needed to know and alienate him from me at the same time, but I was resolved to the fact that any rift had to be real in order to protect him from Cardeli. I'd had the same concerns about how to approach Felix and it had worked out, so I simply waited for his arrival. I didn't have to wait long.

The King Air swooped low over the shoreline and then banked back around toward the airport and Patricio arrived forty minutes later. An assistant wheeled him down the path and when he reached the bottom he stood and walked the rest of the way. He stopped when he saw my face and I thought he was going to fall, but he recovered and shuffled up the steps and held his arms out to me as I stood. We embraced each other, and I gasped with pain at even his weak hug. He immediately stepped back.

"Ribs, too?" he asked.

"Yes."

"It was Cardeli? When did it happen?"

"Yes, it was Cardeli. Sunday night, after I called you. Sometime after midnight I think." I motioned for him to take a chair, and he sat down. I could see the concern on his face as he watched me trying to get comfortable.

"I should have warned you about him more forcefully and a lot earlier, Dexter. I thought his taking your inheritance would be enough. I am sorry. Why did you not call?" he asked. His face had sagged visibly since he saw me, and I prayed he had the strength to withstand what I was about to do to him.

"You were coming today anyway, and I didn't want you to hear of this by telephone and then imagine it to be worse than it is. At least this way you can see I'm up and about," I answered with some semblance of sincerity.

"Is Carol taking care of you?"

"Carol? I don't know anybody by the name of Carol. It's Doctor Spock – Bones – he was a friend of father's."

Patricio smiled, even though it was a tired, care-worn smile, and my heart ached. "His name is Carol, Dexter. He was born on Christmas Day and while he was in the army he was known as Christmas Carol. Not many people know that. I found out by accident after your father died – was murdered – from someone who knew him in Vietnam. It is hard to picture, but I was told he would fight anyone who called him by that name. Never won, but that did not stop him," he smiled. "What is Carol's – sorry – Bones' prognosis?"

"Cracked ribs, broken jaw, sliced scalp and amputated fingertip," I answered, holding up my bandaged hand. "Six weeks."

"I am sorry, Dexter. I should have warned you. I just could not imagine it," he started again.

"It's okay, Uncle. I think he's got it out of his system," I lied.

Uncle Patricio sat back and closed his eyes. I thought he'd dozed off when he asked, eyes still closed, "and how much did Felix tell you?"

"He told me everything. How he found father's body, and how he'd been tortured." I took a breath and recognizing this as the right moment added "and he told me about the smuggling."

Uncle Patricio opened his eyes slowly. "He told you that Jebediah was running cocaine?" he asked.

"Yes, he did."

Patricio sighed, "I did not want to have to tell you that, Dexter. I knew it, but I did not want to be the one to tell you. I figured it out; it was not that difficult. When I confronted Jebediah with it he did not deny it, but he would not discuss it either. I begged him to get out of it, but he would not budge, even when I threatened him with the end of our friendship. I just could not understand him – all those years we spent together."

I understood it. I knew father had done the same thing that I was going to do. He had separated himself from Patricio to protect him from Cardeli, and Cardeli's knowledge of that estrangement had saved Uncle Patricio up until now.

"But that is past, Dexter. Jebediah's lawyer gave me a letter from him within hours of his death – a letter he had been holding in expectation of such a possibility. That letter asked me to forgive him for what he had done, and to take care of you. Believe me, Dexter, I did my best."

"I know you did, Uncle. Did he send you anything else, leave anything with you?" I asked, holding my breath.

"No, he did not. That was all, along with a request that he be buried here on Brac, beside your mother."

"Are you certain he was involved with cocaine?" I asked once again.

"I am sorry, but yes, I am certain. His account here on Brac held more cash than it should have. A lot more, and there were records of numerous, sizable deposits after we split up. I'm afraid that the evidence and his refusal to deny or even discuss his involvement when I accused him directly make it certain." The sadness was written across his face. "I understand the hurt this causes you, Dexter, and why you need to know."

I steeled myself and stood up. I walked over past him, because I couldn't face him when I said what I had to say. It was the only time I was thankful for my broken jaw, since it masked the tremor in my voice as I said what I now knew how to say.

"I needed to know because I didn't want to do anything that would further besmirch father's name."

It took a while for that to sink in.

"What exactly does that mean, Dexter?" he asked hesitantly.

"Smuggling drugs is one of only two things I've ever done half successfully," I started. "You can ask Catalina about it. I told her about how I smuggled marijuana out of Mexico in 1985. And I'm too old to do the other things I did, at least for money." My back was still to him, but I closed my eyes anyway. "I intend to bring cocaine out of Colombia."

"Damn you, Dexter. You are just like Jebediah," he exploded.

I whirled around to see him rising from his chair. I took a half step toward him, and he stopped me with an upraised hand. He hobbled down the steps and made his way toward the path unaided.

"Yes, Uncle Patricio. I am just like my father," I whispered, tears filling my eyes and mercifully obscuring his retreating back.

IX

Felix came on Friday to tell me that there'd been a call from Catalina. It was the call I'd been dreading. She said that if I didn't call back, she would fly here to see me.

Felix took me to his house, and I punched in the number. It only rang once when Catalina answered.

"Dexter?"

"Yes, it's me," I said.

"Are you all right? Patricio told me ..." she stopped, unable to say anything more.

"I'll be fine," I answered. If I didn't know before then I now knew that I was deeply in love and that once again something had been stolen from me. It was no consolation that I wasn't running away, but squarely facing what I had to do. And it made it worse that I couldn't explain it to her.

"Cocaine, Dexter? Please tell me Patricio is confused," she pleaded.

"He's not confused. He got it right. Patricio is always right" I lied, for Patricio had been wrong about my father. I held no malice, as it was exactly the way father had intended.

The last I heard from Catalina was a sob as she severed the connection.

I stood holding the phone to my ear as if it was still a real connection to Catalina and finally whispered 'goodbye, I love you' before I hung up. I turned around and saw Felix standing in the doorway. We locked eyes, and I was surprised to see tears rolling down his cheeks, too.

"Come on, Dex. Bones will be at your place in a while and you can't afford to leave him alone with your rum."

X

It was a long six weeks of healing physically, but nothing compared to the pain I felt in the parts of me that would never heal. I dreaded another call from Catalina or the possibility of a visit, but neither came. And that hurt, too.

12 Cayman Brac and Jamaica: 2004 August

It was the middle of the second week in August and the wires had been gone from my jaw for a month now. In tribute to Bones' skills I felt no misalignment. My phantom fingertip still burned from time to time and my ribs ached periodically, but overall I was in pretty good physical shape.

Whatever excess weight I'd carried before my beating was long gone, and fishing and preparing the *Estrela* over the last four weeks with Felix added layers of solid muscle and a deep-hued color to my hide. In other circumstances it would have been an idyllic existence; honest, hard work wrapped in the scents that reminded me of the best parts of my youth – fresh shrimp, diesel fumes and the tangy salt of the sea. But I could find no relief from the knowledge of what had to be done and the consequences of failure. Any honest evaluation of my track record in life offered little in the way of success to make me feel better.

I decided the *Estrela* would be our base of operations. It seemed appropriate given father had not only prepared her for the task by installing the hidden compartments, but had personally prepared Felix and I aboard her as well by turning us into capable, competent seamen almost twenty years earlier. I knew her capabilities if not her limitations, and she was a palpable, fitting link to father. Felix commented more than once that he could feel Jebediah's presence in her steel plate and the comforting power of her diesel engine. I felt it in the oak spindles of the wheel, worn smooth and stained dark by the sweat of his hands.

At sea and out of the sight of prying eyes we went over her from stem to stern taking inventory of the materials aboard her, jettisoning useless items and inspecting, repairing and replacing where necessary every item that could conceivably be needed for an extended voyage. We spent evenings in the wheelhouse preparing lists of provisions that were nourishing, easy to prepare and had a long shelf life. Under the guise of wanting to have the best-prepared fishing boat in the Caribbean I decided to enlist Bones in restocking the first aid kit.

The electronics were hopelessly outdated. I knew this from my experience of refitting *Party Girl* a year earlier when I exhibited the only interest in her other than ensuring she had every creature comfort conceivable for entertaining.

The Loran radio-signal navigation device was obsolete, and needed to be replaced with a modern global positioning satellite system. This, as I knew from my *Party Girl* experience, could be integrated with compatible radar, autopilot, sonar, and electronic chartplotting components that would simplify not only the installation but offer the added benefit that I knew how to operate them and could teach Felix. They were standard equipment on a modern fishing trawler and would not draw undue attention or interest from anyone familiar with boats. The absence of a fishfinder of comparable sophistication would, however, raise questions so as per Felix' suggestion I added one to our shopping list. The marine radio needed replacement as well, and I decided to order a spare antenna.

"Anything else?" I asked, looking at the list and wondering what it would all cost. I had no idea, and had never even reviewed the *Party Girl* invoices the year before.

Felix thought about it for a minute. "The only thing might be a hand-held portable radio so we can talk to the *Estrela* from the dinghy or ashore."

"Good idea. I'll get two," adding them to the list.

I sat staring at the notes in front of me, but my mind was elsewhere. Felix picked up on it.

"You got another letter before we left, didn't you," he said.

"Yes," I answered quietly. It was a plain brown envelope containing a copy of one of the pictures Cardeli had shown me. The first one came at the beginning of July and scrawled across the picture was '5 months – 1'. I'd received another a few days ago marked '5 months – 2'. I burned it as I had burned the first one.

"Cardeli?" asked Felix.

"Yes. Another picture. To remind me there's only three months left until the deadline." I looked at him briefly and then back at the list.

"Dex, we're doing what we can. The *Estrela* has to be made ready, and we've got that in hand. We're on track with the timetable you prepared. We head to Jamaica next week to sort out that end, and we'll do whatever we have to do there. I have a cousin who will help us, and I'm pretty sure he has the connections we need."

I bridled silently at Felix' words. 'Pretty sure' wasn't good enough, but it wasn't his fault. I needed something more certain, particularly in light of the glaring failure to find any explanation for what it was father had really been up to, and I was stumped. I looked at the oak wheel and wished it could somehow speak to me. I knew the *Estrela* had been part of it, but what?

Felix interrupted my thoughts again, reading my mind. "Maybe we can string Cardeli along by delivering on the cocaine end of things. We can work on that and we just have to get rid of him before he gets pushy about whatever it was Jebediah was working on."

Felix was putting the best spin on it, but I knew it wouldn't work. Cardeli's guard had been up for years, and if whomever he had double crossed in Colombia couldn't get to him I had no confidence we could get close enough without something more than the cocaine as bait. But it was the only angle we had right now, and it would have to do.

"I suppose so, Felix," I said, understanding and appreciating his attempt to reassure me, "I suppose so."

Felix made his way to his berth, leaving me alone in the wheelhouse with my thoughts. I went over everything again for what must have been the hundredth time. Nothing made sense other than the emerging fear that perhaps there wasn't anything at all to father's activities. Maybe we were all reading too much into it. Maybe Uncle Patricio, Felix, even Cardeli and myself were just wrong. The *Estrela* had been searched not once, but twice. Exhaustively. And I'd been over the cottage and the property countless times. I knew the title of every book in the library, and I'd riffled through the pages of each looking for a scrap of paper that might hold a clue. Every map, chart and torn remnant - nothing. It was as if father simply didn't want any clues to be found; or there were none, because there wasn't anything mysterious at all. It all kept swirling around in my mind. Twisting, swirling, changing, shifting.

I went and stood at the old oak wheel and wrapped my hands around the top two spindles, closing my eyes in a vain attempt to get a sense of what it was father had been doing for those last months. He had stood right where I was standing, his hands on those spindles and guiding the *Estrela* – where? Why? I could picture him as he would have been, peering out at the sea. That resolute, uncompromising face that could suddenly break into a smile whenever we met after a long absence, or that could become so animated when he was describing scenes and events from long ago in history.

And then I realized whatever it was - and it was something; the evidence was overwhelming – would not be discovered unless he had wanted it to be discovered. What would father do if he were in these shoes again; in these clothes I'd rescued from the sea chest?

I felt like I was in the middle of a storm. The memory flashed back of the sudden squall in 1984 off the coast of Colombia between Santa

Marta and Barranquilla when we snagged the trawl net and he'd gone over the side instantly, not once but twice. And the story Uncle Patricio told of how father had gone over the side of the *Coroa* in the great hurricane of 1935. Two instances in the middle of a storm, when he'd simply jumped into the sea and done what had to be done.

I was wasting precious time when I needed to be taking action.

I punched the start button. The diesel rattled into life as I flipped the switch on the windlass, hoisted the anchor and swung the *Estrela* toward Brac.

II

I heard the connection going through, and the phone rang only once before it was answered.

"Yeah."

"Shando?" I asked.

"Forty-five minutes," he answered, and hung up.

I was nervous about calling Shando, but had no choice. I needed the name of someone in Jamaica who could connect me with a source of cocaine in Colombia. Felix' cousin could undoubtedly find us the weapons on our list, but I didn't want to waste time rattling around Jamaica working my way through small-time dealers trying to obtain the connection I needed in Colombia.

Three years ago I'd taken *Party Girl* on a whirlwind trip through the Bahamas to the Caicos and then through the Windward Passage to Jamaica. Shando had been aboard along with the usual retinue of thrill-seekers and hangers on, and he'd been a hit in Kingston.

I remembered it as a dangerous place, not at all what the tourists see from the safety of the all-inclusive resorts in Montego Bay or Ocho Rios. Over cocktails with a consular officer angling for an invitation to board *Party Girl* I learned that Jamaica's murder rate consistently puts it right up near the top of the U.N.'s estimates of violence in the world, just behind South Africa and Brazil. That year the murder rate in Jamaica was on course to top 1,100 homicides, the preponderance of those in the ghettoes of Kingston and obviously off the well-beaten tourist paths. In the protective shadow of Shando and the locals he met the first night in town I saw a side of Kingston I stupidly thought at the time was exciting, but now recognized was downright dangerous.

The beating had followed my last call to Shando by just over twenty-four hours, and although the photos Cardeli showed me clearly proved I'd been watched for weeks if not months, I was still unsettled. My ability to judge people during my years in Key West was questionable, and I wondered if Shando was one of those who simply gravitated to people with money, or worse, the highest bidder.

On the other hand, if he was in Niccolo Cardeli's pocket and not just in Mirtha's pants, it couldn't hurt to have him know I was doing as Cardeli wished. There might be an opportunity to get at Cardeli through Shando if that was the case.

Forty-five minutes passed, and I called again.

"Yeah," on the first ring, "no names."

"I understand," I answered, having thought this through. "Do you remember the trip we made three years ago, and the four-day layover?"

"Sure do," he growled. "Nice place, nice people. Thinkin' of goin' back?"

I suppressed the anxiety of telling him where I'd be, and pressed on. "Yes, I'm going back. I need to meet that fellow who gave us the night tour, or somebody like him. Do you remember that excursion – the one out near the edge?" I hoped I wasn't being too obtuse, but Shando caught on and confirmed it right away.

"Let me get this right. You mean the drive through the ghetto, don'tcha?" he laughed.

"Yes, that's the one."

"And you want to meet the social director, or maybe his boss, right?"

"Yes, you got it."

"Okay. D'you remember the jazz and blues place? The place we had dinner the first night?"

"Yes."

"Be there in two days, at the bar, eleven p.m. If I can arrange it, somebody'll meet you."

"And if you can't arrange it?"

"If I can't, I can't," he answered. There was a moment's silence. "I heard you had an accident."

"Yes, where did you hear that?" I asked, surprised he would let on he knew.

"I overheard it. I think you know where. I woulda warned you if I'd known it in time." He hesitated as if he was waiting for a response, which wasn't forthcoming. "Be careful – you're still bein' watched."

I thought about that, and decided to accept it for what it was. "Thanks. And thanks for trying to arrange the meeting. I appreciate it," but he was already gone.

It's two hundred miles from Brac to Kingston, just under twenty hours at *Estrela's* cruising speed. I checked the time and realized I had a lot to do in the next few hours. On top of everything else there was a major tropical storm brewing and I wanted to be away from the anchorage and at sea where the *Estrela* would be safer.

I called my bank on Grand Cayman and arranged for a line of credit at their corresponding bank in Kingston. The manager explained it would be limited to seventy-five thousand US dollars, and a quick mental calculation reassured me that it would do. It would have to do, as my funds were dwindling quickly.

I remembered the name of the Raytheon electronics dealer who had fitted out *Party Girl* the year before and called him in Miami. I went through the list with him, made a few changes, and arranged to have everything I needed air freighted immediately to another dealer near Kingston. He was excited about the size of the order but concerned about my ability to pay, so I gave him the number of my banker on Grand Cayman. Reassured and anticipating the banker would confirm that he'd be paid he offered to fly the same technician who'd worked on the *Party Girl* – at my expense, of course – to Kingston to make the installation. I decided to put that on hold, expecting there would be someone in Jamaica who could do the work if I needed help. It's amazing how a limitation on cash improves a person's attitude toward do-it-yourself projects.

Bones met me at the cottage with a hastily assembled first aid kit. It was in a large cardboard box and I wondered what his idea of first aid was. I soon discovered you don't ask an ex-Vietnam trauma surgeon for a few supplies.

The box not only held the standard items I expected like bandages, ointments, disinfectants and assorted headache tablets, but surgical instruments, syringes, sutures and pain killers including morphine and other drugs I had no clue how to use.

"Bones," I said, exasperated and in a hurry to get going, "we can't possibly need or use all of this. Let's pare it down to the essentials."

"What exactly is it you need it for?" he asked, squinting his eyes in concentration on my face. A warning signal went off in my head, as I'd been careful about disclosing anything at all that might indicate what we were really up to. I'd cautioned Felix about it too, and he agreed the only thing we would talk to Bones about was father's activities and our desire to know more about those.

"It's simple. I've been fishing with Felix, and there's no first aid kit aboard the *Estrela*. There should be one. This looks like a field kit for a MASH unit, and I have no idea what half this stuff is, let alone how to use it." I saw this answer didn't satisfy Bones and decided to simply load it aboard rather than continue the discussion, but it was too late.

"That's bullshit and I know it. You two are up to something. You've supposedly been fishing, but you come back after two or three days with no more than what could be caught in a day. I'm not stupid," he said accusingly, "and I want to know what it is. I didn't patch you up just so you could do something foolish and get all broken up again, or killed."

"Let it go, Bones. It doesn't involve you," I said, closing the box. I realized too late it was the wrong thing to say.

"So you admit you're up to something. Now, as to whether it involves me or not, I suggest you think again. I was Jebediah's closest confidant on Brac, and he entrusted me with almost everything."

Another reference to the endowment father had funded for Faith Hospital, the endowment Bones administered at his behest. It was admirable and possibly even noble, but administering a trust fund was a damned far cry from trafficking in cocaine and conspiring to kill a man in Miami, no matter how morally justifiable Cardeli's death would be. I understood father's need for companionship, particularly that of an educated man with whom he could share his passion for books and history. I could even understand to a certain extent how Bones' eccentricity would appeal to father, as it did to me, but involving him in this was unnecessary and foolish. It would put him squarely in Cardeli's sights if something went wrong and the likelihood was high enough that I didn't care to provide Cardeli with yet another lever to pry on.

"It's not a question of trust, Bones. It's simply that I don't really know what I'm up against and I'd prefer to keep you out of it."

His face went red and I thought he was in danger of a heart attack, which his weight and alcohol consumption more or less eventually guaranteed. He pushed past me toward the door as if to leave, but stopped and turned back to me.

"I want to know who killed Jebediah, who beat you and what you intend to do about it. I know it's the same person or persons. Only an idiot would presume otherwise. And I warn you, I'm no idiot." He was on a roll now. "You better tell me what you're up to when you get back from Jamaica, or ..."

He spun around and left before I could ask how he knew we were going to Jamaica. I was not just perplexed; I was surprised and angry. If Felix hadn't told him, then ... then what? How could he know we were going to Jamaica?

First it was Shando, now Bones. I briefly wondered if I was going crazy with lack of sleep and worry over Catalina and Patricio but then decided I was fully justified in my concerns as I remembered the warning from Shando only an hour or two earlier about being watched. As unlikely as it seemed on the surface, Bones would be the perfect spy. Who had a better excuse for wandering all over Brac than a doctor making his rounds? Now that I thought about it, I had no first hand or factual knowledge of a hospital fund anonymously endowed by father and telling me there was one could be a clever, simple way to get close to me. It's human nature to accept at face value flattering stories about departed loved ones.

I picked up the first aid supplies and the charts from the library and went down to the shore just as Felix was landing the dinghy. He helped with the box and we immediately turned around and headed back to the *Estrela* to hoist anchor and leave for Jamaica.

Amid our last minute preparations I casually asked if he'd mentioned anything to Bones.

"No," he answered, "I thought we agreed not to, didn't we?"

"That's right. Just thought I'd check," I said, deciding not to say anything more.

As we pulled away from Brac I looked back toward the cottage. Bones was standing on the porch watching us leave.

III

The storm blew in exactly as forecast. We were headed directly into it, which is not the worst scenario unless the waves reach disastrous heights and you have to turn and run with it. As it turned out luck was with us for once. The winds although strong at forty miles per hour were nothing compared to what hit Cuba the next day. After it passed us, the storm developed into a full-fledged hurricane named Charlie with winds reaching a hundred and fifty miles an hour.

We were more or less five miles off the western tip of Jamaica when a low-flying plane buzzed us. It crossed in front of the *Estrela* twice before climbing lazily and flying off in increasingly larger circles but never completely out of sight. We continued eastward around the south end of the island toward Kingston and three miles off Portland Point I spotted the cutter approaching on an intersecting course. I pointed it out to Felix.

"Looks like we've got company."

"It's the Jamaican Coast Guard," Felix said. "They'll board and search us now that we're well inside their territorial waters."

We went over our story again and agreed that the truth about refitting the electronics was not only plausible but would arouse the least suspicion. I made sure the marine radio was set to channel 16 and Felix held our course until the cutter came close enough to make their intentions clear. Felix throttled the *Estrela* back and a voice over a loud hailer ordered us to stand to and prepare to be boarded. Two Coast Guard sailors with high-powered rifles stood watch on the bridge of the cutter to ensure we complied as three more crew boarded a launch and approached us.

"How many aboard, Captain?" the leader hailed from about twenty feet.

"Two," answered Felix. We were both outside the wheelhouse and in plain sight. We didn't want to do anything at all to raise suspicion or alarm – not with those high-powered rifles aimed in our direction.

"Permission to board, captain," the leader said. It wasn't a simple request, but wasn't issued in a threatening manner either. We moved to the rear port side to assist the officers in securing their launch and then at their request stood back as they boarded.

"Are you the captain?" the officer asked Felix as his two men moved to check the wheelhouse and cabin to make sure we were the only people aboard.

"Yes, sir," answered Felix.

"I'd like to see your papers, please."

We led the way to the wheelhouse as the officer explained that this was a routine inspection.

He was in his mid fifties and casually dressed. By that I mean he wasn't wearing a cap or jacket, and his uniform shirt was open at the collar. Despite the informal look, he exhibited the calm courtesy and professionalism that suggested he might have served in the British navy.

"Where is your home port, and where was your last port of call?" he asked politely as he inspected our documents.

"Cayman Brac, sir. We left yesterday and came straight here," Felix answered.

"Through hurricane Charlie?"

"It wasn't a hurricane when we came through it, sir," Felix answered.

The officer looked at us both, and continued. "This vessel has been here before, Mr. Smith," the officer said looking at Felix again and comparing his face to the picture on his identification. "Were you in command, and if so, tell me when you were last here."

He was looking at my papers next and comparing my face to the picture. One crewmember was now in the engine compartment and the other was in the supply locker. I knew we were completely clean, but it still made me nervous to be boarded and inspected.

"I was here last September, sir. I came for my cousin's birthday, and there might be a record of that in Port Antonio."

"Yes, Mr. Smith, there is. We already checked," he said matter-of-factly, turning his attention to me. "You look a little different than your picture, Mr. Snell."

"Yes, I do," I answered. "I've cut my hair and lost the beard since I moved to Brac a few months ago."

"I see. You wouldn't be any relation to Jebediah Snell, would you?" he asked.

I didn't try to hide my surprise at the question, and hoped that whatever raised it wasn't going to be a source of trouble. "Why yes – he was my father. Did you know him?"

"Quite well, actually," he smiled, extending his hand. "Welcome to Jamaica Mr. Snell. I'm Commander Jones. Please call me Peter." We shook and he then turned to Felix, offering his hand again. "Nice to meet you, Mr. Smith," he smiled.

"Unfortunate mess, that," he continued. "About your father, I mean. His murder was a shock to all of us who knew him, and I'm bloody sorry they never caught the perpetrator."

"Yes, so am I."

"So what brings you to Jamaica?"

"Well, Commander," I started.

"Please call me Peter," he interrupted. "Both of you," he said, nodding to Felix.

"Thank you. Felix inherited the *Estrela* from father, and I've been helping him fish her. I suppose it's in my blood. We're here to have the electronics updated."

"I see. And you have made arrangements to do that, I suppose?" he asked.

"Yes. The components are on their way here from Miami. I can give you the name of the shipper if you need it," I added.

"That won't be necessary," he said, looking at me more closely. "The *Estrela* is a bit of a step down from the *Party Girl*, isn't she?"

"Why, yes, I suppose so," I answered, surprised again. "But she has - how shall I put it – a more savory reputation than the *Party Girl*."

"That she does, Mr. Snell, that she does."

Felix suggested Commander Jones call us Felix and Dexter, and Peter thanked him before continuing.

"You were here with *Party Girl* about three years ago, I recall."

This time I didn't even try to hide my astonishment, and said as much.

"You seem to be well informed, Peter. I'm flattered that you knew and remember my father, but I'm not certain I'm as comfortable with my own reputation. Suffice to say I'm not as well off as I was, but that I'm enjoying being back on Cayman Brac and aboard the *Estrela* with Felix."

The two crewmen reappeared and reported that everything was in order, except for the box containing the first aid kit. My heart sank as he pointed it out to Commander Jones and explained it held items 'not usually found on a fishing boat'.

The box was still in the corner of the wheelhouse where we'd left it. Peter simply nodded his head toward it, looked at Felix and me and asked, "Well?"

"It's rather simple, really. A doctor on Brac put it together as a favor since there wasn't a first aid kit on board, and I'm afraid he got a little carried away. I don't know everything that's in there, but if there's something that's prohibited we'll be happy to surrender it." I was cursing my foolishness at leaving syringes and vials of morphine and who knows what else in the box.

"That doctor wouldn't happen to be Christmas Carol, would it?" Peter asked.

Felix and I looked at each other stupidly. I was beginning to feel naked. There seemed little the commander didn't know.

"Yes, sir. It was," Felix answered.

Peter looked at him directly. "Well it's probably ok then, but you might want to get rid of anything you don't know how to use. It just raises questions and is of no use to you anyway."

"Yes, sir. I'll do that," Felix answered.

"How long do you plan to be here?"

"As long as it takes us to rig the new stuff," Felix answered. "I hope Dex knows more about it than I do, or we might be here forever."

"I see. I may just drop by to check how you're doing. I'm a bit of an electronics buff myself, and you never know what I could contribute," he said, motioning for his crewmen to leave now.

We followed them back to the launch and untied their lines once they had the engine started. Peter waved goodbye as he throttled up and headed for the cutter.

"Holy shit," was all Felix said we watched them pull away, and I couldn't think of anything more, or better, to add.

IV

Kingston boasts the seventh largest natural harbor in the world and the island is strategically located right between the Cayman Trench and the Jamaica Channel, the main sea lanes for the Panama Canal. The historical significance of the island, I'd learned from father's library, lay in its sugar cane production that for 150 years made it one of the most valuable colonies in the world. The Brits abolished slavery in 1834, and following a referendum in 1962 granted the island its full independence. The Cayman Islands, which up until then were part of Britain's Jamaican colony, chose to remain with the UK.

The most striking aspect of Jamaica's story lies in its violence, beginning with the Spanish occupation in 1510 and the enslavement of the Arawaks who were completely exterminated by the time the British seized the island in 1655. The Spaniards started to bring slaves from West Africa shortly after they began their occupation and the British continued the practice until they completely abolished it in 1868. Prior to that, the colonialists were under periodic sieges led by the Maroons – Spanish slaves who had escaped to the remote, rugged interior when Spain lost control to the British. Following the emancipation of the slaves the history is marred by violent riots fueled by unemployment and patently racial colonial policies. And from what I'd learned from the consular officer during my visit three years ago the violence continues, the only change being the added impact of drug trafficking.

We made fast to a pier in the harbor and cleared immigration. Peter Jones had radioed ahead sparing us the bother of another search, and since it was nearing nightfall we decided to get a good night's sleep which turned out to be impossible.

Twice during the night we were awakened by the sounds of intruders, and twice we chased them off. I've always slept well aboard the *Estrela*, in fact aboard any boat, comfortable in my ability to doze off quickly yet awaken immediately at any change in the wind or other subtle variation in wave pattern or even a change in the way the boat rides at anchor or at a pier. But the boardings unsettled me, probably an aftereffect of the beating I'd sustained earlier and despite Felix' assurances that it was almost certainly kids looking to steal anything that they could peddle elsewhere in the harbor I couldn't get back to sleep after the second occurrence. I sat in the wheelhouse until dawn, thinking about Catalina and Patricio; thoughts that inevitably turned to Niccolo Cardeli and the pleasure I would take in eliminating him.

V

At dawn, Felix set off to meet with his cousin and I went to check on the shipment of electronics. Before we parted we went over our verbal shopping list. We wanted four pistols, at least one of which would be small enough to conceal in a waistband, one high-powered rifle and two shotguns plus several thousand rounds of ammunition. I don't know why, but I added plastic explosive and detonators to the list before Felix set off to find his cousin.

The import brokers' offices were still closed so I wandered around until they opened and then spent another hour locating the right one. It took another three hours to arrange for clearance, payment and shipment of the boxes to the harbor. After making certain the broker was using a reputable delivery service I arranged to meet the truck dockside at five p.m. and headed out to find the combination bar and restaurant Shando had referred to. It wasn't too difficult, except that I couldn't remember the actual name of the club and the additional complication of the language barrier presented by the thick patois of the lad who offered me directions to the blues and jazz spot I described. He led me there for a dollar, instantly solving the translation problem.

I went back to the *Estrela* hoping to grab some sleep, and found Commander Jones waiting at dockside. He was in civvies and walking slowly along the dock surveying the boat. I briefly considered turning away before he spotted me and then changed my mind.

"Hello Peter," I called.

He turned around and flashed a broad smile. "Well hello. I hope you don't mind me dropping by unannounced, but I have a couple of things I'd like to discuss with you."

We went aboard and while I fetched two cold beers he made himself comfortable under the small canvas awning Felix had rigged to provide some shade from the hot tropical sun. After I settled into the other canvas chair he again apologized for arriving unannounced and explained that if we had plans to take the *Estrela* to any other territorial jurisdictions in the Caribbean we should remove the fishing gear – meaning nets – before doing so.

"I never thought about it," I said, "but I suppose that even though we wouldn't fish inside territorial limits it could pose a problem."

"Exactly. Things have changed a lot since Jebediah's time. Strictly speaking, it was the same then, too, but he had a way of circumventing all sorts of rules and regulations with impunity."

"Thank you, Peter. We'll remember your advice although we're not planning to visit any other jurisdictions."

He scanned the harbor with a practiced eye, and I got the impression it was an automatic reflex. "Another thing. If you're planning on coming and going while you're in this harbor I would suggest you leave a guard aboard the *Estrela*, particularly once you have your new electronics."

I told him about being boarded the previous night, and he smiled knowingly. "See? People are desperate here, and bold. You won't mind then that I've taken the liberty to arrange for two trustworthy officers to rotate a 24-hour watch." His eyes narrowed even as his smile broadened. "I wouldn't want something untoward happening aboard the *Estrela*," he said, holding up his hand in anticipation of my objection. "It's the least I can do for the flesh and blood of Jebediah Snell. The first shift will start at sunset tonight. Courtesy of Her Majesty the Queen, of course."

Any objection would further reinforce his already apparent suspicions so I thanked him politely, returning his smile.

"So, did my father visit Kingston often?" I was still curious about father, and so far what I'd learned from his friends and acquaintances only whetted my appetite for more. He was beginning to take shape for me in a way I'd never expected. He was more than a gifted fisherman, skilled mariner and lucky investor, as anyone who had the opportunity to peruse the depth and diversity of his library would soon realize.

"I wouldn't say he visited frequently," Peter answered, "but when he did he tended to stay for a week or more studying original manuscripts in various public and private collections. I've heard it said that the unique interpretations he brought to these, partially thanks to his ability to wheedle access to previously unknown or inaccessible collections, increased the value of those items a hundredfold. He hated the limelight and the Chancellor of the University had a devil of a time convincing him to lecture there."

I was dumfounded. "He lectured at the University?" The memory flashed through my mind of how he had looked so out of place in his faded jeans and windbreaker fiddling with his medallion in the dean's office at my military school, particularly compared to the uniformed and beribboned Colonel Jamieson.

"Yes he did, a number of times, and every lecture was jam-packed. The Governor General – the Queen's official representative here - was particularly impressed and took great pleasure in your father's insights relating to Sir Henry Morgan's place in the legitimate conduct of the wars against Spain as a privateer. Did you know that when the memoirs of a Dutchman named Esquemeling who had served under Morgan were translated in England, Morgan sued the publishers for libel and won an out-of-court settlement? It seems he was most enraged at the suggestion he had arrived in the West Indies as an indentured servant, and as a result in new prefaces to the book Morgan was described as 'a Welsh gentleman's son who was never a servant to anybody during his life, except perhaps unto His Majesty.' I'll never forget Jebediah weaving that fact and many others into a series of lectures that truly brought the early history of the Caribbean to life." Peter paused. "I never missed a single lecture," he said with a healthy display of pride.

I thought about that for a while. "So father was a respected visitor here," I mused aloud.

"Respected, certainly. By one and all. Much like Morgan himself, I suppose. Respected for his public persona and at the same time respected in an entirely different way for the dark undercurrents that swirled about him."

"I'm not sure I understand," I said.

"It's simple, Dexter. Your father was misplaced in time. He was a throwback to the earlier days of buccaneers and privateers, as opposed to the pirates. Jebediah walked a fine line, and would be judged by no man. In fact, unless and until he was caught doing something – and he never was – he intrigued the hell out of people; the same people who flocked to his lectures.

"Many's the time the coast guard laid traps for him, and he outsmarted us at every turn. Don't get me wrong, Dexter, I'm not demeaning your father in any way. I'm just saying he was one of those rare and precious individuals who you know is crossing the line but despite that you can't bring yourself to dislike him for it."

Peter leaned back and took another sip of his beer. "There was always the suspicion, but never the proof. And it made him a romantic figure, particularly among the ladies. Men used to joke about the risk of being off-island when Jebediah was here. But it was only a man who was at home at the time who joked about it, never the man who came home to learn the *Estrela* had been in port during his absence." Commander Jones looked around the *Estrela*. "She's a fine boat, Dexter. And I hope I'm wrong, but if you're out to match wits with me be warned that I'll give no quarter. I gave none to Jebediah, yet I was always welcome aboard. He was a real gentleman, even if a bit of a rogue."

"Thank you for the warning, Commander," I said, draining my beer. "In a strange way, I'm honored. Can I get you another?"

"No, not now. But I'd like one when I come back to see the gear you've ordered. Tomorrow, say midmorning?" he asked.

"I'd like that, Peter," I answered.

Commander Jones disembarked and passed the man wheeling the handcart of boxes down the wharf toward the *Estrela*. To his credit, he never even glanced to see if the boxes appeared to contain what they were supposed to contain. I expect it's the British way of showing confidence and issuing a challenge.

It worked.

VI

Felix arrived back shortly after the boxes were loaded aboard. I told him about Peter Jones' visit and the 24-hour guard. Although it made me nervous to be watched, I should have been getting used to it. We knew it would be too dangerous to take the guns aboard in Kingston anyway so it made sense to make the most of the situation and play it straight.

Felix' meeting with his cousin had gone off without a hitch but some of the items I wanted would take time. Handguns were plentiful and readily available according to Felix' cousin, and the shotguns too posed little problem. The high-powered rifle and plastic explosives were a little trickier, and would take some arranging tomorrow. There would need to be cash up front, which I would get on Monday, and the logistics of smuggling the weapons aboard had to be worked out. I left that part in Felix' hands and went ashore about a half hour before sunset as I didn't want to run into Peter Jones' watchman.

I headed into the area called New Kingston and killed time in a safe, quiet spot until close to eleven o'clock and then made my way to the rendezvous. It being Friday, the club was crowded with late diners and the music – good blues – spilled out of the old converted mansion and into the grounds. The bar, as I remembered, was outside and at the back so I walked through the place and was lucky enough to spot an empty stool at the rail.

It was crowded but neither pushy nor too noisy. The clientele was obviously upper class, similar to what it had been three years ago, and I sat and nursed a rum and coke and watched couples coming and going. Jamaican time is flexible so I was prepared to give it an hour hoping Shando had been able to come through with a connection.

The whole situation with Peter Jones kept coming back to mind and there were a few other things bothering me, not the least being the odds of meeting someone who seemed to have known my father so well. It was one thing to meet someone like Bones on Cayman Brac, but what were the odds on traveling two hundred miles across the Caribbean and running smack into another? Despite my father's extensive voyages through the West Indies, that had to be a long shot. And how did Jones know Christmas Carol? I never asked and realized I should have. Hell, Jones must be thinking the same thing about my apparent lack of curiosity.

The sight of a large woman, immense would not be an exaggeration, making her way across the room with a small man in tow interrupted my jumbled thoughts. She was wearing a flowered tent – there's no other way to describe her dress – and jabbering away in patois to no one in particular. She reminded me of a wave, a big wave that once set in motion moves effortlessly by dint of its own mass, powerfully displacing anything in its path or rolling over anything that won't or can't move out of the way. It was comical to watch people shift aside to let her pass and then close back in behind her as if nothing had happened.

When she was about fifteen feet from the bar the little man darted out from her wake and danced ahead to pull out the empty bar stool beside me and rearrange the people on the other side of it to accommodate her bulk. Once she was settled, he turned toward me with what could only be interpreted as a look of immense pride.

"Doan worry mi son, gwey fix yu up real nice," he beamed.

I have no ear for the local patois, and was embarrassed that I was caught staring.

I mumbled a quick "Pardon me?" as the bartender magically appeared with a tall fancy drink for the woman.

I watched her take a sip from the straw and nod her approval to the hovering bartender, who then moved on down the bar without asking what the little man wanted. It didn't seem to bother him in the least.

She leaned past him and spoke in understandable English, "He said I do what I can." I was taken aback and it must have been obvious as she continued in explanation. "Shando – your friend in the Keys, right?"

"Yes," I stammered.

"He asked I meet you. Here I am," she said matter-of-factly.

"I'm sorry. I was expecting to meet someone I would recognize from three years ago. You've caught me by surprise."

"Right. Shando said it be preferable you meet someone up the ladder. That's me – I'm Tun, this's Gunnaz," she said, offering her hand. I shook her massive hand, and Gunnaz just nodded to me, moving out from between us and facing the room. "I doan talk here, doan do business here. Too many ears."

She got up without saying anything more and I followed her and Gunnaz through the bar and restaurant like a water toy being pulled in the wake of a boat. An old van was waiting out front and Gunnaz

motioned for me to stand aside while he helped Tun up and in the back
and into her chair. When he was satisfied she was comfortable, he
waved me in and then got out and slammed the door shut.

The vehicle was actually bigger than a full-sized van; more the size
of a small panel truck and the driver's compartment had been separated
from the rear by a plywood bulkhead and sliding window. Gunnaz
stuck his head through from the driver's seat and announced that we
were off before closing the window and leaving me alone in the back
with Tun.

The truck was comfortable; air conditioned and equipped with
several small wooden chairs and one large recliner that reminded me of
a La-Z-Boy, which was where Tun was ensconced. The La-Z-Boy was
mounted on a platform that elevated it about a foot, presumably to
make it easier for Tun to ease her bulk in and out, and if it wasn't for
the fact that we were in the back of a truck I got the impression of a
queen on a throne.

Tun pointed to a small fridge and asked me to get two Red Stripes
while she arranged herself. She pushed on the arms of her chair until a
footrest popped up and the back reclined to forty-five degrees. She
fixed her eyes on my face and I swear they didn't move off me for the
next two hours. I handed her a beer and sat in one of the wooden chairs
arranged in front of the throne.

"How my friend Shando?" she asked, taking a big swallow of the
Red Stripe, smacking her lips and wiping her mouth with the back of a
massive arm.

"He's fine, as far as I know. I haven't actually seen him for a few
months," I answered.

"Good mon," she said, holding my eyes with hers.

"Yes," I answered. I wasn't sure what else to say, it being apparent
Tun controlled every conversation. I felt the truck pull onto the street
and move away slowly.

"You want sumting. I tell Shando I listen."

I thought for a second about how to broach the subject, and decided
that under the circumstances anything but a direct request was a waste
of time. "Yes. I need to make a connection. I need a name in
Colombia."

Her eyes narrowed, but never wavered. "You talk cocaine. Must be
cocaine. No other reason for Colombia. No other reason to meet with
Tun."

"I hope you don't take this the wrong way, but I don't know who you
are. I just asked Shando to try to arrange a meeting with someone here

in Jamaica on the expectation he – sorry – or she could aim me in the right direction."

"Tun can do it, if Tun wants," she said. She reminded me of Shando in the way she referred to herself by her name. I mentally compared that to the way a queen uses 'we.' I decided Tun's usage was infinitely more direct and powerful.

I sat and waited, the obvious question of whether or not she wanted to give me a name hanging in the air.

"Shando ask Tun to educate you, Dexter Snell. I do that now."

And educate me she did.

She started with a historical run down on the use of narcotics, and although it wouldn't impress the US Drug Enforcement Administration, it sure as hell impressed me.

According to Tun the use of coca, as opposed to cocaine, goes back thousands of years, obviously predating the Spanish conquering of the Incas in South America. The coca plant in it's raw form was used much like caffeine is used by some people today, and the image of supercharged, caffeine-jagged yuppie stock brokers came to my mind. The Incas chewed the leaves, which don't contain much cocaine in their raw form, the drug releasing slowly over time. Tun stated that the leaves contain considerably less than one percent of the drug, and in order to get the equivalent of a good Wall Street toot an Inca would have had to jam a whole pint of them up his nose and then somehow get the cocaine to release all at once – an impossibility given the limitations of chemistry at the time. In fact, she said, it took 'the civilized western world' to figure out how to do it.

The best the Incas could accomplish was chewing a small handful of leaves into a wad and then carefully adding something with high pH content – burned roots or crushed seashells for example – to the center of the wad so it didn't burn their mouths. They then simply held the wad in their cheeks as their saliva mixed with it and released the cocaine to be absorbed into the bloodstream over time, suppressing hunger and giving them an energy boost. The Spanish conquerors soon discovered that by encouraging this practice and in fact accelerating it they could drive up the gold production from their captured mines by providing their Inca slaves with less rest and little or no food. The hungrier and more tired the Incas became the more they turned to the coca leaf to stand up to the ordeal and it became a vicious cycle leading to their eventual extinction. The similarities to both the enslavement and elimination of the Arawaks on Jamaica and the economics of the opium trade in China were not lost on me.

"Sig Freud and friends figure out how to 'tek good ting mek bad.'" Tun said, slipping into pure patois for an instant.

Then she launched into a treatise on marijuana – ganja – and provided a similar but in my opinion less inspired historical perspective, ending that part of her dissertation with the conclusion that only a white man could take otherwise worthless plants that grow wild and elevate them into a 'mega-billion' dollar industry by declaring them illegal, and then spend billions more on futile enforcement efforts that make them more valuable still.

It was as if I was on trial somehow as she stared at me. I really didn't know what to say and was overwhelmed by the feeling I was trapped in some kind of warp between Cardeli, father, Patricio, Catalina, my own past and now centuries of relentless struggles between the developed and third worlds; the 'haves' and the 'have-nots.' Were the spirits of the Inca gods in Macchu Picchu laughing at us, having unleashed their own reckoning?

I swear Tun could read my mind, and satisfied at the turmoil she'd unleashed within me she launched into a recent history of drug trafficking.

"You see movie called Blow?" she asked.

I said I had and off she went again.

"George good man, but foolish," she said. I assumed she was referring to George Jung, whose story is told in the movie.

Tun provided more background, giving me her version of what happened on Norman's Cay for five years from 1977. Norman's Cay lies just over 200 miles from the Florida coast, at the northern end of the Exumas – part of the Bahamas chain. It seems that Carlos Lehder, George Jung's original partner, took over the entire island by evicting the residents and then built a 3,300 foot runway protected by radar, bodyguards and dogs to accommodate incoming DC3's loaded with cocaine from Colombia, then dispatching smaller, single-engine planes to tiny airfields along the south east coast of the US. Tun said each shipment was between 500 and 1,500 kilos and at his peak Lehder handled thirty planeloads a day, clearing a million dollars every 24 hours for simply handling the transportation logistics. The US government eventually forced a crackdown on his operation by a reportedly reluctant Bahamian administration rumored to be benefiting from Lehder's largesse. Lehder fled to Colombia, where he lived like a king until the US finally managed to have him extradited.

The upshot of all this was that the US poured millions, then billions, into interdiction efforts. Sea and air patrols along the coast were reinforced, and military technology including satellite surveillance was pressed into service. A network of dirigible-mounted radar devices permanently tethered offshore along the Florida coast – I'd seen those from *Party Girl* – were perhaps the most visible sign of the increased defense of the US coastline.

"So smuggling change again. Move to California and up through Mexico. And Jamaica," Tun said. "Mek new business for poor people."

Tun explained how large shipments were now being delivered from Colombia to Jamaica and Mexico, whose coastlines were less effectively guarded, and then broken down into small packages of one or two kilos and smuggled individually into the US by 'mules' – desperate people who risked stiff penalties in return for the chance to make one or two thousand dollars as couriers. The traffickers were simply playing the odds – for every five shipments according to the USDEA, ten according to Tun, one was discovered and seized - and the smugglers simply absorbed the loss as a cost of doing business. Of course the unfortunate couriers lost more than money, facing stiff prison sentences. But there seemed to be an endless supply of wretched individuals waiting to take their places.

"Plane still fly, but not like in de time of Lehder and Norman's Cay."

Instead, many of the shipments to Jamaica were being delivered offshore, transferred at sea and at night to small Jamaican fishing boats or simply dropped overboard and then picked up by the same fishermen. Tun laughed as she described the occasional kilo package found floating loose as a 'square tuna.'

"One square tuna feed big family," she added.

Tun tossed her empty Red Stripe into a bucket and motioned for me to fetch two more from the fridge. I opened them, handed one to her and sat down in my wooden chair again. The truck was still moving, and it felt like we were on a mountain road judging from the twisting and turning. My wooden chair bounced around constantly, and it took a fair amount of effort to maintain my balance and concentrate on Tun's narrative at the same time. Her throne was bolted down and she was comfortable, chuckling now and then at my attempts to keep from being thrown to the floor.

I wondered why Cardeli didn't simply avail himself of the same connections out of Jamaica. This might be easier and less risky than I'd thought. I asked Tun how the business was organized.

"Doan know exactly. Colombians control supply and traffic in US. Jamaica just link in de chain," she said.

"So you can't sell directly to me?" I asked.

"Tun doan sell. Just run service. White Gold Express," she offered, laughing, "No paperwork, no hassle."

I realized with a sinking feeling in the pit of my stomach that I would in fact have to go to Colombia and make a connection further up the chain. And I would have to somehow figure out how to get the cocaine into the States. I didn't have enough time left to organize something like Tun described, and was sickened further by the thought I would have to run the narcotics blockade myself carrying a substantial amount of cocaine aboard the *Estrela*. I only had a little over ten weeks left to get at Cardeli, and I couldn't see any other way. And on top of that, I still didn't know what it was father had been up to. I didn't believe he was smuggling cocaine, and neither did Cardeli. As if that wasn't enough I had to acknowledge to myself that deep down inside, despite the threats, I did not want any part of a scheme that might actually result in narcotics landing in the US – or anywhere, for that matter. At the same time I just had to keep going and hope for a break.

"What about a connection in Colombia?" I asked.

"Dangerous place," Tun answered, the smile disappearing from her face. She switched her lecture to the Colombian end of things.

I'd heard of the Medellin cartel, and Pablo Escobar. Who hadn't? And the Cali cartel as well. Tun's story started there.

The market opened by George Jung in the US and expanded exponentially by Carlos Lehder had incredible repercussions in Colombia. In the beginning, there was little stigma attached to coca because of the centuries-old traditions of its use in a relatively benign form. The European discovery in the late nineteenth century of how to process raw leaves and extract the cocaine was only the first step in the tragic explosion. It took the wealth and appetite of the American consumer coupled with the subsequent prohibition efforts of the government to drive the price up to the point where cocaine became a hundred billion dollar industry.

In Colombia, Peru and Bolivia the governments initially turned a blind eye to the growing predicament. After all, coca thrived everywhere in their countries and had forever. Coca and cocaine were simply not the same thing to them, and they saw cocaine as a uniquely American issue - without the American market there would be no problem. On top of that the rising market value of coca leaf provided them with a solution to one of their own pressing domestic problems: how to employ millions of people in a third world country. A family of four could exist on the six or seven hundred dollars a year they could earn by living near and tending as few as two remote acres of coca plants. In so doing, they actually alleviated the deadly influx of humanity into increasingly overcrowded and ghettoized urban centers that offered no employment and even less hope. Bananas, coffee and other crops required more sophisticated cultivation techniques and more arable land – both beyond the reach of the peasant population and both dependent on a market infrastructure that didn't exist in those countries. Not to mention the vagaries of foreign-controlled coffee prices that frequently fell below the cost of production, leaving families to starve to death. The coca leaf market was a solution that appeared to be heaven sent.

Despite the increasing pressures brought by the Americans, initially on Peru and Bolivia, those governments weren't committed at first. And once they were, production shifted to even more remote areas of the Andes Mountains and to Colombia where it became an even bigger business helped by the rise of people like Escobar.

Colombia was different than Peru and Bolivia, being relatively more sophisticated. The members of the cartels had greater influence on their own government, and the wealth they created was in part used to ensure their safety from the increasingly long reach of the Americans. Escobar himself even managed to get elected to the Colombian parliament for a short time.

It wasn't until reform-minded politicians in Bogota began to flirt with the idea of extraditing leading members of the cartels to the USA that things erupted.

Apparently Escobar, using his billions in cocaine-fueled wealth, embarked on a campaign of kidnapping or assassinating those politicians he saw as a threat. The campaign reached a peak with the assassination of the Minister of Justice and it was downhill for Pablo from there. However, the private armies he and other drug lords had created soon found new employment.

The exigencies of the American cocaine market are such that if supply is threatened or falters, the price simply rises to the point that new means of supply come on stream. The Revolutionary Armed Forces of Columbia – FARC – a Marxist guerrilla movement that had been in existence for more than twenty years stepped in and took over, providing protection for the cocaine trade in return for what amounts to little more than a taxation system that funds their ongoing battle with the government. It seems FARC controls a big slice of Colombia, and the legitimate government is more or less powerless to do anything about it although it receives massive aid and assistance from the US government. Tun said the Colombians have grown dependent on the aid money, and that if they were really successful in defeating FARC another whole segment of the Colombian population would be unemployed.

"So are you saying I will have to deal with an armed guerilla movement?" I asked, overwhelmed.

"Look on de bright side. No haffta deal wit Tun," she grinned.

The truck jolted to a stop, and the door slid open. The interior was immediately filled with the stench of rotting garbage, and I saw we were in the middle of a slum.

"Get out," ordered Tun.

I was stunned, and she repeated the order. I still made no move.

"Out!" shouted Gunnaz.

I stepped into the road. The stench was even worse outside and I saw an endless collection of ramshackle, dilapidated hovels. Gunnaz helped Tun down from the truck.

"We walk," she said, rolling down the littered roadway. I caught up to her, with Gunnaz a few steps behind.

"You look. See poverty here," she said as she waved an arm in a big arc. "People desperate. No hope."

She stopped when we were about a hundred feet from the truck, paused and then turned back. I followed again, and took in the sights around me. I had to agree with her assessment.

When we got back to the truck Gunnaz helped her up, then stopped me from following her. Tun turned around to face me. "Unnerstan?" she asked.

I nodded, processing everything she'd told me and trying to make sense of the ridiculous set of circumstances she'd laid out. Demand driving supply, and efforts to interrupt that supply simply ensuring prices stayed high or higher, further ensuring that someone would always take the risk to satisfy the demand. The conditions in the slum around us told me the rewards didn't even have to be terribly high to encourage people to risk imprisonment. This was a prison in and of itself.

"Tun," I asked, "how do you know so much about all of this?" It was a question that had been nagging at the back of my mind.

Tun laughed, and answered in now-perfect English. "I graduated at the top of my class from the London School of Economics. I was there in the sixties when Mick Jagger was in attendance, only I never met or saw him," she smiled. "My training in economics relating to supply and demand applies to and explains the narcotics trade, and I'm just naturally curious."

The smile disappeared, and she stared at me.

"Why are you meeting with Peter Jones?"

The question shook me. Once again I was overcome with the desperate feeling everything was out of control.

"We were intercepted and searched by the coast guard off Portland Point on our way here. There wasn't anything aboard except for some medical supplies that raised a question, but he seems to have taken an interest in me," I answered, "and I simply don't know what to do about it."

She thought about that, as if she was considering whether or not to believe me. She must have reached a conclusion.

"Peter Jones is both an honest and a worthy opponent. Don't underestimate him. At least you won't be shaken down for a bribe or have drugs planted on your boat as long as the police know he's taken an interest in you."

Tun moved away from the door and settled back onto her throne.

"I'll get you a name in Colombia, Dexter Snell. But I hope you know what you're doing. I like you."

Gunnaz slid the door closed and pointed me to a car that had pulled up behind the truck. I went to it, got in the front seat next to a silent, taciturn Rastafarian and was driven back to the harbor.

VII

It was nearly two in the morning when I was dropped off, a fact I knew would be reported to Peter Jones. If he asked about it, I decided to give him part of the truth and then stonewall him. There was no sign of a guard around the boat but I had no doubt he was somewhere where he could watch us.

Felix was awake and sitting in the wheelhouse when I boarded. The look of relief that flooded his face showed how worried he'd been.

"Damn it, Dex. Where the hell have you been?"

"Relax. I was in good hands. I met Shando's contact at the bar and I've been given a lesson in the economics of the cocaine industry. It's a little frightening to say the least. And as a bonus I was given a quick tour of a Kingston slum."

"You were in the slums? Who the hell was this guy?" Felix exploded.

"It wasn't a guy, Felix. It was a woman."

"That's even worse, man. You were wandering around a Kingston slum with a woman? What the hell were you thinking? Who was it?"

"It was a woman who goes by the name Tun," I said, "whatever that means."

Felix stared at me wide-eyed. "You met Tun?" he asked, "and you don't know what her name means?" He broke out laughing. He laughed until the tears rolled down his cheeks. I didn't understand what was so funny all of a sudden, and waited for him to explain.

"You met Tun," he laughed, "and don't know what that means. Wait until I tell my cousin this one."

"So? Tell me what's so funny."

"God, Dex. Don't your eyes work?" he asked, waiting for me to somehow figure out what the joke was. I just sat there until he couldn't hold out any longer. "Just how much do you think she weighs?"

It finally dawned on me. "A ton, I guess," finally getting it. "And what about her man Gunnaz?"

Felix stared at me. His eyes went wider and wider as if he expected me to understand at any second. I tried, but couldn't figure it out.

"Dex, he has a gun. Gunnaz, get it?" He broke out again into gales of laughter. "So you went on a tour with Tun and Gunnaz. I'd sure like to meet this guy Shando. He knows some important people."

We talked until just before dawn, the levity fading quickly as I told him about the realities of what we had to do.

VIII

Peter Jones showed up just before noon to find us surrounded by a pile of electronic components, our faces buried in installation manuals. He thought it amusing and again offered his assistance, producing a toolbox full of wire cutters and strippers, pliers, connectors, testers and other paraphernalia. He took a visual inventory of what we'd purchased and soon had Felix and I busy removing the old gear and running the new cables following the same routings as the ones we were replacing. It only took about four hours, since we were lucky that most of the existing brackets were easily adapted to hold the new stuff, and then Peter set about testing the connections with some kind of meter before announcing we were ready to turn it all on. The only item that presented a problem was the through-hull fitting for the new fishfinder/sonar unit and Peter promised to have a diver available the next day to do the underwater work.

He began switching everything on and we watched while he fiddled with and adjusted knobs and dials. I was familiar with the actual way most of it was supposed to work and offered the occasional piece of advice when I could.

Everything appeared to be in order with the exception of the sonar fitting and the necessity of taking the *Estrela* out to sea to calibrate the auxiliary gyrocompass for the autopilot, which he suggested we do after the diver fitted the through-hull sensor. Peter then called for a beer break and Felix went to fetch some from the icebox while Peter and I settled into chairs under the canvas shade on the work deck.

"You were out rather late last night, Dexter. Seeing the sights were you?" he asked casually.

"As a matter of fact I was. I went to a jazz club and took up the offer of a night-time tour of Kingston from a couple I met there."

"I hope you realize just how dangerous Kingston is at night. Who did you meet?"

"Is this an official inquiry, Peter?" I asked.

"Why no, it's not. It's just a conversation and curiosity. You aren't hiding anything, are you?"

"Why no, I'm not," I parroted him, smiling politely.

"That's good to hear, Dexter. You sounded exactly like Jebediah there, by the way."

"Shouldn't be surprising, I suppose," I answered and switched the subject. "I was wondering about the history of Port Royal. I understand it sank into the harbor during an earthquake around 1690 – do you know anything about it?"

Felix was surprised to hear Peter and I discussing the history of Jamaica when he emerged from the cabin with the beer and we spent the rest of the afternoon in a pleasant discussion about Port Royal and Sir Henry Morgan while Felix grew increasingly edgy as the time grew closer to meet his cousin again. I knew it was bothering Felix but couldn't figure out how to hurry Peter along without raising suspicion. He finally solved the problem by excusing himself and headed off to prepare for a night patrol.

As soon as he was safely out of sight Felix left, telling me to not expect him back until morning, and I headed to the *Estrela* for a nap. That proved to be a waste of time as I just tossed and turned thinking about what had to be done in Colombia and worrying about how I was going to get at Cardeli before I ended up in over my head. I finally got up, showered and headed back to the jazz club. It was around nine when I arrived and went through the restaurant to the bar.

It wasn't crowded yet and the band was either on a break or hadn't started. I had just ordered a drink when two men took the stools on either side of me.

"You look better than last time, Dexter," one of them said, and I looked to my right and saw Nestor. A quick look to my left confirmed Diego was with him.

"What, no hello for old friends?" he asked.

"What do you want?" I spit out.

"It's not us who wants to see you, Dexter. It's somebody else. Drink up and let's go."

"Why should I go with you?" I asked.

"Simple. You don't want us to go back without you and report that you don't give a shit about your Uncle and that nice little girl Catalina, do you?" he smiled menacingly.

I tossed some money on the bar and stood up without waiting for my drink. "Let's go," I said, cursing myself for the lack of a weapon. I was about to miss an opportunity to settle this immediately, and my mind spun trying to figure out what I could do.

Nestor and Diego walked behind me as I left the club and then shoved me against the side of a waiting car, searching me before pushing me into the backseat and climbing in on either side. I had to force myself to remain calm, at least outwardly. My heart was racing and I fought to control my breathing. Nobody spoke a word until we pulled up in front of the Pegasus hotel, a luxury high-rise facility in the financial district.

"Come on," ordered Diego, leading the way through the front doors and into the lobby to the elevators, Nestor close behind me. We rode up to the suites floor at or near the top and I was pushed out of the elevator and down the hall. Diego knocked twice on the door and then opened it with a key.

The lights were dimmed but I saw it was a large, luxurious suite. Diego patted me down again, more thoroughly this time, and told me to go and wait on the balcony. "He's here," he called out before they left. I was certain they wouldn't be far away, probably standing right in the hallway outside the door, but I wondered why Cardeli would take a chance like this. I could have him over the balcony and plunging to his death before they could possibly stop me and I began to figure out exactly how I would do it.

"Hello, Dex," she said, and I spun around. It was Mirtha, standing in the doorway to the balcony. The soft light of the suite spilled out from behind, silhouetting her. She was holding a glass of champagne and wearing nothing but a towel. "Have you missed me?"

"I've been too busy to miss you. You may not know that I'm working for your husband now," I answered facetiously.

"Oh yes, I know. And that's one of the reasons I'm here, dear Dexter. Help yourself to a drink from the bar and come and join me," she said, moving out onto the balcony and toward a sitting area at the opposite end.

I poured myself a stiff scotch and walked back toward her. She was sitting on a chaise and pointed to a wicker chair across from her. She sipped her champagne and stared at me as she made a show of crossing and then uncrossing her legs. The barest hint of a smile appeared on her wide mouth. I sipped my scotch and stared back in anger.

I had to get myself under control. Showing any hint of rage or resistance would not further my goal of getting close enough to Cardeli to kill him.

"Niccolo wants to know how you're doing – I hope you realize he's concerned about you," she said.

"I wish I could believe that," I said. "But I'm beginning to see how I can move significant quantities of cocaine and I'm certain I can prove my value to him."

I discarded the notion of mentioning Shando. If she knew I'd been in touch with him, then fine. And if she didn't, then it would continue to work in my favor. I stood to lose nothing either way, as she either knew or she didn't. It was still bothersome that someone was able to keep track of me. It had to be either Shando or Bones.

"So you think you can really do this?" she asked, toying with her champagne glass and moving her crossed leg up and down slightly but continuously. A few months ago and under other circumstances I would have looked forward to a romp with a woman who threw herself at me. I had to be careful to play this convincingly.

"Yes, I'm certain I can. And quite frankly, I'm looking forward to it. I've had a taste of being broke and it sours quickly."

"So," she said, her eyes narrowing, "you've had second thoughts about leaving me for that stuck-up little bitch, have you?"

"Well, let's just say I miss my house, boat, plane and helicopter," I said with what I hoped was a fair imitation of my old cockiness, "and although I'll probably never see them again, I'd like to think I can at least make enough money to enjoy myself."

"You're still a bastard, Dex. But you're an interesting bastard. Let's get the business out of the way. Niccolo wants a progress report."

I gave a rundown of what I'd learned, making it sound like significant progress. I told her about the coast guard patrols around Jamaica, the way the fishermen retrieved the shipments and how they were broken down and shipped by mule into the US. I explained how FARC controlled or was heavily involved in the business at the Colombia end, and that I'd made contact with one of the top people in Jamaica who was providing me with a Colombian contact. I assumed Niccolo probably knew all about the changes in the way cocaine was smuggled now and all about FARC, but it certainly wouldn't hurt to let him think I'd discovered it myself by dint of diligent preparatory homework. I concluded with what I'd done to refit the *Estrela*, omitting the fact we'd found false compartments in the fuel tanks. I leaned back in the chair and took a swallow of the scotch.

"I'm impressed, Dex," she purred, "There may be more than one reason to keep you around. And believe me, unless at least one reason makes Niccolo happy, you'll be gone." She uncrossed and crossed her legs again, more languidly this time and making sure the towel slipped a little higher on her thighs.

"Niccolo wants to know what you've done about the other little task as well."

I knew she was referring to father's activities, and I had no choice but to bluff.

"I think I'm onto something there, too, but I'm not prepared to talk about it yet. I'll have it before the end of October though. I guarantee it."

What damage could that do, I reasoned. I knew the deadline wouldn't change, and I would either have it figured out or not. No use sending out alarm signals. If anything, Cardeli might become curious enough to want to see me in person. I'd sure as hell be ready next time.

"Well, Dex, it looks like you're on track. I'm surprised, but Niccolo said you'd either completely collapse or get it done. I guess he was right. You'll need money at the Colombia end, and it'll have to be cash. When are you returning to Cayman Brac?" she asked.

"I was actually thinking about going straight to Colombia from here and arranging for the money after I have everything set but you're right, I may as well do this in one fell swoop. Why can't the money be delivered here?"

"There are reasons you don't need to know about. It's got to be on Cayman Brac. Niccolo said for you to be there in five days."

Why Brac? Was it Bones after all? Shit, it could be Bones *and* Shando. I wasn't getting anywhere other than simply getting closer to crossing over the line that would make me a cocaine trafficker.

"Okay, he's the boss. I'll be there," I confirmed.

"That's nice, Dex. And how are things with Cat and Patricio?"

"I don't know, Mirtha, and quite frankly I don't care. I haven't heard from them since shortly after Niccolo visited me on Brac."

"Oh?" she asked, a smile playing across her face. "Would you like to know what your precious little girl has been up to?"

"I told you I don't care," I lied.

"Are you sure? I've got some pictures of her with her new boyfriend. She's moved to Atlanta and she's cutting a pretty wide swath. Poor old Patricio is all by himself in Brunswick."

I struggled to keep the pain and hurt from showing on my face. I stood up and leaned forward toward Mirtha, smiled and said, "I told you I don't give a shit," and then turned my back on her on the pretext of refilling my glass at the bar at the other end of the balcony.

I shouldn't have been surprised Catalina had found someone new. I had hurt her terribly, and for all she knew I had reverted to my previous selfish persona. I had gone to extreme lengths to alienate both her and Patricio, and now freed of her twenty-year fixation on me she could get on with her life. It did surprise me however that she had abandoned Patricio, and the thought of him sitting alone in that house in Brunswick without either of us there to keep him company in his final years was unbearable. My gut twisted thinking about it. Hell, who was I kidding? My gut twisted with pain not only for Patricio, but for the possibly irretrievable loss of Catalina as well.

I refilled my glass and took a deep swallow.

"Dexter."

I turned around slowly. Mirtha was halfway across the balcony, and she stopped and looked at me.

"There's another reason I'm here," she whispered, letting the towel drop.

She moved her shoulders back, proudly thrusting her breasts forward to display them prominently. Her nipples were swollen even more than I'd remembered, and I could see the moisture on her thighs, her bare pubis glistening with the evidence of her excitement.

"Isn't Shando enough for you, Mirtha?" I asked mockingly.

She challenged me with her eyes as she reached between her legs, exploring her own wetness with her right hand as she teased a swollen nipple with the other. "He's bigger and stronger than you, but he can't do what you do."

I closed the distance between us in three steps and struck her squarely across the face with my open hand. My fury boiled over and I didn't hold anything back. I wasn't worried about marking her as I'd been the first time and even as I slapped her harder and harder, working down her breasts then to her inner thighs and finally taking my leather belt to her ass, she erupted in orgasm after orgasm, begging for more.

I don't know how long I kept it up, but she was still begging like a bitch in heat when I left.

IX

Felix returned to the *Estrela* just after sunrise and said his cousin would have the weapons, ammunition and Semtex plastic explosive for us the next day, and that the upfront money had to be handed over that morning. The transfer itself was to be made at night, at sea off the coast by Port Antonio.

I told him about the meeting with Mirtha, leaving out the parts about Catalina and what I'd done to Mirtha. I left it that I'd convinced her I was looking forward to the prospect of making some serious money.

Peter showed up at eight with a diver in tow and explained how the old sonar fitting would be removed and the new cable and sensor quickly fed through the hole from the bottom to minimize the inflow of seawater into the hull. It went as he described, although Felix was nervous until the hole was plugged and the influx of seawater halted. We ran the cable up to the sonar/fishfinder and cranked up the engine so we could seatrial and calibrate everything.

Peter certainly knew his way around marine electronics and I readily admitted I would never have been able to calibrate the gyrocompass. We were playing with the autopilot and checking out how all of the devices were interconnected when he asked where I wanted the arrival alarm mounted.

"What's an arrival alarm?" I asked.

"It's a remote horn that sounds when you've arrived at a preset destination, warning you to take over from the autopilot," he explained.

I thought about it and concluded it was unnecessary in the wheelhouse since the autopilot itself had a built-in speaker that did the same thing.

"Just wire it up and leave about fifty feet of cable in a coil. We'll decide where to put it later," I said. While Peter was doing that I noticed the box of medical supplies still in the corner of the wheelhouse and it jarred my memory. "Peter, how do you know Christmas Carol?"

"I wondered why you didn't ask before," he said, still concentrating on hooking up the alarm. "He lived in Kingston for a few months after he mustered out of the army, but he didn't exactly fit in here. He met your father, who told him about tramping around the Caribbean and next thing we knew he was aboard the *Estrela* with his one suitcase and off to god knows where with Jebediah, eventually ending up on Cayman Brac. Brac's gain, Kingston's loss."

"So you know him well?"

"Well enough to know he can be a royal pain in the ass when he sets his mind to it. He hounded the establishment in the Caymans and even the Governor-General here in Jamaica relentlessly after your father's murder, completely dissatisfied with their failure to find the perpetrators. Only the threat of revoking his license silenced him, and even that only after it appeared continuing investigations might smear your father's reputation. He's a tenacious little son of a bitch; I'll say that for him. And loyal to a fault."

"Do you know anything about an endowment to Faith Hospital Bones administers?" I asked, feeling Felix' eyes on me.

"Yes, although few people do. Your father made another little known endowment as well. It funds two full scholarships a year for underprivileged children from the Caymans or Jamaica to attend the University of the West Indies and study Caribbean issues. Bones is the one-man selection committee for the Caymans and he comes here twice a year to meet with his Jamaican counterpart. We always get together for a drink – or two." He turned to me and smiled.

"That's it, boys. Everything is hooked up and working as intended," he concluded, putting the last of his tools away. "I suppose you'll be on your way now?"

"Tomorrow, Peter. We're heading home," I answered, "but we may swing around the east end of the island and back along the north shore just so that I can say I've circumnavigated Jamaica."

"Remember what I said, Dexter. I don't want to catch you two up to no good."

I let that comment go and we headed back to the harbor. As we tied up and Peter disembarked, he turned to me once more.

"I'll be the only patrol out tomorrow night, Dexter, and I regret that since I've decided to concentrate on the southwest coast I'll not come across you. Do I have your word that whatever it is you're up to tomorrow night won't fit up a nostril?"

I looked at him squarely, stuck out my hand and he took it. "You have my word, Peter. And thanks – for everything." I watched him walk down the wharf and climb into his car.

Later that night, a boy on a bicycle delivered a pizza to the *Estrela*. Felix spoke to him and after he insisted it was no mistake he gave him ten dollars and he peddled off. Scrawled in pencil under the lid of the pizza box were the words 'Juan Gomez, San Vicente.' I had my Colombian connection.

X

We made the deposit the next day and the transfer from Felix' cousin was accomplished without incident at 4:00 a.m. We headed immediately for Brac and Felix stowed the shipment in the hidden compartment in the port tank while I manned the wheel. I stood alone in the wheelhouse of the *Estrela* and contemplated the good my father had accomplished, and how many people he'd touched. The more I thought about it, the angrier I became at the way he'd died.

Hurricane Danielle swirled harmlessly on the far eastern edge of the Atlantic while closer to home, a more dangerous storm raged inside me. It was a storm that would swirl through the Caribbean and descend on Niccolo Cardeli.

13 Cayman Brac: The Secret

We made Brac late the next evening. Bones was there on the porch, waiting for us.

Peter Jones' talk had me less nervous about Doc's ghostly ability to materialize from nowhere at my cottage whenever we arrived back at Brac, but no less curious about how he fit into all of this. Something was still not kosher.

"You're just in time to join me for a drink," he announced, tossing the ice from the one – or ones – he'd consumed prior to our arrival and refilling his glass. He wasn't smiling. I wasn't, either.

"I need some answers, Carol," I said, using the name that he probably didn't suspect I knew. It didn't throw him in the least.

"Good. Then we've got something to trade," he shot back, "because I need some, too."

I passed on the drink, and started right in. "How did you know we were going to Jamaica?"

"The charts were in plain sight on the desk in the library, you ass," he fired back. "Now, my turn. What were you doing there?"

I was instantly deflated and on the defense. His answer as to how he knew we were headed to Jamaica was so obvious I now doubted my ability to carry off what I'd set out to do. And now I was trapped into dragging Bones into the quagmire. I looked at him sheepishly.

He softened a little, but not much. "Look, I know you're in the middle of a hell of a mess and I've done my best to try to help you. I stood by your father through thick and thin and although that hasn't impressed you so far – maybe because you don't believe me – I'm going to give you something entrusted to me by Jebediah." He spun on his heel, grabbed the bottle of rum and led us into the library.

A canvas sack lay in the middle of the chart table. It was old and dirty, and tied closed with a piece of rope. The thought crossed my mind that it might hold a particularly precious bottle of vintage rum, but I wasn't certain Bones would have shared that with us.

"Once I show you what's in this sack, I want some answers," he said, squinting through the tiny glasses that had somehow been bent since his last visit and now sat crooked on his round, pudgy face.

An uneasy feeling spread through me. Over a number of weeks I had come to understand that this man, despite his appearance, was no buffoon. And despite his alcohol intake I had never seen him in any condition that even approximated impairment.

"I want to know who killed Jebediah, who beat you and what you intend to do about it. I know it's the same person or persons. Only an idiot would presume otherwise."

I looked at Felix. He shrugged his shoulders nervously.

"It's dangerous, Bones. I'd prefer not to involve anyone else."

"And that's why you did whatever you did to your Uncle Patricio and that lovely girl Catalina?" he demanded.

That caught me by surprise. "I know you've met Patricio, but how do you know Catalina?"

Bones looked at me. "This is a small island, Dexter. I met her at the Inn the first time they came here and again the second time she was here, before she moved her things down to your cottage. She reminded me of your mother. You might not be aware of the likeness, but it's amazing. Here – look at this," he said, removing a picture from his shirt pocket and flipping it across to me. I caught it in midair, and stared at him before slowly turning it over and looking at it.

It was uncanny, and it tore at me. This was the only the second picture of my mother I'd ever seen, and she would have been about the same age as Catalina when it was taken. They could have been sisters.

"There is a popular theory that men are attracted to women who remind them of their mothers, particularly if they had a close and loving relationship. Ditto for daughters and their choice of husbands. Rather unusual however for someone who couldn't have known their mother. You can keep that picture, by the way."

He stared at me and then made a decision. "I'm going to take it from your silence you've agreed to my terms." He picked up the sack, and went on. "Jebediah gave me this to hold for you. He said it was your legacy, and I wasn't to look inside it even though he said it wouldn't mean anything to anyone but you or possibly Felix. I have never opened it," he said, taking a drink. "Jebediah also told me I wasn't to give it to you unless I felt you had earned it, but I'll be damned if I know what he meant by that." Bones tossed the bag across the table to me and I caught it in one hand. "There, it's yours. Let's see what's in it."

I looked at Felix and hesitated before untying the rope that held the bag closed. The rope was rotten and fell apart, and the contents spilled out onto the table. I stared at what appeared to be another piece of canvas with a rope through a series of loops and picked it up, puzzled. There was a sheath with a knife in it attached to the rope, and as I spread out the material I realized it was an old pair of canvas work pants that had been cut off roughly above the knees, and that the pockets had been sewed shut by hand with twine. I held them up for Felix and Bones to see, and then it hit me. I looked more closely then my legs gave out and I sagged into a chair.

Felix and Bones looked at me like I'd gone crazy, and I actually felt the blood draining from my face as I withdrew the knife from its sheath and carefully sliced open the twine that sealed the pockets. I stood again and upended the pants over the table. Gold coins – old gold coins – spilled out and rolled everywhere. There were about twenty and Bones and Felix picked them up.

"They're old Spanish coins, Dex," Bones said, "and although there are lot of them, I don't understand all the secrecy. And what's with the pants and knife?"

I turned to Felix. "Don't you remember these pants?" I asked him.

Recognition finally flooded his face, and he grew excited. "I sure do, Dex!" he exclaimed. We stared at each other wide-eyed and looked again at the coins.

"They're all from 1715 or prior," Bones said, his eyes narrowing. "They must be from the 1715 Spanish plate fleet that sank in the hurricane off the east coast of Florida. But that's already been discovered, claimed and pretty well worked over. Jebediah had a fixation with that fleet, and he and I did a lot of reading about it."

I looked at Felix again. "Tell him Felix."

"The coins aren't from the wrecks off Florida," he said.

"How the hell do you know that, and where do you think they came from?" he asked, thoroughly exasperated.

I held the pants up again. "Father put these on, cut off the legs and fastened the sheath to this rope and through these belt loops just before he made his second dive over the side of the *Estrela* in 1984. The try net was caught on something underwater, and we were in a squall. Felix and I were both with him, and he made us memorize the exact location." Bones' eyes were now almost bigger than the lenses of his glasses. "Father is telling us where the rest of these are."

"It's the *Griffon*," Bones whispered reverently.

"The *Griffon*?" Felix asked.

"Yes, the *Griffon*," he repeated

II

Bones started to pull books from the shelves and Felix and I located the appropriate charts from the drawers.

"It's the *Griffon*, sure as hell," hollered Bones, letting out a whoop as he held up a mildewed book. "Old Jebediah knew it all along, and he roped me into studying up on it just for this very moment," he beamed. "He knew this would happen some day; that we'd all be here looking at his pants and gold coins, and he set the whole thing up. I thought we were just studying history all those nights, while he was secretly making sure I would be able to tell you about the *Griffon*!"

"Well are you planning to tell us or just whoop and holler?" Felix asked, grinning.

Bones started in as he poured himself another drink. "The Spanish dispatched ships every year to the New World – the Spanish Main – to gather the riches plundered from south and central America. They went to Cartagena Colombia, Veracruz Mexico and Portabello Panama, offloaded supplies for their colonies and took on the gold and silver they'd looted the previous year. The ships would then rendezvous in Havana so they could sail back together as a 'plate fleet.' It was the idea of safety in numbers; protection from their enemies – the Brits and the Dutch at that time - plus privateers who followed in the earlier footsteps of Sir Henry Morgan and common pirates like Blackbeard. The biggest threat though was the weather."

He was pacing now, back and forth in front of the stone fireplace and taking frequent slurps from the glass he held in his stubby fingers.

"The Spanish king needed the gold and silver to fund his wars against the English, and he was on the verge of bankruptcy because there had been no shipments in 1713 and 1714. The fleet of 1715 was therefore particularly rich in cargo, carrying everything that had piled up for those years." Bones stopped and looked at us, beaming again. "I can't believe Jebediah got me to learn all this, and that the books are still here," he said, pointing to one book in particular.

"Cut the crap, Bones, what happened with the fleet?" Felix pushed him again.

"The fleet met in Havana and left on July 24. The route was straightforward: up the Florida coast on the Gulf Stream and then out into the Atlantic for the voyage to Spain. The hurricane caught them off Florida and drove eleven of the twelve ships onto the shoals at Cape Canaveral, wrecking them between what is now Sebastian Inlet and Stuart. The only ship to escape was the *Griffon*, a French ship that was under lease. Your father speculated that it would have been of slightly different design than the Spanish ships and that it was able to sail a few points closer to the wind and escape the shoals. In any case, for centuries it was believed that either the *Griffon* went down unnoticed or it was unremarkable because it wasn't actually carrying treasure."

"Nobody looked for it?" Felix asked.

Bones shook his head while he swallowed. "Not even all of the wrecks that have been found there have been positively and specifically identified. So your father questioned how anyone could know the *Griffon* did or didn't sank off the shores of Florida, or whether or not it was carrying treasure. There were careful records kept of what was aboard each ship to prevent pilferage, but who would be foolish enough to believe that somebody didn't find a way to dip into the royal treasury?"

Bones tilted his head back and laughed long and hard. "Dexter, your cagey old man kept me looking through and reading everything I could find on the *Griffon*, knowing full well where it was all along. He made me into an expert on a ship that only he knew for a fact escaped with a load of treasure." Bones smiled as if he was now in on a joke that had been had at his expense.

"Where is it?" he asked, then not allowing us the time to answer. "It can't be Havana – even Jebediah wouldn't have taken the *Estrela* there. No, and it can't be Jamaica. The Brits controlled it in 1715. That leaves Panama or Mexico, and I'm not sure that makes sense, either. The *Griffon* would have had to sail right back past the site of the wrecks and would certainly have put ashore looking for survivors," he ruminated, pouring himself another rum. "No, that's not it. There's only one answer," he said, turning and raising his glass, "the *Griffon* rode out the hurricane by heading northeast, away from the coast, then swung back in an arc to Cartagena!"

I was impressed by Bones' thought process and told him so.

While Felix and Bones were congratulating each other and slopping back rum, my mind was working overtime. I now had the last piece of the puzzle I theoretically needed to ensure the safety of Catalina and Patricio, but the treasure had to be recovered and I had to set up the cocaine buy as well. If anything, the complexities served to clear my mind. Father had laid out the path.

The only permanent and certain solution was to eliminate Cardeli. The cocaine and the treasure simply provided the opportunity to do that. Just as I had resolved I would never actually land cocaine in the US, I felt a new determination to ensure father's treasure never fell into Cardeli's hands. I pictured father's death, tortured and staked to the beach here on Brac with this secret locked inside and I knew I could not betray him.

I spread the charts out on the table and quickly found the exact one I needed. The location father had burned into my mind twenty years ago, almost to the day I realized with a start, was still fresh. I not only remembered the coordinates but could also recall exactly which landmarks should be visible on the coast and where the reefs lie in relation to the wreck.

"Congratulations, Bones. You figured it out, but with all due respect that's the easy part," I said, drawing an immediate end to their celebration. I felt the calmness spread through me, along with cold determination. I looked Bones squarely in the face. "Are you sure you want to know the rest? There's a chance you could end up dead with Felix and me."

He straightened his glasses, considered what I'd said carefully and then spoke. "Dex, there's something you don't understand about Jebediah. He not only had a passion for the Caribbean, but he had a passion for life and people in general. If he believed in something, or in a person, nothing got in his way. I felt it, in fact still feel it to this day, and I know there are others."

I thought about Peter Jones. And Uncle Patricio's stories of how, despite the contrived differences between he and father at the end, he could still tell the stories of how father had applied relentless energy to any task that demanded it. He told those stories with passion and a sparkle in his eye.

"You can't keep me from this," Bones continued, "no matter how hard you try."

I spun the chart around so it was facing Felix and Bones and stabbed my finger at a point between Santa Marta, Colombia and Barranquilla, less than a hundred miles northeast of Cartagena. "This is where your *Griffon* went down," I said. "And if you're in, Bones, you'll do as I say. This is too dangerous for everyone to be running off half-cocked."

I watched Bones nod his head in agreement and then gathered up the coins, put them back in the pockets of the canvas pants and rolled them up. "Go check the lobster traps, Felix, and while you're doing it weight these down with a rock and sink them. Assume you're being watched, so be careful."

Felix left and Bones and I put the books and charts away. Then I told Bones to sit down. "Here's what I know."

I told him about Niccolo Cardeli and Mirtha, and about how father had scarred Cardeli so many years ago in Key West. I told him how Cardeli had sworn to never set foot in Key West again until he was satisfied his vendetta was complete, and how he had made a fortune trafficking in narcotics until he double-crossed somebody in Colombia and father had somehow destroyed his network. And then I told him about the beating, filling in the details about Cardeli's demands on me backed by the threats against Catalina and Patricio, and how he lived in Miami behind a phalanx of bodyguards.

"So where do you go from here?" Bones asked, visibly shaken. "I understand now why you didn't want the police involved."

"The police can't ensure Catalina and Patricio's safety, Bones. You know that as well as I do. The only way to neutralize Cardeli is to kill him."

"How?" he asked.

I looked at him and then reached behind my back and pulled out the small, flat black pistol tucked into my waistband and slapped it on the table. "I'll do as he wishes until I can get close enough to kill him."

Bones whistled, reached across the table and picked it up. He expertly tipped up the barrel to check for a round in the chamber and then ejected the magazine. "Beretta .32 caliber Tomcat, the rust-proof titanium model, 7-shot magazine loaded with hollow points," he said. "This packs a wallop for its size." He saw the surprise on my face. "I'm a weapons nut – have been since 'Nam. I know it may not be consistent with being a doctor, but I subscribe to a half-dozen or so gun magazines and am fairly up on what's out there. This must have cost a fortune – did you get it in Jamaica?"

"Yes, I did. Along with three larger pistols, shotguns rifles and plastic explosives – Semtex. Do you know anything about explosives?"

He nodded. "As a matter of fact, I do. Plastics were a big deal in Vietnam. What do you plan to do with that?"

"I'm not sure yet, let me think about it."

Felix came back with three lobsters, telling us it would cover his trip to the traps for anyone who might be watching. He left to get the fire started and fetch the water, and I continued filling Bones in.

"We got the name of a Colombian contact while we were in Jamaica and refitted the electronics on the *Estrela*. And in the middle of all that, plus buying the guns, figuring out how to smuggle them aboard and dealing with a curious Jamaican coast guard commander Cardeli's people abducted me again. It wasn't as bad this time - no beating - they wanted to make arrangements for the cash I'll need to do the cocaine deal."

Bones looked sheepish, and I knew why. "You put Peter Jones onto us, didn't you?"

"Yes, I admit I did. I told him you were up to something and asked him to try to prevent you from doing anything stupid," he said, only half apologetically.

"It turned out fine, Bones. But no more freelancing, right?"

"Agreed."

I sat back in the chair and thought about the changed circumstances. "We'll need to do some homework, and do it quickly. Maybe you can help."

Felix came back in and sat down, waiting for the water to boil. I began to sketch out what I thought we had to do.

"Cardeli is scheduled to make contact with me again here tomorrow or the next day. Felix, I want you to get the diving gear ready. Have it inspected and get the tanks filled. Load them aboard the *Estrela*, and if anybody asks just say we're planning a diving trip and maybe even thinking about starting a charter service. Can you do that?"

"Yes. I have another cousin who runs a dive shop here. He'll do it for me."

"If you have to, buy replacements for anything that's worn out. Do you know how to run the compressor on the *Estrela* to refill the tanks?"

He assured me he did, and I asked him to remove the main nets from the *Estrela* but to make sure we had enough smaller nets, slings and tackle to be able to rig the winch for heavy lifting.

"Bones, can you find out what the situation is along the coasts of Venezuela and Colombia?"

"I think so, what do you want to know specifically?"

"Status of marine patrols, interdiction efforts, anything you can find out. May as well include Trinidad in that, too. Any chance of doing it without alerting our friend in the Jamaican Coast Guard?"

Bones held up his hands. "You made your point, Dex. I won't do that again. Leave it with me. I'll figure it out."

That was all I could think of at the time, and twenty minutes later we were eating Felix' lobsters. I sent them off just after two in the morning, Bones carrying the old sack away with a half bottle of rum and some dirty laundry in it just in case someone had seen him arrive and wondered what was in the bag. I told him to leave it on the front porch of his house in plain sight just to make it easier for them.

After blowing out the lanterns I went to bed and got the best night's sleep I'd had in months.

III

Cardeli did not show up the next day or the day after, and there was no message from him. I didn't actually expect him in person, but was prepared nevertheless. The Beretta was becoming a natural part of my attire, and I was getting antsy and tired of waiting.

On the third day Bones sent a boy to ask me to come to his place at eight that night. I gave the boy a dollar and sent him back to tell Bones

I'd be there, and set off to find Felix. I arrived just in time to catch him climbing into his old truck to go and check on the diving gear and decided to go with him.

His cousin's dive shop was down by the wharf. It was cluttered with equipment and I wondered how he kept the used stuff he had for sale separate from the gear that belonged to his customers. Like most activities in the islands, precision and timeliness were not high on the list of priorities and my anxiousness only made it worse.

Felix found our equipment lying untouched in the corner and I exploded in frustration, stomped down the wharf and stood staring out at the sea. The days of inactivity were taking their toll on me, and Felix wisely left me alone while he remonstrated with his cousin. He came down to collect me forty-five minutes later with the news his cousin had traded him fully reconditioned equipment, piece for piece. I felt badly about my outburst and went back and paid him more than I should have, and helped Felix load the truck.

It was still early afternoon, so we took everything out to the *Estrela* and arranged it properly in the forward equipment locker before heading out to do an hour or so of test diving. It didn't take me long to remember how to assemble the apparatus, scuba diving being one of the more interesting things I'd learned at the military academy, and we were soon diving in forty feet of perfectly clear water. I watched Felix closely and was pleased to see he was a natural diver, comfortable in the water and breathing in a normal, controlled rhythm.

We put in a little less than an hour and surfaced to wash the equipment with fresh water and stow it. Felix showed me how the compressor worked and then we made for the anchorage and I headed over to Bones' house.

Bones lived in another old cottage, closer to the hospital. It wasn't as old as mine but was comfortably appointed if cluttered.

"Any contact with our friend?" he asked as I came in through the front door.

"Nothing yet, and I'm getting edgy. I need to be doing something."

Bones waived me over to a chair piled high with books and old magazines, and I moved them onto the floor. He was sitting at his desk, at least I assumed it was a desk, so covered in papers and assorted junk to make it invisible. Amid the confusion sat his computer and he waved an arm at it and explained how he kept in touch with the world through an internet satellite hookup on his roof.

"Keeps me sane," he said, "I can keep up with world events and any interesting medical advances with this. And it's a perfect cure for my insomnia."

"You have something for me?"

"Yep. Found some interesting things. First, the good news. Those coins aren't really coins. They're called cobs. The ones recovered from the wrecks along the coast of Florida have a market value right now of about three thousand dollars each, so the cobs lying down by the lobster traps are worth sixty thousand dollars.

I whistled long and low. "I wonder how many were aboard the *Griffon*?"

"According to old Spanish records, there weren't supposed to be any. But that's beside the point. We know differently.

"The rest of what I learned isn't exactly good news. First, as to Colombia there is a 'no travel' advisory in effect from the State Department for U.S. citizens. Second, the situation there is a little more complicated than your friend in Jamaica described it. It's not just the FARC rebels, but there's also another group called ELN. And then there's the AUC plus the drug lords. They're all fighting over the same patches of ground. Nice people, and they hate Americans. Throw the police and the Colombian government troops in, too. You could run afoul of any or all of them."

I'd really thought I was almost home free. "I'm counting on the contact name to help me work through all this, Bones. It's lucky I got that in Jamaica."

Bones tilted his head and looked at me over the rim of his glasses. "I'm not through yet. There are the U.S. government people who work with the Colombian military, and if the Colombian armed forces choose to look the other way, the U.S. guys sure as hell won't. America has dropped about six billion dollars into that country since 1999 and every dead Marxist or kilo of seized cocaine counts on the score sheet of the U.S. bureaucrats who make their living messing around in foreign countries. Kidnapping, extortion and drug dealing, and it isn't like a basketball game where you can tell the players by the color of their jerseys."

It was overwhelming, and the more I thought about it the more I realized I just had to get going. Sitting and over-thinking this wasn't getting me anywhere. "So I just have to watch out for the police, the military, FARC, ELN, AUC, the drug lords and U.S. government interests. Sounds easy," I said sarcastically.

"Now for the extra complications," he smiled sadly.

"Extra complications?" I stood up and began to pace back and forth. "What are those?"

"Piracy. The Venezuelan and Colombian coastlines have terrible records for attacks on private vessels. These aren't all drug related, either. A lot of them are attributed to poor fishermen who see the chance to rob and loot lone vessels. Yachtsmen are warned to travel in groups and to not anchor at night. Cartagena itself is considered safe, but attacks have been reported within fifty miles of that harbor. And you can't just waltz into Colombian waters and recover a treasure. The government will tie it up for years and the chances are good you'll never get to keep a single cob after you to go to the risk and expense of recovering it. All things considered, Dex, I don't like your chances," he concluded, leaning back in his chair and crossing his arms.

I stopped pacing and snapped at him. "Worrying about it doesn't improve the damned chances, and neither does sitting around here. The contact I have in Colombia is in San Vicente – where in hell is that?"

Bones looked at me for quite a while before answering. "I realize it's frustrating, but you aren't any better off heading in there unprepared." He pulled out a map of Colombia and looked at it for a few minutes before spreading it out on top of the mess on his desk. "It's right here," he pointed and I saw it was in an area named Caqueta, in the south of Colombia and just east of the Andes.

"Does that location tell you anything?" I asked.

"Yes, it does," he answered, pushing his glasses up onto his forehead and rubbing his eyes. "It says 'FARC' to me. A big chunk of the Andes and virtually all of the area east of the Andes is controlled by FARC. This area through here," he said, sweeping his finger in a northeasterly direction from the border of Peru up toward Venezuela along the east side of the Andes range, "is the Llanos frontier – one of the principal coca growing regions and almost certainly under the control and protection of FARC. The towns might be held by the military or possibly by the AUC, but I'll bet the countryside belongs to FARC."

"Okay, Bones. How did you gather all of this information?" I asked.

"Internet, mostly. The US State Department has a great site; so does the United Nations, and it's not hard to find more. I just did searches on FARC, Colombia, USDEA and a few other links and it's all there. Simply a matter of sifting through it and deciding what makes sense," he said, obviously pleased with himself. He should have been, too. I wouldn't have known where to start.

I looked at his computer with a little more respect. "Can you get that thing to tell me the quickest and best way to get to San Vicente?" I asked.

Bones grinned and started typing on the keyboard. "I'm not just another pretty face, you know."

It wasn't long before he had the answer, and it wasn't good either. The choices were limited. The closest major city was Florencia, the capital of Caqueta, about a four-hour drive. And once again Bones had bad news.

"Colombian presidential candidate Ingrid Betancourt was kidnapped in 2002 while driving from Florencia to San Vicente," he said. "She's still being held by FARC. It's been two years – time means nothing to these people"

This latest news had no further impact on me. I was deadened to anything short of doing something, anything.

"Bones, I can't sit around any longer. I'm going crazy here."

He looked at me for a bit, and then changed the subject again. "I don't understand why they want to meet you here on Brac. Jamaica makes far more sense, particularly from the money end. The Jamaican banking system still has massive loopholes in it that makes it easy to launder cash, and the drug people know it and use it. It would be a lot easier to make your connection in Colombia and then arrange payment in Jamaica."

That's all I needed to hear. I headed for Felix' house to make use of the phone.

Shando answered on the first ring, and didn't put me off this time.

"I need to know how to get hold of that package I left with you," I said impatiently.

"You can reach her at your old house. The number was never changed," he said. "She just got back from Jamaica, and he was havin' fits. Couldn't reach her, or she wasn't returnin' his calls. You didn't have anythin' to do with that, did you?"

I avoided answering directly. "I've been back here for four days. And I'm leaving again tomorrow. The contact came through, thank you, and I'm heading a little further south this time."

"I hope you know what you're doin'," he said. "These people are dangerous."

"I know. And they seem to know every step I'm taking," I said curtly. I could hear him saying something else as I cut the connection.

I dialed the house immediately and asked for Mirtha. The woman who answered asked who was calling.

"Just tell her to come to the damned phone. Tell her it's someone who knows she doesn't bruise easily." I was put on hold, and waited for almost three minutes before she picked up.

"Hello, Dex. Where are you?"

"I'm where I was supposed to be three days ago, and I'm not waiting here any longer."

"That's not for you to decide. I suggest you sit there like a good little boy until you're told otherwise," she said, anger creeping into her voice.

I took a deep breath. "You can fuck off. This isn't Shando you're trying to push around. In case you've forgotten, I've got a timetable that was given to me by your husband. I need to know he can handle everything at his end." I closed my eyes and prayed I wasn't making a big mistake, but I didn't think I was. It was make it or break it time.

"Are you suggesting he owes you some kind of a deal?" She sounded incredulous.

"That's exactly what I'm saying. This is business, Mirtha, and if he wants more then he better be ready. He can threaten all he wants to, but he's missing the biggest motivator he's got – greed. Mine and his. But quite frankly, mine is enough by itself because I don't give a shit about the rest of his threats. And if he doesn't want to cut a deal for future deliveries, then I'll find somebody who does. We both know what I'm doing is valuable, so it won't be difficult. He's not the only tough guy around, and maybe he's not even the toughest." I let that sink in. "And don't forget that if I go somewhere else then you lose your little fringe benefit, too. Have you told him how you beg for it, Mirtha? How long did it take you before you could sit down again?" I asked mockingly.

She was silent for a long time. Long enough that I began to worry I'd overplayed my hand. Then she spoke up, more quietly this time, almost apologetic. "Come on, Dex, you know you don't need to go anywhere else. Niccolo just had to get this thing out of his system; it's been consuming him for years. I know I can get him to listen to reason, particularly when it's business. And there's no need for difficulties between you two to come between us, is there?" she asked, almost sweetly.

I breathed a sigh of relief. If she had any influence at all with him, I knew she'd use it. I decided to press further. "Just tell him I'm on my way south, and I intend to set this up right. The minimum transaction I'll consider is a million, and it's got to be ready for deposit when and where I say. It's a little over a week to the first of September. I suggest he have the money available in three weeks, where you and I met last week. The deal can be done by bank transfer. He'll know how to do it, or can find out how. I suggest you plant your ass at that same hotel and wait until you hear from me. And don't get smart about it. It might take another three weeks after that – around the sixth of October - and you'd better be there for the duration. And when I'm ready to make the final delivery I want him there." I hung up before I had to go any further. I was wrung out and beginning to sweat. As I put the receiver down, I realized my hands were shaking.

14 Colombia: 2004 September

Due to the US State Department warnings about American citizens traveling to Colombia, I decided use my Caymanian papers. I'd carelessly allowed those to lapse and it took a week and a half to renew them, so despite my anxiety to get started it was the first of September when I flew into Mexico City to connect with the Avianca flight to Bogota. At least I wouldn't be on Brac to receive the next picture of Catalina or Patricio with '5 – 3' scrawled across it.

I had to collect my single valise from the Aero Mexico carousel and then recheck it with Avianca after their own security went through the contents again, far more thoroughly than it had been inspected previously.

The departure lounge was crowded and I looked around trying to guess why different people were traveling to Bogota. Some reasons were obvious; families traveling together, probably returning home, and some were young enough to be students. Three men in what appeared to be Colombian military uniforms could have been meeting with their brethren in the Mexican armed forces. The rest were less easy to categorize.

Lost in thoughts about what a narcotics smuggler or terrorist would look like I realized someone was speaking right next to me.

"Are you looking for somebody?" she asked again.

"Sorry, are you speaking to me?" I asked, turning to the woman standing to my left. I hadn't noticed her in the crowded lounge and was now aware I'd been staring at people.

"Your first visit to Colombia?"

She was petite, about five foot five, and her chestnut colored hair just touched the top of her shoulders. Sparkling dark brown eyes – almost black – complemented full, sensual lips parted in an engaging smile that showcased her gleaming white teeth. It was a smile that would fit nicely in an orthodontist's advertisement. Her cinnamon-colored complexion was unencumbered by makeup and I guessed her to be in her mid twenties.

"Yes, this is my first visit," I answered, "and no, I'm not looking for anyone. I was just wondering why different people travel to Colombia."

"Is there something wrong with traveling to Colombia?" she asked, traces of a smile playing at the corners of her mouth. "Some of us are just going home for a visit. That's a good enough reason, isn't it?"

I wasn't sure what to say, and she knew it. She laughed at my discomfort and her smile widened even further as she watched me.

"I'm sorry," she said. "I can guess what you were thinking, and I took advantage of you." She offered her hand. "I'm Nina."

"Dex," I replied, relieved to be off the hook. "So you're going home," I said, shaking her hand.

"Yes, I was born and raised in Colombia and my father is still there, but I live in Miami. Miami is the unofficial capital of Latin America, you know. I decided to stay there after I finished school, much to my father's distress."

Miami again. The mere mention of the city I'd once enjoyed so thoroughly now only served to remind me of Cardeli. Immediately but irrationally suspicious, I wondered why she was traveling to Bogota through Mexico City when there was a direct flight from Miami, and asked her.

"I've been visiting my brother. He's another family disappointment, a doctor who also decided he wanted to live outside Colombia. It's not easy to move back once you've gone to school somewhere else." She had an engaging and open way about her, and I chided myself for looking for hidden motives.

"And you? Where are you from, and what takes you to Bogota?"

"I live in the Cayman Islands, and I'm interested in Caribbean history," I improvised slightly. "I visited Cartagena in 1984 with my father and I'd like to see it again, along with a little more of the country."

"You know it's dangerous, don't you?" she asked.

I acknowledged I did, and that I knew a little about the current situation from reports a concerned friend – also a doctor like her brother – provided me from the internet.

"And didn't those reports suggest you should perhaps be traveling straight to Cartagena? And staying there?" she asked.

"I suppose that's what my friend was trying to get me to do. I'm just naturally curious, I guess."

"And naïve," she added. "What seat are you in?"

I took my boarding pass from my pocket and checked it. "16A."

"And you're not with anyone?" she asked again.

When I repeated I wasn't she laughed and snatched the boarding pass from my hand. She turned toward the Avianca customer desk, grinning at me over her shoulder.

"Well you are now."

I watched her shapely backside as she strolled over to the desk. It was round, not plump, and it certainly did something for her designer jeans. The high-heeled leather boots accentuating the sway of her hips didn't hurt either.

It took her a few minutes with the service representative before she came back with a new boarding pass.

"You're in 2A now, beside me. I hope you don't mind."

I pretended to consider whether I minded or not and she playfully swatted me on the arm. "You have no choice now anyway," she grinned, "you're stuck with me." That was one way to put it, but the envious glances of the other male passengers waiting to board the flight told me otherwise.

The flight left on time – a minor miracle according to Nina – and I was soon learning more about Colombia, and about her. She was a regular flyer on the Mexico – Bogota route and routinely returned on the direct flight to Miami.

Nina's smile and outgoing nature were infectious, so I shouldn't have been totally surprised to find the cabin crew knew her by name and she seemed to know them. I learned through her banter with the flight attendant that she always had the same seat on this flight – 2B – and more often than not, the seat beside her was kept open. It seems I wasn't the first person that she'd had switched to sit beside her, and she showed no sign of embarrassment at the fact.

"So you make a common practice of picking up interesting people in the departure lounge, do you?" I asked accusingly.

Her eyes went wide in mock alarm, and she answered with a straight face. "No, Dex, absolutely not," she protested, leaning closer to me as if to share a secret. "I never pick up *people*, just attractive single men!" she whispered, those dark eyes dancing in amusement. "Have I made a mistake in your case?" she asked, wide-eyed.

No I thought, I certainly hoped not.

And then the memory of Catalina intruded, and I instantly became more reserved. I thought about her being in Atlanta with someone new, and my demeanor soured. Nina felt it too, burying herself in the book that had been sitting in her lap unopened.

We landed in Bogota and as we taxied to the terminal, Nina turned to me and apologized.

"I'm sorry for joking about meeting people on the plane, Dex. Please believe me I said it in fun, and it has been a long time since I met someone as nice as you."

I smiled, sadly I suppose, and told her it was my fault; I was trying to get over someone.

"And does this trip to Colombia have something to do with that?" she asked.

"Yes, I suppose it does."

She smiled back at me. "Then Colombian hospitality demands I do what I can to make your stay here pleasant and your visit a success. No strings attached."

"No strings attached," I agreed, and told her the name of the hotel I had booked in Bogota.

We deplaned and made our way to immigration where there were separate lines for 'Visitantes' and 'Residentes'. She waved to me as she was expedited through her line and I had little time to wonder if I would ever see her again before I was sidetracked by the bureaucratic process of entering Colombia.

The process wasn't cumbersome, just time consuming and I felt intimidated by the foreign language, the preponderance of armed military personnel and the no-nonsense approach of the immigration officers. I surrendered my passport and the officer made quite a display of flipping through it and checking for entry stamps. There weren't any, since it was new, but then he began to flip through a huge computer printout checking for some type of record, I suppose. I had a fleeting fear he would find an entry made in error that would result in hours of interrogation in a locked room with people who spoke no English. Before my anxiety could overwhelm me he stamped my papers with a huge 'wham', passed them back to me and waved me through.

I claimed my valise, went through a green door that was for people with nothing to declare and followed the signs to the taxi exit.

Bogota is in the mountains. The elevation of 8,700 feet not only makes it cooler than you would expect so close to the equator but causes shortness of breath until you become acclimatized. I was immediately aware of both and stopped to fish a jacket out of my valise and catch my breath.

I spotted a man waving to me from beside a plain black, full-sized Ford and walked over. As I got close, Nina poked her head out of the back.

"Can I give you a ride to your hotel?"

"If it's not out of your way ..." I said, relieved I wouldn't have to use my broken Spanish to explain to a taxi driver where I wanted to go.

"Don't be silly. This car belongs to my father, and it's no trouble at all," she said, sliding over so that I could get in beside her as the driver put my valise in the trunk. I climbed in the back and the driver closed the door behind me. Because of the dark tint on the windows, I hadn't seen the other man sitting in the front passenger seat.

"He's a security man," Nina offered. "It's common here. In the U.S. you'd call him a body guard." Nina leaned forward and gave the driver the name of the hotel, and we were off.

"You didn't have to do this," I said, "but I really appreciate it. I've never been through immigration before where I couldn't speak the language, and I'm a little overwhelmed."

Nina smiled. "It's natural. The bureaucracy takes some getting used to, but the reality is they only intimidate people who don't know better. You need to be forceful with them. You'll learn."

Nina kept up her chatter until we arrived at a gate guarded by two uniformed, armed security men. I had to present my passport and a printed copy of my reservation so they could check it against a printout of reservations, and then they inspected the trunk before they opened the gate and let us in. At the main entrance a porter took my bag and headed into the lobby while I leaned back inside the open window of the car and thanked Nina again.

"You're welcome, Dexter Snell," she said and laughed at my surprise that she knew my last name. "Relax – I saw your name on the hotel reservation form. Mine is Garcia Lopez by the way, just so you know when I call you tomorrow."

And with that Nina Garcia Lopez smiled, rolled up the window and pulled away.

II

I had to complete a lengthy form at the check-in desk to which they stapled a photocopy of my passport and entry visa and it occurred to me that clandestine travel, at least for a foreigner, would not be easy in Colombia. A bellhop who spoke passable English took my valise and showed me to my room.

He told me registered hotel guests needed to have their identification with them at all times, particularly in order to pass the front gate security. Visitors to guests also needed identification and were not admitted to the grounds without first being cleared at the gate.

He suggested that if I wanted to visit a restaurant or other place after nightfall I check with the front desk and arrange a car through them. The hotel had a list of restaurants and clubs considered safe, and for a fee the car could wait or return at a prearranged time to pick me up.

Under no circumstances, he warned, should I consider making my own arrangements or wander the streets after dark. He pointed out the safest alternative was to avail myself of the excellent bars and restaurants in the hotel compound. I tipped him, thanked him for his advice and locked the door behind him.

I flipped on the TV – the first TV I'd watched in months – and found CNN. Pouring a scotch over ice, I went out on the balcony to take a look at the city.

Bogota is a modern capital, particularly as I viewed it at night. High rises separated by smaller buildings marked the downtown area, surrounded by a mixture of residential and commercial zones. The downtown streets were busy – at least judging by the headlights of the traffic – while I noticed the streets around the hotel were much quieter, almost empty by comparison.

It seemed foggy, and although I learned later it was pervasive smog that clears only after a good rainfall I could make out two mountains rising to the east. I couldn't see the peaks but knew from Bones' research they rose another 2,000 feet above the city's already impressive altitude.

For a city of ten to twelve million people, depending on official or unofficial estimates, at night and from this location it seemed safe and friendly as opposed to the impression I got first from Nina and then the bellhop. The security at the hotel certainly suggested, at least for the Americans who frequented it, all might not be as tranquil as it appeared from my balcony.

I turned back into the room, took a quick shower and changed into fresh clothes before wandering down to the second floor lounge. It was large, and one wall was made up of sliding glass doors that led to a patio, presumably open during the day when it was warmer. I took a seat at the bar.

The bartender's nametag identified him as Luis, and once he realized I spoke no Spanish he immediately switched to English.

"Drink, señor?"

I ordered a Glenfiddich on ice and spread out a map of Columbia on the bar top.

"Iss familiar with Colombia, señor?"

I admitted I wasn't, and he proceeded to point out various places he thought would appeal to a 'turista.' They included the principal cities like Bogota, Cartagena, Barranquilla and Santa Marta, and he extolled the virtues of all of them. I led him on by asking polite questions, and when he finished describing the sanctuary of Monserrate atop one of the two mountain peaks I'd spotted to the east of Bogota I pointed to the Llamos frontier and asked about San Vicente.

"No, iss no place for turista," he said quickly and then started back again on all of the advantages of Bogota.

I listened politely for a while and then asked again about San Vicente, explaining I wanted to see 'the real Colombia.' His expression conveyed his concern as he made it clear it was dangerous in San Vicente. He put his hands on the bar, spread his fingers wide open and leaned forward, shrugging as he explained that it was too 'precarious.' I asked whether it was FARC or the AUC and he immediately turned away with anger in his eyes and went to work dusting the bottles displayed behind the bar, his back to me.

I looked at the map again, drained my scotch and decided to try a different tack tomorrow. I left twenty dollars on the bar, returned to my room and stood on the balcony for an hour or so nursing the same scotch, deep in thought. I went to bed exhausted, but tossed and turned thinking about Nina. My last thoughts, however – and dreams – were of Catalina.

III

Morning arrived with a light rain shower before the sun broke through and the skies cleared completely. I had coffee on the balcony before ordering a taxi to take me to a shopping district recommended by the concierge.

Bogota in daytime, in the right places, is a disarmingly friendly city. I wandered through the district for an hour until I found an interesting restaurant with an outdoor patio where I could watch the street. The waiter was particularly helpful, and offered numerous suggestions on native cuisine as well as places I should visit in Bogota. While I waited for my brunch to arrive I spread out the map of Colombia on the table. The waiter brought my meal and we then played out virtually the same scene I'd experienced the night before with the bartender at the hotel. As soon as I asked about San Vicente he explained the danger, and when I asked a second time he left me alone. This wasn't going to be easy.

I took the obligatory tour to Monserrate that under other circumstances would have been fascinating, and then returned to my hotel. I went through the security procedure at the gate and strolled into the lobby where the concierge promptly intercepted me.

"Señor Snell – if you please, sir – there is someone here to see you. Please follow me."

I did a poor job of hiding my surprise and followed the concierge around behind the front desk to a small office. He stepped aside and waived me through, then closed the door without following me.

Two men in uniforms sat at the desk and one of them pointed to an empty chair. They did not introduce themselves.

"Señor Snell?" the one I presumed to be in charge asked.

"Yes, I am. Who are you?"

"Policia, Señor Snell, and we have questions." He clearly indicated he was in charge, and had my registration documents on the desk in front of them. "You are turista, Señor Snell?"

"Yes."

"And what iss it you are doing here?"

"Visiting. As a tourist. I was in Cartagena twenty years ago and I want to go back there. And I'd like to see more of Colombia while I'm here. I was up to the monastery this morning."

"But you have also interest in the Llamos frontier and San Vicente? You have left those out, Señor," he said helpfully. The helpful bit didn't fool me.

"I was, until I talked to a few people. They convinced me there are far more interesting places in Colombia," I lied.

"Iss that so?"

"Yes, it also seems San Vicente is dangerous." I maintained what I hoped was an open face as the officers sat there smiling at me silently. I recognized it as the Patricio treatment and subdued the natural impulse to break the silence until I realized that was provocative in and of itself.

I reached into my jacket pocket and pulled out the map of Colombia, and unfolding it showed them that San Vicente was near the capital of the State of Caqueta, and that I was simply curious about smaller centers off the beaten path.

"Department, Señor Snell," said the junior officer.

"Pardon me?" I asked, not understanding his comment.

"Iss a Department in Colombia, not a state. Caqueta Department."

I thanked him for pointing that out and folded the map.

"You are from Caymans?" he asked, picking up another piece of paper and looking at it.

"Yes."

"But you are also Americano?" he asked. "How iss this?"

That question caught me totally by surprise and I'm sure it showed on my face. "I was born on Cayman Brac. My mother was Portuguese and my father American. It was suggested to me that I travel to Colombia using my Cayman papers."

"Because iss dangerous here for an Americano?" the senior officer asked, his eyebrows rising higher on his forehead.

"Yes, I suppose," I answered.

"Ah, Señor Snell – but then already you knew the Llanos and San Vicente can be extremely dangerous," he smiled, pleased that he had trapped me with this tacit admission. "Can you explain?"

"No, I can't, other than to say that I am known to be rather foolish as well as impetuous. And that the warnings from friends before I left combined with what I've been told here have since convinced me that those places are no longer of interest to me."

I sat back at that point and resolved to volunteer nothing more unless asked directly and specifically.

"So, Señor Snell, you would have us believe you have no interest here other than being safe turista?" he asked. I had the feeling there was more, but for the life of me couldn't imagine what it could be. He answered that for me with his next question. "You are not, what you say, an agitator for human rights?"

I felt a wave of relief wash over me. "No – absolutely not. Why would you think that?"

"Because no narco trafficker need to ask perfect strangers in Colombia how to get to San Vicente, so you are not one of those. That means you are either human rights agitator, a left-wing Marxist sympathizer or particularly stupid turista," he said. "Do you have preference how I describe you in my official report, Señor Snell?"

I smiled coolly. "You have trapped me into admitting my stupidity," I answered. "May I know your name? You have me at a disadvantage," I added.

He regarded me carefully. "But of course, Señor Snell. How rude of me. I am Capitán Luis Torrano, at your service." He made a point of neither standing nor offering his hand, merely bowing his head slightly as he said his name.

"Is there anything else, Capitán?" I asked, attempting to draw this to a close.

"Yes, Señor Snell, there iss," he said with a smirk. "I would like to say that any man who receives an invitation from Nina Garcia Lopez could not be a fool. Unless he refuses that invitation, of course."

With that, the Capitán rose to his feet and went to the door, followed closely by his subordinate. Just as it seemed he was leaving he turned back to me with one last remark.

"Please be careful while here, Señor Snell. We would not like anything to happen to our turistas Americanos."

It took me a minute to compose myself. How did they know so much so quickly? I left the office and headed to the elevators but the concierge intercepted me again, this time with a small envelop. I opened it on the way up to my room.

It was a message from Nina received shortly after I'd left the hotel that morning. She was picking me up at nine p.m. – in twenty-five minutes. That explained how the Capitán knew about her and an invitation, but it didn't explain how he knew her.

I hurried down the corridor to my room to shower and change and immediately discovered my personal belongings had been searched. The search was done in such an obvious way that it must have been the police. It was another warning, no less clear than the one I'd received in person.

I had brought little, and nothing of value other than cash and the identification documents both of which I carried with me so it took no time at all to determine nothing was missing. Forcing back the stress I was feeling from the interrogation and now this, I jumped in the shower and then threw on casual slacks, loafers and a polo shirt, all the time wondering why my life continued to be driven by events – and people – beyond my control.

IV

I was surprised to see Nina waiting for me in the lobby after the bellhop's admonitions about visitors, but relieved to see that she, too, was casually dressed. And once again her clothes looked better than they would otherwise simply because of the way she wore them.

"Hola," she called to me, "I wasn't sure you would get my message. I hope you didn't have other plans."

She tilted her cheek up for a kiss then took my hand and pulled me toward the door. "We must hurry. My father doesn't like to be kept waiting."

I stopped in my tracks. "Nina – you're taking me to meet your father?"

"But of course. He is the most important person in my life and he constantly worries that I am not married and perhaps seeing the wrong kind of man. He is extremely jealous, and even more protective," she said brightly, as if that would put me at ease.

"You don't even know me. We only met yesterday and I don't know anything about you. I'm not sure this is a good idea," I protested.

Nina pouted then tilted her head slightly and worked some kind of magic with those dark eyes. "But certainly you can tell everything about me by meeting my father. He says breeding counts in everything – not only horses – and he has a discerning eye when it comes to the men I bring to meet him," she said as if that made perfect sense and would instantly put me at ease. "So far, he has found the faults with every one of them and saved me from making a silly mistake."

In some obtuse way, the absolute lack of logic in what she said intrigued me. What the hell, I thought, I have nothing better to do. It certainly didn't cross my mind that the irrationality of my own decision to humor her was driven by that pout and those sparkling, almost-black eyes.

"Let's go," I said.

The pout vanished instantly and she pulled me again toward the exit while calling goodbye to the concierge, who was watching me enviously. There seemed to be extra doormen standing around too, and they were all transfixed on Nina as if she were some kind of celebrity. Her exotic beauty and self-confidence were consistent with that impression.

The drive to her father's house took about thirty minutes and she chatted nonstop while the driver and bodyguard pretended to hear nothing. We went down an avenue whose expansive width seemed to serve no purpose other than to display statues, and Nina explained that statues were common in every city in South America. She told me that was one of the few things she found lacking in Miami.

We turned off the avenue at a corner dominated by a large colonial mansion partially hidden behind a wall. To my surprise, we pulled up to an arch in that same wall along the side street and the two guards stationed there swung the gate open and let us pass after a quick glance inside the car.

The wall had hidden the classic splendor of the courtyard, and I was overwhelmed by the impulse to try to take everything in at once. A spectacular fountain dominated the front and center of the area with everything else laid out to draw focus to it. Hidden spotlights played on the jets of water, slowly changing colors and directions, making the fountain itself appear to be moving. The front of the mansion was also tastefully lit, accented is more accurate, in a way that did not detract from the fountain.

We pulled up to a portico where I could imagine horse-drawn carriages arriving over a century ago, and the driver and bodyguard opened our doors.

"Kind of fancy, isn't it," Nina commented as if noticing it for the first time. "Come inside." She took my hand again and led the way.

The foyer was no less impressive; a full two stories in height and lit by a huge chandelier. Oversized, colonial furniture was arranged in groupings on ancient carpets that ran up the center of the marble floor. Nina pulled me toward a massive set of ornate wooden doors and we entered what would best be described as a reception area. A fire roared in the fireplace and I followed her toward it. I didn't appreciate the size of the fireplace when we first entered because it was proportional to the room, but as we got closer I realized it was huge.

A servant appeared from nowhere with a tray holding three glasses, a bowl of ice and a decanter, all in crystal.

"I noticed you drank Scotch on the plane, Dex. I hope this is okay," she said. The servant deftly balanced the tray on one hand and with the other used silver tongs to add ice cubes to two of the glasses and then pour the scotch. I was impressed.

"Salud," she toasted, clinking her glass against mine. It was single malt and the smell and taste of the peat were in perfect balance.

"It's excellent," I complimented her. "Thank you."

"Hola, Nina and Nina's friend." I turned to see a man – presumably Nina's father – striding toward us from the other end of the room.

He was in his mid to late fifties and like me, casually dressed. He wore taupe corduroy slacks and an open-necked dress shirt with a sweater draped over his shoulders European-style. I saw with pleasure he was also wearing loafers. As he drew closer it became obvious where Nina got her eyes; they sparkled in his round, open and friendly face. His smile, too, was instantly recognizable as a family feature.

I guessed his height at five ten or so, and he carried a few extra pounds but was by no means overweight. He bent slightly and offered his cheek for Nina to kiss while quickly looking me up and down.

"Did you cheat, Nina? Tell me the truth now," he scolded.

"No, Papa, I didn't. He dressed this way on his own," she insisted in response to some secret game they played.

"Ah, then welcome to my home. Mi casa es su casa," he said, offering his hand. "Please call me Jorge." His grip was strong, and his hand warm.

"And please call me Dex. Mucho gusto," I answered, expending my entire Spanish vocabulary in one shot.

"You must excuse Nina and me for our little game. I alternate randomly between formal attire and casual when I meet her friends, and their reactions can be rather amusing depending on their expectations. And of course it is particularly cruel when the young man, knowing our family background, has set out to deliberately impress me for I can tell right away by his obvious discomfort. I know it's a naughty trick, but I warn you – I have more," he smiled.

"Thank you for the warning, Señor Garcia Lopez, but I had no idea when I dressed I would be meeting you and, no offense, your name means nothing to me anyway."

Nina and her father laughed, and once again I failed to understand what was so amusing.

"Dex," Nina explained, "My father's name is Jorge Garcia Ramirez, but you would normally call him Jorge Garcia. It is Spanish tradition to add the mother's maiden name to form a child's new surname. My paternal grandmother was a Ramirez, so father is Jorge Garcia Ramirez. My mother's maiden name is Lopez, making me Nina Garcia Lopez. I know it's confusing to a norteamericano."

Her father was now smiling indulgently as he continued to inspect me, taking his drink from the servant who then placed the tray on a sideboard and left.

"No offense taken, Dex," he said, sipping his scotch.

He may not have been offended, but I was. I didn't care for the undercurrent here, and it didn't at all fit with his open, friendly face. I remembered the contemptuous attitude Colonel Jamieson had exhibited toward my father so many years ago in the dean's office at my military school, and the pride I felt that day as father tolerated the insults only to a certain point.

Maybe it was the stress I had been subjected to earlier with the police interrogation, but I had little patience for more.

"My bloodline, Señor Garcia Ramirez, may not be apparent in my teeth like a horse," I said, "but I am the proud son of Jebediah Snell, a shrimp fisherman from the Florida Keys and Cayman Brac; a self-educated, self-made man who had the misfortune of leaving a sizable inheritance to his only child, who managed to squander it through profligate living. I am now primarily concerned with accepting the consequences of my actions without bringing further shame to my father's memory. And if that doesn't suit you, then fine."

I expected the outburst would conclude the evening and the shocked look on Nina's face certainly suggested it might. But her father's expression changed little, if only to soften somewhat as he took my now empty glass and refilled it from the decanter. He handed it to me and held up his own in toast.

"Well spoken, Mr. Snell. I'd like to hear more of your father Jebediah. Salud," he said. "Nina, please go and see to the setting of the table while I show our guest through the main floor of the house."

Nina's surprise mirrored mine but she hesitated only briefly before, without a word, leaving us. Jorge took my arm and led me on a tour.

It was soon obvious that showing me the mansion, although impressive to say the least, was secondary to Jorge's interest in my father. He said little about the house or its contents as we strolled through and instead exhibited genuine curiosity about shrimping and the early days of the Marques Snell company. He was an excellent listener, and whenever I ran out of words he would ask a question that set me off in a new direction.

I wasn't used to talking like this about my father and as his questions led me through the stories of the 1935 hurricane, the incident at military school and my recent discoveries of the scholarly and humanitarian sides of my father I found a new pride in his accomplishments. I have no idea how long we'd been walking and talking until a servant came and tactfully suggested that Nina was waiting for us. As Jorge led the way to the dining room it hit me just how big this house was, and the depth of the history represented by the paintings and other artifacts scattered through it.

The dining room, like the rest of the house, was massive. One end of a table that could easily accommodate thirty guests was set for three. The candles in two magnificent silver candelabra were ablaze. And so was Nina.

"I didn't bring Dex here for you to monopolize, father," she complained.

"No, you brought him here hoping I would tear him apart like the others, proving to you I'm jealous and that I love you," he said. "I like him."

Nina's eyes went wide in disbelief. "You like him?" she asked as if that was impossible.

"Yes, and I think you do, too," he answered indicating with a motion of his hand that we should be seated, "don't you?"

Nina reddened visibly as she sat in the chair her father held out for her.

Dinner was delicious, if somewhat elaborate. It rivaled anything I've had in fine restaurants and was complemented by a carefully chosen selection of Chilean wines. The company didn't hurt either, even though Nina was subdued throughout the meal. Her father told me a little about his family, a family whose roots could be traced back to the early Spanish times in Colombia, and how one of his ancestors had been a governor. The estate dated to the colonial period and at some point the family came into a large tract of land in Antioquia Department and began to breed horses.

"Do you know of Antioquia?" Jorge asked.

I admitted I didn't, and he paused. "Perhaps you have heard then of its administrative capital – Medellin."

"Of course I've heard of Medellin," I answered. "I can't imagine that there are many who have any interest at all in South America who haven't heard of the Medellin cartel and Pablo Escobar. I didn't realize it was a capital city."

"Yes. It is a sad commentary on Colombia that in the eyes of the world Medellin and Cali are the most recognizable places, and the production and export of cocaine is arguably our biggest industry."

Jorge returned briefly to the story of his family but with the mention of the drug cartels he lost his enthusiasm. He ended with a comment that the family had prospered with each succeeding generation until his, a point I took to heart.

"And now I sit in this house that has been in my family for many generations and lament the fact my daughter and son – the last to bear the Garcia name – are effectively exiles from the country of their birth."

"And your wife?" I ventured to ask.

"She found life here too difficult," he said, "and when I refused to leave she found happiness with an Occidental Petroleum executive. She now lives in Houston."

"She abandoned you, father," Nina said furiously. "I visit you regularly and so does my brother."

Jorge held up his hand, instantly silencing her. "Enough. Circumstances are circumstances and some are such that we cannot change them. In those cases we must do what we must do. I cannot leave Colombia, yet I will not begrudge those who find they can. Each person makes a decision, and I will no more sit in judgment of those who leave than I will accept their judgment of me for staying."

Jorge picked up a small silver bell from the table and rang it, and a servant appeared. He asked that coffee and brandy be readied in the library and apologizing, excused himself saying he would join us there in a few minutes.

Nina took me by the arm and led me to the library, her favorite room in the house. My entire cottage would fit inside it, and the collection of books was staggering. The shelves were in sections ranging up the walls to a height of about twelve feet, and the sections were separated by paintings of people I assumed to be Garcia ancestors. Nina guided me to one particular section.

"These books belonged to the Garcia who built the original portion of the house in 1720, shortly after the city became the capital of New

Grenada," she said with obvious pride. She continued to explain that in the early 1800's another Garcia, then allied to Simón Bolívar, helped liberate the city from the Spanish and it became the capital of the new country of Great Colombia that included Ecuador, Panama and Venezuela.

"New Grenada was dissolved in 1830 and Bogota became the capital of what is essentially Colombia as it exists today," she said, continuing the history lesson.

I learned how each successive Garcia, prominent in the politics of his time, added to the house; faithfully retaining its colonial style until it was 'completed' in about 1900. And each Garcia also expanded the library and added to the book collection.

The books were priceless, many hand bound in tooled leather. I couldn't help but imagine what my father would have felt not only seeing them, but knowing they were in the hands of the original family that collected them.

Nina picked up on my fascination with the contents of the room and walked me around it, using little bits and pieces of family history and personal anecdotes to bring the various pieces to life. We ended up in front of another massive fireplace where a fire blazed warmly. Over the fireplace hung a painting of a Spanish officer in ornate armor, mounted on a magnificent horse.

"He was the first Garcia to arrive in Colombia," she explained. "And that was one of the early Spanish horses that have since formed many bloodlines throughout the Americas. The Garcias have had a love affair with their horses for countless generations. The ranch in Antioquia Department is one of two near Medellin that are world famous for their Paso Fino horses." She looked at me as if that might mean something to me, and when it was obvious it didn't she went and poured coffee.

We sat in the oversized leather chairs in front of the fireplace and watched the flames silently for a while, each deep in thought. I was wondering about Jorge Garcia and the rather abrupt ending to his recounting of his family's story. I sensed undercurrents suggesting there was more, and I speculated what it might be.

"I apologize I had to leave you," Jorge said as he entered the library, closing the door behind him. "I had to make a call to the ranch. We are considering the purchase of some new breeding stock and I wanted to make sure the bloodlines are properly documented."

He poured himself a brandy and joining us in front of the fire picked up roughly from where he had left his story with the mention of Medellin and the cocaine cartels, before the exchange with Nina over her mother.

"Colombia has changed dramatically in the last forty years, and it is a regressive change," he began again.

"Colombia is at war with and within itself, and the vast majority of the casualties are civilians – at least 3,500 every year are killed. The armed factions portray most of these as enemy 'collaborators' and 'sympathizers', yet it is impossible to be neutral. One can display neither allegiance nor aversion toward whatever particular group that controls one's region at the moment. What makes it worse is that there are no fixed boundaries, no front lines or other demarcation of territory. The positions shift almost daily.

"Am I boring you Dexter?" he asked.

I assured him he wasn't, and he continued.

"There are four armed groups, and some of these have factions within themselves. First, there is the government represented by the police and the military." Jorge paused just long enough to sip his brandy. "Then there are the leftist guerillas, primarily FARC although there are others. In direct opposition to the leftists, and just as ruthless or perhaps more so, are the right-wing paramilitaries the largest of which is the AUC. The paramilitaries are sworn enemies of the leftists and are therefore loosely allied with the military and therefore the government but have an advantage over the army in that they are not subject to the scrutiny of international human rights activists. They are often accused of performing dirty work on behalf of the military. Finally, there are the drug lords who hold no political agenda or allegiance other than what is required to protect their businesses. Making it worse is the fact that the lines between all four armed groups is becoming increasingly blurred when it comes to profiting from narcotics in one way or another."

I had heard bits and pieces of this, from Tun in Jamaica and in Brac from Bones, but this was the first time I was hearing it from a Colombian.

I noticed Jorge's snifter was empty, so I took it from him and refilled it as he continued to speak.

"The guerrillas see any wealthy Colombian as fair game. Kidnapping funds a lot of their activities, along with the 'taxes' they collect by protecting the coca growers and processing labs in the areas they control. The army is incapable of covering all of Colombia, with the mountains and the part of the country to the east of the Andes being good examples. There are portions of Colombia that have never known a police or military presence until recently and even now, with the massive resources of the U.S. being thrown into the fray, they cannot exert effective influence over the entire country."

I handed the snifter to him and he took it without seeming to notice.

"This is where the paramilitaries enter the picture, fighting the leftists for control where the military cannot, or will not.

"It is at best a fluid situation, with positions shifting constantly. And when these shifts occur, civilians are invariably accused of abetting the previous occupying group. The accusation can spring from something as simple as a shopkeeper selling goods to the 'enemy' in the normal course of his business or a peasant having sold chickens or pigs to the wrong person. And the inverse is also true – refusal to sell to or trade with members of the group holding sway at the particular moment can also be considered as taking a partisan position. The consequences of such actions – or inactions – be they real or simply perceived, can be instant execution. There are no appeals."

Nina interrupted. "I'm not sure Dex wants to hear all of this."

"Yes, I do," I assured her. "It's all a part of the world Americans are insulated from, and I'm very interested."

Jorge looked at me. "You are sure? I have few visitors and I fear I am rather long-winded when I have the opportunity."

I told him once again I found it fascinating and specifically asked him to continue.

He nodded and then after a pause to gather his thoughts, spoke again. "In many cities and towns areas are contested neighborhood-by-neighborhood, or even block-by-block. That is the case in the working class neighborhoods of Medellin but is not unique.

"The economies of smaller towns are tied to the rural areas around them, and vice versa. Even where the government, or a paramilitary group, manages to take control of a town the roads and countryside around it are invariably controlled by the guerillas. You cannot travel in and out of these towns without crossing numerous checkpoints operated by one of the factions, and each time you do so you are in danger of being accused of collaboration and summary execution. The campesino – you would call him a peasant - must cross these checkpoints to bring his goods to market and then return home. And every time he crosses a line he is questioned; the nature of the questions dependent on which group controls the checkpoint. 'What did you do in town? Are there guerrilla checkpoints on the road? Did you tell the army we were here? Do you sell pigs to the paramilitaries? Do you sell vegetables to the guerillas?' Every time he is questioned the peasant runs the risk of saying the wrong thing and jeopardizing not only himself but also his family and possibly even his entire village.

"The AUC – the largest paramilitary - sees all union members and human rights workers as guerilla collaborators, a view that also seems to be held by many of the police and military commanders and is even implied by senior members of the government. These union members and human rights activists are at extreme risk. Just over four weeks ago three trade unionists with close ties to an international commission on human rights were killed in Arauca, a disputed area with heavy military and paramilitary presence. There are already rumors swirling they may have been victims of extra-judicial 'justice.' And a high profile is not even necessary to be caught up in this. Attendance at a church rally that marginally supports a certain position can be construed as collaboration.

"The end result is that the average non-aligned Colombian is effectively disenfranchised – there can be no free political discourse. Espousing a middle road through Colombia's troubles places one squarely in the sights of every group. If one doesn't get you, another will."

Jorge talked about his family ranch in Antioquia Department and how he could no longer risk going there except by private plane, and then only rarely and briefly.

What it boiled down to was many people with resources had simply chosen to leave Colombia, or as in Jorge's case chosen to stay but maintain their silence and a low profile.

We sat quietly, deep in our own thoughts. It struck me that Nina's father was caught up in circumstances which paralleled mine to some extent as he too was no longer in control of his own destiny. By remaining in Colombia he lived in fear of his personal safety, although it was in a larger sense and less specific than my own situation. While Jorge's family was safe as long as they stayed outside of Colombia he seemed to be trapped here by ancestral ties just as strong as the bonds that connected me to my father.

Jorge was the first to speak, breaking the solemnity.

"I'm afraid I have ruined the evening by dwelling far too long on Colombia's problems. I apologize," he said. "It is late, and if you do not mind I will leave you now."

Standing, he turned to me. "It has been a pleasure meeting you, Dexter Snell. I hope to see you again while you are in Bogota. I promise next time we will speak of something more pleasant."

Nina and I both stood. I shook hands with him and Nina kissed his cheek before he left, again closing the door behind him. We sat back down and watched the fire. Nina broke the silence this time, still staring at the flames.

"My father likes you. I've never seen him so open with anyone I've brought here."

"I like him, too. At least after I passed the initial inspection."

Nina glanced at me, embarrassed. "I'm sorry. I realized during dinner that it has been just as my father explained. I have taken pleasure in our little game, as he called it, where I bring men home for him to tear apart."

"And was that your plan for tonight?"

She hesitated, gathering her thoughts before answering. "I suppose so. But there's more." I allowed her the time to continue at her own pace while reflecting on the fact it was the first time since I'd met her yesterday that she didn't simply blurt out whatever it was that was on her mind.

"Dex, I was thrilled you stood up to my father the way you did. I guess I hoped you would, but I was shocked when it happened. It was new ground for me, and for my father. Every one else I have brought here, how do they put it in America?" she asked. Then, answering her own question said, "Everyone else kisses his ass. You did not."

I was secretly pleased at least one trait I'd inherited from my father was recognized and appreciated.

We made small talk for a while longer but it wasn't the same. Nina had lost the bubbly edge that made her such an interesting companion on the flight the previous day, and I was feeling overwhelmed again by my own situation.

Nina finally stood and said she thought the evening should end now. She walked me back through the house and out the side door to where the car was waiting.

"Good night, Dex," she said, rising on her tiptoes and presenting her cheek for a quick kiss. When I leaned down she turned her face toward me and threw her arms around my neck, pressing her lips to mine. Her mouth opened and her tongue burst into life as she pressed herself closer to me. She gave a little moan and shiver before she pushed herself away and, without saying a word, turned and ran back into the house.

V

The next day I decided to throw caution to the wind and placed a call to Felix from my room. I was worried about a tap on my phone as a result of the interview with Capitán Torrano, but as it turned out it didn't matter as there was no answer at Felix' house. There was no answer at Bones' house, either.

Making contact with Juan Gomez without traveling to San Vicente was clearly impossible and I was stymied as to how to get there. It crossed my mind that Bones might have an idea, and I decided to try him again later. And using the room phone was definite folly; I'd have to figure a way around that, too.

I turned my thoughts to the retrieval of the Spanish treasure from the *Griffon*, and the best way to go about it. Would it before loading the cocaine or after? And I still didn't even know how to go about making the connections I needed. Hell, I was getting nowhere. I finally admitted to myself I was killing time simply to avoid thinking about Catalina. And now Nina.

VI

The days took on a pattern over the course of the next week. I would meet Nina for a late breakfast – an early breakfast by Latin American standards – and we would set off on a day of visiting museums, art galleries and buildings of note. Always using the plain, black Ford and always with the driver and bodyguard close by. We ended every day with a late dinner at her father's house, which I must admit I greatly enjoyed. Jorge was never around. Nina simply said he was busy.

Nina was recognized often, particularly whenever we had our mid-afternoon lunch at a café or restaurant. My curiosity finally got the best of me and I asked about it.

"That is something I like about you, Dex," she smiled, leaning closer to me. "You are unaffected by my family history and reputation.

"Three years ago an important magazine did an article on the most eligible bachelors in South America, and despite the fact my father refused to speak to the writer he ended up near the top of the list. And his picture, with me on his arm, appeared on the cover. Inside there were more pictures along with a side story that identified me not only as the daughter of one of the most eligible men in South America, but suggested I was one of the most eligible single women as well. My father considered the article a major invasion of his privacy if not a risk to his safety and mine, and although his notoriety has faded mine has not. I seem to be a continuing item of interest in Colombia simply because I do not live here."

I thought the explanation a touch too complicated. Nina's physical beauty combined with her natural intelligence and outgoing personality would attract attention even if she weren't Jorge Garcia's daughter. I stifled the impulse to say so, at the same time realizing her semi-celebrity status accounted for her easy access to the hotel and other places.

I was aware of a current between us, and I know Nina was too. I caught her stealing glances at me when she thought I wasn't looking and she would redden slightly whenever she took my arm and her body touched mine. I never mentioned that first kiss. Yet I knew she was waiting for me to initiate another.

And it wasn't that I didn't want to kiss her again. At first I desperately wanted to just hold her in my arms and feel the closeness of another person without complications. I wrestled with how to do that, but something kept telling me not to. As each day, each hour and each minute went by my inner turmoil increased as my appreciation of Nina grew. And I sensed she felt it as well. Her patience only made it worse.

VII

"My father would like to see you," Nina announced matter-of-factly as we finished our dinner one night toward the end of the week. I hadn't seen him since the first visit to his house and had stopped inquiring about his absence. "He has asked you to join him in the library," she said, "and I will see you tomorrow."

I thought it strange he was there in the house yet hadn't dined with us but I reigned in my curiosity as Nina offered her cheek for a goodnight kiss. I made my way to the library and found Jorge there, sitting in front of the fire.

"Hola," I said, "I understand you have been busy this past week."

Jorge rose and extended his hand formally, then offered me a drink.

"Yes, as a matter of fact I have been busy," he said. "Please sit here with me. I would like to speak with you frankly."

I sat and sipped the brandy, waiting for him to begin.

"I apologize for this, but I have done some checking on you." He glanced at me as if expecting me to object or to protest. When I didn't, he continued.

"The Colombian community is small, Dex, particularly the portion of it representing what you might call the aristocracy although I hate that term," he began. "I asked about you through friends in Miami. You were well-known there."

I nodded. "Yes, I suppose I was, although I'm not proud of it," I answered.

"I understand. I found what you told me the first time we met is the truth," he said, shifting his gaze from the fire to my face, "as far as it goes."

I locked eyes with him, and waited.

"Please tell me what your connection is with Pedro Arroyo Montoya."

I was surprised, since the name meant absolutely nothing to me. "I'm sorry, but I don't know anyone by that name," I said. "Should I?"

Jorge continued to hold my eyes with his while sipping his brandy. "His daughter is Mirtha Cardeli. Surely you do not deny you know her husband, Niccolo?"

Now I was surprised, although I shouldn't have been. If the Colombian community was as small as Jorge said, and given the high profile I'd maintained in Miami it only made sense the connection could be made easily.

"Yes, I know them both. Niccolo Cardeli now holds the Florida property I inherited from my father. All I have is my home on Cayman Brac," I answered truthfully. "I told you that."

"Yes, you did." Again a long pause, "But you did not tell me your father was murdered. And then there is the fact you are here in Colombia where Niccolo Cardeli has many enemies, including his estranged father-in-law Pedro Arroyo."

I watched the flames in the fireplace. It was as if they were consuming me. They jumped and leapt in unexpected directions, reaching out and singeing, then burning, consuming everything they touched.

"Do you deny your father was murdered?" he asked.

"No, I don't deny that," I answered quietly.

"Did Niccolo Cardeli murder your father?"

I watched the flames. They were relentless. Never hurried, simply relentless; engulfing everything within their reach. It was hypnotic.

"Yes."

Jorge's questions were burning me as surely as the flames in the fireplace seared the logs piled there. I felt helpless, unable to move away.

"Was your father involved in the cocaine trade?"

It was too much. I turned toward Jorge and I knew he could see the pain and anger in my eyes. And what I saw in his eyes gave me strength. I saw compassion in those dark eyes; pain, too. And in his open, friendly face I found what I would have expected from my own father.

I told Jorge Garcia Ramirez everything and whenever I faltered he would ask a simple question, just as he did that first night, and more of my story would tumble out. He paced back and forth in front of the fireplace, absorbing everything, never passing judgment. When he had it all, he took my glass and refilled it.

"This has been an emotional week for me," Jorge said. "First, you came here and took my daughter by storm. You must know she is quite infatuated with you – no, that is not fair. She has been infatuated with an endless string of men. This is different.

"Then you stood up to me in a way no one has before, particularly Nina's so-called suitors. And as a result you won my admiration as well."

I wondered where this was going but was still too emotionally overwrought from sharing my predicament with a relative stranger to think clearly.

"The connection to Pedro Arroyo was most troubling for me," he continued. "He is a known drug trafficker and has close ties to, if not control over, one of the AUC paramilitary factions. It is people like him who are destroying Colombia and I feared it was him specifically you came here to see."

"Jorge," I interrupted, regaining a semblance of control over my emotions, "please understand I would use Pedro Arroyo or someone like him if it helps me get close enough to Cardeli to kill him. I will not hesitate."

He continued to stand in front of the fire and watch me. He seemed to reach a decision.

"Revenge is a particularly strong motivator in the Latino psyche, Dex. It must be the Portuguese blood in you. It is something I understand very well, and I respect it.

"And the hot temper you described in your father a week ago also troubled me. Temper is perhaps the wrong word. A better description might be his bias toward taking action rather than sitting idly by and allowing circumstances to unfold around him, as I have done. It is a choice a person makes, Dex – one you have made, and one I have made poorly. My complacency is unworthy of the Garcia name."

Jorge began to pace again, and it was obvious he had more to say.

"I owe you a debt of gratitude for arriving here and shaking me up. It is a debt I would like to repay," he said, stopping his pacing and looking directly at me, "by helping you do what it is you need to do here in Colombia."

At first I wasn't exactly sure what to say. For once circumstances had transpired to my advantage. "Thank you, Jorge. I can't refuse your offer, even though I shouldn't drag you into this. I just don't know what else to do," I said simply.

"There are two conditions attached to my offer, Dex."

I nodded my agreement before I even heard what they were.

"The first is I must have your word the cocaine will never land in the United States. And the second is you treat Nina honorably. She is a grown woman, Dex, and whatever happens between you two is your own affair. Simply promise me you will not lead her on."

I stood and shook Jorge's hand. And then he embraced me.

I moved into the Garcia house the next day.

VIII

Nina's pleasure at my arrival at her father's house, luggage in hand, was short lived as rather than spending more time with her I spent less. Jorge and I were preoccupied with the details of arranging things and although he clearly knew his way around Colombia the cocaine trade was unfamiliar ground for him. I left those arrangements to him, and re-established contact with Bones and Felix using a landline Jorge provided. A phone that he assured me was secure, as opposed to a cell phone that had been my first impulse. I had a lot to learn about government surveillance.

I called Felix first, and this time he answered.

"Damn, Dex, where have you been? Bones and I have been worried sick."

I apologized for the lack of communication and explained as best I could that I was safe and on track. Then I went through a list of things he had to do, including installing a false bottom in the fish hold in the *Estrela*. I'd decided we would put the gold from the *Griffon* in the compartments in the fuel tanks and hide the cocaine separately in the bottom of the hold. Mixing the two cargoes somehow made no sense.

And I told Felix to bring the *Estrela* to Trinidad by the twentieth of September and wait there unless he heard differently from me. We agreed he would find dockage at the boatyard we'd visited with father twenty years ago.

"And there's one last favor, Felix," I said before hanging up.

I asked him to paint over the name of the *Estrela de Marques* before he reached Trinidad. I did not want that name on her while she was carrying cocaine.

I called Bones next, and he too remonstrated with me about the lack of contact. His words were stronger and more profane than Felix' but he brightened considerably when he heard I might not have to go to San Vicente. I kept the conversation short, which wasn't easy as he had endless questions about what was happening. I finally got him off the line and decided to call Mirtha. It was a few days before she was to be in Jamaica, but I thought I'd try anyway.

The connection went through to Jamaica and the hotel operator confirmed she was there, but not in her room. I left a message saying I would call back in an hour.

I went to Jorge's private office, a smaller room off the library, and found him there yelling at someone over the telephone in Spanish. When he hung up the anger left his face immediately and he smiled.

"That was the manager of my ranch. For too many years he has had things his way, knowing I only travel there reluctantly and believing I cannot manage without him. I told him things are going to change, and I will be there in two days."

"Is that wise, Jorge?" I asked. "Is it safe?"

He smiled. "Many wealthy people still live in Medellin, including other horse breeders. So I have decided it is a matter of determining how to do it. I will figure it out."

I went back to my room and tried Mirtha again, and this time when the call was put through she answered. I didn't even attempt small talk. I had no appetite for it when it came to either Mirtha or her husband.

"Do you have the money?" I asked.

"I can get it with twenty-four hours notice. You simply have to give me the details, and then I need final clearance from Niccolo," she said. "But I have some additional instructions for you."

"What? I thought his instructions to me were crystal clear."

She hesitated, and then started. "Niccolo wants to know what it was your father was after – what it was he was doing before he died."

"Murdered, you mean," I snapped.

"Have it your way. Do you know what it was?"

I said I did know, and that I was working on it.

"That won't be good enough. He wants something tangible – some kind of proof you have it figured out, and that it's worthwhile. He told me to tell you not to screw around, that he still knows where your uncle and that stuck-up little bitch are."

I thought about it for a minute and then asked her what else there was.

"The goods you are buying have to be inspected before Niccolo releases the money. You need to call me two days before your final arrangements are made, and I will tell you how it is to be done. There will be no transfer otherwise."

"What else?" I asked.

The tone of her voice changed subtly but noticeably. "Dex, dear, I don't like the way you're talking to me. This problem between you and Niccolo doesn't have to interfere with us, does it?"

I didn't answer, and she continued in the same placating tone.

"I've been here for two days, in the same suite as last time. You remember the last time, don't you Dex?" she purred.

"Yes Mirtha, I remember," I answered, instantly disgusted with myself again.

"It's so lonely here, Dex. I wish you were with me. I get excited just thinking about it. Can we come back here when this is all over? Just you and me. I want you so badly."

I wanted to reach through the phone and strangle her. I felt dirty just talking to her, worse than I'd felt in Tijuana fifteen years ago when I'd done similar things for money. That seemed honest now in comparison to this.

"I don't think so, Mirtha." I struggled to hold the emotion out of my voice. "I've got lots to do."

She spat back instantly. "It's that bitch, isn't it. You're still not over her, are you? Well, just so you know, she's marrying the guy in Atlanta. It was in the papers."

I felt as if I'd been stabbed, and recovered as quickly as I could. "I already told you I don't give a rat's ass about her, and I meant it. I just don't want anything to screw up my business with your *husband*," I lied.

"It's a good thing you don't care about her, Dex, because Niccolo said that if you don't come across with something worthwhile on what your father was up to, he'll kill her. He says he'll do it in a way that makes sure your uncle dies of shock. What do you think of that?"

I closed my eyes and tried to shut everything out. All I could see was Catalina, and the filthy hands of Cardeli and his men on her, debasing her before they killed her. And I knew what that would do to Uncle Patricio.

"What does he want?" I asked, the resistance gone from me.

"That's better, Dex dear. So much better. Save your rage and passion for me. At least I appreciate it. He says you can decide what kind of proof to give him, but it better be good."

I thought again furiously, but couldn't come up with anything other than sending him the coins I already had and telling him there were more.

"Where do I send the proof?" I asked, scrambling for a pen and paper as she gave me an address. I wrote everything down and hung up as soon as I had it.

The call, and what I'd learned, exhausted me as thoroughly as if I'd run a marathon. I stood for a while on the small balcony off my room and then went to see Jorge. I needed to talk to someone.

IX

Jorge was still in his office, on the telephone again. He took one look at me and hung up.

"What is it, Dex? Are you okay?" he asked.

I told him about the call to Mirtha, and Cardeli's insistence on some type of proof my father's secret project was worthwhile. We discussed sending him the coins, and I confirmed I could do that.

"Will you tell me the rest, Dex?" Jorge asked shrewdly. "There must be something else to make you so agitated."

I had already told him about Catalina and Patricio, and Cardeli's threats. I hesitated, but one look at Jorge's face told me I needed to tell him the rest.

"Catalina is engaged to be married," I said quietly.

Jorge came from behind his desk and put his arm around me, guiding me out the door and into the courtyard. He took me to a secluded alcove with a view of the main fountain and its jets of water accented by the hidden lights. It was just after sunset, and the stars were appearing in a sky that had been washed clean by an afternoon downpour.

"I used to sit here with Nina's mother," he said. "This was our favorite spot, and although it was enough for me – this house that has been in our family for many generations, and living in the country that speaks the purest Spanish in the world – for her it could not offset the realities of Colombia today. I know she loved me, and God knows I love her still, but the cruel truth is I had to let her go or watch her wither and die here, just as I would die living in exile anywhere else.

"If you love Catalina, Dex, you must let her go. You must complete the course you have set out on. You have done the only thing possible under the circumstances, and you must see it through. If it turns out badly and you are killed it is better she believe the story you have fabricated than have her live her life in remorse."

I sat silently watching the lights playing on the fountain below the stars. I knew Jorge was right and I was thankful he was there and understood what I was going through. He got up without saying a word and left me in the alcove, sensing I needed to be alone.

Stars are noticeably different at high altitudes. They are brighter and shimmer more obviously as their light travels through less atmosphere than at lower altitudes. As I watched the sky I wondered which of these brilliant stars were visible in the heavens over Atlanta, and if Catalina was watching those same stars right now. I sat for hours alternately watching the jets in the fountain and the stars in the sky. I finally stood to go inside to try to sleep when I saw her.

Nina was sitting on the other side of the fountain from me, across the courtyard under an arbor near the wall. I hadn't seen her go there and had no idea how long she had been sitting watching me. When I stood and saw her she came across the courtyard toward me, stopping a few feet away.

"My father told me tonight why you are here Dex, and what has happened."

I started to say something but she held up her hand to silence me.

"Please let me speak. And then you can go and leave me if you wish. Just hear me out please," she asked quietly.

I nodded my head.

"You told me from the beginning there was someone else. I'm under no illusions, and although I said there should be no strings attached to whatever happens between us, that is not the whole truth now. I see my father in you – more than in any man I've ever known – and I love you for that, Dex."

I tried to stop her, but she lifted her hand again to silence me.

"I am a grown woman, and you are a grown man. I know you like me and that is all I ask. I promise I will not try to displace your Catalina, Dex, but can we not acknowledge we are deeply attracted to one another and as long as we are at least friends nothing that happens between us can be wrong? Only North Americans are so … so hung up."

She turned her back to me and looked at the fountain for a long time before spinning back around and stamping her foot. "Damn you, Dexter Snell. Can't you see I'm inviting you into my bed? I've never had to do this before," she blurted in exasperation.

I closed my eyes for a second and took a deep breath. I reopened them only as I began to take a step toward her, but before I could move an inch she was in my arms.

X

I didn't know what to expect the next morning but was surprised to awaken alone. I wasn't even sure when Nina had left me.

A knock at the door announced the arrival of breakfast, and a servant came in with a tray and nonchalantly but purposefully proceeded to set a table for two people by the window. I decided there were certain advantages to a more liberal outlook in these matters, at least more liberal than what American society is used to. Not that I'd ever felt personally constrained by society in general. I climbed into Nina's shower and tried to make sense of the last thirty-six hours.

Confiding in Jorge Garcia and his subsequent offer of assistance had been an incredible relief. I realized now there was no practical way I could accomplish what I needed to get done in Colombia without some type of help, and he was confident he could do it. Simply having someone to talk to was reassuring.

Felix would be in Trinidad in ten days or so and I knew everything was, or would be, ready to go with the *Estrela*. The location of the *Griffon* and the Spanish treasure was firmly fixed in my mind thanks to father's actions in the squall twenty years ago, and I had Felix' memory as a backup.

I was oversimplifying things but the recovery of the treasure and the procurement and loading of the cocaine were the necessary steps toward maneuvering Cardeli into a position of vulnerability. Just a few weeks ago it had seemed impossible. Without minimizing the dangers and risks still ahead I should have felt better than I did, but the news of Catalina's engagement lay over me like a pall.

In certain ways Catalina and I were alike. The pain I'd put her and Patricio through in my determined ploy to distance them from my predicament with Cardeli probably drove her to run, much like I had run after the death of my father. As agonizing as it was, I had to admit this was a fitting penance for my years of neglecting Patricio. But if there was a god in charge of reward and punishment, what had Patricio ever done to deserve this? I had now abandoned him twice and was certain my actions had also driven Catalina from him. The best I could hope for in the end was they would reconcile and be protected by either Cardeli's death or that he believed they meant nothing to me anymore. As much as I tried, though, I had a difficult time wishing for Catalina's happiness with her fiancé.

And that finally forced my thoughts around to the previous night.

Nina had proven to be an enthusiastic and uninhibited lover, and after an initial, frantic coupling she gently but intently set about exploring my body, probing and examining me purposefully while she asked about my likes and dislikes. She demonstrated the same excitement and pleasure normally ascribed only to the male in his purely physical, emotionally detached exploration of a new, unfamiliar female. I found the role reversal to be both striking and erotic and I wondered if it was a deeply repressed desire in other women. It brought into question the assumption of the naturally monogamous nature of the human female struggling to dominate the wandering nature of the male.

The thought that Nina could share a physical relationship with me without the entanglement of an emotional one was reassuring in some confused way, but I still had nagging doubts.

I no sooner toweled off and dressed than Nina burst into the room like sunlight breaking through a cloud-filled sky. She was glowing, and I had a fleeting stab of regret as she ran into my arms and kissed me. But just as quickly she turned away and danced over to the table.

"Hurry, Dex. Father wants us to throw some things together and join him. He's moved his trip to the ranch ahead and wants us to go with him," she said, the excitement apparent in her voice. "I haven't been there in two years, and I can't wait to show it to you."

She busied herself pouring coffee and juice as she launched into descriptions of her favorite horses and how much she wanted to go riding again, asserting her father's Paso Fino horses were among the finest in the world. I resisted the impulse to explain I was not the most accomplished rider but she was already beyond that topic and telling me about a special place on the ranch where she wanted to take me swimming.

"Nina," I interrupted, "I think we should talk about last night."

She stopped talking but continued to busy herself at the table with her back to me. I watched her, thinking about what to say and how to say it. She spoke first.

"Did you not enjoy what we did last night?" she asked, still not turning to face me.

"Yes, I did, Nina. Perhaps too much."

"So did I, Dex," she said, turning toward me. "But it was not too much. It was exactly what I needed, and I think you did, too. Am I wrong?"

I hesitated. "Well, no. You're not wrong. It's just …"

"Stop right there, Dex," she broke in. "If you say one more word, you'll be attaching strings. And didn't we agree not to?"

"Yes, we did," I nodded.

"Then leave it. Hurry up and eat, my father expects us in twenty minutes."

We ate quickly, and I went to my room and gathered up my things. I didn't have much so it wasn't a matter of picking and choosing, I just threw it all in my valise. Then I called Bones on the secure line.

"I hear nothing from you for over a week, then two calls in two days," he grumbled, but I could tell he was pleased to be back in touch.

I quickly explained I wanted all but three of the coins we'd found expressed to the address Mirtha had given me. I asked if he could do it in a way that would prevent him from being identified as the sender, possibly without the shipment even being traceable to Cayman Brac. Bones assured me he could do it, and I re-emphasized how important it was.

As an afterthought, I asked for his email address and rooted around in my bag for a pen and paper to write it down before disconnecting and heading downstairs.

If Jorge had any concerns about what had happened between Nina and me, he didn't show it. I was starting to believe I was the one who had the morality hang-ups, which was a completely new position for me to be in. Yet I still had a nagging worry I might be getting in over my head somehow. The smiles Nina and her father exchanged when they thought I wasn't looking didn't help and I hoped I wasn't the pawn in some new game they were playing.

We were in Jorge's plane and heading northwest by noon.

It was a relatively short hop, a hundred and twenty miles. The pilot circled the ranch before we landed and Jorge excitedly pointed out his favorite spots as he tried to give me an idea of how big the ranch was. A rough calculation from hectares indicated it was between seven and eight thousand acres, probably closer to eight.

We landed on a grass strip and taxied up toward the modest – compared to the mansion in Bogota – hacienda. Two vehicles came to meet us, and there were smiles and greetings all around. I wondered which one was the manager Jorge had the argument with on the telephone, but it was not clear amid all the chatter and excitement. I did, however, notice Nina received more than her fair share of the attention.

As the luggage was removed from the plane and loaded into the back of a jeep Jorge suggested Nina show me the stables and the horse breeding operation while he attended to some business. Nina took me by the arm and we headed toward the collection of large, well maintained buildings that were the focal point of the ranch.

A ranch hand, presumably a foreman, met us at the gate and after exchanging pleasantries left Nina to show me inside the stables. I've not been inside a lot of stables in my life and never one dedicated to breeding, but I was impressed. It was much more modern and clean than I expected. In fact, it was a showcase.

The stalls were meticulously kept and roomier than any I'd seen before. Each had a plaque with the name of the horse, and under the plaque there were charts and records similar to those you would expect to see at the foot of a hospital bed. There were notes on feeding times, type of feed, exercise times and other data I didn't understand. Nina explained that these handwritten records were logged into a computer database every night and then sent by satellite internet connection to her father's computer in Bogota for his review. It was obvious from Nina's excitement that horses were in her blood too, and she said she often reviewed the records herself from her home in Miami.

The farm office was attached to the stables and we went through it to get to the paddock where two grooms were exercising horses. I don't exactly know what I expected to see, but Nina watched my face expectantly and then laughed with pleasure as she took my arm. The first horse to catch my attention was also the closest, and the rider seemed to be floating along at a speed slower than a person would normally walk yet the horse's feet tapped a clear, unbroken and steady four-beat rhythm faster than you can tap your hand against your leg, not unlike the roll of a drum. Nina said this was the Classic Fino gait attainable by only the finest Paso Finos.

"The Conquistadors bred these horses from the original Barb Andalusians and Spanish Jennets brought by Columbus on his second voyage," she said. "There weren't any horses here before that.

"Those first horses were the start of the Paso Fino breed, and it was a point of pride for the Dons to own and ride only the best. They could carry a three hundred pound rider for hours, and were much prized for their endurance."

Nina continued to tell me about the horses without taking her eyes from the two in the paddock. "The original breeders were in the Dominican Republic, Cuba, Venezuela, Puerto Rico and of course here in Colombia, but there are now breeders in the U.S., Canada and other countries. The Garcia horses maintain the relatively smaller size that was a characteristic of the breed a hundred years ago, but the Paso Finos in the States are bred to be larger due to preferences there."

We stood for another few minutes mesmerized by the horses before she pulled on my arm. "Come on, let's go to the hacienda and see what father has planned. I want to make sure there is time for some riding," she said.

The hacienda was modest in size only compared to the colonial mansion in Bogota, but the rustic luxury and obvious value of the furnishings could stand up to any comparison. Everything was wood, leather, silver and brass, and elegantly complemented the stonework that dominated the interior of the house. The main entrance opened directly into the great room that soared to the beamed and vaulted ceiling two stories above us. An open staircase led from the main floor up to an open balcony along the back, separated from the great room only by a wrought iron railing.

The natural tranquility of the room was violated by two voices raised in anger, one belonging to Jorge, spilling over from the balcony. Although they were yelling in Spanish the heat burned through, requiring no translation. The argument stopped abruptly with a loud crash and pieces of pottery flew through the bars of the railing and fell to the floor at our feet as a red-faced, swarthy man appeared at the top of the staircase. He paused long enough to turn and shake his fist at Jorge, who was only steps behind him, before running down the stairs with short, choppy steps. Jorge descended calmly while the man made his way directly to the front door, rudely pushing Nina aside with another Spanish expletive. The slam of the heavy door signaled the end of the exchange, with only the shards of broken pottery on the floor left as evidence of the altercation.

"I apologize for that display," Jorge said, walking across the room and opening the front door. "I am afraid it did not go as well as I had hoped."

A vehicle was roaring away, the spinning of its wheels on the gravel of the laneway drawing further attention to Jorge's understatement. When it was gone, he closed the door and tried to change the subject.

"I have some positive news, Dex. Things are moving quickly. I will explain it to you a little later," he said. "How did you find things at the stables, Nina? Do they meet your approval?"

Nina gave him a big hug. "Are you okay father?"

"Yes, I am fine, but I need to find a new manager or make other arrangements. It seems Manuel does not care for my renewed interest in assuming a more active role in the operations of the ranch. I suspected that might happen when I told him yesterday I wanted to review the accounts," he said, glancing at the broken pottery. "There are – how should I put it – some irregularities in certain cash payments. But I do not want to trouble you with that, dear. Tell me about the stables."

Nina's face brightened. "They're wonderful. It's just like I remembered, only better somehow. Thank you for agreeing to bring us here."

I smiled. "I thought this trip was at your father's request, Nina. That's the way you put it to me."

Jorge smiled indulgently. "She was at me first thing this morning, Dex, when she found out I had moved my visit ahead. Despite appearances, I still worry about being here and it was my intent to come by myself, conclude what it was I had to do and then rejoin you in Bogota."

"But father, if it's safe enough for you to be here then it must be okay. And it's been so long. I like the house in Bogota, but it is the ranch and the horses I miss the most," she wheedled, hugging him again. "And besides, nothing bad has ever happened here. I think you are overcautious," she said, quickly adding "but I love you for it."

Not to suggest she was insincere, but it was apparent to me how Nina manipulated her father's moods by flattering and reassuring him. It was a pattern that probably developed between them after her mother left.

Jorge moved back from her, holding her at arms length while looking directly into her eyes and then reached some kind of decision. "I need to explain something to you, Nina. Dex, you may as well hear this, too. Please come upstairs."

He moved toward the staircase. Nina hesitated briefly, clearly perplexed by the subtle change in the tone of his voice and the break in their usual pattern of protective father, adoring daughter. This was obviously new to her. She took me by the hand and we followed Jorge up the stairs.

The balcony was all that could be seen from the main floor, and when we made it to the top step I was dumbstruck. The center of the second floor was open, with rooms opening off either side. A massive stone fireplace dominated the center of the open space and it was constructed in such a way that the fire was open to view on all four sides. This area was clearly Jorge's personal space and held a desk as well as comfortable leather couches and chairs. Bookshelves and display cases lined the walls, filled with trophies, awards and pictures of many generations of Garcia horses. I assumed the one door off the left side of the room led to his private suite and the two doors to the right might lead to guest accommodations. Jorge didn't offer a tour as he had of his house in Bogota, but went directly to his desk indicating with a wave of his hand that we should sit in the two leather chairs in front of him.

"The situation here in Colombia is every bit as dangerous as I have explained to you, Dex," he started. "I have explained it to you as well, Nina, but perhaps not as clearly as I should have," he smiled indulgently.

"You don't need to be so protective, father," Nina started, only to be cut short by a wave of Jorge's hand.

"Please, let me finish. I have indulged you during your visits here for my own selfish reasons. That must stop if you intend to continue coming to Colombia. I can no longer sit back and watch silently while this country deteriorates, and anything I feel compelled to do or say will increase the danger here not only for me, but for you as well."

Nina's concern showed plainly in both her face and in the way she sat bolt upright on the edge of the chair.

"There have been certain payments made from the accounts here with my tacit if unspoken approval, to ensure the ranch operations continue as close to normally as possible. Manuel handled those payments and I have long suspected he was not only directly involved with paramilitary activities but feathering his own nest as well. That was confirmed when I told him I wanted to make the next payment myself. Judging from his violent reaction, it is apparent some of the money he claims he needs for this is going into his own pocket. I would estimate as much as half."

"So he's probably in hot water not just with you, but potentially with whoever he's been paying off," I suggested.

"Exactly. And I am hoping it is enough to make him leave Antioquia and not cause me any trouble. But I am not counting on that completely. I have never trusted him; I simply found it convenient to use him so I could hide in the house in Bogota, which I am no longer prepared to do."

Nina was clearly agitated, the concern apparent in the tremor in her voice. "Are you sure you need to do this, father? Why can't you just leave all of this to other people?"

"No. I am the only Garcia in our family history who has sat back complacently and watched events in Colombia unfold. I cannot go on this way, and it is only fair I tell you."

Jorge turned back to me. "I have to leave immediately, Dex, and I will be gone for two or three days," he explained. "I will be in Medellin for a day, and then on to Cali. I just have to finalize this other matter for you in person."

"I'll come with you, Jorge," I said, feeling guilty he was doing this for me.

"No," he said politely but firmly. "This business will be conducted in Spanish, and the fewer people involved, the better. Besides, I would like you to stay here with Nina. It has been years since I have seen her so happy," he said, and then noticing my expression added, "Please, do not be embarrassed. I am aware she spent last night with you. Nina told me she has no expectations and as long as you do not lead her on, and I have no reason to believe you would, then I am content."

Nina's face was crimson, and I felt awkward as well. She stood up and walked over to the railing and stood with her back to us looking out on the great room.

"Thank you, Jorge, but I still feel terribly guilty about you doing this for me in Cali and Medellin by yourself. This isn't how I pictured this working."

"You have no choice in the matter, Dex. And excuse me for being blunt, but this is the last I will hear of it. I am leaving immediately, and I do not care to discuss it with either you or Nina. If I am delayed for any reason, I will call you here. The telephone on this desk is secure like the one in Bogota. By the way, it seems delivery will be made in either Cartagena or Barranquilla. Can you see any problem with that?" he asked.

"No, I can't. Other than Cardeli insisting on some type of inspection before he releases the payment," I answered.

Jorge narrowed his eyes and looked past me toward the great room. "I understand. Let us agree simply that delivery will be made somewhere along the northern coast, say between Cartagena and Santa Marta – that gives us a little more flexibility."

"I'm certain that will be fine," I said.

"Nina," Jorge called out, "I would feel better if you and Dex returned to Bogota."

She wheeled about and strode back toward her father, stopping in front of his desk and leaning toward him, both of her hands flat on the desktop.

"I heard everything you said, and I understand better than you want me to. The Garcia blood runs in my veins just as strongly as it flows in yours and if you choose – as you put it – to stop running, then so do I. I'm not leaving the ranch until you come back."

Jorge smiled, stood and walked around the desk to put his arm around her shoulders. "I expected this. I think my little girl has decided to grow up. Just the same, what I told you this morning still stands. If you insist on staying here I want you to take no chances." He kissed her cheek and then took his briefcase from the top of the desk and headed for the stairs. We followed him down and to the front door.

"Nina, tell the foreman it is my wish that he report to you until I return. I will see you in three days," he said as he climbed into the waiting jeep and headed for his plane, which was already running and spinning around for takeoff.

XI

Nina's displeasure at her father's abrupt departure was gradually replaced by an appreciation of the impact of the changes he'd announced. She went to the stables to see the foreman and then spent several hours in the ranch office going over the books with the administrator, leaving me to use Jorge's desk and the phone he'd assured me was secure.

It was now late afternoon, and I called Bones.

"Hello," he answered curtly.

"It's me, Dex."

"Thank god. What a damned day this has been."

"What's going on?" I asked, alarmed.

"It's Felix, Dex. He's in a bit of a jam. Nothing that can't be fixed."

"Is he ok?"

"Yes. The police are holding him. But he should be released soon."

"Stop pissing around and tell me what happened," I said.

"About the same time you called this morning, Felix was beating the hell out of a photographer he found snooping around your cottage. Judging by how long it took me to stitch the photographer up and set his broken arm, I'd say Felix gave him more than he bargained for."

"Was he the one who took the pictures of Catalina and me?"

"Yes. The police let me talk to Felix and he confirmed it. The guy panicked when he caught him, and Felix said it took a lot of physical persuasion to overcome his fear of his employer before spilling everything. He's been watching you for months."

My mind was racing as I thought about the possible implications of having caught this guy. "Bones – is there any way we can keep the news we caught him from getting back to Miami?"

"Felix thought of that already. He said the man is so afraid of Miami he'll do anything to keep them from finding out he's been discovered. To explain the extent of his injuries he agreed to back up the story that Felix caught him actually breaking in to your cottage and he put up a struggle. He'll keep his mouth shut about everything else, but you've got to agree not to press charges on the break-in. That should end this quickly and keep everything relatively quiet."

"Then why are the police still holding Felix?"

"They don't exactly buy the struggle bit since Felix doesn't have a mark on him. But as long as they both stick to the same story, the police will have to let Felix go. I have a lawyer friend at the police station right now."

"Do I have to call anyone about dropping charges?" I asked.

"No. The lawyer will tell them you want the charges dropped. It's taken care of, but the police are getting a little curious about the activities around here since you've come back."

"We can't help that. Let's just hope this puts an end to being watched. It was spooking me. Did this guy have anything to do with my father's murder?"

"No, he didn't, Dex. He only moved here two years ago. He's a freelance photographer who just got in over his head."

"Well, we might be able to use him later. Make sure he keeps reporting to Miami there's nothing happening on Brac. Did that package get off?" I asked.

"Yes, it's gone. An anonymous intermediary at the other end will take care of it. Should be delivered the day after tomorrow. Untraceable."

"Thanks, Bones. And thank Felix for me."

"One more thing," Bones laughed, "Felix said if you called to tell you this was the most pleasurable thing he's done in years."

I said goodbye and hung up. At least one loose end was tied up and accounted for, and it made me feel a little better knowing it wasn't one of Cardeli's goons sneaking around on Brac. A hired hack with a camera was bad enough but the thought it might have been someone with a gun was something else entirely.

I had been sitting with my back to the staircase watching the fire as I talked to Bones, and when I swiveled the chair around to hang up I saw Nina was sitting there.

"Good news?" she asked.

"Yes, in a way. How about you?"

"I went through some of the accounts with the administrator. The amount of cash that's been taken out of here is amazing, and I have a feeling it wasn't just the ranch manager. I think she was in on it, too."

"What makes you think that?" I asked.

"A woman's intuition. I sense more between her and the manager than just the money. I'm going to replace her."

Interesting. It was obvious Nina intended to take more than just a two or three-day role as caretaker in Jorge's absence.

"Do you have someone in mind?" I asked.

Nina looked surprised. "Well, I haven't thought it all the way through yet. It won't be easy to find someone who is competent and who can live here on the ranch. The foreman seems to be good, and although he didn't say so directly he seemed relieved to find out Manuel is gone. He assured me there won't be any problems with the day-to-day operations and he manages most of them anyway. I got the impression Manuel was away a lot."

I watched Nina's face as she looked past me at the fire. I could see her mind was working overtime, and there were a lot of thoughts whirling around in that pretty head. Her life had been turned upside down in the last few days, and it wasn't just me. Her father's stated intention to emerge from his self-imposed exile was already having an affect on her, and she was too smart not to realize there would be more. At least she was of an age and maturity level that would allow her to deal with it

"I've arranged with the cook for an early dinner, Dex," she said, shifting gears. "I hope you don't mind, but I'm tired."

I certainly understood.

XII

I was right about the upstairs of the hacienda. The two doors to the right of the open area each led to a luxurious guest suite. A shared bathroom about half the size of each suite with an oversized whirlpool tub situated in a gable with a view out over the ranch separated the suites. Each bedroom had an oversized walk-in closet that made my valise look out of place, plus what I was beginning to believe was a Garcia trademark – a huge fireplace.

Dinner was simple compared to meals at the house in Bogota and it was a subdued affair as Nina was preoccupied with her own thoughts. It wasn't an unwelcome situation as I had a lot to think about as well. Nina asked me to take a walk with her while the dishes were being cleared. She took my arm and led me to the stables.

"Are you okay?" I asked.

She didn't answer.

"I understand the changes your father is making will affect you, Nina," I said. "I only wish I'd had the chance to adjust to adulthood while my father was still alive. You and Jorge have a wonderful opportunity ahead of you."

She let go of my arm, walked to one of the stalls and stood looking at the foal inside, facing away from me. Then she whirled around and I caught a glimpse of the tears streaking her cheeks before she ran past me and back to the hacienda.

XIII

Nina came to me at some point during the night, sliding silently under the sheets and then waking me with her soft caresses. We made love without speaking, gently and unhurried, and she left me again some time before dawn.

XIV

The light streaming through the windows woke me at sunrise and I went through to the bathroom. The door to Nina's suite was closed so I showered, dressed and went downstairs to find something to eat. The cook poured me a cup of coffee while chattering away in Spanish and then chased me out of the kitchen only to reappear ten minutes later with a big smile and a tray piled with covered platters of fried eggs, bacon, potatoes and toast.

'Norteamericano,' she said, standing and watching me eat, the smile never leaving her face. Not having the Spanish vocabulary to explain I don't usually have a large breakfast, I polished everything off and went back upstairs. Nina's door was still closed so I began to examine the pictures of the Garcia horses, the trophies and awards. And then the books.

Private libraries always remind me of my father, and this was no different. I chose a couple of books written in English, sat in a big chair by the fire and began to read, but I couldn't concentrate. I was restless and my mind kept jumping back and forth between what Jorge was doing, Felix' discovery of the photographer, the coin delivery tomorrow in Miami and Nina. Always back to Nina. But overlaying all of this was the ominous reality of the final confrontation with Niccolo Cardeli. Everything was in motion now, and it certainly looked like I would have my reckoning.

I thought back to those first seven months after my flight home to Cayman Brac, and those relatively few months before Cardeli burst into my life. The peace and contentment I'd found in father's little stone cottage surrounded by those who meant the most to me – Felix, Patricio and Catalina – seemed so far away now, like a dream. Curiously, my previous life in Key West held no more meaning for me other than to serve as a counterpoint to those months on Brac. If anything, my relentless but aimless fifteen-year pursuit of pleasure had simply established the capacity to appreciate fully the depth of what I'd experienced in those months, making more acute my sense of loss.

I couldn't help but wonder what Jorge was going through. In a way, his story was similar to mine. A family inheritance that allowed him the luxury to live in splendid isolation from the reality that surrounded him and then a sudden realization there was more to life. And with that, the recognition he was caught up in a dangerous political and social situation over which he had little control. I harbored some guilt for being the catalyst for Jorge's change in perspective, but rationalized it against the firm belief he had already known deep inside himself what he had to do. I decided any guilt I felt should be limited specifically to what he was doing for me, not for his decision to restore his family tradition of involvement in Colombia's affairs.

And that brought me back around to Nina, but not before she interrupted me herself.

"Hola, Dex," she said, coming up the staircase from the great room.

"Nina – I thought you were still asleep."

"Silly man. I've been up since before dawn going over the books again," she laughed, planting a kiss on my cheek. "And I was right about the administrator. She packed up her things and left some time during the night."

The sparkle was back in Nina's eyes, and in her smile.

"So that leaves you in the lurch. You now have no manager and no administrator."

"And no problem, relatively speaking," she said. "I've told the cook to prepare a picnic lunch. The horses are being saddled and you and I are going for a ride."

"Is that wise? I mean is it safe?"

"For your horse, or for you?" she laughed. "It will be a short ride, not far. I want to show you my secret place. Did you have anything better planned for today?"

As much as I felt the need to be doing something, there was nothing I could do. I had to wait for Jorge, the coins weren't due to be delivered to Cardeli until tomorrow and it seemed Bones and Felix had things under control at their end. I had to consider the possibility I was afraid of horses.

"No, I suppose not," I answered, trying to think of another way out of this.

"Let's go," she said, grabbing me by the arm and pulling me toward the stairs.

The horses were saddled and ready, with a leather satchel attached to the one Nina mounted. She was already riding away as I climbed onto the other horse, desperately trying to remember what little I knew of horseback riding from my days at military school. What I remembered most was having a sore ass.

To my surprise, I had nothing to do other than sit and maintain my balance. And maintaining balance wasn't even an issue as the horse seemed to glide along as if on rails. There was only the clatter of hooves and the gentle forward motion to remind me I was on a horse and it didn't take long before I was completely absorbed in the view. With all due respect to the breathtaking beauty of Colombia, it simply doesn't compete with the view presented by Nina's backside in her tight riding pants.

Once we were out of sight of the hacienda Nina slowed until I drew up alongside her.

"I miss this, Dex. It's so easy to get caught up in all the glitz of Miami."

"I feel the same about the open sea and Cayman Brac," I answered. "I suppose that a horse, a backpack and the mountains give the same freedom as a boat on the Caribbean."

We rode along in silence as Nina led the way up the middle of a shallow, meandering stream that cut between the mountains, forming a gorge. Before long I thought could hear water rushing, and as it grew louder I realized it was the sound of rapids or perhaps a waterfall. We rounded a turn in the stream and Nina stopped. As I rode up beside her I saw it.

The gorge along which we'd ridden opened into a small glen and the stream was flowing toward us from an oblong pool, perhaps thirty feet in length and half that at it's widest point, bounded on three sides by cliffs. But the most striking feature was the waterfall at the far end. It was a sparkling, silver ribbon that fell sixty or seventy feet before breaking the surface of the clear, dark pool.

Nina sat on her horse watching me while I took it all in.

"Isn't it beautiful, Dex? There is no place like it in the whole world," she said as she dismounted.

I had to agree. It was so private, and the only sound was the splash of the waterfall as it broke the surface. The late afternoon sunlight played on the cascading water at the eastern end. Nina began to laugh as she ran the sixty feet to the pool, shedding her clothes as she went.

"Come on, Dex," she yelled as she stopped to pull her boots off and then the rest of her clothes before diving cleanly into the pool. I wasn't far behind her, and she surfaced midway to the waterfall as I dove in. The shock of the cold water jolted me. I surfaced and quickly struck out after her.

Nina was an accomplished swimmer, and she was already climbing up onto a small ledge beside the waterfall when I caught up to her. I grabbed her by the ankle and pulled her, laughing, back into the pool. She surfaced immediately and wrapped her arms and legs around me, pressing her lips to mine and holding onto me until we sank slowly below the surface. She finally broke away, pushing herself backwards and up and I watched her surfacing before I kicked and came up, too.

We climbed onto the ledge and I could feel the reflected heat of the sun from the surface of the water and the rock wall behind us warming me. Nina took my hand and pulled me along the ledge and into a small grotto behind the waterfall.

"Look, Dex," she exclaimed.

The sunlight played through the falling sheet of water, dappling Nina's skin and highlighting her chestnut-colored hair. She took a step back and faced me, her arms spread wide to allow the sunlight to play on her body, watching me watching her.

"I told you this was a special place," she whispered, the sunlight reflecting deep in her dark eyes like diamonds set in coal. "Do you like it?"

I didn't know what to say. My senses were overloaded. It wasn't just the pool and the waterfall or the natural serenity and purity of the place; it was as if those were all just backdrops and that Nina herself was the jewel in the setting. I struggled to find something to say, but I didn't have the words. Any attempt to voice what I was feeling could never do justice to what she was sharing with me; what she was offering. I turned away from her and dove through the ribbon of water and swam back to the other end of the pool.

The satchel Nina had brought contained a towel and blanket as well as a bottle of wine and the picnic lunch. I spread out the blanket and then dried off and dressed before Nina emerged from behind the waterfall and swam back. I was busying myself unpacking the lunch when she walked up behind me and spoke.

"Dex? Is there something wrong with me?"

"No, Nina," I turned toward her. "There's absolutely nothing wrong with you. In fact, everything is right about you. There must be something wrong with me."

She hesitated briefly, then picked up the towel and went to gather her clothes from where she'd strewn them. I couldn't watch, and resumed laying out the lunch. I was opening the wine when she came back and sat on the blanket, wrapping her arms around her knees and staring out at the waterfall.

"We need to talk, Dex."

"I don't know what to say, Nina. I'm not very good at this."

She patted the ground beside her and I sat.

"Most men aren't, you know. The more important or stronger their emotions, the less they're able to talk about them. It's like they're afraid of saying something wrong or somehow showing their feelings. Women, on the other hand, tend to spill everything out whether the words match what they're really thinking or not."

She let that sink in.

"Are you afraid of me, Dex? Do you not find me attractive?"

That was easy to answer.

"Any man would find you attractive, Nina."

"Wait, Dex. I'm not interested in *any* man. I'm asking about you. Do you not find me attractive?"

I glanced at her before answering. "Yes, Nina. I find you attractive. Isn't that obvious?"

"Yes, the physical attraction is obvious. But is there something else about me you don't find appealing?"

"No. Not a thing. I already said there must be something wrong with me."

If I thought I could hide behind that statement, I was wrong. Nina was relentless.

"So what is wrong with you? What do you think it is?"

I continued to stare at the waterfall. I saw the way the ribbon of water twisted and turned on its fall from the top of the gorge, before plunging into the pool.

"I'm afraid, Nina. Everything I've ever cared about ends up being taken away."

"Taken away, or driven away?" she asked quietly. "There's a difference, you know."

"Both, I suppose. I've never thought of it that way."

"Do you care about me, Dex?"

"Yes."

"Do you realize you're driving me away?"

"Yes, I suppose I do. At least I do now."

"Is it Catalina?"

There. She said it, but I suddenly understood that wasn't all of it.

"I've accepted she's marrying someone else. I guess I just can't let go."

Nina put her hand on mine.

"Dex, if you could just let go then it wasn't real to begin with. I have a feeling that whatever you had with Catalina made you a much better person. You have to decide whether you are going to build on that or revert back to the person you once were. Or simply wallow in self-pity for the rest of your life," she said. "You don't have to forget how you felt about Catalina in order to go forward. I suspect she will be part of you forever." She squeezed my hand. "It's up to you to decide. I just don't want you to think I'm trying to displace Catalina, or that I can't accept what she meant to you."

I felt better somehow, but still couldn't find the words.

"I'm going to tell you something, Dex. And I don't want you to say anything. But I'm not running anymore, either. I love you."

We only sat a few more minutes before she got up and smiled at me. I should have felt awkward, but I didn't. I was simply puzzled at the sense of peace that came over me.

"Let's pack up and go back to the hacienda, Dex. Today has been perfect for me."

XV

As we rode closer to the hacienda I could see five vehicles pulled up in front; an old canvas-covered stake truck, three jeeps and a car. The ranch staff was gathered on the front porch guarded by about fifteen men with rifles. Nina rode straight to the house, bypassing the stables.

"Who are you?" she demanded.

"AUC, Señorita Garcia," answered a man who appeared to be in charge. "At your service."

"I doubt that," Nina said, dismounting. "What do you want here? And why are my people being held?"

"Please, Señorita. We mean you no harm. Where is your father?"

"What do you want with my father?"

The man in charge stepped down from the porch and walked toward Nina as I dismounted.

"Pedro," Nina called to one of the ranch hands on the porch, "take these horses to the stables and rub them down."

Pedro hesitated before moving, uncertain as to what to do.

"Let him go," the leader said. "Now where is your father?"

"He's in Bogota. You can deal with me. What is it you want?"

"His plane is not in Bogota, Señorita. Are you suggesting it is missing?"

"I'm not suggesting anything. I'm telling you that whatever it is you want, you will have to deal with me."

The man stared at Nina, and I stepped forward to stand beside her as Pedro took the horses to the stables.

"Let's go inside where we can talk," he said.

Nina whirled around and strode toward the stables. "If you want to talk to me it will be in the ranch office. The hacienda is private," she said over her shoulder as she walked. "And tell your men to put their guns away. I will not talk to you while you are holding my people."

As I walked with Nina I heard the man issue orders in Spanish and glanced back to see they were doing as she'd ordered. Nina never hesitated and never gave them the satisfaction of even indicating they might do otherwise. I remembered what she'd said about dealing with the bureaucrats at immigration but would not have believed she would display that attitude in this situation. When we reached the office she stepped aside and waited for the man to open the door for her.

Inside she turned on him again.

"What is it you want?"

The exchange switched to Spanish and went on for some time. It was a heated conversation and I sensed it ended with some type of agreement before switching back to English.

The man walked to the window and spoke while looking out at the paddock, his back to us. "And what is Señor Snell doing here?"

Nina raised her hand to signal me to be silent.

"He is my guest, and no concern of yours."

"But he told Capitán Luis Torrano in Bogota he was going to Cartagena, Barranquilla and Santa Marta. Why is here, outside Medellin?"

"I repeat," she said, "he is my guest. I do not need your permission to have guests at my ranch."

The man turned around and narrowed his eyes.

"Your ranch Señorita Garcia? Is Señor Garcia giving you the ranch?"

"You know exactly what I mean," she said, "and you have what you came for. Now leave."

The man walked forward and leaned across the desk. He spoke in Spanish and Nina went white before he turned and left the office. I heard him call to his men and the vehicles started shortly after. I walked over to the window and watched them leave, the car stopping to pick him up.

"Are you okay?" I asked.

Nina had tears in her eyes, and she was trembling.

"They will never break me. They are pigs."

She met me half way across the office and I wrapped my arms around her.

"I don't know everything that was said, but he knows you're one hell of a woman, Nina."

"Do you think so? He openly threatened my father at the end, Dex. He said it would be a shame for something to happen to him just because of me. He told me to go back to Miami."

"I don't think you left him much choice. You berated him in front of his men, and I was afraid it was all over right then. Did you know how dangerous that was?"

She turned her face up toward me.

"Dex, I didn't have any choice. And I wasn't just being brave, either. I was more afraid two hours ago," she said, her eyes going wide.

"Two hours ago?" I asked stupidly.

"Yes," she said, "two hours ago." She continued to stare at me, and when I didn't understand she stepped back and stamped her foot. "Damn you, Dexter Snell. When I told you I loved you."

"Oh, that," I answered. I held her stare long enough to watch the anger creep into her face, and then broke into a laugh and held my arms out to her again. "I think I might be in love, too," was all I could say.

XVI

The hacienda was buzzing when we walked in the front door. The cook and all of the household staff were there, plus the foreman and a few others. The men were holding their hats in their hands in respect.

The foreman stepped forward and began to speak to Nina. He was obviously the spokesperson and I gathered from his tone and the way he kept bowing his head that he was complimenting her. Nina said something in response, then offered her hand and kissed him on the cheek saying "Muchas gracias," and they all trooped out.

The cook chased the rest of the staff from the room by clapping her hands, then came over and gave Nina a big hug before heading for the kitchen.

"What was that all about?" I asked.

"It's a little embarrassing, Dex, particularly for the men. They wanted me to know how proud they are I am here and how I stood up to the AUC. They are also glad the manager and administrator are gone."

I smiled at Nina and thought about how frivolous she'd seemed when I first met her in the airport lounge in Mexico City two weeks ago. It seemed like a lifetime had passed since then.

"I'm proud of you too, Nina."

Her face lit up again. I have never met anyone whose face is so expressive. Not just her eyes and her smile, but her entire face.

"Come on," she said, "let's get ready for dinner."

We ate a casual meal in front of the fireplace in the great room as Nina explained the Spanish portion of what had happened in the ranch office. It seems the manager had told the AUC that Jorge, Nina and I were at the ranch, and that he'd been fired. The visit had been to ensure the monthly 'tax' payments to the AUC would continue.

Jorge and Nina had guessed right – the manager had been padding the payments and lining his own pockets. Nina figured less than half had been going to the AUC, and took a chance by telling him she was prepared to continue paying what had been paid previously, and named an amount that was forty percent of that shown in the books.

"Weren't you worried?" I asked.

Nina smiled and told me negotiating was in her blood. She knew right away she wasn't far off the mark, and the fact he settled relatively quickly told her the amount was enough in excess of what had actually seen its way to the AUC that the previous manager would be in trouble with the paramilitary. That, she explained, was her hope, ensuring he would have to leave Antioquia for his own safety and cause them no more trouble.

The condition Nina attached to the agreement was that one person only would make the monthly collection. There was never to be more than one AUC representative on the ranch at any time. I had a brief mental image of paramilitary commandos arguing over who would make the collection in the hope of catching a glimpse of Nina.

I was still troubled by the fact they knew so much about me but Nina said it was to be expected, that the police and military were rumored to be in collaboration with the paramilitary groups and this simply confirmed it. That I was suspected of being either a human rights activist or a drug smuggler – two opposite ends of the spectrum in my books – did little to ease my mind.

XVII

I was up early the next morning, anxious to confirm the coins had been delivered to Miami and anticipating we'd hear from Jorge. I called Mirtha's hotel in Jamaica just before noon and was put through to her room. She answered on the first ring.

"I was hoping it would be you," she gushed, "I just got off the phone with Niccolo. He got the package – he wants to talk to you directly. How much gold is there?"

"I don't know for sure. All I can assume is that there's a lot."

"Dex dear, I can't tell you how excited I am. Do you know what it's worth? Where did they come from? How old are they?"

I couldn't think of a reason to play it cute. The gold was obviously the key to accessing Cardeli directly and whatever I could do to stoke the fire of his greed would only bring me closer to my goal of a face-to-face meeting with him.

"Slow down, Mirtha, one question at a time. The value of the actual gold is minimal compared to the value of the coins themselves. They're called cobs and they date from around 1715. They're quite rare."

"You mean they're worth a lot more than if they were just melted down?"

The greed and ignorance sickened me.

"Yes, similar cobs sell for about three thousand each. It's possible these may be worth more because the story behind them is so interesting."

"I knew you would come through, Dex," she lied, "but I'm so lonely here. Can you sneak away for a few days and meet me?"

"No, Mirtha. I can't."

I resisted the urge to tell her what I really thought about her and her vicious husband.

"Can I come to wherever you are? Please?"

I closed my eyes, revolted by the thought of seeing her again. I fought to keep my voice under control and still keep her on my side.

"No. There's too much to do. Maybe once this is all over. Give me a phone number so I can call Niccolo."

I got the number and rang off. At least now I had a way to contact Cardeli directly. I paced back and forth for a few minutes composing myself before I dialed.

A woman answered the phone. I told her I needed to speak to Niccolo and to tell him it was Dex. He was on the line in seconds.

"How many of those do you have?" was the first thing he said.

"You have them all," I answered, "but I know where they came from."

"How many are there?"

I ran through the same information I'd just given Mirtha, and if anything Cardeli's voice indicated he was even greedier than his wife. There is something about gold that excites some people more than others and I judged Cardeli was at the extreme end of the scale.

"How do I know you aren't lying, or you don't intend to keep some of these for yourself?" he asked.

"Look, Niccolo, I'm not in a position to fork out over fifty thousand dollars for gold coins just to scam you. I know where those came from, and I intend to recover the rest. I have no idea how many there are, but you can have whatever I find. I'm more interested in making money from the other part of this deal."

Cardeli considered that.

"I want one of my people with you when you go for the rest of these."

I hadn't expected that, but should have. I mentally kicked myself for not thinking of it but was damned if I was going to ever let Cardeli get his filthy hands on my father's treasure.

"No good, Niccolo. I won't go for it. And besides, can you trust your own people with the gold?"

He was silent again, probably thinking as fast as I was.

"Listen to me, you bastard, and listen good," he finally said. "You're taking one hell of a risk here. If you don't come up with a pile of these cobs or whatever it is you call them, then I'm going to assume you cheated me. And what I did to your father will look like a birthday party compared to what I'll do to you."

I had no doubt he meant it, but at least he hadn't threatened Catalina and Patricio this time. Then he said something that told me I was on the right track.

"I don't want any of my people to know about the gold. Will it be on the boat with the other stuff?"

I took a chance.

"Yes."

"Then you make sure my people don't find out about it. When is the deal going down?"

"I don't know yet, but it's getting close. Do you want me to call Mirtha or you when I know?"

"Call Mirtha on that, but call just me as soon as you have the gold."

And then he hung up.

As with almost every call to Mirtha, I was physically and emotionally drained when it was over. It was worse this time, having spoken to Cardeli as well. At least I was a step closer to dealing directly with him which I reminded myself was my main objective. I went to the ranch office to look in on Nina.

"Any word from Jorge?"

"No, but he said he'd be two or three days, and he'd call if he was delayed. I'm not worried."

Her expression indicated otherwise, and it was another ten days before we heard from him.

XVIII

Nina was completely stressed when Jorge called on the twenty-fifth, and I wasn't doing much better. He assured us over a terrible phone connection that he was okay and would be at the ranch in another day or so. He wouldn't – or couldn't – provide any further details, but the call established he was alive.

I was also worried about Felix. I'd asked him to be in Trinidad by the twentieth, five days ago, and I had no way to get in touch with him. I'd called Bones every day to see if he'd heard anything, and he hadn't. Bones wasn't at all worried and I began to wonder if I was simply overwrought by Jorge's situation.

On the afternoon of the twenty-seventh we heard the sound of an approaching airplane. Nina recognized the plane before it landed and she ran toward the grass landing strip. The plane taxied halfway toward the hacienda before stopping. The pilot deplaned first and then helped Jorge climb out. He looked terrible.

He must have lost twenty-five pounds and his disheveled clothes hung on his emaciated frame. He had shaved, poorly, missing some spots and cutting himself in others and his left arm was in a sling. But the most striking change was in his eyes. The sparkle and luster were gone; his eyes looked dead.

Nina was crying before she reached the plane and he winced in pain as she threw her arms around him. I walked up and stood awkwardly as they embraced.

"Hola, Dex," he said. "Can you help me to the hacienda please?"

Jorge put his right arm over my shoulder. As he leaned against me and I put my left arm around his waist to support him I could feel his thinness through his clothes. It was a slow, painful walk to the house. I got him onto a leather couch while Nina ran to get him a brandy and tell the cook who was hovering in the doorway to prepare some food.

"Ah, that's so good," he said, taking a drink. Nina sat next to him.

"What happened to you father? Where have you been? Why didn't you call?"

Jorge turned his sad eyes toward Nina.

"A bit of foolishness, dear, that's all. I feel better already."

"I shouldn't have let you go alone," I said.

"No, this had nothing to do with your situation, Dex," he said, taking another drink.

"I'll send for a doctor, father."

"No, please Nina. I just need some rest and then we must leave here and go to Bogota tomorrow." He took another sip of his brandy. "It is not safe here."

"Yes it is," Nina said, "I made new arrangements with the AUC while you were gone. Please tell me what happened to you."

Jorge looked surprised.

"You made arrangements with the AUC?"

"Yes, but please tell me what happened to you first, then I'll explain."

Jorge managed a little smile, but there was still no spark in his eyes.

"I flew to Cali when I left here and made the necessary arrangements for Dex. It was quite simple, really, and led me to believe perhaps the situation in the outlying areas was not as desperate as I had thought. So I decided to see for myself, which was a mistake."

"You went into the mountains outside of Cali?" Nina asked.

"Yes, dear," he answered, "I know how stupid of me it was. I drove only about twenty miles before I came across a checkpoint. It looked so inept – two men and a decrepit old truck – and I did not handle it well. It was a FARC roadblock and there were more men on both sides of the road."

"They took you?" Nina asked.

"Yes, but only after I berated them for what they were doing. They took the jeep and I was forced to walk with two of them up into the mountains. We walked for a day and a half before we came to a primitive encampment where I was to be held until a zone commander could be summonsed, but there was some kind of fight on the third or fourth night and they moved me further up into the mountains."

"You could have been killed," Nina cried.

"Yes, I could have, but I was not. I could hear automatic rifle fire all around us as we made our way further up and then it gradually faded into the distance. They set up another camp. We were there for a few more days before word came I was to be moved again."

"Were you tied up?" Nina asked.

"Sometimes, but not all the time. There was another attack in the night, only this one caught my captors by surprise and I managed to escape in the confusion. I was stumbling down the mountains in what I thought was the direction of the road when I was found by part of the paramilitary squad that was after the FARC group who had been holding me."

"And they took you back to Cali?" Nina asked.

I took Jorge's empty glass to refill it as he continued.

"Not immediately. I was taken to a small ranch that seemed to be a temporary operations base and questioned. They were as bad as FARC, in some ways worse. At least the FARC people were able to spout Marxist rhetoric, as misguided as it was. These people have no political motivation at all other than to kill every person they could find who gets in the way of their cocaine operations or who is not against FARC."

"But surely they realized you had been held captive and weren't part of FARC?" I asked.

"That did not enter into it, Dex. I was somewhere I was not supposed to be. And according to their narrow view of the world since I was not there on business they had sanctioned, I was by default against them. My explanation that I simply wanted to see for myself what was happening only made it worse, implying I was going to form my own conclusions. They took me to Cali after a few more days. I was interrogated again before being turned over to the police. It was the same routine all over again with the police, only they let me call you and had a doctor look at me before they let me go."

"And your arm?" Nina asked.

"It is my shoulder. Torn ligaments. I fell when I was running down the mountain, away from FARC. I will have it looked at again when we fly back to Bogota first thing tomorrow."

Nina hugged him again, taking care not to put too much pressure on his left arm.

"I'm staying here," she said.

Jorge looked at Nina, and then at me.

"No, you are not. It is not safe here, and you are coming to Bogota where I can protect you."

Nina stood up and walked over to the fireplace before turning back to face him.

"I'm staying here. There is no manager and the administrator left with him. I've made a deal with the AUC for less than half of what was being taken out of here before, and I feel it's as safe as it can be given the situation in this country. I won't run and hide in Bogota."

"Ah, so that is it," Jorge said. "You are berating me for hiding in Bogota all these years."

Nina ran back to him and hugged him again, this time forgetting about his shoulder and he winced.

"That's not it, father. I would never do that to you. I just feel like I belong here."

"And not in Bogota?" he asked.

"I feel like I belong there, too. But not if I allow the AUC, FARC and the police to decide for me."

"And what do you think about this?" Jorge asked, turning his sad eyes on me.

"I understand your fears, Jorge, and I share them, too. But I also understand what Nina is trying to say to you, and quite frankly, I don't think there is anything either of us can do to change her mind. Or if we even have the right to try."

15 The Griffon: 2004 October

I called Bones the day after Jorge arrived back at the ranch and he confirmed Felix was in Trinidad. Felix had been as worried as I was, and had called Bones to find out if he knew anything about my whereabouts. Bones agreed to relay a message to Felix saying I'd be there in a few more days, but he seemed reluctant to hang up.

"Is something bothering you, Bones?"

"Yes. I don't know how to tell you this," he said.

My heart stopped.

"It's Uncle Patricio, isn't it? Is he all right?"

"He's okay, Dex, he called here last night. It's Catalina. She was married last Saturday. I'm sorry."

I closed my eyes and took a deep breath.

"I knew she was engaged, Bones. What did Patricio say?"

"He wanted to know if I knew where you were. I told him I didn't, Dex, but that I'd pass along a message if I heard from you. Then he told me about Catalina."

"Anything else?"

"Yes. He asked me to tell you that he still loves you, and to be careful. He said he never told your father that and he's regretted it ever since."

I felt the tears coming to my eyes.

"Bones, if this turns out badly and I don't get a chance, will you tell him that I love him, too?"

"I won't have to, Dex. You'll tell him yourself. I just know it."

I thanked him and hung up.

It took me a few minutes to compose myself and then I set about cleaning up the details with Jorge.

Jorge and Nina reached an uneasy truce over her staying at the farm and in the end Jorge decided to stay, too. A doctor was flown in from Medellin and advised Jorge to take it easy for a few weeks before beginning to exercise his arm and shoulder.

We reviewed the arrangements Jorge had made for the cocaine buy and agreed on a code we could use over the telephone to set up the actual delivery once I'd retrieved the gold from the *Griffon*. Nina was fully involved in the planning and contributed more than Jorge, a situation I attributed to the lingering effects of his ordeal at the hands of the AUC, FARC and the police.

I worried that Nina might hold me responsible for what had happened to her father but it never came up. If anything, she seemed more upset at his naiveté and with concern over what I was about to do. It was a tearful parting and she promised to meet me in Cayman Brac when it was all over. I pushed aside the sense of foreboding that overtook me and presented the most positive attitude possible.

II

Jorge's plane took me to Trinidad and I cleared entry formalities without a hitch. I grabbed the first taxi and spotted the *Estrela* as soon as we entered the boatyard, tied up to a pier close to the fuel dock with her stern toward land. The name had been changed as I'd asked, and she was now identified as the *Pelican*, home port Santo Domingo. It looked strange painted on the stern, and I wondered what my father would think. Despite the name change she would always be the *Estrela* to me.

Felix spotted me climbing out of the taxi and ran down the pier, almost knocking me off my feet as he rushed to embrace me.

"Man, you're a sight for sore eyes. I've been worried sick," he said.

We boarded and once safely distanced from prying eyes and out of earshot of the people on the pier immediately got down to business.

"Any problems so far?" I asked.

There were some minor complications obtaining fake registry papers for the *Estrela* that now identified her as the *Pelican*, registered in the Dominican Republic, but Felix had resolved them quickly with cash. He'd fitted the false bottom in the fish hold himself and everything else was ready to go. I was itching to be at sea so Felix went to clear up the account at the boatyard office while I prepared to depart.

I did an engine room check, dipped the fuel tanks and started the engine before finding the charts we'd need and plotting the route. The first leg, 467 miles west along the coast of Venezuela from Port of Spain, Trinidad to Curaçao, would take us just over 45 hours. We had four thousand gallons of diesel fuel and the trip to Curaçao would consume only 370 gallons. I made a note of that along with minor course changes, their positions and time estimates. Once we were approaching Curaçao we could decide whether to pull in or continue straight on to the *Griffon* – another two hundred miles.

Felix stepped into the wheelhouse and declared we were ready, so I went and untied the lines. We cleared the harbor and Felix and I began to fill each other in on the details of what had happened over the last four weeks. Felix' story of how he'd come across the photographer and the details of his interrogation technique would have been amusing if not for the fear we'd felt about being spied on. As it turned out, Felix was convinced the photographer himself posed no real threat to us other than he'd been watching us and reporting back to Cardeli.

We were fifteen miles from the harbor and talking about what had happened in Colombia when the VHF radio crackled into life.

"*Estrela de Marques, Estrela de Marques, Estrela de Marques.* This is the *Mariel*, over."

Felix and I stared at each other in shock. No one should even know we were here other than as aboard the renamed *Pelican*, let alone the *Estrela*.

The call came in again as I looked around, trying to see if I could spot a boat named the *Mariel*.

"*Estrela de Marques, Estrela de Marques, Estrela de Marques.* This is the *Mariel*, over."

I spotted a boat off our portside, roughly astern of us and grabbed the binoculars for a closer look. It was a steel shrimper, much larger than the *Estrela* but about the same age. It had an elevated wheelhouse and was painted in similar colors to our boat.

Because of the position of the shrimper relative to us I couldn't see the name but as it quartered astern of us it obviously saw ours, and the radio came alive again.

"*Pelican, Pelican, Pelican,* this is the *Mariel*, over."

I answered the call this time, identifying us as the *Pelican* and requesting a switch to a working channel.

"*Pelican,* this the *Mariel*, over."

"*Mariel,* this is the *Pelican*," I answered. "Go ahead."

"*Pelican,* I thought I recognized the lines of your boat. Do you know if it was ever named *Estrela de Marques*? Over."

My mind was racing. Whoever was at the helm of the *Mariel* and recognized the *Estrela* at a distance might become suspicious if we tried to put him off and denied any knowledge of the *Pelican's* previous name.

"Yes, *Mariel.* This boat was previously the *Estrela de Marques*, over."

"I thought the *Estrela* was in Cayman Brac. I see your home port is Santo Domingo, over."

This was too close for comfort.

"I don't like this, Dex," Felix said, echoing my own unspoken concern. "And I don't like the way he's swung around and is coming up on us."

The captain of the *Mariel* had turned to follow directly in our wake, and was making about two miles an hour more than our ten. He would be on us in a few minutes.

"Remember when we were here with Jebediah in '84?" Felix asked.

The same thought had crossed my mind. It was like a flashback, with father meeting the Marques Snell boats and carefully rendezvousing with them while Felix and I stood watch aboard the *Estrela* with the rifles.

"The rifles are in the hidden cabinet there behind the cabin bulkhead," Felix said.

It was the same cabinet we'd used in 1984 and I went and took out a rifle, shotgun and my pistol. I stuffed the pistol in back of my khakis under my shirt and after checking the rifle and shotgun to be sure they were loaded propped them in the corner where we could get at them quickly.

I thumbed the mike and answered the *Mariel*.

"Please stand away, *Mariel*. Do not come any closer, over."

There was no answer, and we watched nervously as the *Mariel* continued to close on us before swinging a few degrees to her port and crossing our wake, clearly intent on coming up on us.

"*Pelican*, will you back down and launch your dinghy? I'd like to meet you half way, over."

"This is weird," Felix said. "It's just like it was twenty years ago. What do you want to do?"

My curiosity, or maybe it was my stupidity, outweighed my desire to run but if it was the *Mariel's* intent to run us down she had the size and speed to do it.

"Back down, Felix. Same drill as father put us through. I'll launch and meet with him while you stand watch."

I scanned the *Mariel* again with the binoculars and saw only two crewmen on deck. The size of her dictated there were more, and I had to assume they were armed and standing watch in the same way we intended. I took one of the handheld radios with me and launched the dinghy but waited to set off until I saw there was only one person approaching in the other boat.

The man in the other boat was in his mid to late forties with long, graying hair and a walrus moustache that drooped down over his mouth. His weather-beaten face framed a pair of cold, gray eyes that squinted in the sunlight reflecting from the sea. He wasn't a large man judging from what I could tell from his seated position, but was stringy with clearly defined muscles in his arms and neck. He wore a dirty, light blue t-shirt with the word '*Mariel*' stenciled on the left breast.

'Ahoy, captain,' he called as we both slowed and then shut down our engines. "I'm Justin, owner of the *Mariel*."

"What do you want?" I asked.

He looked at me through his squinty eyes as if he was deciding whether or not to answer me. "I wanted to meet whoever owns the *Pelican*," he answered. "Do you know the previous owner?"

"Yes. Do you know him?"

"No, but I knew the owner before him. He was a shrimper out of the Florida Keys and Cayman Brac. The last I'd heard, the *Estrela* was still in Brac."

It was eerie, sitting in a dinghy in the Caribbean verbally fencing with someone who had some degree of knowledge about my father and the *Estrela*. I wasn't sure how to proceed.

"Not very talkative, are you?" he said.

"Mister, I don't know who you are and I'm still not sure about your intentions. My partner and I are simply cruising the Caribbean, doing some diving and exploring. You must know we can't be too careful here."

"I'm well aware of that. I'm just curious about the history of the *Estrela* since I last saw her in '85. Like I said, I heard she belonged to a man in Cayman Brac. An Englishman," he said casually.

I wondered why he added that bit about the Englishman. If he was trying to put me at ease he just blew it. Felix could never be described as an Englishman.

"That's bullshit, mister. The owner on Brac was not an Englishman." Justin didn't bat an eye.

"I assume there's someone on the *Pelican* with me in the sights of his rifle," he said. "Just like you're in the sights of a rifle from the *Mariel*. I suggest we cut the shit. What was the name of the man who owned that boat before Felix Smith?"

"Jebediah Snell," I answered.

He was surprised.

"Maybe I misjudged you. I worked for Jebediah a long time ago. What was the name of his company?" he asked.

"Marques Snell."

He kept his eyes on me. If he thought I was going to add anything he was mistaken, but I was genuinely curious as to what this was all about. And how did he know Felix' name? He obviously knew the *Estrela* and my father, but I was not prepared to make any assumptions as to his intent or accept his explanation at face value.

"I told you my name," he said. "It's only polite to let me know who I'm talking to."

"Dex," I answered.

"Dexter Snell?" he exploded. "I'll be damned. Your father talked about you all the time. He used to tell all his captains that his son Dex was a better captain at the age of six than any of us would ever be," he laughed. "I should have known somehow. And I suppose that's Felix Smith aboard the *Pelican*?"

I was completely off balance. This was a little too much to handle, given what we were up to and our attempts to disguise who we were.

"Look," Justin said, "I understand why you're being so cautious, and you should be in these waters. With your permission I'd like to go back to the *Mariel* and tell my men to stand down, then come back alone to the *Pelican* or *Estrela* or whatever it is you want to call her. You'll have me at a disadvantage, which should tell you something."

I couldn't see what harm that would do. It was the only thing that would make me feel easier than if we hadn't come across each other in the first place.

"Okay Justin. I'll see you in a few minutes. And don't think about bringing a weapon."

Justin laughed as he pulled the rope to start his outboard.

"Just like your old man," he yelled at me as he headed back to the *Mariel*.

Felix waited at the wheelhouse door, rifle in hand, until I made fast to the stern and climbed aboard. I told him about the exchange and he felt the same way I did; nervous and cautious, but curious.

We watched the *Mariel* and Justin was soon heading back toward us in the dinghy while his trawler turned and moved further away from us. He was going out of his way to remove any threat.

We settled in the wheelhouse to talk but before we did Justin walked around looking at everything. He seemed familiar with the boat and stood at the wheel for a few minutes before taking a seat at the chart table.

"I owe your father a great debt," he started. "How much do you know about what happened to the Marques Snell fleet?"

"Not much. I just know the boats were all sold at my father's insistence and over the objections of my uncle."

"Would that have been Jebediah's partner Patricio Marques?"

"Yes, that's him. Did you know him, too?"

"No, I wouldn't say that. I never met him but Jebediah talked about Patricio almost as much as he talked about you. He must have been quite a man."

"Still is," I said to Justin's surprise. "He's ninety-eight this year and still sharp. What do you know about the sale of the boats?"

"Well, it was a messy situation. Jebediah found out some of the captains were running drugs aboard the Marques Snell boats and he had no way to stop it. It had gotten too out of hand by the time he realized what was going on, and all I can figure is that he decided the best way to extricate Marques Snell was to sell the boats. That was in 1984, and he made a run down through the Caribbean and met with almost all of us one at a time, much as you and I did today."

I looked at Felix and he nodded at me.

"We were aboard the *Estrela* when that happened," I said.

"I thought so. I knew he had someone aboard, or he wouldn't have insisted on meeting that way. He didn't even mention the drug running, just said the boats were being sold and each captain had ninety days to come up with the money if he wanted to buy. Every single captain took him up on it, and I guess it didn't surprise him that some – most – had the money immediately. Those were obviously the ones involved in the drug smuggling. The rest of us had a tougher time of it."

"But you obviously came up with the money," I said.

"Not really. At least not with all of it, and not within the ninety days," he said. "And that's why I owe a debt to your father. The captains who couldn't come up with the money were offered extended terms and a lower price. In my case, he sold me the boat for well below its true value and financed it for me on nothing more than a handshake and a promise to never smuggle drugs. I sent payments to his bank in the Cayman Islands for another three years after his death until I'd paid what I owed. I heard he personally gave Marques Snell the full price for the boat out of his own pocket before he sold it to me for what I could afford. And I know I'm not the only one he did that for."

That explained the comment Uncle Patricio had made about the payments flowing through father's bank account. Payments he'd mistakenly thought were proceeds from drug smuggling.

"What happened after that trip in 1984?" I asked.

"I don't know all the details, but Jebediah spent a lot of time down here on this boat, alone. He would see me once in a while, but he wouldn't talk about anything other than how I was doing. I later figured out that it was to protect me from any fallout resulting from information he was passing to the U.S. government about the movement of the boats involved in the smuggling ring. The ring was completely busted up in 1985, and I heard there was a price – a big price – on Jebediah's head."

Justin looked out the wheelhouse window.

"A few of us got together after he was killed and talked about how to get even for him, but other than talk it's never amounted to much."

"Do you know who did it?" I asked.

"Yes, at least we think we do. An Italian who lives in Miami. Niccolo Cardeli."

"Why didn't you go to the authorities?" I asked.

Justin laughed. "A bunch of shrimp fisherman who at best manage to stay on the right side of the law only about half the time? Up against a millionaire drug dealer in Miami? Don't make me laugh."

I digested that and had to agree it would have been futile.

"Then why didn't you come to me with that information?"

Justin stared at me for a long time, and I felt his cold, gray eyes penetrating mine.

"By the time you were old enough and we knew where you were we also heard about your high living ways. You would have pissed on us from the deck of that fancy yacht of yours. Someone who knew you in Key West said that other than as a target to draw Cardeli out and someone to have a hell of a good time with, you were as useless as a rubber crutch."

That hurt, but I was way past the point of being shocked or insulted at my well-deserved reputation.

"Pretty blunt, aren't you," I said.

"Yep. Jebediah said he liked that. Sort of inspired me to greater heights of bluntness, if there is such a word."

"Who was it knew me in Key West?" I asked.

"I think if they'd wanted you to know then they'd have told you themselves," he answered.

"How do we know who the hell you are and even if you weren't one of the drug smugglers?" Felix interjected.

"You don't," he said, turning to face Felix. "But I'm telling you there are lot of us out here who'd avenge Jebediah's murder if we could. Maybe the flame doesn't burn as hot as it once did, but the embers are glowing. We still refer to ourselves as 'Jebediah's Boys' and I'm not even sure if there's any one of us who knows who everybody is, but one way or another if you were a friend of Jebediah's you can find another friend in any port in the Caribbean."

He let that sink in. "Now, do you mind telling me what you're doing here aboard the *Estrela* instead of your fancy yacht? And how you have the goddam nerve to rename her?"

I watched Felix struggling to control himself and once again realized how lucky I was to have such a loyal friend. And how my father had earned and deserved every one of his.

"I don't have a fancy yacht anymore," I answered him. "Except for my father's cottage on Cayman Brac I pissed it all away. And Felix was kind enough to offer to retrace the voyage we made with my father in 1984."

Justin's eyes narrowed.

"Why the name change?" he asked.

"Let's just say that even as kids in 1984 we knew there was something going on down here and we felt it would be smarter to rename the *Estrela* before we set out. We're just noodling around, rekindling memories."

Justin continued to stare at me, and then stood up.

"Have it your way, mister. But I know bullshit when I hear it and that's quite a load you're hauling," he said, leaving the wheelhouse.

We followed him out and helped him cast off. He traveled about a hundred yards before he turned his dinghy around and came back, shutting down his engine and coasting up close.

"Whatever is it you're up to – and I know you're up to something – be careful," he warned before restarting his outboard and heading back to the *Mariel*.

III

After allowing for the time we'd spent with Justin, we made Curaçao right on schedule and decided to go directly on to search for the *Griffon*. It wasn't a difficult decision since the boat was running perfectly, we had plenty of provisions and enough fuel to cruise all the way around the Caribbean a few more times. Besides, we were both anxious to begin the search.

Justin's comments about me upset Felix until I reminded him what he'd said himself shortly after I'd reappeared on Brac after all those years. That calmed him a bit, but he still held the opinion that Justin, a stranger, had a lot of nerve.

The new information answered the remaining questions about my father and the cocaine trade. It explained the payments flowing through his accounts and added another piece of lore about my father to my growing collection. The reference to 'Jebediah's Boys', though, stung me as much as it pleased me. The fact that so many people had positive memories and feelings about him was the nice part; the fact I was

Jebediah's only son – that I knew of – and was not part of that group, hurt.

I wondered just how many people in the Caribbean knew or knew of my father. It seemed I kept stumbling across them without really trying. I could understand finding people like Bones on Cayman Brac but Peter Jones and now this Justin character were a little further off the beaten path. And Justin said there were more. He said there was someone in virtually every port in the Caribbean, which may have been an exaggeration but I was certainly starting to wonder. In his own way, my father may have been almost as well known in his own time as Sir Henry Morgan was in his.

It was another four hundred miles to our search site and I plugged the coordinates of the course legs into the chartplotter and switched on the autopilot. I was becoming fairly adept at using the electronics and kept finding new features every time I used them. The radar was straightforward and the only limitation was the relatively low mounting height of the beater bar on the aluminum mast affixed to the roof of the wheelhouse. The curvature of the earth is such that the distance to the horizon from that point was only about twelve miles, even though the theoretical range of the unit was upwards of forty miles. In order to detect anything beyond that twelve-mile horizon, the object had to be of a size that extended above the horizon. Thunderheads, for instance, were easy to pick up at a distance beyond twelve miles because of their elevation.

I was curious about the arrival alert feature that Peter Jones had wired to a remote speaker and I set it to sound when we reached the end of the first leg. Sure enough, it sounded right at the point we needed to alter course. The remote speaker was still connected to the main unit, its fifty feet of wire coiled behind the chartplotter. I thought again about mounting it on the work deck but decided to leave it for the time being.

Felix had brought a file folder of information on yacht piracy in Venezuelan and Colombian waters Bones had run off the internet and time and again there were warnings based on documented evidence of solo boats being boarded and robbed. Traveling in groups and avoiding remote anchorages at night, options not available to us, apparently afforded the best protection. We decided that whenever possible we would keep moving at night with one of us constantly watching the radar to avoid being surprised by approaching vessels of any size.

We passed Aruba in the night much as we'd done twenty years earlier and I mused about Sir Henry Morgan's exploits at Maracaibo, which now lay south of us. It was the Maracaibo tale that had gotten me into trouble at military school and even though it seemed a lifetime ago it simply emphasized that my father's spirit lived everywhere in the Caribbean.

The boat was on autopilot, which does not relieve the helmsman of keeping a close watch. But it did allow me to pull the chart of the area of our intended search and plot a grid on a piece of plain white paper. The center of the grid was our target location expressed in the latitude and longitude Felix and I remembered. That point had been established by Loran, the best navigation device available at the time, but I knew the chance of the Loran-generated coordinates matching up exactly with the more accurate GPS-generated coordinates was remote. It would therefore be necessary to start with our GPS position, adjust it for what we could recall about visible landmarks, and then work an underwater grid search from there. My plan was to anchor the *Pelican* at the center point and do a circular dive within underwater sight of the boat hull and then reposition the boat to the next grid point. We would repeat the process until we found the remains of the *Griffon*. From my research – Bones' research – we knew that at most we would find a pile of ballast stones. Any wood would have rotted away or been eaten by teredo worms, the termites of the sea, long ago. It was simply a matter of luck. And if that failed, perseverance.

IV

We reached our target position on the fifth of October and by rights should have checked into a port of entry since we were now in Colombian waters. We weighed the risks of alerting government officials to our presence and decided to find the *Griffon* and secure the gold in the hidden saddle tank compartments before heading for a port.

I explained to Felix the discrepancy between Loran and GPS coordinates and we reviewed the other information at hand. The landmarks had not been clearly visible during the squall twenty years earlier, but father had asked us to visualize them as marked on the chart. We soon found that didn't help, as it simply told us we were in the right general vicinity. The one thing we did decide was not to search any areas deeper than forty feet since father had been free diving.

We hauled the tanks and other gear up onto the work deck and I made the first dive. It took over twenty minutes to swim a circle around the boat and I didn't spot anything. I surfaced and climbed into the dinghy while Felix moved the *Estrela* to the next point on the grid. While we were moving I estimated that with repositioning the boat and all of the associated tasks we could make about ten dives a day. Given the area covered by each dive and the overlap needed to make sure we didn't miss anything a quick guess told me it could take somewhere between twelve and sixteen days if our starting point was only a quarter mile off target. I looked around me. A quarter of a mile didn't seem like much; it could easily be more, and my spirits sank.

When Felix stopped to anchor at the next grid point I took off my dive gear and climbed from the dinghy onto the *Estrela*.

"What's wrong?" he asked. "Am I in the wrong spot?"

"No, you're not. This isn't going to work. I just figured it could take us sixteen days if we're only a quarter mile out and we have to allow for the recovery of the cobs after we find the *Griffon*. We don't have that much time. There has to be a better way."

Felix followed me into the wheelhouse and I sat back down with a pencil and paper. I drew out a new grid half a mile square. With our starting point in the middle, it gave us the quarter mile to each side. I quickly saw the problem of searching the area with circular dives was that the dives had to overlap in order to get the coverage. It was a waste of time.

I started to draw lines through the square, and the answer hit me. I felt stupid.

"Look, Felix. If we do the search in straight lines, we can cut the time down."

I scribbled away on the paper trying to remember my geometry lessons. From the surface it was roughly forty feet to the bottom. With visibility of a hundred feet, I drew a right-angled triangle and then it hit me.

"The square on the hypotenuse," I mused aloud.

"What?"

I laughed. "The square on the hypotenuse is equal to the sums of the squares of the other two sides. That means we can see about a hundred and eighty feet of bottom from a point on the surface."

"Damn Dex, I'm glad I'm not the one figuring this out. Geometry wasn't my strong suit."

I quickly calculated it would take fifteen passes of a half-mile each to cover the grid. "How fast do you think we can go being dragged behind the boat?" I asked Felix, sitting back.

"Maybe a mile an hour?" he answered. "Without losing the dive mask."

"That's what I guessed, too. It'll take seven and a half hours without rest breaks. Let's say a day to search a half-mile block."

I felt better again.

"We'll need to use the *Estrela*," I said. "That way we can use the GPS and autopilot to hold the pattern. It's bound to wander a bit at slow speed but we'll have to live with it."

The day was half over by the time we had everything sorted out. Calculating and entering all the coordinates took the most time and I was frustrated long before I dropped over the side with mask, snorkel and flippers. Slowing the *Estrela* to a mile an hour was also a challenge we solved by dragging a small sea anchor that resembles a parachute.

We made four passes, alternating at the end of every other pass to change places. Then I noticed the blip on the radar screen. It appeared to be another boat ten miles to the east of us, and it wasn't moving. I pointed it out to Felix when he climbed aboard and he suggested it might be a fishing boat.

We waited for an hour watching the screen and decided to move away from our grid location and see what happened. The other boat sat until we'd moved two miles and then began to follow us, closing the gap to ten miles again. We continued for another hour and then stopped and watched the blip continue toward us and then it stopped again, too.

"That's not a coincidence," I said, and Felix agreed.

It's a strange feeling to be out on the sea, in the middle of nothingness, and know you're being watched. Even if it's just electrons bouncing back and forth between green-screened devices there's a sense of intrusion. Eventually the sense turned to one of violation as we were drawn back to the screen time and again to see if the blip was still there. It always was. And then so were the signs of a storm gathering off to the northeast.

We decided to head back eastward toward the boat that was watching us.

"Let's see what happens when we turn the tables," I said.

We made two miles before the other boat began to move away from us. It was now clear that whoever it was wanted to keep us in radar range, but didn't want to make physical contact. At least not yet.

The thunderheads were now clearly visible and we changed course back to the west. It was another ten minutes before we realized the other boat was no longer following us. It was headed eastward and soon disappeared from our screen.

The sun set as we realized the thunderheads too were disappearing. Perhaps it was a harbinger of better luck to come.

V

We were at it again at first light and covered our original grid by noon with no success. We decided to expand our grid by running square patterns around the perimeter so the search area increased around our original target point rather than take a chance on starting an entirely new grid. Felix laid out a cold lunch of sliced meat, cheese and bread while I entered the new coordinates.

Around mid afternoon I spotted what looked like a pile of rubble well off to the right. It wasn't the first time I'd seen something, so I didn't get my hopes up. I dropped the towline and snorkeled along the surface toward it.

As I swam closer I felt my excitement building. There was not just a pile of rubble, but something else positioned on top of it. It looked like a triangle.

When I was almost directly above it I recognized what it was. I tore off my mask and waved my arms frantically over my head while treading water. Felix had already turned the boat to come around and pick me up again as he had so many times before after a false alarm, and saw me waving. He drew to within twenty feet and emerged from the wheelhouse.

"Drop the anchor," I yelled, swimming toward the *Estrela*. "This is it, Felix. Get out the tanks!" We both donned diving gear and jumped over the side. The depth sounder showed thirty-two feet, and the visibility was excellent.

The triangle on top of the rubble was a pair of shrimp doors. They were pulled together to form a tent shape that was unmistakably intentional, left as a marker. Small, brilliantly colored fish swam around them and in and out of the openings between the stones that made up the rubble. The doors and the stones were well encrusted with marine growth and if not for the shrimp doors positioned as they were it would have been easy to miss the stones. They were scattered about and although they were recognizable once the doors drew attention to them, they were unremarkable otherwise.

I don't know what I was expecting, but it dawned on me this wasn't a simple case of diving down and recovering some old treasure chests holding gold coins. In fact, I didn't even know how to begin. I swam over the rubble looking for something – anything – that looked different. Nothing stood out. I overturned some of the stones and out of the corner of my mask saw Felix doing the same thing.

The stones were actually spread over a large area, which didn't make sense to me. The ballast stones should be in a pile where they would have settled as the wooden hull of the *Griffon* rotted away over the centuries. Perhaps the hull had been spilt open somehow and the ballast was dropped as the *Griffon* was driven, sinking, by a storm.

I swam around the area and realized that explanation didn't make sense, either. If the stones had been dropped from a storm-driven vessel then they would be laying in an elongated pattern, and this was more circular. I signaled to Felix to surface.

Disappointment showed on Felix' face as we clambered aboard the *Estrela* and stripped off our gear.

"Maybe this isn't it, Dex," he said.

"It's it. Those shrimp doors didn't get there by themselves."

I took a quick look around to make sure there were no unwanted visitors and then went inside to check the radar. It was clear.

I was standing at the wheel of the *Estrela*, gripping the stained oak spindles when Felix came in. He didn't say a word, turning around quickly to leave me with my thoughts.

It was just over twenty years since we'd last been in this exact spot with my father, and he'd stood with his hands on this very wheel after his second dive before we headed toward Cartagena. And then he'd come back here again, who knows how many times, in the year before his death.

I made my way back to the work deck and found Felix setting up another set of tanks.

"Are you okay?" he asked.

I sat down on the transom and looked out over the sea. Why did father make so many trips here and only recover twenty cobs? It didn't make sense to me.

"Yeah, I'm okay. Just a little puzzled," I answered.

"I think you should go down again, Dex. I'll stay up here and keep watch. If a boat shows up on the radar I'll shut the engine down as a signal for you to surface."

I couldn't think of anything better to do, so I dove again. This time I concentrated on the shrimp doors.

The doors had clearly been arranged leaning against each other in a tent shape. They would not have ended up that way by chance after fouling on the ballast stones. As I looked them over I noticed there seemed to be stones piled up beneath them in a conical arrangement. I also saw something hanging down between the doors over the cone and reached in to see if it was just seaweed.

It was a wire of some kind, attached to the top of one of the doors. And there was a round disc at the end of the wire. I pulled the wire loose and surfaced with it.

The wire must have been stainless or it would have corroded and broken long ago. I went to the toolbox and retrieved a stiff-bristled brush to clean off the disc. It was the medallion father used to wear around his neck on a leather thong, the one he'd threatened to garrote Colonel Jamieson with so many years ago. The medallion removed any doubt that father had arranged those doors.

I yelled to Felix and when he came running from the wheelhouse I tossed the medallion to him.

"It's your father's!" he exclaimed. "Where was it?"

"Attached to the shrimp doors. I want to lift those doors back aboard the *Estrela*. Help me get the cable over the transom."

Felix started the winch and I positioned the boom over the back of the boat. When there was enough cable I jumped in and dove down again, fashioning a loop through the apex of the doors and then resurfacing to signal Felix to hoist them. The doors broke the surface and hung precariously as Felix swung them over the work deck. As he began to lower them to the deck they broke apart and fell with a crash, splintering into rotten pieces.

I climbed aboard and we went over the pieces for almost an hour before conceding they could tell us nothing. Something was still playing in the back of my mind. It was the way the ballast stones were spread in a circular pattern.

"Felix, I'm going down again. I need a net attached to the cable this time."

"What is it? Is there something else?"

"It's the damned stones. If the *Griffon* broke up while being driven by a storm the stones should be spread along the path it followed until it sank."

"That makes sense," Felix said. "But if it sank in one piece, then they wouldn't be. It must have sunk more or less intact."

"If that was the case," I said, "then the stones would be in a large pile roughly the length of the hull. And they aren't. They're spread out in a circle, an oval actually."

Felix thought about it, nodding his head.

"Then they've been moved, like someone set them aside to search under them. Jebediah already searched here, didn't he?" he asked, the smile leaving his face again.

"I think so. In fact, I'm certain. If the gold was here, then he recovered it. I just don't know why he left those clues to bring us back."

I dove down again and concentrated on the area that had been covered by the shrimp doors. I began to fill the net with stones from the conical pile, intending to move them out of the way and work down to the bottom. The exertion increased my air consumption and as it became harder to breathe I pulled the reserve lever and surfaced to change tanks.

While I went below to get a fresh tank I heard the winch start and assumed Felix was lifting the net to drop the stones away from where I was working. Then there was a huge crash and I scrambled up from the storage locker to find Felix standing sheepishly amid a pile of ballast stones on the work deck.

"I hauled the stones aboard, and the net broke," he said. "I don't know what I was thinking."

I looked at the pile of stones scattered about the deck and felt a huge wave of relief sweep over me. Some of them had been split apart by the force of hitting the steel deck and it was a wonder Felix hadn't been injured. As I looked closer at the pile something caught my eye, and I sat and down and started to laugh. I couldn't stop, and kept at it until the tears rolled down my cheeks.

"I could have been hurt, you know," Felix complained.

I was of course relieved he wasn't, but that's not why I was laughing.

"We're out of here, Felix," I managed to say between laughs. "Father beat us to the gold. Let's get the cocaine and finish this thing."

Felix started to laugh too, thinking we'd been tricked.

I knew better.

VI

We cleared customs and immigration in Barranquilla, but not until after we'd been thoroughly searched.

Felix had hidden our weapons in one of the saddle tanks along with my Cayman Islands documents. I used the American passport Felix had brought along for me. There was no way to reference that passport to the Cayman documents I'd used to enter Colombia four weeks ago so as far as the local authorities were concerned this was the first time I'd ever entered their country.

The cell phone Jorge had given me showed a signal and I used it to call the ranch while Felix went to find fresh fruit and vegetables. I got through to the ranch office and asked for Jorge. I was put on hold, and then Nina came on the line.

"Dex, thank god you called," she burst out.

"What is it?"

"It's my father. He's missing again. He's been gone for three days, and I can't get hold of him. I'm worried sick."

"Slow down," I said. "Start from the beginning."

"I don't know him anymore, Dex, he's become a complete stranger. All he could talk about after you left was the years of hiding in the house in Bogota. He got drunk and said so many stupid, awful things. We had a huge fight and when I woke in the morning there was just a note saying he'd gone to Arauca."

"Where? Arauca?"

"Yes. It's one of the most dangerous places he could go - all of the factions are fighting there. He just took the plane and left."

"Did he say why, Nina? Anything to do with me?"

"No, it has nothing to do with you. It's like he's determined to prove to himself he's not afraid. It's as if he thinks I'm looking down on him since he found out I stood my ground against the AUC. I'm worried sick, Dex."

I thought back to the first time I met Jorge and how much pleasure he took from his role of father-protector to Nina's innocent naïveté. It was as if their roles were now reversed, without the pleasurable part.

"Have you called your brother?"

"No. I'm not going to call him until I know more. He's too much like my father and he'll just get in the way. He'll want to call the police."

I got an uneasy feeling in the pit of my stomach.

"What are you planning to do?"

"I'm meeting with the AUC commander in an hour. The one who was here when we came back from the ride to the waterfall."

"Damn, Nina. I don't like the sound of that."

"I don't like it either, but I've thought this thing through. I have every reason to believe the police and the military are collaborating with the AUC anyway. In the end if anything is going to happen it'll be the AUC who can help. If I can convince them it's in their best interest."

"How are you going to do that?" I asked.

"I don't know yet. I'll think of something. I have to."

I could tell Nina had made up her mind and I couldn't think of anything better to suggest.

"Will you call me after you've met with him?"

"Yes, I promise," she said. "And thank you for not trying to talk me out of this."

Then she hung up.

I sat and thought about the mess we were in. I had no gold aboard the *Estrela*, Jorge was god-only-knows where and probably in the hands of FARC or the AUC, and I didn't have any final arrangements for the cocaine. On top of that we'd been followed by another boat until the storm struck and we had no idea who it was or why they'd been tracking us. It occurred to me this must be what it's like to be caught in quicksand, where every move only results in sinking deeper. On top of everything else I seemed to be dragging more and more people in with me.

I busied myself refilling the dive tanks and then spilled my guts to Felix when he returned. As the hours went by I became more and more agitated worrying about Nina's meeting with the AUC. I realized I hadn't even asked whether the meeting was taking place at the ranch or someplace else and fought the urge to call her. I finally decided to give her one more hour when the cell phone rang.

"Hello," I blurted.

"It's me, Dex. I'm okay."

It was then I realized how stressed I was. I collapsed in one of the canvas chairs on the work deck and switched the phone to my other hand.

"Are you there?" she asked.

"I'm here. You're okay?"

"Yes, I'm okay. I've made some progress. They located my father's plane in Arauca and the pilot is bringing it back here now."

"Do they know where he is?" I asked.

"No, not yet. He took a four-wheel-drive vehicle and drove out of town three days ago. The man I met is making inquiries, but it'll be a few days before he knows anything more."

"He's going to help you?" I asked.

"Yes. It's complicated, and I can't explain it over the telephone. Listen carefully," she said. "I've made new arrangements for the other matter."

I wasn't expecting this, believing my situation would take a back seat to the disappearance of her father. Nina proceeded to use the code we'd worked out to tell me where I was supposed to pick up the shipment in thirteen days. I wrote down the code words and numbers in pencil on an envelope and read them back to her to make sure I had it right. I did, and she added it was all subject to final confirmation two days prior to the delivery.

"Can you send the plane for me?" I asked. I was worried about her and what she was going through.

"No, Dex. I'll take care of this myself. He's my father and I'll deal with it," she answered.

This certainly wasn't the same Nina I'd met five weeks ago on the plane from Mexico City and I wondered what other changes might have taken place in the last weeks.

"But I love you for offering," she said, "and I'll call you to confirm as we agreed."

I went ashore and found a telephone to make the call to Jamaica.

Mirtha was in a foul mood.

"I've been stuck on this island for four weeks while you screw around," she complained. "And I'm fed up."

"Why don't you call your husband and tell him?" I asked. "Or do you want me to tell him?"

That calmed her a little.

"Do you have everything?" she asked.

"I've got one thing taken care of," I lied about the gold, "and the other is due in thirteen days. I'll call to confirm forty-eight hours in advance."

"You're cutting this awful close," she threatened.

"It can't be helped. Do you want it called off?"

"Don't be trite, Dex. It's just that I'm so lonely. If it's going to be almost two weeks, why can't you come here?"

I hung up and called Cardeli. All he wanted to hear about was the gold, and I simply told him it was aboard and there was more than I'd imagined.

"And the other cargo is due in thirteen days," I said, switching the subject.

"Where?"

"Somewhere along the northeast coast. I'll confirm forty-eight hours in advance, as you asked."

He seemed anxious, and I attributed it to the greed over the gold.

"My men will meet you when you take delivery. No payment will be made unless they confirm the cargo is as it should be."

"I understand that to mean the second cargo, right?" I was starting to sweat.

"That's right. There is to be no mention of the other. Do you understand?"

"Yes, I do. Where am I to make the delivery?"

"Deliveries," he corrected me. "There will be two deliveries. My men will tell you where and then I'll tell you where to make the second delivery. That cargo is mine. Do you get my meaning?"

I correctly interpreted that to mean he would personally take delivery of the gold after delivery of the cocaine. That would be my only chance at him since I wouldn't be able to bluff him again once he discovered there was no gold aboard.

VII

The next eleven days were hell. I called the ranch every other day, but Nina wasn't there and they didn't know, or wouldn't tell me, where she was. Felix recognized my black mood and steered clear of me.

She called the morning of October sixteenth.

"It's on," she said as soon as I answered.

"Your father?" I asked.

"Got a pen and paper?" was all I got in reply.

Nina ran through the code quickly and dispassionately. I took it down, writing as fast as I could and read it back to verify it. Then she hung up.

I sat there breathing slowly and deeply. I don't know how I'd expected to feel, but I felt nothing. All the months of preparation, false starts and stops plus the emotional turmoil were boiling down to this. Then my missing fingertip began to burn again, something that hadn't happened in months, and it brought back the memory of the beating on Cayman Brac. I closed my eyes and thought about my father and wondered for the millionth time if this would have turned out differently if I'd lived my life more responsibly and heeded Uncle Patricio's advice; if somehow this wasn't all some kind of penance for my lifestyle. Or maybe it was the price I had to pay to learn about my father. Either way, the wheels were once again in motion.

I went to look for Felix and found him studying the chart we'd used to locate the *Griffon*.

"It's on," I said. "The day after tomorrow, 11:00 p.m. in Santa Marta."

He didn't say anything or even acknowledge me.

"I know I've been a jerk for the last week and a half, Felix. I'm sorry."

He finally spoke without turning around. "Any news about your friend Jorge?"

"No, nothing. Nina just gave me the information about the delivery and hung up."

"Damn. Something has to start going right for us, Dex." He looked at me briefly then looked out the wheelhouse window. "Let's get moved."

I called Miami to tell Cardeli the buy was on and that we were moving the renamed boat to the commercial docks in Santa Marta. The conversation was short and as soon as he confirmed again that the gold was securely aboard he said we would be met in Santa Marta and rang off.

We didn't speak much on the six hour crossing to Santa Marta. The sea was relatively calm, smooth rolling waves in an even pattern. They imparted a sense of tranquility that belied the tension that hung between Felix and me in the salty air.

It seemed like the harbormaster was expecting us. He directed us to dockage against the main breakwall at the end of a line of tugs and fishing boats, between two rusty old scows. We secured the *Estrela* to the stanchions, allowing for the rise and fall of the tide, and set about washing her down. The longer we scrubbed, the more worried I became.

The area where we were docked certainly afforded privacy but at the same time left us exposed to an attack. There was about a hundred feet or so of broken concrete between the edge of the breakwall and a row of unlit, dilapidated buildings. Although there was activity elsewhere in the harbor there was nothing at our end and it would be easy to approach at night, particularly through the abandoned buildings or even by climbing over the rusting hulks that hemmed us in.

As far as Cardeli knew we had a substantial amount of gold aboard and due to my own goading he seemed to be more interested in the cobs than in the cocaine. I went and found Felix.

"I'm worried about this spot," I said.

Felix looked around at the harbor and the buildings. The sun was setting and it was obvious we'd soon be in darkness and vulnerable. We had maybe another forty-five minutes.

"You're right," he said. "We don't have much time."

I went and checked the old buildings across the wharf while Felix got out the shotgun and pistols. The buildings were more or less empty except for the junk piled everywhere. I gathered up an assortment of cans and pipes and propped them up against the doors from the outside so that if someone tried to come through the buildings and surprise us we'd hear the clatter. Satisfied it was the best I could do I went back to the *Estrela*.

Felix had the same idea and was finishing the rigging of monofilament fishing line across the fore and aft decks and tying it off to cans filled with stones. We went to the wheelhouse and decided to shut the generator down so we could hear anyone approaching.

"We'd better have a talk," I said. "Do you want out? I won't blame you if you do."

"Out? What's out?"

"You can just pack up and head back to Brac."

"You mean run?" he asked, and the unspoken implication hung there between us.

"I didn't mean it like that," I said.

He stared at me. "No, I don't want out. I just want this to be over. And I want it really over. I feel awful I even thought Jebediah was running dope, and the more I think about it the madder I get. That bastard in Miami has to die, Dex. I want a piece of him."

I was relieved Felix was still committed. I let the heat of the moment pass and waited five minutes before breaking the silence.

"What will you do after this is over?" I asked.

Felix turned those big, chocolate brown eyes on me. "I don't know. I don't think I can ever go back to fishing."

I sensed he had an idea, and I was right.

"Don't laugh, but I'm thinking I'd like to run dive charters."

"Why would I laugh?" I asked.

"Well, you know those two boys that work for me? They don't have fathers. Like me when I was growing up. All I had was Bibi and Jebediah. And don't get me wrong, but there was a little too much Bibi and not enough Jebediah."

I laughed at the memory of Bibi's loving but overpowering presence. I knew exactly what he meant, particularly the too few times either of us had with my father.

"I'd like to do something for kids who don't have fathers. Like Jebediah did for me when he took us on that trip in 1984. That was probably the best thing that ever happened to me, Dex. And I keep thinking about the thing Jebediah set up to send kids to school. Not every kid has what it takes to go to school like that."

"What are you driving at?" I asked.

"I'd like to take kids on diving trips through the Caribbean. Kids that don't have fathers, and who don't know anything other than getting into trouble."

I was surprised. I never pictured Felix as anything other than a carefree fisherman. And I suppose that said more about me than him. I was so caught up in my own problems I hadn't spent any time at all thinking about Felix' world other than how it was tied to mine.

"But that's just a dream," he said. "I don't have the money it takes to do it. What about you? What do you want to do?"

I was immediately uncomfortable, and tried to think of a way to change the subject.

"You didn't laugh at me, Dex," he said. "I won't laugh at you."

The discomfort became more acute, like a stick poked into my guts. The trouble was that I knew what I wanted but had avoided even thinking about it. I was too conditioned to losing the things that meant the most to me to put my dreams at risk by consciously thinking about them let alone verbalizing them.

"It's Catalina, isn't it?" he asked, unintentionally twisting the stick. "And Patricio, and your past," he continued as the stick wound my guts into a knot. "I know it's not the money, Dex. I saw that before you took the beating. Are you going to run again after this is all over?"

"I don't know if I am or not."

"I know," he said, pulling the stick out. "You're not going to run."

My guts spilled out and with them my words. "I just want someone to love and who loves me," I choked, "I've lost Catalina, and I just want this to be over."

"It's Nina, isn't it?"

"I lose everybody who matters to me, Felix. I always have. And how the hell can I even think about Nina when I just lost Catalina. There must be something wrong with me."

"Dex, listen to me," he said. "I'm just a dumb fisherman from Brac and I don't always get the words right, but maybe you spent so many years only loving yourself that you're trying too hard to make up for it. Maybe you don't even recognize when someone loves you."

I was struck by his choice of words. It immediately brought to mind another fisherman from Brac who I'd underestimated.

"Maybe Catalina wasn't right for you. Maybe you weren't right for her. Maybe you both just had to get that out of the way. You can still love her, you know. But you can't make her come back to you – she's gone. And you can either accept it or spend the rest of your life thinking about people who aren't with you anymore instead of thinking about the ones who are."

I couldn't even speak. I'd already said more than I wanted to.

VIII

The clatter woke me some time after two in the morning. Felix had relieved me of my watch at midnight and it felt like I'd just fallen asleep.

I crept from my berth and into the darkened wheelhouse. Felix was standing at the starboard windows, staying in the shadows of the moonlight and watching the warehouse. He had a shotgun in his hands.

"Do you see anybody?" I whispered.

"No, not yet. I think the noise came from the doors down to the right but I can't be sure."

I picked up the second shotgun and moved over beside Felix. The front of the old building was in complete darkness and it was difficult to make anything out in the direction he pointed.

"I'm going to check the port side to make sure nobody's coming at us from the water," I said.

The moonlight was better in that direction but it was still tricky trying to separate the shadows and reflections from what could be a small boat. I could see to the side and forward, but the view to the rear was obstructed by the structure of the boat. When I was satisfied it was clear to the side I checked behind us through the smaller windows set high in the aft bulkhead of the wheelhouse. The wheelhouse was two feet higher than the galley and crew quarters behind it, and I could see over the roof. I looked closely at the abandoned scow tied up behind us but its high bow made it impossible to see anyone crouching there. To make it even more difficult there was a mess of old machinery piled on the scow's foredeck.

"Dex," Felix whispered. "I thought I saw something move down the dock. Over where the sound came from. The third set of doors down. Can you see from there?"

I shifted my position to get a better view but I still couldn't see anything. The front of the building was completely protected from the moonlight. Then I thought I saw a form slip out the door and move along the wall toward us. It was just a momentary glimpse and I almost convinced myself it was my eyes playing tricks on me when I saw the same movement again, and then again.

"There's at least three of them moving along the wall toward us," I whispered.

Felix nodded. "You watch them. I'm going out the other wheelhouse door and around to the work deck."

I moved from the back of the wheelhouse and over to the side window where Felix had been. I just got there when all hell broke loose.

I heard a yell and then a thump at the back of the boat at the same time the three people in the shadow of the warehouse broke and ran for the side of the *Estrela*. I kicked the door open and stepped out.

A shotgun blast erupted from the work deck, then another, echoing off the walls of the warehouse. The three forms didn't even break stride and I leveled my shotgun and fired. Two of them went down but the third dodged to the side and kept coming.

The last thing I remembered was a crash at the front of the boat and then waking, sputtering from being doused with a bucket of water. My head was throbbing and I couldn't focus.

"Dex, wake up," I heard Felix calling through the fog.

I tried to get up but my arms and legs refused to cooperate. An arm went around my shoulders and propped me into a half-sitting position.

"Felix?" I asked. "What happened?"

"Damn, Dex. You sure had me worried there." He said. "I can't leave you alone for a second. Come on, get up."

Felix hauled me up and back into the wheelhouse. My legs were still like rubber and he had to help me into a chair.

"How many fingers?" he asked, holding his hand in front of my face.

"Eight," I answered, "like a goddam octopus."

"I guess you're okay, then," he laughed. "I always wanted to do that."

"How long was I out?"

"Ten minutes, maybe. Just long enough for those bastards to haul their wounded away."

"How many were there?"

"Seven. Three came at you from the side, two came over the back and two over the front. I filled the two at the back full of buckshot and you got two of the three from the warehouse just as two more came over the bow. It was one of those two that hit you with a pipe just as I came around and got the drop on them."

"Where are they now?"

"One spoke decent English and we decided it would be best for them to get the hell out of here. They didn't have any guns or I'd bet one or both of us would be dead by now."

"Me, anyway," I said, feeling the lump over my left eye. "Any chance they'll be back?"

"I don't think so. At least three of them won't – they're too badly hurt. I told them it wouldn't be buckshot next time." Felix went and got some ice and wrapped it in a towel before pressing it to my forehead. "And I'd guess if there's any such thing as harbor security on duty they'd be here by now. I'd bet it'll be quiet until morning."

"What do you think they were after?"

"Anything they could get their hands on. The electronics, probably. They were pretty scruffy looking. Not the type someone would hire to go after something specific."

I felt the lump over my eye and realized I was lucky I wasn't bleeding.

We nailed the warehouse doors shut the next day and spent another boring day and half until just before the cocaine was to be delivered.

IX

"We've got company, Dex," Felix said.

I looked up and saw three men walking toward us along the wharf. Two had small satchels and one carried a briefcase. As they drew closer I recognized the two carrying the satchels and my blood ran cold.

"It's Cardeli's men," I said.

"The bastards that beat you?"

"Yes."

Felix' voice was cold. "Dex – were these the ones that killed Jebediah?"

I took Felix' upper right arm and squeezed hard. His bicep was taught with tension, and my fingers didn't go even half way around. "Easy. Remember that if we don't get Cardeli too, then we've got nothing."

"Answer me, Dex. Did they kill Jebediah?"

"Yes, they were there. But Cardeli and others were, too."

I felt Felix relax but a dark, ominous glow replaced the spark in his eyes. He turned toward me and I saw something in his face I'd never seen there before. "I'm a fisherman, Dex. Two in the net is just a start. I want the whole school, but at least I've got these bottom feeders where I can play with them."

I stared at him, eye to eye, and understood he would bide his time. A fisherman is nothing if not patient and Felix could sense the time wasn't right.

As they came even with the side of the *Estrela* I stepped out and faced them.

"Well look here, Diego," Nestor said. "It's our amigo Dexter Snell."

"Yeah, what a coincidence; Cayman Brac, Jamaica and now Santa Marta. All the best places," Diego laughed.

Nestor and Diego climbed onto the work deck and set their satchels down with a clunk as Felix walked up behind me.

"Just you and your trained monkey aboard this scow?" Nestor asked. If there was a leader between the two of them, it was Nestor.

I don't know which comment bothered him the most – calling the *Estrela* a scow or calling him a trained monkey – but Felix scowled back at them. "Just Dex and me and now two harbor rats."

"Funny, real funny," Nestor spat.

"Cut the shit, Nestor. We've got a job to do," I said.

The third man was still standing on the wharf. He was slightly built and watching the exchange nervously, his eyes jumping behind his round, wire-framed glasses as he clutched his briefcase with both hands. He wore a light colored sports jacket with pens sticking out of the breast pocket where a handkerchief belonged. The jacket was wrinkled and stained, as were his pants.

"Get your ass aboard, Einstein, and sit down over there until we need you," Diego ordered.

Nestor pulled a pistol out from under his jacket and waved it at us. "Inside, boys. We need to explain the rules."

I looked around the harbor before finally moving back to the wheelhouse, followed by Felix. Diego picked up both satchels and followed Nestor who kept his gun on us.

When we were inside Diego produced two sets of handcuffs and secured us to the wheel. I noted with pleasure he had trouble fitting the cuffs around Felix' massive wrists and that it made him nervous.

"Where are the guns?" Nestor asked, patting us both down.

"What makes you think we have guns?" I answered. Felix and I had already talked this through. We'd decided to put the shotguns and one rifle in the hidden wheelhouse cabinet and leave the rest, except for my Beretta pistol, in the saddle tank. The pistol was tucked up behind a mass of wires under the shelf that held the electronics, and we assumed whomever Cardeli sent would find the hidden cabinet.

"Don't play it cute, Dexter. The word around the harbor is that you have shotguns aboard. I want them, and the rest, too."

I knew they'd never find the compartments hidden in the saddle tanks, but chances were good they'd find the bulkhead cabinet. And Felix had said that when he inherited the *Estrela* the guns were gone, so it was even possible Nestor and Diego knew about the cabinet from their earlier searches. Finding the shotguns and rifle might convince them they'd found everything. I decided to make it easier.

"They're in a cabinet in that bulkhead," I said, nodding toward the rear wall that separated the wheelhouse from the galley and berths. "Press down on the shelf and pull."

Nestor nodded to Diego who went and easily opened the cabinet, suggesting to me they knew it was there.

"A regular arsenal, isn't it? Expecting trouble?" Nestor laughed. "Looks like you already found some, Dex, from that lump on your forehead. Where are the rest?"

"That's it. There aren't any more," I answered, staring at him.

"We're going to search the boat so don't play it cute."

"Search away. That's it."

Nestor stared back at me, thinking. "We're not going to let you out of our sight you know. And you'll both be handcuffed most of the time, so don't plan on pulling anything fancy."

It was as I suspected. Nestor and Diego were basically lazy and they felt they had the upper hand. Granted, handcuffed to the wheel we were definitely at a disadvantage but they would have to learn soon enough they needed us to run the *Estrela*. At least I hoped they needed us.

"I just want to get this done," I answered. "And prove to your boss we can all make some money at it. But you're welcome to run the boat if you want."

Nestor's eyes narrowed as he stared at me. "We'll see. Diego – bring Einstein in here and get him set up. Then get a lock on that cabinet."

Diego brought the one they called Einstein in and he set about taking things from his briefcase and arranging them on the chart table. Nestor went to search the boat while Diego produced a hasp, shackle, hand drill and bolts from one of the satchels and padlocked the cabinet shut. They were obviously prepared for that, and I looked at Felix as he rolled his eyes in amusement. So far, so good.

Nestor wasn't gone more than ten minutes. I remembered the hours Felix and I had spent searching the *Estrela*. He told Diego the boat was clean except for the knives in the galley.

"I tossed them over the side," he said as an affirmation of his thoroughness. I was afraid to look at Felix in case he broke out laughing. There are enough sharp objects aboard a fishing boat to stab a whale to death. And barring that, heavy blunt tools that would do a much better job than the bat Nestor and Diego used to break my ribs in June.

"Are you planning to leave us cuffed here forever?" I asked. "Because in that case you need to decide which one of you is going to cook, who'll run the boat and who'll take on the cocaine in another hour or so. Plus, you might want to decide who is going to enter the coordinates into the navigation system to get us to wherever it is Cardeli wants his shipment."

Nestor and Diego exchanged glances. It was apparent neither of them had a clue about running a boat.

"Look," I said, "I'm sure one of you is capable of running the boat but it'd be a lot easier if we decide right now to do this together. You have the guns and the backing of your boss and if we weren't planning to go through with this then we wouldn't be here."

Diego began to fidget. "What about it, Nestor?"

"Shut up, I'm thinking," Nestor answered.

I pressed my advantage.

"Otherwise, let's call this off right now. The connection is mine," I bluffed, "and these people won't deal with you. We both know that, otherwise your boss would have you doing this on your own."

I held my hands up as far as I could. "Undo these things and let's get ready."

"I figured all that out, Snell. We just had to get the rules straight. Uncuff them," Nestor ordered Diego. "But if I even suspect either of you are trying to pull a fast one, one of you gets his kneecap shot off as a warning. Understand?"

I nodded.

"And what about you, monkey?" he asked Felix.

"I get you. I'm just along for the ride anyway," Felix answered.

Felix and Diego went to the work deck to prepare the fish hold while Nestor got out a scrap of paper with latitude and longitude scribbled on it. I recognized the coordinates as being close to Jamaica and got out a chart.

"It's right here," I said pointing to the Pedro Cays south of Jamaica. "Five hundred miles across the Caribbean from where we are now."

Nestor looked at the chart. "Do you have one that shows the whole Caribbean?"

I retrieved another chart and spread it out. "Here we are in Santa Marta," I pointed, "and here's the Pedro Cays," I said, drawing my finger slowly across the Caribbean. "Five hundred miles of open water."

"Christ, what about all the damned hurricanes this year? It seems like every time we turn around there's another one," Nestor said, the bluster gone from his voice.

"Can't be helped. Felix and I ran through Hurricane Charlie on the way to Jamaica in August. You remember that one, don't you? We missed the hundred and fifty mile an hour winds by a day, so we didn't have to deal with more than twenty-five foot waves. It was a snap," I said, trying to keep the smirk off my face. "And if we hit another one it should be a lot easier with four of us aboard. Felix and I can use an extra hand on the deck."

"On the deck?"

"Yeah. Things always seem to come loose in a hurricane. Either on deck or down below. You can't afford to have something fall overboard and take out the prop or break loose in the engine room and puncture a fuel tank or disable the engine. The boat would broach and sink in an instant."

Nestor looked around nervously. "I always wondered how all this steel stays afloat. Isn't there some kind of foam or something to hold it up?"

The urge to laugh out loud was tempered by the fact we were trapped on the *Estrela* with two homicidal sadists. Cardeli didn't employ them for their intellect, but I had to be careful not to underestimate their capacity for violence.

I pointed out that Hurricane Ivan crossed directly over the Pedro Cays just three weeks ago and Nestor lost even more of his bravado. I traced Ivan's path with my finger, pausing directly over the Pedros.

"Well, I guess we just make a quick run across," he said.

"I suppose. The *Estrela* cruises at nine knots – ten point three miles an hour. We'll make it in just over forty-eight hours."

"Two days?" Nestor said, looking at all the white and blue on the chart indicating water.

I let that sink in and set about punching the necessary coordinates into the nav system, making notes of legs, times and positions. It struck me that nothing scares a bully more than being confronted with his own fear. You just have to find out what that fear is, and I'd found Nestor's. I wasn't sure what Cardeli's fear was. Maybe it was just pure greed that would be his downfall. At least that was what I was counting on.

"Dex," hollered Felix. "More company."

I checked the old wind-up clock that was still screwed to the shelf in front of the wheel. It was only 10:25. They were early.

A truck and car were moving slowly down the wharf. The headlights bounced up and down as they crossed the sections of broken concrete, making the shadows dance about like marionettes. They pulled around in an arc to face the *Estrela* and shone their headlights into the wheelhouse and onto the work deck. It was impossible to see past the lights into the car or the truck.

"What the hell," Nestor said, pulling his pistol.

"Put it away," I ordered. "You can't even see them and it's not like you've got the money with you."

Nestor was sweating and his hand was shaking. I began to wonder what kind of a mess we were in.

"Put it away. Now!" I yelled.

I headed out of the wheelhouse and held up my hand to shield my eyes. "Shut down the lights," I called.

Vehicle doors slammed shut and one man stepped out into the light. He looked vaguely familiar, but I couldn't place him.

"How many aboard?" he asked.

"Five," I answered.

"Everybody out where I can see them," he ordered. He then turned toward the lights, ordering his men to search the dock area.

Felix and Diego were already on deck, and Nestor and Einstein joined us. Einstein looked like he might faint. We stood for fifteen or twenty minutes until someone gave the all-clear signal, and the man came aboard. He brought one other with him.

He walked directly up to me and took my hand. "Nice to see you again," he said, winking. "I assume everything's set, as we agreed?"

His back was to Nestor and Diego and he whispered to me. "Just say yes."

"Yes, it's all set," I said. I wondered what was going on but had no choice but to play along.

"Good. And the money will be transferred to my boss's account in Jamaica?"

Nestor spoke up. "Once we check out the shipment it will be. Not before."

The man turned to Nestor. "Are you going to check it?"

"No. Einstein here is the chemist. He'll do it."

"Fine. Where does it go?"

Felix stepped forward, indicating the open fish hold. "Down here."

The man turned and whistled toward the truck. "Back it around."

The truck turned around and backed up to the edge of the wharf. The rear doors swung open and two more men jumped out. They began lifting and carrying cartons over to the *Estrela* and Nestor opened the first one. It was filled with plastic-wrapped packages a little bigger than half a loaf of bread, the 'square tuna' Tun had told me about.

The car was still facing us and I couldn't see past its headlights. It made me nervous to be handling cocaine with the lights on us like this but nobody else seemed bothered by it.

Nestor grabbed the middle package from the top row of the first carton and held it out to Einstein. "Here, test this."

Einstein's hands were shaking. "I don't think you want to test from the first box," he said. "I usually pick one from somewhere else in the shipment."

"Well, pick one then," Nestor snapped. "How many in a box?" he asked no one in particular.

"Ten," answered one of the men from the truck.

"How many boxes?"

"Seventeen."

Half the boxes were loaded when Einstein pointed to one. "Bring that one over and open it." He removed the first layer and took a package from the middle. "We'll test this one."

"Get the rest stowed," Nestor ordered. "And then get ready to close the bottom of this hold once Einstein's finished."

The familiar-looking man, Nestor and I followed Einstein into the wheelhouse.

"Have you seen this done before?" Einstein asked.

"Just get on with it," Nestor said. "That's what you're being paid to do."

Einstein looked at us over the top of his glasses and then got started.

"I'm interested," I said. "I want to know how this works." Anything to cut the tension.

"Cocaine has to be kept dry," he began. "It has a shelf life. That's why it's wrapped so well." He put the package on the table in front of us and cut a one-inch slit in the topside. "See? Three layers of plastic."

"Cocaine dissolves in water," he explained, pouring water from a thermos into a glass beaker. "Impurities don't. And you need to use cold water. Amateurs make that mistake. Warm water can dissolve some of the impurities," he said, dropping about half a thimbleful of the white crystals into the beaker. He watched as they sank into the water, fully dissolving before they reached the bottom.

He picked up the beaker and held it up to the cabin light. "You look for a film or slick on the surface of the water. That indicates impurities."

Apparently satisfied, he lit an alcohol burner. "The second way to find impurities is with a burn test." Einstein placed another half thimbleful of crystals on a piece of foil and held it up to the flame of the burner. "Pure cocaine bubbles – sort of melts – and then leaves a nice, even, light brown film." He watched the cocaine over the top of his glasses, holding his breath. "Like this!" he said, grinning. "Impure coke, which this isn't, turns black and the residue is lumpy."

"Are you saying this passes?" Nestor asked.

"Ninety percent pure, or better. It's first grade stuff."

Einstein was clearly in his element. It's always nice to meet someone who enjoys his work. I breathed easier.

"Don't you even snort it?" Nestor asked.

"No, I don't. You can't tell much from that, although lots of dealers and users will tell you they can. Clinical tests show the effects of good cocaine versus bad on the average user are too subtle to serve as a reliable indicator of the quality of the coke. What the average cokehead remembers is the effect of whatever the coke was cut with before he got his hands on it. I've heard idiots talk about the 'freeze' they get from good coke. That's the Novocain or Lidocaine that someone up the line stepped on the pure stuff with. By the time this gets on the street Stateside it will have been stepped on so many times it'll be down to only twenty percent pure. It'll have been whacked with everything from milk sugar, dextrose and borax to maybe even a laxative that's popular in Europe. Real smart dealers cut it with an amphetamine so the cokehead gets a speed kick and a burnt nose, and even pays more for the shit because he thinks it's purer than the stuff his friends buy."

Einstein re-wrapped the package using plastic and tape from his briefcase and tossed it to Nestor. He put everything else away and stood up. We followed Nestor back to the work deck. The truck was turned around again and together with the lights of the car we were unable to see who was behind them.

"Put this back in the box and seal up the bottom of that hold," he ordered Diego. "I'll call the boss and tell him the shit's aboard and better than ninety percent. Where does the money go?" he asked.

"This is the account and bank in Jamaica," said the man from the truck, handing him a scrap of paper.

"It'll be in there the day after tomorrow at the latest," Nestor said. "Now let's get out of here," he said turning to me. "I'm nervous as hell about all these lights and I don't like the idea of sitting at this dock anymore with the shit aboard."

"You're not going anywhere," the man said.

"What do you mean? I'm not staying here like a sitting duck with a million bucks worth of coke aboard."

"You're not sitting here," the man said. "You're coming with us until that money's in the bank."

"What? No way," Nestor yelled, pulling his pistol.

"You might want to put that away. There's five men with rifles behind those headlights and they'll blow you away in a second."

Nestor looked around frantically. "I'm not going."

"It's you or Mister Snell. Take your choice."

I wasn't counting on this. I looked at Felix and then back at Nestor. I felt everything sliding out of control.

"I'll go," Felix volunteered.

"No good. My instructions are it's either you or you," he said pointing first at Nestor, then at me.

"Take Dexter, then," Nestor spat. "And you'd better have him back here in two days – 6:00 a.m. on the twentieth. Daylight. Right here. And make him walk along the wharf. I don't want to see a car or a truck coming this way."

My brain and heart were both racing. I should have known something like this would happen but I couldn't see any way out. The original plan was that Jorge would put up the money. Something was wrong.

"Take Dexter, but we're still not sitting here," Nestor said. "Get this barge out of here, monkey," he spat at Felix. "I'm not sitting here for two days like a sitting duck. And don't try any funny shit."

I looked at Felix, then at Nestor. "His name's Felix. I'd suggest you get that right or you'll end up running the boat yourself. And I have a feeling your boss has told you to keep your hands off both of us unless we do something stupid. So far, I'd say you've cornered the market on stupid."

Nestor's face went bright red but he put his pistol away.

"You too, Einstein. We're done with you. Get off the boat," Nestor said.

I climbed off the *Estrela* and watched as Felix showed Nestor and Diego what they had to do to prepare to leave the wharf.

"I'll be okay, Dex," he called out. "Don't do anything stupid yourself, and I'll see you back here in two days."

The man told Einstein to get in the truck and they'd drop him off. "You get in the car," he said to me. "In the back."

I heard the *Estrela's* engine fire up as I walked toward the car. It was a full-size Lincoln and except for the windshield the windows were tinted so that I couldn't see inside.

The man held opened the back door. "Inside, Dex. The boss is waiting for you."

As I ducked to climb in I saw a woman's legs on the far side of the car.

X

I didn't think anything else could surprise me, but I was wrong.

"Dex!" she sobbed, throwing herself at me before I was even in the seat. I heard the door slam behind me and then we were moving, my arms wrapped tightly around Nina as she cried onto my shoulder while Jorge's driver and bodyguard kept their eyes straight forward. I couldn't speak at first. It was all too much.

Nina leaned back, wiping the tears from her eyes with the backs of her hands. "I'm sorry for kidnapping you. I'm just so relieved you're okay."

"I wondered what was going on, but if I have to be held hostage a million dollars seems about right," I said. "And I can't imagine a better choice of captor."

She smiled, regaining her composure.

"Where's Jorge?"

"He's still missing Dex. I'm working on it."

"Who set this up then?"

"I did. It took a lot of work, but I didn't have anything else to do. The search for my father is going so slowly. I would have gone crazy if I hadn't had this to keep me busy," she started.

"Slow down, Nina. This is too much all at once – you'll have to start at the beginning."

I sat back in the seat and looked at her. She had changed somehow, and despite the initial outpouring of emotion she was clearly back under control. She looked at me almost shyly and I realized she was easily the most attractive woman I'd ever met. A big part of that was her ever-developing confidence.

"We're going to my hotel. I've been here for three days finalizing the details and I'll tell you all about it once we're there."

"Three days? You were in Santa Marta before I was?"

She took my hand in both of hers and leaned forward to speak to the driver and bodyguard. "Good work. Thank you. Please check on the people in the truck as soon as you drop us off, and then take care of the chemist. Call me in my room when you're done."

"The chemist?" I asked. "Einstein?"

She patted my hand and then wiped away the last of the tears on her cheek. "Relax, Dex. I think I have everything covered and I feel better now."

I was overwhelmed. So much had happened in such a short period of time, and here Nina was reassuring me.

We pulled up in front of an expensive hotel and the bodyguard jumped out to open the door. A few minutes later we were in her suite and she was ushering me toward the bathroom.

"Take a quick shower, Dex. There's a robe on the back of the door. I'll fix drinks and tell you what's been happening when you're done."

I took her in my arms and kissed her and then she pushed me away. "Please hurry and shower, Dex. I need someone to talk to."

It was the quickest shower and shave I'd ever taken, and as I stood under the spray I realized I probably stank of diesel and sweat. I lathered up again and then wrapped myself in the robe and went to find Nina. She was on the balcony, two drinks beside her on the railing.

The balcony overlooked the sea and I wondered which of the lights out there was the *Estrela*. Nina must have read my mind.

"Will a radio reach your boat from here?" she asked.

We were about twenty floors up and the height of an antenna is the most important determinant of the range of a marine radio. I looked at my watch. The *Estrela* couldn't be more than eight or nine miles away.

"Probably," I said, "if I had one." I kicked myself for not bringing one of the hand-held units, but how was I to have known I'd be in a position to use it?

"Will this one work?" Nina asked, retrieving an expensive-looking portable from the bedroom.

I stifled the urge to ask how and why she'd acquired it and fiddled with the buttons until I figured out how it worked.

"Pelican, Pelican, Pelican, this is the *Bibi, Bibi, Bibi,* over."

I hoped Felix wouldn't mind my using his mother's name as my call sign, but I couldn't think of anything else at the moment. I was preparing to call again when Felix' voice broke through.

"Bibi, Bibi, Bibi, this is the *Pelican,* over."

I switched him to a working channel and reestablished contact.

"My host has asked me to maintain radio contact with you every eight hours. Is that a problem? Over."

There was no answer for a few minutes, and I stared at the lights on the sea again.

Then the radio crackled with Felix' voice. "No problem, *Bibi.* What do you estimate as the range of your radio? Over."

"Ten miles from harbor, maybe fifteen, over."

"That's good. The charter wants to stay close in case of weather problems, over."

I started to laugh and Nina looked at me like I was crazy. My worries about Felix' treatment at the hands of Nestor and Diego evaporated as I pictured them thinking about trying to run the *Estrela* by themselves.

"I read you. This is *Bibi* over and out."

"What's so funny?" Nina asked.

"It's Cardeli's men, Nestor and Diego. The vicious bastards who killed my father, beat me and cut off my fingertip," I said, holding up my hand. "They're afraid of the water."

Nina hugged me again.

"You think a lot of Felix, don't you," she said.

"Yes, I do. I couldn't have gotten this far without him. Or without you for that matter." She smiled at me in appreciation. "Now tell me what's going on. I need to understand."

Nina picked up our drinks and led me back inside the suite. Once we were seated on the couch, she started.

"I told you about my father going to Arauca and how he disappeared after renting a car. And that I met with the AUC."

"Yes, but no more than that."

"I struck a deal with the AUC commander for the Medellin region. He has his counterpart in Arauca trying to get my father back."

"What kind of a deal?" I asked, wondering how deeply Nina was mired in this mess.

"He gave me new contacts here to set up the delivery. I had to start all over because I couldn't piece together everything my father had arranged. And that's where it got complicated." Nina stood up and walked over to the window, then came back and sat down again. "I need to know something, Dex." She looked at me with those big, brown eyes and I realized they were like Felix' eyes, only darker. I was having trouble concentrating. "You and my father agreed the cocaine would never reach the States, right?"

"That's right," I said, wondering just where this was going.

"Good, because there's less than a kilo of cocaine aboard the *Estrela*."

I must have been suffering from stress or exhaustion because what she said didn't sink in immediately.

"No, Nina. We loaded it. There were seventeen cartons. With ten packages in each box. I saw most of it come aboard and it's in the hold."

"It's not cocaine, Dex. It's sugar and borax."

My head was spinning. Here I'd thought Nina had set this up and she'd somehow pulled everything together. I didn't know how but she was clearly involved in something even she didn't understand. She'd been duped by the AUC or whomever they'd put her in touch with. I felt lost, worried about exactly what was happening around me, around us and to us. It was almost too much to try to stay ahead of Cardeli and that end of things and now the backside of the scheme was sliding out of control. How could she think she could make an arrangement with revolutionary groups and drug dealers? They must have seen her coming and had an easy time of playing on her naïveté.

"Nina, I don't know how to tell you this, but it's cocaine. I watched them test it." She smiled at me and tilted her head forward slightly. I felt so sorry for her. "The dealer, Nestor and I all saw it." It still hadn't hit her yet. "The money's being transferred to the dealer's account in Jamaica." She was still smiling at me.

"The dealer isn't a dealer, Dex. He's the foreman from the ranch."

My mouth dropped open in shock. Now I knew why he looked familiar.

"The account in Jamaica belongs to me," she continued. "I set it up a week ago. The chemist you call Einstein is a real chemist, though. He's one of about six in Santa Marta who freelance. I paid them all off in advance counting on Cardeli to arrange for someone local to do the testing, and I knew within hours of you calling Miami which one it would be."

I still couldn't believe it. "So the test was fake?"

"No, it was real. I couldn't take a chance on Cardeli's men not knowing something about testing cocaine. That single package Einstein tested was the only real one in that carton, and even *it's* not completely filled with coke. Only the outer layer of the package is cocaine, and the chemist knew which box and which package to choose. He prepared and packed it himself."

She sat back, waiting for me to absorb it all.

"I know it's a lot to take in, Dex. I told you I've been busy."

"And what if something had gone wrong?" I asked, knowing now she would have an answer.

"The men in the truck were all from the ranch, too. They were armed and there were rifles aimed at Cardeli's men through the whole thing. From behind the lights."

I took a big swallow of scotch.

"The AUC runs cocaine through Santa Marta. They're not the only ones, but they are here. They put me in touch with the freelance chemists and convinced each of them it was in their best interest to cooperate with me. I paid the AUC sixty percent of their normal profit on a transaction of this size for their help and for what they've supposedly done to help me find my father."

Jorge. How could I have forgotten about him? "I'm sorry, Nina. We should be talking about your father. I'm just a little stunned by all of this."

She stood up again and went to refill my glass. "There are two groups who claim to have him. One is a FARC unit and I really don't know who the other group is. It's not clear to me yet. But it doesn't really matter who they are if they have him."

"It's not the AUC?" I asked.

"I don't know for sure, but it could be. Both groups have made ransom demands."

Nina handed me the glass and sat down again.

"A week ago I asked both groups for proof they have him and he's still alive. All I've received in return are more demands for money and threats they'll kill him if I don't pay." She picked up her glass and held it in both hands, twisting it around and around without drinking from it.

"And?" I asked, trying to understand.

"I'll pay to get my father back. I'll pay any amount. But I won't pay one peso until I know who has him and that he's alive."

I felt like I was an observer to what was happening. It was all too fast, too complicated. All the pieces of what I'd seen as my problem had shifted, mixing in with pieces of other puzzles. I remembered a picture of an English garden with hedges arranged to form a maze, but this was infinitely more complex.

"Isn't that risky?" I asked, not knowing what else to say.

Nina turned fully toward me, shifting her legs up onto the couch and leaning forward to look at me. She searched my face while I watched her, as if she was seeing me for the first time. My hair, my forehead, nose, mouth and then my eyes; she locked onto my eyes.

"He's dead, Dex."

"What? How do you know? Are you sure?"

"Look at me, Dex," she demanded, taking my hands in hers again. "I know. I've done my mourning. I know he's dead."

I sat there and looked into her eyes and it finally hit me. I saw it deep inside her. She knew.

I'd been holding my breath and I let it all out now. "I'm sorry."

"Thank you. I know you are," she said, still holding my eyes in a lock. "It's not your fault, Dex."

Again, I didn't know what to say. It was all too much, too fast. Nina had had time to work through all of this, and she'd done it on her own. The girl I'd met in the airport lounge, seemingly years ago, was gone, replaced by the woman who sat in front of me holding my hands in hers.

"I've decided I'm staying here in Colombia. I'm not running. I'm a Garcia, and I'll stand my ground. It's what my father would have wanted."

I needed to think, to clear my head. I went to the balcony and leaned against the railing, watching the ships' lights blinking in the distance. One of those lights belonged to the *Estrela* and she'd been riding this sea for as long as I could remember. And my father had lived his life in these waters too, in boats that preceded the *Estrela*. The *Coroa*, the *Flor* and the *Catherine the Great* – boats I'd heard of but never seen. Sir Henry Morgan had sailed these seas in the *Lilly* and perhaps even crossed swords with Nina's Spanish ancestors. Such a glorious heritage lives in the Caribbean; an indomitable spirit that saturates everything touched by it, bounding it. From Colombia and Venezuela up past Cuba, into the Straights of Florida and the Keys themselves. Centuries of struggle. Good versus evil, always defined by points of view and perspectives as fluid as the Caribbean itself. It is the setting of a never-ending struggle for survival, and if not survival, then for dominance and wealth. It is the story of life itself. Greed, passion and love. And it holds people like me in its thrall.

Nina came up behind me and wrapped her arms around my waist.

"I know it's what Jorge would have wanted, Nina. Is it what you want?" I asked, still looking out at the sea.

I knew the answer before she spoke. It was all there before me. Nina was as much a captive as I.

"Yes," she answered simply, "but no more than I want you. And I know I can't have both."

I felt the sea pulling at me.

"I wouldn't be happy at the ranch, or in Bogota, Nina."

"I know that, too."

I turned in her arms and held her close. We stood that way for a while and I felt the rhythm of her breathing, the warmth between us.

She leaned back in my arms so she could look into my eyes.

"I love you, Dexter Snell," she said at the same time she held a finger to my lips. "Don't say anything. Just listen."

She leaned against me again, the side of her face against my chest.

"For a while I wished I'd met you in Miami, before all of this. Then I realized it wouldn't have worked. We weren't the same people we are today.

"Colombia is my home. My roots are here in the mountains, whether it's Bogota or the ranch. I never understood until I heard you talk about Cayman Brac and the love you have for the islands and the sea. The house and the ranch are my islands, Dex, and the mountains are my sea."

Her voice was calm and soothing but her words were coming from her soul and connecting directly with mine. It was as if she was bypassing my mind and touching me someplace I'd never been touched before; someplace I never knew existed.

She tightened her arms around me for a moment as if to tell me she could feel it, too.

"I'm not the same as my father, Dex. I'll never be trapped inside Colombia, but she'll always pull me back. Do you understand?"

"Yes," I whispered, sensing I was losing in a new way someone I loved.

"I told you there were no strings attached. But there are. All kinds of strings. My heart belongs to you, and it belongs to Colombia. Simply knowing that about myself is enough for me.

"I can't ask for something I can't give in return. And right now, I'm as tied to this country as you are to the sea. All I ask is that you hold my love someplace inside you, wherever you go, and whoever you are with – and I know there will be others or you wouldn't be you – until you can't hold it any more, and then tell me. Up until you tell me differently, I want to imagine I can always come to you. That is the only string I really need."

I closed my eyes and waited for the pain to hit me, but it didn't come. My mind told me I had lost Nina but something else told me she was giving herself to me in a way no one else ever had, or could.

I started to speak but she leaned back and held her finger to my lips again. "Don't say anything unless it's that you can't live with that."

She stared into my eyes for a long time and found her answer.

Then she took me by the hand, leading me back inside.

"Make love to me, Dex."

XI

Nina's driver dropped me off at the harbor two days later and I walked along the wharf toward the *Estrela* with murder in my heart. Our idyll had been shattered the evening before when I called Bones to let him know the deal at this end was completed and we would be on our way to the first rendezvous the next morning.

"Bad news, Dex," he'd blurted out. "Patricio is missing."

My first thought was that he was with Catalina but it had been her who had reported his disappearance and the police on Brac had been asked to check and see if he was there.

I called Miami and couldn't reach Cardeli, and then I called Jamaica. The switchboard put me through to Mirtha's room and Shando answered. I didn't even acknowledge him, demanding to speak to Mirtha.

She'd as much as said that her husband had Patricio and taunted me with the fact that Shando was there with her. I didn't care any more about Shando, and my concern about Patricio was answered simply by suggesting I follow through with my end of the deal.

Nestor and Diego were standing on the wharf beside the *Estrela*, and they looked tired. I had no time for small talk.

"Let's go," I said, jumping on board.

"Not just yet, hotshot," Nestor said. "We need to stand here for a while."

I looked at them and recognized the green cast to their faces. It's an old saying that there are two kinds of people when it comes to being at sea - those who get seasick, and those who haven't been seasick yet. It was some small measure of satisfaction that they'd had something to think about other than tormenting Felix.

I turned my back on them and went inside half expecting to find Felix cuffed to the wheel. I was surprised to find him in the galley whistling and preparing breakfast.

"Eggs and grits, Dex. Grab a plate."

I watched Nestor and Diego through the porthole while we talked and ate.

Felix told me that except for the company the two days at sea were pleasant. That made me feel less guilty about the time I'd spent with Nina.

"How'd they get so sick?"

Felix laughed. "The seas weren't big enough on their own, so I kept setting the course so we quartered the waves and got as much rock and roll as I could. And then they got the stupid idea they'd be better off in their berths instead of standing in the wheelhouse and watching the horizon. I didn't tell them otherwise and even opened the rear port to give them some fresh air," he chuckled.

We always keep the rear port closed because it draws the diesel fumes in and the thought of Nestor and Diego getting sicker and sicker amused me, but not enough to lighten my dark mood.

"Are you okay, Dex?"

"No, I'm not. They've got Patricio. They're holding him somewhere until the deliveries are completed."

Felix slammed his plate down. "We're screwed then."

"Not yet we're not," I answered. "I told Mirtha I'd sent a letter to someone detailing what's happening. The letter is to be opened only if Patricio is not released alive within fourteen days, which gives us enough time to do what we have to do. I'm counting on the fact if I kill Cardeli his organization will fall apart and whoever is holding Patricio will just run for it. Judging from the intellect of these two goons I'd say that's a safe bet."

"And if he kills us?" Felix asked.

"In that case, I'm counting on him having vented his rage and fulfilling his vendetta on us. He can justify to himself that letting Patricio go is of no consequence knowing that letter is hanging over him."

"So then he'd get away with this whole thing, and Jebediah's murder, too."

I smiled at Felix, and he read the menace in my eyes. "No, he won't. Even if he kills us and lets Patricio go, he'll die." I thought about what I'd left in Nina's hands, and what she'd do. "The person who holds that letter is unstoppable. Cardeli is a dead man, no matter how this turns out."

XII

We finally left Santa Marta at 9:00 a.m. over the protests of Nestor and Diego. Although the weather was clear and the forecast favorable I told them we had to hurry because a storm was on its way. Felix fought to hide his smile as I explained to them that if we were very lucky only the edge of it would catch us.

I followed Felix' example and set the course to maximize the roll of the *Estrela* to the extent it wouldn't appreciably delay our arrival at the Pedro Cays and settled in for what I hoped would be a routine crossing. My mind was on what I had to do and thinking about Patricio when Felix tapped me on the shoulder. He nodded at the radar screen.

A blip indicated we were being followed at a distance of ten miles, the same way we'd been followed when we were searching for the *Griffon*. This was not a coincidence; we were heading directly out to sea, not along the coast. Within a few miles of changing course slightly, the boat following us would make the same change. It never varied in its distance from us and we had no choice but to simply keep track of it.

By late afternoon Diego was seasick again and excused himself to go to his berth. It must have been the power of suggestion because Nestor followed him thirty minutes later, abandoning all thoughts of keeping Felix and I under close watch.

Seasickness is the result of a disagreement between the body and the brain. The body senses rolling and pitching but the brain, through the eyes, detects no movement relative to the inside of the boat because the boat is moving, too. The only cure is to get yourself ashore or to move into fresh air and watch the horizon. When the eyes fix on the horizon, the brain realizes there is in fact movement taking place, and the sickness subsides eventually. The best spot on a boat to avoid seasickness is at the helm, which Aunt Isabel laughingly used to explain was why Uncle Patricio never let her steer the *Sol de Marques*. My father used to say that if your mind was weaker than your body you were in no danger of seasickness, but Nestor and Diego put the lie to that theory.

The Pedros lie 430 miles north, northwest of Santa Marta and allowing for the slight course deviation to provide the roll that made Nestor and Diego so sick we would be there shortly after dawn on the second day out.

Our two gangsters made periodic visits to the wheelhouse to check on the storm situation and, like little kids on a car trip with Mom and Dad, ask how much further it was to our destination. Felix came up with the idea of frying bacon and eggs for a snack whenever it looked like they were getting their sea legs, and opened the appropriate portholes to make sure the smell wafted back through the berths. It worked like a charm.

On the second night I decided to remove the remaining rifle from the hidden saddle tank. We talked about the risk of being discovered and decided it was worth it if we took some precautions.

The next time they came up for air I suggested they might want to try some seasick pills.

"Seasick pills?" Nestor yelled. "You've got seasick pills and never gave them to us you son-of-a-bitch?"

"Sorry. I forgot about them. I never need them. They're in the cabinet in the head – Dramamine."

Nestor wobbled back to the head and retrieved the bottle, taking a double dose and giving the same to Diego. It's been my experience that Dramamine taken after the onset of seasickness does nothing to relieve the symptoms, but it will make you sleep. We waited until they were out.

We'd found the portable radios wouldn't work down in the hold where they were surrounded by steel so we had to find another way for Felix to signal me if Nestor or Diego reappeared. I spotted the remote speaker for the arrival alert and confirmed the plug also fit the main radio. I strung the wire back along the edge of the shelf and out along the wheelhouse, tucking it up inside the drip ledge to the work deck and then down into the engine room. Felix only had to key the mike, not speak, to make an audible signal.

I quickly undid the rear strap on the starboard saddle tank and wrestled the end plate free. The rifle was wrapped in plastic and I slit the coverings open and then concealed it in a space between the front of the saddle tank and the bulkhead that separated the engine room from the gear compartment. I took out a box of ammunition as well and was about to close the compartment back up when I spotted the container of Semtex. I grabbed it and stuck it in the bilge where it was covered with oily water and then hurried to close the tank. I had the plate up and the lower bolt fastened when the speaker snapped twice. There was no way I would have time to fasten the top bolt so I pushed the strap in place and put the bolt in my pocket.

"He's on his way back. It's generator trouble," I heard Felix say over the speaker.

I looked at the strap again and just leaned over the generator when the hatch opened and Nestor came down, pistol in hand.

"What in hell are you doing down here, Snell?"

I pretended I was surprised and snapped my head around. "Oh, it's you," I said before turning back to the generator.

"What are you doing?"

"Generator trouble. I'm checking it out."

"Your partner said it was engine trouble, Snell."

"Then you heard him wrong. It's generator trouble."

I suddenly realized the speaker was sitting back behind the steps from the work deck and that if someone – anyone – from another boat used their radio Nestor would hear it. Even an idiot would be able to figure out Felix had signaled me.

"Engine. He said engine," Nestor insisted.

I turned around and threw the wrench on the steel floor as I pushed my way past Nestor.

"Where the hell are you going?" he yelled.

"I'm going to the wheelhouse. If you think it's an engine problem, you fix the fucking thing."

Nestor looked around. The engine and generator were both running and there were belts and pulleys spinning, plus the prop shaft clattering away at our feet. The boat was rolling normally, but to Nestor it must have seemed like a nightmare.

"In fact, Nestor, show me which one's the engine and show me which one's the generator."

He looked around in increasing fear and bewilderment as the boat rolled even more than usual. He pushed me out of the way and climbed back up the companionway.

"I'll sit here while you fix it," he said.

"It's already fixed. It was just a loose wire." I went up the companionway and closed the hatch behind me. Nestor was on his hands and knees on the work deck, retching, and I went back to the wheelhouse.

"Should be working okay now. It was just a loose wire," I said to Felix as Nestor came by us and went back to his berth.

"There's a loose one here, too," Felix said, showing me that he'd unplugged the remote speaker from the radio. "And the boat that was following us is gone."

I looked at the radar screen. It was all clear but we'd been followed long enough to leave no doubt where we were headed and it would be relatively easy for another boat to pick us up as we approached Jamaican waters. There wasn't much to be done about it at any rate.

XIII

Felix nudged me awake at 5:00 a.m. We'd taken turns dozing fitfully in one of the wooden chairs in the corner of the wheelhouse by the chart table and my neck and back were sore from the awkward position.

I was alert instantly, tense from thinking about the possibility of meeting with Cardeli. All I knew was the cocaine was to be unloaded before the gold and I wasn't going to miss any chance at him.

"There's a target on the radar, Dex. About nine miles ahead, right on the coordinates. Should we wake our friends?"

"No. They'll probably wake up on their own when we arrive. Let them sweat it out and worry about their boss finding out they've been dogging it."

We watched the horizon and the radar over the next hour. As we got within the last few miles we spotted the boat. It was big – well over a hundred feet. And as it started to take on shape and form I recognized it.

"It's the *Party Girl*, Felix. That's our rendezvous. Take us to within a hundred yards and we'll hold there. We'll see what happens."

Felix took the *Estrela* closer and when we were where we wanted to be he throttled down and we drifted while I scanned the *Party Girl* through the binoculars. Nestor and Diego came charging into the wheelhouse.

"What's wrong? Why are we stopping?" Nestor yelled. I simply pointed to the *Party Girl*.

"Shit. It's the boss," Diego said. "Call him on the radio."

"I don't think that's a good idea. They can call us if they want radio contact. It's not like they aren't expecting us," I said still looking through the binoculars.

I could see some activity on deck, although I didn't recognize anyone. They were preparing to lower the launch and I watched to see if Cardeli would appear. Nestor and Diego went to the work deck and were waving and shouting at the *Party Girl* as four men climbed into the launch and headed toward us.

"Are any of those Cardeli?" Felix asked.

"No. And I don't recognize them. I haven't seen anyone aboard I recognize." I put the binoculars down and went back to the work deck. Felix stayed in the wheelhouse where he could get at my Beretta quickly.

Diego had hold of the bow line of the launch and Nestor was arguing with the man in charge. The argument was in Spanish and I had no clue what it was about, but Nestor was highly agitated. I walked over to the side of the *Estrela* and waited.

Diego began to shout now, too, his voice rising a full octave in his anger. Nestor tried to climb aboard the launch and was pushed back by one of the crew. The argument was escalating quickly and I still had no idea what it was about. The only thing clear to me was that Nestor wanted off the *Estrela*.

Nestor made another attempt to board the launch and the man he was arguing with pulled a pistol and aimed it at him. Nestor backed up, sputtering what I took to be obscenities.

"Snell?" the man said to me.

I nodded yes.

"The boss wants you to head for Mexico. You'll be met by another boat and unload there."

"Unload what?" I asked.

The man swore at me in Spanish before switching back to English. "The fucking cocaine, you asshole. Here's the lat and long," he spat, tossing a small, watertight container at me. I caught it and put it in my pocket. "Do you think you can handle it?"

"I found this spot, didn't I? Where's Cardeli?"

"That's what I want to know," Nestor yelled.

"That's none of your damned business," the man said. "You do what you're told, and he'll meet you after you've dropped the load in Mexico. Not before. He doesn't want anything to do with you or this boat until the shit's gone. Understand?"

I thought about bluffing, somehow using whatever Nestor and Diego were agitated about to force a meeting. The man was still holding his pistol on Nestor and now another member of the crew pulled one and aimed it at Diego.

"You will not try to contact us by radio under any circumstances. If you do, I've been ordered to tell you someone will die. If we need to contact you we'll call you the *Gallo*, understand? *Gallo*," he repeated.

"I understand."

"What's the cruise speed on this tub?" he asked.

"Nine knots," I answered.

"Damn. There's a storm on the way, and it'll catch us before we can make our destination. Do have enough fuel for sixty hours or so?"

"Sixty hours!" shouted Nestor. "I want to see the boss!"

The man waved his pistol at Nestor again. "The boss says if you or your partner give me any trouble, I'm to shoot one of you. He doesn't care which one."

Nestor glared at the man then looked at Diego. He obviously had nothing else to say.

"We'll be following you the whole way, Snell, just so you know. If you make any strange detours from here to the destination the boss said he'd take it as a sign he's to terminate the deal. He said you'd know what that means." The man turned to the helmsman, shouted something in Spanish, and then they pulled away. I watched them head for the *Party Girl* as I went to see Felix.

"Did you catch that?" I asked, picking up the binoculars again.

"Everything except the Spanish parts," he said.

I was scanning the *Party Girl* again when I saw her. Mirtha was on the upper deck facing the *Estrela*, both hands on the rail and wearing nothing but a thong. But that wasn't what made my blood boil. There was a huge black man behind her and when he turned around it confirmed what I already knew. It was Shando.

I hung the binoculars back on the hook and pulled the little canister from my pocket. There was a scrap of paper with latitude and longitude on it, and a picture of Uncle Patricio holding up a Miami Herald with a date of four days ago. I passed the picture to Felix and looked at the charts.

"It's Xcalak, Quintana Roo," I said. "Have you been there?"

"I've been to Chetumal and remember rounding the point to get into the bay," Felix said. "Xcalak is on the point, isn't it? On the Mexican side of the bay, across from Belize."

"That's it. Just about straight west from here," I confirmed, punching the coordinates into the nav system. "Let's go."

Felix powered up and swung the *Estrela* westward as Nestor and Felix came into the wheelhouse.

"Where the hell is this place?" Nestor asked.

I showed him on the chart.

"Sixty hours, a storm on the way and Mexico of all places," he muttered to himself.

"Do you know what happens if we're caught in Mexico?" Diego asked.

"I sure as hell do, and so does the boss. Shit," he said.

"I told you not to kill that Mexican bastard, Nestor."

"Shut up," Nestor snapped. "How the hell was I supposed to know he was related to the chief of police? Maybe they've forgotten about us."

Diego said something in Spanish and headed for the galley. "I'm going to eat something while I can."

The *Party Girl* didn't move until she was almost off our radar screen, then picked up a course that took her ten miles to the north of us and parallel to our route. She stayed there, on the edge of our radar screen, for the next fifty-five hours until the storm swept in just north of Roatan. And the edge of the storm wasn't all we picked up.

Shortly after I swung the *Estrela* northwest on the final leg to Xcalak I picked up another target on the radar. This one was to the south and west of us on the opposite side of our track from the *Party Girl*. I watched it for twenty minutes or so and then pointed it out to Felix. Nestor saw me and came over.

"What's that? The boss's boat?"

"No," I answered, showing him the other target. "That's the *Party Girl*. I don't know who this one is."

"Are we in Mexican waters yet?"

Felix showed him on the chart where we were, and which direction we were headed. The *Estrela* was rolling a little more than she had been before we made our last course change and the seas were starting to build with the approaching storm. I could see the thunderheads to the east of us and pointed them out to Nestor.

By 9:30 that night we were fully engulfed by the storm and still several hours from Xcalak and the protection of Chetumal Bay. Nestor and Diego had consumed the better part of a bottle of rum and were arguing about something in Spanish when two targets appeared directly north of us on an intercept course. The *Party Girl* was still east of us but had closed to within six miles in the storm, and the other target that had been following us since Roatan was southwest of us. I was certain that *Party Girl's* bridge would have spotted the two targets approaching from the north on their own radar screen but was doubtful they would be able to pick up the other target because of their distance apart. The *Estrela*, being roughly between them, was able to pick up all. Four boats surrounded us, only one of which – *Party Girl* – we recognized. I wished I could have labeled her friendly.

"What do you think, Dex?" Felix asked.

"Think about what, you monkey?" Nestor shouted, staggering over to the screen while trying to counter the pitch and roll of the boat. "What's that? What are those two dots ahead of us?"

"I don't know. But they're on a direct course to intercept us," I said without taking my eyes from the screen.

"Are we in Mexican waters? They can't touch us if we're not in Mexican waters, right?" he asked.

A bolt of lightning lit up the wheelhouse and the immediate crash of thunder told me it was close. The wind was still picking up and a glance at the barometer showed it had dropped to 28.2 inches. It was falling fast.

"I don't think it matters where we are right now. We're close enough to be taken under escort and hauled in to Mexican waters, and from what I've heard it'll all be over then," I said.

"Turn this tub around and get the hell out of here. What are you waiting for?" Diego yelled.

Felix laughed nervously and Nestor swatted him in the back of the head. "What's so funny?"

"Those boats are making at least fifteen knots, Nestor. We run at nine. We can't outrun them," I pointed out.

Nestor and Diego stared at the screen, watching the boats close on us. Another bolt of lightning lit us up and I could see the look of terror on their faces.

The fact that well over ninety percent of the cargo was powdered sugar and borax didn't make me feel any better. The presence of two murderers and the weapons we had aboard made it almost certain Felix and I would spend most, if not all of the rest of our lives rotting in a Mexican prison.

The wind was whipping the tops off the waves now and sending them in sheets across the *Estrela*. Combined with the rain it limited our visibility to about a hundred yards, but even that was intermittent at best. The noise level of the storm was rising also and it was now necessary to shout to be heard.

"Radio the boss. Ask him what we should do," yelled Nestor.

I ignored him.

"Are the bow anchors lashed down?" I shouted to Felix.

"If you hadn't asked, I'd say they were. Now I'm wondering. It's been over two weeks since we used them," he shouted back.

"I'll go forward and check."

I grabbed one of the red inflatable jackets from the locker and pulled it on. We had two of them and they were great for working in a storm since they weren't bulky until you pulled the tabs to inflate them. I remembered trying to talk Felix out of buying them because they weren't as visible as the yellow ones that were out of stock and I was now glad that he prevailed.

"Where are you going?" Nestor yelled.

"Forward to check on the anchor lashings. Want to come?" I answered, slamming the wheelhouse door shut before he could answer.

The roll of the boat was bad, but I've been through worse. A lot worse. I worked my way forward and found the anchors double lashed to their mountings. A quick look around confirmed there wasn't anything loose the foredeck so I worked my way back to the aft deck. If anything had been loose back there, it was already gone. I checked the line locker and then put a pin through the hasp. Next to an anchor sliding off the foredeck and wrapping around the prop shaft or holing the bottom, a loose line was the hazard I most wanted to avoid.

Another lightning bolt lit the sky and I thought I saw a naval cruiser to the starboard side, but it could have been my eyes playing tricks on me. I made my way carefully back to the wheelhouse.

Felix was wrestling with Nestor and trying to keep the *Estrela* under control at the same time. I jumped across the wheelhouse and pulled Nestor away, knocking him to the floor.

"What in hell are you doing?" I yelled.

"I want that radio. I want to get off this boat right now. He better come and get me or I'm blowing the whistle," Nestor screamed.

A flare shot past us just in front of the wheelhouse, silencing him for a second.

"What was that?" Diego hollered.

I looked at the radar. The two boats were off our starboard side and almost on top of us. I knew now I had in fact seen a patrol boat in the lightning flash.

"It's a warning to stop."

The radio burst into life as I checked the barometer. It had dropped two more points.

"Blue and white fishing vessel, back down. Repeat, blue and white fishing vessel, back down. This is the Mexican Coast Guard, over."

"Get the rifle," Nestor shouted to Diego. "And keep this boat headed straight. Don't stop or I'll shoot you," he yelled at Felix, pulling his pistol.

"Blue and white fishing vessel, back down. Repeat, blue and white fishing vessel, back down."

Another flare burst in front of us as the rain cleared briefly and Diego yelled at the sight of the two vessels. Each was trying to spotlight us but the pitching of the sea made the lights hard to aim.

There was a crash and clatter from below deck as something broke loose.

"Hold course, Felix," I yelled. "I'm going to check the engine room."

I went out the wheelhouse door on the side away from the coast guard cruisers and wondered how this could get any worse. And then it did. Diego opened fire on them.

The footing was no better than it had been a few minutes ago. The rain-slicked steel deck combined with the pitch and roll of the boat to make moving around treacherous, but I finally made it to the engine room hatch and heaved it open. I could still hear the crack of Diego's rifle but now it was joined by bursts of fire from the deck guns of the patrol boats.

I hit the switch for the engine room lights and half-staggered, half-fell down the companionway and immediately found the source of the crashing. The top end of the strap I had left unbolted earlier had popped loose and the end plate from the saddle tank was clanging back and forth against the empty tank, booming like a huge kettle drum. I managed to wrestle it inside the tank where it couldn't cause any damage to the running gear and started back up the companionway when I had an idea. It was desperate, probably insane, but it was the only option I could think of. It took me about five minutes to rig and I could now hear the unmistakable sounds of high-powered shells hitting the *Estrela*.

I scrambled back up the companionway and made my way forward to the wheelhouse. Nestor and Diego were both clinging to the opposite railing, firing at the cruisers. The muzzle flashes from the cruisers' deck guns confirmed the battle was fully engaged and I had no doubt about how it would end. The storm was lifting and it was easier to see the lights of the cruisers now.

"I've been hit, Dex," Felix yelled. He was standing in a pool of blood still holding the wheel, the lower part of his left trouser leg torn and blood-soaked.

"How bad?" I yelled, kneeling to take a look. I ripped the material away and saw a clean wound through the middle of his calf muscle.

"I can still stand," he hollered. "Tie it off."

I rigged a tourniquet from my belt and tightened it.

"Get into the other inflatable jacket," I yelled at him, taking the wheel.

Party Girl was still showing on the radar, but she had moved further away. There was no doubt they'd heard the orders from the coast guard to back down and were probably watching their own radar to see what would happen. The other target was still to the southeast of us and holding its distance. I thumbed the key to the mike so *Party Girl* could hear the sounds of gunfire over their radio while I looked at the nav display. Then I ripped the cord from the radio and dropped the mike on the floor.

I looked back at Felix and saw he was almost in the life jacket. It took me a few more seconds to punch the coordinates I wanted into the autopilot and plug the remote arrival alert into the back of the unit. After another look to make sure Felix was ready I hit the engage button and felt the autopilot take control of the wheel.

Nestor and Diego were still firing at the cruisers as I ran to Felix and pushed him out the far door to the rail.

"Jump," I shouted. He only looked at me for a second before he went over the side. I was right behind him.

The hull of the *Estrela* shielded us from the spotlights and the gunfire for five or six seconds and then she was past us. I was counting on the confused seas and the fact all of the combatants were focused on each other to remain undetected and it worked.

I swam over to Felix. "Are you okay?" I asked, pulling the cord to inflate his jacket before I pulled mine.

"Yeah. When did you cook up this one?" he asked.

"When I was down below. I didn't know what else to do. I'm sorry."

"Sorry? Damn, Dex. I was thinking the same thing and just had to hang on until you came back. I didn't think you'd go for it and I was trying to figure out how to knock you out and throw you over the side."

"How's your leg?"

"Sore, must be how a whale feels when he's harpooned." We watched the lights heading away from us. The cruisers were firing tracers and we could see that most of the bullets were missing the mark as the boats rolled back and forth.

"It must have been a ricochet that caught your leg."

"No, it was that bastard Nestor. He shot me when he saw me with your pistol, and I dropped it. I don't know where it went, Dex. I'm sorry. But I hope he gets what he deserves. I wanted to watch those two die."

The wind was dropping and it was quieter closer to the surface of the sea. The tops of the waves weren't being torn off anymore and the rain was past us. I could actually see a break in the clouds to the east and stars were beginning to show.

I held up my wrist and checked the time on the luminous dial of my watch.

"Watch closely, Felix. Keep your eyes on the lights." I held my breath.

The explosion lit the entire sky to the north, followed closely by the concussion as the sound reached us. All of the lights were now gone, which I hadn't expected. It was only a few seconds however before the remaining wind carried the smoke away and we could see the searchlights of the cruisers. The lights of the *Estrela* were out forever.

"Shit, Dex. What was that?"

"We got them, Felix. Whatever else happens, we killed those two. I rigged the arrival alert to the Semtex in the engine room and plugged it into the autopilot while you were getting into the life jacket. It was set for a mile and a half."

Even in the darkness I could make out the white of Felix' grin as he wrapped his arms around me.

The coast guard vessels circled the area for about a half hour before leaving. There wouldn't have been anything more than an oil slick, and even that would have broken fairly quickly in the waves.

We floated silently watching the departing vessels, each deep in thought. Felix broke the silence first.

"Do you think you die quickly when a shark attacks?" he asked.

The same thought had been nagging at me. The blood from Felix' wound would act like a beacon.

"There are pocket flares in these jackets if you're having second thoughts," I said. "They might see them and come back for us."

"What do you think the chances are we can make them believe we were kidnapped?" Felix asked.

"None. It would be too easy to track where we've been and put two and two together. I don't think we can count on a Mexican court to rigorously apply the burden of proof, and I don't think the U.S. or the governor of the Cayman's will help us, for the same reasons. We just look too damned guilty."

Felix looked at the lights disappearing over the horizon. "I can't spend the rest of my life in jail, Dex. I just hope the sharks make it quick. Why don't you swim away? There's no need for you to stay near me."

"What for? So I can be desert? If we're both shark bait, then I'd rather we go at the same time."

After two hours the initial tension of watching for sharks was replaced with a fatalistic resignation to our fate. The water was warm but Felix began to shiver from loss of blood and shock. He drifted in and out of consciousness and we talked whenever he awoke.

The storm was completely past us now and the stars were coming out. The waves had changed to gentle rollers. I thought about how satisfying it always was to come through a night storm aboard the *Estrela* and watch the sky reappear. And I remembered the storm twenty years ago when Felix, father and I had been caught off the coast of Colombia and father had discovered the *Griffon*. I began to sing the same pirate ditty father had sung when the storm had passed, realizing now of course he had been celebrating the crowning discovery of his life.

Felix rallied from unconsciousness and joined in. We sang louder and louder and then began to laugh with the memory. Despite the laughter I could feel tears ready to break out. It wasn't just the memory of my father, but the memory of everyone who had ever meant anything to me. Patricio, Aunt Isabel, Catalina, Bibi and Nina. Ah, sweet Nina.

I now regretted leaving the letter with her. I knew whether Patricio was freed or not she would avenge my death. And I felt guilty about setting her on that course. She didn't need that burden. I would like my last thoughts to be of her riding her Paso Fino horse to her secret pool and waterfall, and finding peace there.

Felix broke into my thoughts. "The stars, Dex. Look at the stars."

"Yes, Felix. They're beautiful."

"The stars are coming for me. They're taking me to Jebediah and Bibi," he whispered.

The tears washed down my cheeks as I realized the end was near. I prayed the sharks would come so I didn't have to watch Felix die.

"Look, Dex. Over there. That star is coming for me."

I followed the direction of Felix' stare and had to rub my eyes to clear them. There was a light coming toward us from the southwest; a light, not a star.

"Felix, hang on," I shouted, shaking him at the same time. "It's a boat, man."

The adrenaline surged through me and with it the will to live. I grabbed Felix harder and shook him again. "Hang on, Felix. For god's sake hang on!"

The light was maybe a mile off and I couldn't get an easy fix on whether it was headed for us or not. If I waited too long and the helmsman was not headed for us, he might easily miss a flare. I felt in the jacket pockets for the small rocket and pulled it out.

It was a simple device. I unscrewed the cap, held it over my head with one hand and pulled the chain with the other. Nothing. I pulled the chain again and it fired but the flare sputtered out before it had reached fifty feet. It was impossible to tell if the light changed direction.

I searched Felix' jacket and located another flare. It was now or never, there was nothing to gain by waiting. I fired it straight up so that if it was spotted it would be clear where it came from. This time the flare worked perfectly, the first time. And this time it was easy to spot the boat changing direction and heading toward us.

I held Felix for the ten minutes it took the boat to reach us and watched in shock as it drew closer. It was the ghost of the *Estrela*. Blue and white paint and identical lines. When I closed my eyes I could even hear the same throaty rumble of the single diesel engine, a sound I'd recognize anywhere.

The engine shut down and a flashlight pierced the darkness from the port side.

"We need some help here," was all I could think to say. "My partner's injured."

The man tossed me a line and hauled us around to the transom. He reached down and grabbed Felix' jacket with both hands and hauled him up before turning back and helping me up onto the illuminated work deck. I felt like I was in a dream, back aboard the *Estrela*.

He was about an inch taller than me and had short, dirty blond hair and green eyes. Lean and wiry, I later guessed him to be about a hundred and ninety pounds.

"Can you help me move your partner inside?" he asked and we hoisted Felix between us and dragged him into the wheelhouse.

"He's lost some blood," I said, ripping his trouser leg higher and taking a good look at the wound. It was grayish white around the edges and swollen shut, but not bleeding. The man poked at it with his finger causing Felix to moan. Then he felt his pulse before fetching a medical kit, preparing a syringe and stabbing it into Felix' buttock. He swabbed the wound with some kind of ointment before wrapping his calf in a bandage and securing it with tape. After checking Felix' pulse again he undid the tourniquet and suggested we put him in a berth.

"It doesn't take a doctor to see that he's strong," he said. "And I don't see any signs he's in immediate danger. The shot will help him sleep."

I took another look at Felix and then followed the man back into the wheelhouse.

"Thank you," I said extending my hand. "I'm Dexter Snell."

"I know," he smiled. "I'm Jesse Brady. I didn't expect to find anyone alive after that explosion."

He was about my age, maybe early thirties, and I wondered if I'd met him somewhere before. He must have noticed the puzzled look on my face and pointed to the rear bulkhead wall before turning to the helm and starting the engine.

"We'd best get out of here," he said as I stared at the words in the frame bolted to the wall. I read them in silence and confusion.

JEBEDIAH'S LAW

1. *Find something you like to do, and get good at it.*
2. *Find somebody who will pay you to do it.*
3. *If you can't find somebody to pay you to do what you like to do, prepare to starve or do something else part-time.*
4. *Never give up your dreams.*

"You've been following us since Roatan, haven't you?" I asked. "Or since Santa Marta?"

"Roatan," he said. "A man named Justin followed you from Santa Marta until he was certain you were headed for Jamaica."

"So you know Justin?"

"No, I've never met him."

"Then how did you find me?"

"Justin handed you off, so to speak, to Commander Peter Jones in Jamaica. Jones then tracked you long enough to be confidant of your course west toward Roatan, called me, and I followed you here."

"I didn't spot anyone on the radar following me from Jamaica."

"No? What about *Party Girl*?"

So he knew about that, too. "Other than *Party Girl*, I mean."

He looked at me. "I don't think you're that stupid. You know as well as I do the height of Jones' boat gives his radar a greater range than yours."

I knew that was true but was too tired to explain my line of questioning or even defend myself.

"Jebediah's Boys?" I asked.

"Yep."

"And did my father give you that?" I asked, looking at the wall plaque.

"No, I put it together myself from what I learned from Jebediah. What happened out here? The explosion, I mean. My radar picked up the two patrol boats as they approached you."

"How did you know they were patrol boats?" I asked. I still didn't know whether it was happenstance they'd found us.

"They called you on the radio. Remember? I picked that up."

"I'm sorry. They did. I'm afraid I'm not thinking straight."

"Understandable under the circumstances. What happened? I saw that explosion from a long way off. Was it you who keyed the mike and broadcast the gunfire?"

"Yes. There were two men aboard who decided to fire on the Mexican boats. One of them shot Felix, and we decided to bail out. The *Estrela* exploded about twelve minutes after. It must have been a lucky shot by the coast guard."

"Lucky shot my ass. Diesel powered boats do not go up like that. What were you carrying in addition to the cocaine, explosives?"

I closed my eyes. It was all too much. Why did it always seem strangers knew more about what I was doing than was possible?

"Why were you following us?" I asked. "I mean it's lucky for us you were, but why?"

"You're just like your old man," he sighed. "Trying to do everything on your own. He was always helping other people but something in him just wouldn't let those people help him in return. Is it a family trait?"

Maybe it was, I thought. But then the only family I knew was my father. Blood family, anyway.

"I guess it is. Did Justin know what I was doing?"

"He didn't know exactly, but he didn't buy that story about cruising around the Caribbean for old times sake. He followed you for a few days while you and Felix zigzagged around the coast off Colombia until he figured you were on to him and then he took off. But he didn't go far and he saw you loading what he decided was cocaine in Santa Marta. Are you going to tell me what the hell's going on or not?"

I still felt uncomfortable. I wished Felix was there beside me to give me his reading on this guy.

"How did you know my father? You're too young to have worked for him," I said.

"Wrong. I ran away when I was fourteen and ended up working on one of the Marques Snell boats in the Honduras just as Jebediah sold them all off. I don't know why, but he took an interest in me."

I knew why. Jesse was the same age then as my father was when he met Patricio.

"How did you get this boat?"

"It was 1986 and I had, shall we say, a falling out with the captain. Jebediah underwrote a highly leveraged buyout." He looked me in the eye. "It was on a handshake, no supporting documents. I learned he was murdered exactly five weeks later."

"I can see this boat isn't fished," I said, wondering exactly what it was Jesse Brady did for a living. For all I knew, this was the boat I was to transfer the cocaine to in Xcalak.

"That's correct, it isn't fished anymore. It hasn't been fished since about 1990, when I laid her up. I put her back in the water two years ago and live aboard her now."

"Independently wealthy? It takes money to keep a steel trawler afloat."

"I already told you Jebediah made it possible for me to buy this boat. You probably know there were only three – now two – sisterships to the *Estrela*, the *Sol* and this one, the *Rough Draft*."

"The *Rough Draft*?"

"I know it's not Portuguese, but I had to rename her and it sort of fit in with what I do. I got the boat in 1986 and it wasn't easy, by the way, being a 16-year old shrimp boat captain. Jebediah seemed to understand that somehow and told me to grow up fast. I kept sending the payments to Jebediah's account after he was killed and had it paid off by the end of 1990."

I felt like I could tell this part of the story myself. I closed my eyes thinking about how hard people like Justin and now Jesse had had it compared to me, but how they considered themselves so lucky because of my father. I immediately sensed the ring of truth to what Jesse was telling me.

"I drydocked the boat fourteen years ago and moved to Toronto, Canada. Married, went to school, divorced. It's a long boring story. I'm trying to make a living as a writer now, and this suits me."

"Which part of your writing involves following me through a storm?" I asked, but with less suspicion now. Genuine curiosity was replacing doubt in my mind.

"None, but my writing will never get in the way of helping nail the guy who killed Jebediah. That's what this is all about, isn't it? At least I hope it is. If it isn't, I'll just drop you two off wherever you want and send the word out to the rest of Jebediah's Boys that you're as big an asshole as everyone thought you were."

"There's one more thing bothering me," I said. "Why didn't the coast guard come after you or the *Party Girl*?"

"After the explosion they made radio contact with both of us. *Party Girl* identified herself as a private yacht headed for Cancun, and the Mexican coast guard knows this boat. I told them I was heading for Chetumal when the storm hit. They told *Party Girl* to check in with the port authorities when she reaches Cancun and just wished me a safe trip. As for why they picked you initially, I can't answer. Luck of the draw I suppose."

I looked at the wall plaque again, and thought about my father's love of the sea, of fishing, boats, history and pirate gold. That plaque captured the essence of my father, and it took someone who knew him to write it.

"There's rum in the cabinet back there if you want it," Jesse said. "And under the bottom shelf there's a little coke if you prefer. Help yourself. I'm no angel, but I don't need it."

I had a large rum and then spilled my guts to Jesse Brady about Niccolo Cardeli, and how I'd set out to kill him. I left out the parts about the *Griffon* and the gold cobs but told him about the threat to Patricio, my beating, the fake cocaine shipment and how I'd blown up the *Estrela*. It took an hour to tell the story and answer Jesse's questions, and then he swung the *Rough Draft* around and headed north toward Chetumal where he knew a doctor who could keep his mouth shut for a fee.

XIV

The doctor poked and prodded Felix' calf, rewrapped it and then gave him another shot. The instructions were for Felix to stay off the leg for a week or so to give the torn muscles a chance to begin to mend, and to change the bandage daily. The doctor never questioned the cause of the wound, which Jesse explained was a diving accident involving a spear gun, and we set out for Cancun.

The *Party Girl* had a sizable head start on us, compounded by the fact she could cruise at just over twenty-five miles an hour compared to our ten. By the time we reached Cancun, she was gone.

Jesse tied up at the fuel dock and after instructing the attendant to top up the tank we left Felix in charge and went to find a telephone.

"A friend of mine has an office down the pier," Jesse explained. "He used to work for Marques Snell, too." Somehow I wasn't surprised.

The office was in the back of a rundown shack that handled commercial fishing supplies, and Jesse suggested we keep my name out of any conversations. He spoke to the owner for a few minutes and then we were left alone to use the telephone.

"The *Party Girl* refueled here at 11:30 yesterday morning," Jesse said. "It caused quite a stir."

"Why?" I asked. "There's bigger yachts than her that call here."

"Not with a barely clothed owner who acts like she owns the whole country," Jesse smiled. "She put on a real display. The word is that when the immigration officials arrived to check the papers she refused to let them aboard. They agreed, but only if everyone came onto the wharf with their passports."

"Cardeli? Did he mention a man with a scar on his face?"

"That's where it got messier. She agreed to have everyone on the wharf except for one. Apparently he never leaves the master suite. It must have been him."

"What happened?"

"Everyone came ashore, and then she escorted one official aboard who apparently checked Cardeli's papers. It was all over in less than ten minutes. I might be able to confirm it was Cardeli but we run the risk of arousing suspicion if I start asking too many questions, particularly at the immigration office."

I thought about it for a minute while I looked out the office window at the junk piled behind the building.

"No, it was Cardeli. Was there a big, black guy with her?"

"He said something about a big guy. He seemed to be with the woman, but he didn't say a word. They left for Key West as soon as they were refueled."

I looked at my watch. *Party Girl* would eat up the six hundred miles or so to Key West and be there in the next hour or two.

"Do you know anyone there?" I asked Jesse. "Someone you can trust with something a little edgy?"

"You mean illegal, don't you?"

"Yes."

"Tell me what it is, and I'll take care of it."

Jesse placed the call and made the arrangements for a pistol, some cash and a few other items I wanted to be delivered to me on the pier at Mallory Square along with a key to a hotel suite I knew was kept open for the highest bidder during Fantasy Fest. It would take us fifty-eight hours to reach Key West, which would make it near midnight on the twenty-ninth. It was perfect timing for an anonymous arrival.

"It's set," Jesse said after hanging up. "He'll have the stuff you want in a sailor's bag that matches one I'll loan you. You're to meet him along the sea wall by the pier. He'll ask you for a smoke and you can switch bags. I promised him he'll be more than adequately compensated."

"Thanks, Jesse. I owe you."

"No you don't. Just kill that bastard for Jebediah."

I turned to leave, wondering how I'd get close enough to Cardeli when Jesse took my arm.

"There's something else," Jesse said. "*Party Girl's* been in Miami for the last year and the word is out she's returning to Key West. There's a big function planned aboard by the owner the night after we get there, and nobody knows who it is. It's rumored it's somebody who is returning to Key West after something like sixty-five years and everybody's scrambling for an invitation."

Now I knew how I'd get to Cardeli. And his return to Key West would be remembered for a long time.

16 Key West: The Reckoning   October 30, 2004

It was dark, just before 11:30 when I made my way to meet with Shando. I was still unsettled from the phone call earlier and the pistol tucked in the back of the cummerbund of the tuxedo I'd bought that afternoon provided little comfort.

I didn't know exactly what to expect. A year ago I would have trusted Shando with my life but now I was actually putting myself in that position, and with a lot less confidence in him than I'd had then. His earlier call had forced my hand. He was either with me or against me, and if he was against me then showing up for the meeting didn't make any difference since he could kill me any time he wanted to as long as I was somewhere in the Keys.

And there was a third possibility, the one I was counting on; that Shando just didn't care one way or the other.

The room Shando used as his office was up a back staircase behind a little bar and restaurant on Whitehead Street, the first street west of Duvall. I went down the alley and picked my way around the trash to the stairs. There were no lights, just the way Shando liked it, and I took a deep breath before I headed up.

They heard me climbing the stairs and the door swung open as I reached the top, bathing me in light. I couldn't see past the light into the room but I stepped inside just like I'd done so many times before and the door closed behind me.

Shando was sitting behind his desk, leaning back in his chair with his hands clenched behind his head. The gorge rose in my throat as the man who'd opened the door began to pat me down before Shando spoke, stopping him. "He's okay. Leave us alone."

The man, who I didn't recognize, grunted and went out the door.

Shando stood up and came around the desk. He was in a tuxedo as well and he wrapped me in those massive arms and hugged me quickly before he stood back.

"You've lost weight, Dex. You're lookin' good. You're lookin' dangerous," he said, retrieving a big cigar from the ashtray on his desk.

"You look about the same, Shando. The same as you looked on the deck of the *Party Girl* when I saw you a week ago in the Pedro Cays."

He laughed that deep laugh and showed his white teeth as he exhaled a cloud of smoke. The smoke curled upwards, swirling around the bare bulb hanging from the ceiling.

"Things aren't always what they appear, Dex. You remember Shando said that. Will you remember that?"

"I'll remember."

"You do that, 'cause you and Shando are gonna talk about this again. I promise you. You told Shando to take care of that little package you left behind a year ago, didn't you? That's what I was doin'," he said, smiling. It wasn't a big smile. On any one else you'd call it a smirk, but Shando doesn't smirk. Despite the heat in the room I felt cold. "You ready to go?"

"Go where?" I asked.

"To the party, Dex. Shando wants to see the fireworks. Been waitin' a while for this. You want me to get you aboard the *Party Girl*, don't you?"

"Yes."

"I've been hearin' stories second hand for a year now. Shando wants to be there for the finale. Interested bystander status. Ringside seat. Let's go."

He stepped past me and opened the door to let me out, then ducked through and closed the door.

Shando's car was waiting for us on the street and we climbed in the back.

"*Party Girl's* docked at the pier. No class. I liked the way you brought your guests out in the launch. These people have no class, Dex," he repeated.

He looked out the window during the three-block drive, puffing on his cigar. "You ready for this?"

"Yes, I am," I said, staring him in the eyes.

"I mean really ready. You can still run, you know."

"I'm through running, Shando."

"I think you might just be at that, Dex." Our eyes were still locked together, but Shando's had narrowed perceptively, as if he could see right inside my head.

We pulled up at the pier and got out. I looked at *Party Girl*. I'd wondered whether I would feel anything, any resentment or regrets about not owning her any more. I didn't.

We walked over to the gangway and Shando told the two men standing there I was with him and they let us pass. They reminded me of Nestor and Diego and I wondered if any of the men who'd been with Cardeli when he had me beaten on Cayman Brac would be there, and if they'd recognize me. There was the crew from the *Party Girl* who'd come over to the *Estrela* in the Pedro Cays to worry about, too.

Before we reached the top of the gangway Shando put his arm around my shoulder. "You know those men are packin' heat, don't you?"

"I assumed as much," I said truthfully.

As quick as a flash, Shando had his hand behind me and under my jacket and my pistol was gone.

"Keep walkin', Dex. Just keep walkin'. Remember I told you things aren't always what they appear?"

"I remember," I spat.

"Just be cool. What'll be will be."

Two more men appeared at the top of the gangway; the same types as were at the bottom. "Evening, Mr. Shando. Can you step this way, please?"

"It's okay, boys. He's with me," Shando said.

"Boss's orders, Mr. Shando. No exceptions," the taller of the two said as they took me aside and discretely patted me down.

Shando stepped over and spread his arms.

"You're okay Mr. Shando. I'm sure he didn't mean you."

"Thank you, boys. Shando will be sure to put a good one in for you when he sees Mrs. Cardeli," he laughed. The crude joke wasn't lost on the two goons who rolled their eyes and stifled their laughter.

I was alternating between sweats and chills and wondered why I hadn't just bought a high-powered rifle with a scope and picked Cardeli off from the roof of one of the buildings near the pier. It was too late now, and I stepped up beside Shando and grabbed him by the arm before we reached the stairs to the upper deck.

"Are you going to give me back my pistol?"

"Not yet, Dex. The timing just isn't right," he said. His eyes were cold and flat. "When we get to the top I'm going to head for the bar at the back of the boat. You stay on my right, and wherever I move, you stay on the side of me away from Cardeli and Mirtha. Do you understand me?"

I looked at him. Had he just stopped dropping his g's? I know he hadn't referred to himself as Shando. I had known him for sixteen years and never once heard him talk like this.

"What the hell's going on?" I hissed.

"Think of this as a show, Dex. I've got the ringside seat and you're the star attraction. You've thought about this for the last what, five or six months? I've thought about it for a lot longer, and you're not going to ruin it for me. Do you have a choice?"

I felt a cold fury tearing through me. What the hell was going on?

"You can still run, Dex. But you won't. You've got too much of your father in you."

"What do you know about my father?"

"I know Cardeli hated him. I also know he thinks you're dead and that he's convinced he's settled the score. If he knew you were alive you'd be worth a lot of money to whoever brings you to him. Are you a gambler, Dex? You aren't the Dexter Snell I knew a year ago, and now you're learning I'm not the Shando you thought you knew. It's fair in a way isn't it?"

I looked at the pier. It was near where Aunt Isabel had picked me off the *Estrela* in 1975 to start school. And it was probably near where Uncle Patricio had plucked my father from the water in 1934 and hoisted him dripping up onto the deck of the *Sol de Marques*. 'Don't think, act' I imagined my father saying.

I gave Shando the Snell smirk, and he stepped back in surprise. "Let's go, Shando. Let's see what happens. I'm ready."

We emerged onto the upper deck and I stayed to Shando's right as we walked toward the bar at the rear. A band was playing a waltz; the deck crowded with people in black tie and evening gowns.

"Two double scotches, straight up," Shando ordered. I was discretely trying to see what was happening, but there were too many people. It seemed like they were in a ring around the deck and they were watching someone in the center.

The music ended and the crowd began to applaud. When the applause faded, Shando yelled for attention and he raised his glass in a toast.

"To our gracious host and hostess," he said and people began to move aside as he took a step forward. Then he stepped aside himself and I saw Cardeli and Mirtha in the center of the deck.

As people raised their glasses Shando moved back a step so he stood beside me to my right. Every eye on the deck was on Shando, just like it used to be when he made his entrances. Every set of eyes except for mine. I was staring at Cardeli.

It seemed like a moment frozen in time. An eternity. Then Mirtha noticed me with a gasp, her hand flying to her mouth. Cardeli looked at his wife and then followed her gaze until he saw me, too.

Cardeli's face contorted instantly, transforming his features into a grotesque mask. He screamed something in Italian and the crowd's attention immediately shifted from Shando to Cardeli, who reached inside his jacket and pulled out a gun. The crowd scrambled to get of the way, women's screams drowning out Cardeli's stream of invective.

As he aimed it at me, I raised my hands and looked sideways at Shando.

An evil grin contorted Shando's face as he kept his eyes locked on Cardeli. "No," Shando yelled. "No!"

Shando's left arm lashed out and hit me in the right shoulder with the force of a wrecking ball, knocking me sideways at the same instant I heard the shot. I remember wondering why I was also spinning backwards as the second shot followed the first in a split second, and then I felt the pain.

Shando was kneeling beside me, propping me up. He still held his own pistol in his right hand and I could smell the cordite. It was pandemonium now as people screamed and fought to get down the companionway to the lower deck. Some were jumping into the water and I could hear the splashing.

"Hang on, Dex, I'll get you to a doctor," Shando said. I could see Cardeli's inert form sprawled on the deck twenty feet from me, a pool of blood seeping across the teak. My right shoulder began to ache and I could feel something warm soaking down the inside of my jacket. I tried to speak, but nothing came out.

I looked at Shando and finally managed to croak out a few words. "All the doctors in Key West have jumped overboard."

"Look out," somebody yelled. "She's got his gun!"

I looked just in time to see Mirtha aiming her husband's pistol at me. She was holding it in both hands and the last thing I remember is the sound of two shots and being struck in the left side of my head by a baseball bat.

II

Regaining consciousness is not something I will ever look forward to, having experienced it three times in five months. Of course the alternative is not acceptable, either.

I remembered pieces of my unconsciousness, but not all of it. It was like a dream, but not like a dream. There was no trace of or interference from the rational side of my brain, no questioning or nagging doubts lurking in the murky depths. It was a place devoid of reality and fact. It was a comforting place.

I had been aboard the *Estrela* with my father and mother and Aunt Isabel. Bibi was there, too. And a huge black man I didn't recognize, who father referred to as 'captain.' There was no hunger, thirst or other basic needs to drive anyone or impose any kind of timetable. More than that, there was no time at all. No division of days or weeks. Rather there was a permanent condition of the most glorious sunrises and sunsets that occurred simultaneously and never ended. I was just there, with those people aboard the *Estrela*, and everything seemed peaceful and satisfying. Whatever conflicts that might have existed had either been resolved and forgotten or had been banished to another world.

I still have a sense there may have been more, but the details escape me. I lost them as I slowly regained consciousness. The only abiding thing I carried with me as I woke was the feeling they were all happy and that the *Estrela* had been delivered to them. They were cruising off into the mist as I became aware of pain and voices and the re-emergence of the rational functions of my mind.

"Dex, wake up," I heard, but the words initially held no meaning. It was like they were just there somehow. There in my mind. "Dex, wake up Dex."

My head throbbed and I could feel a pulsing in my right shoulder. A pulsing and an ache.

"Dex, wake up."

The mist cleared and the *Estrela* was gone. I opened my eyes and tried to focus.

"He's awake," I heard. So I must be alive my brain told me. "Dex, Dex, it's me, Nina. Wake up Dex."

Nina's face swam into view, and I knew I was back. Beautiful Nina. I tried to move my right arm, but I couldn't. With the shock of the pain came the memory of being shot aboard the *Party Girl*, and then being hit in the head.

"How long have I been out?" I asked.

"Three days, Dex. I came as soon as I could."

I closed my eyes, trying to put everything together. I remembered more details, but they were coming slowly. "Shando," I said with a start. "Where's Shando?"

"He's just outside in the hall, Dex."

"He's okay then?"

"Yes, he's okay. And you will be too, Dex."

I closed my eyes again and then wondered how Nina had gotten here. How had she known? I remembered the letter. "Patricio!"

"He's okay too, Dex. Just relax. Felix, Doc, Jesse Brady. They're all okay. Try to pull yourself together. Shando has to talk to you before the police are told you've regained consciousness."

"Bring him in."

"Are you sure? The concussion was a bad one."

"Yes, I'm sure. Please get him for me."

Shando filled the doorway and then stood beside the bed. My left hand disappeared inside his.

"Thank you, Dex. I never thought I'd see that day. I've waited my whole life for the chance to kill that man."

I wasn't quite with it yet. He couldn't have waited his whole life. My father wasn't murdered until 1986. I needed to concentrate.

"The police?" I asked.

"Listen closely, Dex. We don't have much time. The witnesses all saw an unprovoked attack on an unarmed man. The police know Cardeli took over your assets, and that he held a grudge but they don't know anything else. Nothing. You were my guest and Cardeli's men let you on the boat after searching you. You didn't want to attend the party, but I talked you into it, suggesting it was an opportunity to bury the hatchet. I told the police I didn't know the hatred ran so deep, since I've never met Cardeli. They know or suspect I was involved with Mirtha, but they also know she was involved with lots of men and that Cardeli didn't care. Have you got all that?"

"Yes, I think so. How did you explain your gun?"

"I have a license for it, Dex. I threw yours overboard the first chance I had. The police found cocaine aboard the *Party Girl*. Enough to justify trafficking charges if he was alive. Cost me a fortune," he laughed.

"Won't Mirtha cause a problem?"

"Mirtha's dead too, Dex. I killed her. I was a second too late to get her before she shot you. Lucky it just creased that hard head of yours. Again, the witnesses all saw her go crazy. It was self defense."

I struggled to try to make sense of it. I had too many questions.

"Don't fight it, Dex. Just go with it. If the police get any deeper, pass out or something. The rest is all taken care of, but you don't need to know it right now."

"Nina?"

"Yes, Dex. I'm still here."

"Thank you," I said.

Two police officers came in along with a doctor who flashed a light in my eyes and took my pulse and blood pressure. "Five minutes," he said to the police who then chased Shando and Nina from the room.

It was pretty simple and straightforward. I only answered a few open-ended questions and confirmed the facts that Shando and others had presented to them, and after advising me to let them know before I left Key West they walked out.

I slept again and when I woke Nina came and took my hand.

"There are some other people here who want to see you, Dex. Are you up to it?"

I supposed I was, but I didn't want any more police or, perish the thought, lawyers.

"I think you'll want to see them, too," she said.

The door swung open and Catalina maneuvered Patricio's wheelchair into the room. Tears rolled down my cheeks and I couldn't speak.

"I'll wait outside," Nina said, closing the door as she left.

Catalina was crying as she rolled Patricio to the bedside. My heart was pounding as I looked into her pale blue eyes and saw the pain and remorse hiding there.

"I'm so sorry, Dex. I didn't know."

"It's okay, Catalina. You weren't supposed to know. It's my fault."

"No," Patricio interrupted. "If anyone is to blame it is Jebediah and me. And mostly me, I am afraid. He tried to warn me sixty years ago this would not end until Niccolo and his father were dead and I would not listen to him. He was right. He was right about so many things, and I was a pig-headed fool. I suppose I still am," he said.

"Don't punish yourself over the past, uncle, it isn't worth it," I said, wondering at the same time if I'd ever be able to free myself from my own past.

"I should have recognized your father in you the last time we met on Cayman Brac, Dex. I should have known there was more. I let my temper and selfishness take over and it was not until shortly after Catalina married I finally understood and called Bones looking for you."

Catalina sobbed at the mention of her marriage.

"I was angry, Dex," she said, tears rolling down her face again. "I was so angry. I ran away from both you and Patricio. I never even gave you a chance to explain."

"I wouldn't have, Catalina. I couldn't. I'd already made up my mind about what I had to do. I knew the risks."

"But you didn't count on me running away, did you?" she said between sobs.

I realized painfully there was nothing to be gained from this. The sad look in Patricio's eyes told me he knew it, too.

"Is he a good man?" I asked, cowardly avoiding the real question I wanted to ask.

"Yes, he is, Dex. You'll like him," she said, wiping away her tears with a tissue.

"I'm sure I will," I lied.

"Cardeli's assets have been seized by the authorities on racketeering charges, Dex," Patricio said after a few seconds of awkward silence. "I have instructed my people to look into acquiring those he took from you."

I smiled at him, knowing it was his way of trying to make up for the rift between he and my father. "Don't do it, Patricio. I don't want them. I just want to go home, and my home is on Brac."

I could see the understanding in his face, and the satisfaction.

"Then you have no objection to me helping Mr. Shando acquire the house on Caroline Street?"

That caught me totally by surprise. "The house on Caroline Street? Why would he want it?"

"I suspect it is because of the many good times Jebediah and his father shared there, but I never asked him"

"His father?" I asked, shocked. "Who was his father?"

"You did not know? He did not tell you?" Patricio asked.

"No, he didn't."

"The house on Caroline Street belonged to the widow we bought the *Catherine the Great* from, and was where Jebediah met your mother."

"Yes, I knew that when I bought the house twelve years ago."

"The night we bought the boat from her was the night your father cut Niccolo Cardeli. And the man who stepped forward when things got really ugly and told the crowd we had bought the boat fair and square and paid more than anyone else was Mr. Shando's father."

My mind was awash with the thought that Shando's father had known my father and Uncle Patricio. And that Shando had never told me.

"Mr. Shando's father came to work for us as a captain and was murdered years later by Niccolo in revenge, but we could never prove it," Patricio said. "Mr. Shando was just a little boy when it happened, and he and his sister were sent to Jamaica to live with relatives. I did not even know he was here in Key West until this happened."

I remembered Shando's comment earlier that he'd waited all his life for revenge, and now understood he hadn't meant revenge for my father's death but revenge for that of his own. And following right on top of that thought was the recognition of the curious speech pattern he had where he referred to himself as Shando in conversation, the same way Tun had in Jamaica. If that wasn't unsettling enough, I remembered the dream I had while I was unconscious.

"Was Shando's father a big man?" I asked.

"Huge. Just like Mr. Shando. And as black as coal."

"What was his name?" I asked.

"I am embarrassed to say I do not know. Jebediah always referred to him simply as 'captain', which pleased him to no end."

I looked at Catalina and then back at Patricio. "I want to go home. I want to go home to the cottage on Brac."

"Will you marry Nina?" Catalina asked.

"I don't know. She's made it clear to me it wouldn't work right now. And too many things have happened too fast, to me and to her."

"She loves you, you know," Catalina said, her eyes flashing defiance. I recognized behind that look the same cowardice I'd felt moments earlier, and the same unasked question.

"I know," I said, stifling the urge to add that it was an unconditional love.

Patricio let that hang in the air for a long time before suggesting it was time to leave. "I will send the plane to take you home as soon as the doctors release you, Dex."

"Thank you," was all I needed to say.

Sparks flashed between Nina and Catalina as they passed in the doorway, and in the brief instant they glared at each other they missed the big wink Uncle Patricio shot to me.

17 Cayman Brac: 2004 November

It was two more days after Patricio and Catalina visited me in the hospital before I was released, and Nina insisted we use her plane. I agreed to spend a night in her penthouse condo in Miami to help her pack some things she wanted to take back to Bogota, and she managed to keep me over for one more night. By then she seemed to sense I needed to get home and hustled us out the door by mid afternoon.

As we flew over the blue waters toward Brac I thought of all the people who had touched my life in the last year and how much had been done in the days after the shooting aboard *Party Girl* to cover my tracks.

Cardeli's gangsters had all either disappeared or told the police they didn't know anything, and Shando had spoken to the crew of the *Party Girl* to make certain none of them could remember seeing another boat in the Pedro Cays. Shando said they were now more afraid of him than they had been of Cardeli. He apologized for never telling me about his father and for using me to draw Cardeli out into the open. He'd hoped to get at Niccolo through Mirtha, but even while he was aboard the *Party Girl* in the chase through the Caribbean Cardeli never emerged from the master suite. And Shando thought it was hilarious I'd never connected him to his older sister, Tun.

He had nothing but admiration for Jesse Brady, who it turned out had come up with the ideas for most of the pieces to cover our tracks. 'He must be one hell of a fiction writer' was Shando's take on him.

Felix had been flown to Jamaica on Patricio's plane within twelve hours of the shooting and was placed aboard a boat that an official from the Jamaican Coast Guard later said was named *Estrela*.

And the police had what they really wanted, a neat package closing the books on Niccolo and Mirtha along with the publicity of a major cocaine bust. As for his kidnapping, Uncle Patricio told them he'd gone on a vacation and forgotten to tell anybody. Nobody wanted to hassle a ninety-six year old man.

"A peso for your thoughts?" Nina asked.

"I'm thinking about all the effort everybody went to over so many years to get even with Niccolo Cardeli," I said. "Particularly at the end."

She smiled. "It couldn't have happened unless you'd done what you did, you know."

"Thanks, Nina. But I think it was more than that. There were too many people trying to get him."

"All of them connected in some way or another through you. You were the catalyst."

I thought about that some more as I looked down at the Caribbean again.

"There's something else, isn't there," she said.

"Yes. Patricio told me they had two daughters. I wonder what happened to them."

Nina took my hand and squeezed. "Everybody in Key West is talking about that. They were having a party in the house on Caroline Street when their parents died. The police came to tell them and they didn't even care enough to stop partying. They apparently turned it into a celebration."

It still bothered me. "But they have nothing now. The authorities have seized all of the assets."

Nina laughed, which surprised me. "Do you remember my father asking you about Pedro Arroyo Montoya?" she asked.

It took me a second, but then I remembered Jorge telling me Pedro Arroyo was Mirtha's father, Niccolo's estranged father-in-law, a reputedly notorious Colombian drug lord.

"Yes, I remember now."

"He held a celebration, too, when he heard Mirtha and Niccolo were killed. He disappeared after having the girls flown to Colombia and the rumors are the three of them are in Rio living under false names. Those girls will be the death of him there," she said. "A fitting end."

We swung low on the approach to Brac and I was disturbed to see a mass of boats in the waters near the cottage. I had told Nina so much about the solitude and privacy, and I supposed I had been deluding myself Brac would somehow escape the hordes who have ruined so many of the other islands in the Caribbean.

A car dropped us off and we walked down the path. Nina was pulling on my hand to get me to go faster and when I reached the clearing I saw why.

"Welcome home, Dex!" a crowd yelled, and I stopped dead in my tracks.

Patricio was standing, shakily, in front of the group. He was leaning on Shando who was smoking one of his huge cigars. Tears ran down my face as I picked out Felix, Bones, Commander Peter Jones, Jesse Brady and Justin, the sharp-tongued fisherman with the walrus moustache from Trinidad. They were scattered among other people I didn't recognize, some of whom held a banner that read 'Jebediah's Boys." There must have been thirty or forty people.

Nina hugged me, careful not to pressure my shoulder. "Do you forgive me for keeping you in Miami for two days?" she asked. "We needed the extra time so everyone could get here. Some of those boats have been traveling for three days."

"Come around the front and I'll get you a drink," Bones yelled. "I need one myself."

Shando helped Uncle Patricio into his wheelchair and pushed him around the cottage to the porch. He picked up the chair, Patricio still in it, and deposited him in the center of the porch. Patricio handed me a pair of binoculars.

"Have a look, Dex," Patricio said. I could see all of the boats without the binoculars, but I took them and stood with them in my hand while I looked out over the water. I could see Justin's big trawler, the *Mariel*, and instantly recognized the lines of Jesse's *Rough Draft*, the sistership to the *Estrela* that now lay beneath the sea near Xcalak Mexico. I saw other trawlers of various types all from different ports of call around the Caribbean, and then another boat with the same lines as the *Estrela* caught my eye. It couldn't be.

I lifted the binoculars to my eyes and ranged in with shaking hands. '*Estrela*' was clearly painted on the transom, and below, in smaller script above the words identifying the home port as Cayman Brac, were the words '*Sol de Marques Snell*'.

I turned toward Patricio, speechless.

"She is yours, Dex," he said.

Tears gathered at the corners of my eyes. "Thank you, uncle. Thank you so much. But I can't accept your boat."

Patricio's face fell, and I quickly explained. "She must belong to Felix."

I turned to Felix, who was laughing along with Bones and everyone else.

"Look at the boat beside the *Estrela*," he said.

I turned again and focused on the white boat riding at anchor beside the *Estrela*. It was a dive boat, a big one. It looked new, and I wondered whose it was. Then I saw the name: *Pelican*. Homeport Cayman Brac, Captain Felix Smith.

That did it. I couldn't hold the tears back any longer and I knelt beside Uncle Patricio and hugged him as tightly as I could with one arm.

"Careful, Dex," he said. "These old bones break easily."

"A toast," Bones yelled. "As soon as I get another drink!" Then he thought better and simply held up the bottle. "A toast to Dexter and Jebediah Snell, two of the finest buccaneers who ever sailed the Caribbean," he proposed, chugging the rum directly from the bottle.

"Aye," yelled everyone else, joining him.

I felt the need to say something, and stepped up onto a stool.

"I want to thank all of you, particularly those who have traveled so far to get to Brac, and those I've never met and are here because of my father." I raised my glass in a lone toast to them.

"I've learned things about my father in the last year I would never have known without you. And I'm looking forward to learning more.

"There were many," I continued, "and at times that included me, who thought my father was engaged in something nefarious in the last years of his life. That is, something more sinister than what you suspected him of, Commander Jones."

"Guilty," Peter Jones hollered to laughter all around.

"And thanks to Bones – Christmas Carol to those who dare – I can say my father found one of the most interesting treasures in the history of the Spanish plate fleets, the wreck of the *Griffon*."

There were murmurs of interest all around, but sadness on the faces of Felix and Bones.

"In true buccaneer fashion, my father buried the treasure and left a trail of clues only two people could follow. Those two were Felix and I. Neither of us realized it then, but we were with father when he discovered the wreck in 1984."

I paused for effect. "Felix and I found the wreck, at least what's left of it, about four weeks ago. And with it, another clue." Felix and Bones looked at each other in puzzlement.

"I couldn't have deciphered the clue without Felix' help, but I daresay this clue was intended only for me." I took the medallion from my pocket and held it up. "This medallion was suspended from a pair of shrimp doors over a pile of ballast stones. It didn't mean anything to me other than the fact it had belonged to my father until Felix winched up those stones and dumped them on the work deck of the *Estrela*."

Both Felix and Bones were staring at me now, mouths agape.

"Some of those stones split apart, and it finally hit me they were not from the *Griffon*, but from the same ballast stones used to build this cottage. The stripes of lighter-colored stone through them were another clue. Just like some of the stones you see here on the front of the cottage," I said pointing to one.

"If that's the case, then where in the cottage did they come from?" asked Bones.

"They didn't. They came from the well. The treasure of the *Griffon*, of the plate fleet of 1715, is hidden in the well behind the cottage."

Bones and Felix looked at each other in disappointment and shuffled about nervously.

"The well's been searched, Dex. You and Felix searched it and so did others," Bones said gently. "And Felix and I dug it out again while you were in Colombia."

"No, it hasn't been searched. And I of anyone should have realized it. Follow me."

I led the crowd around to the back of the cottage to the hole and the pile of stone beside it.

"We searched here," I said, pointing to the hole that appeared to be the remnants of a partially repaired well. "But as I should have known, as my father intended and as Sir Henry Morgan taught us at Maracaibo, something can appear to be there when it isn't."

"That's right, Dex," Bones said sadly. "The treasure appears to be there, but we know it isn't."

I smiled and held up the medallion again. "And my father left this medallion to remind me of something I already knew."

Patricio broke out in laughter, and everyone looked at him like he was crazy. "Military school, 1984," he finally said. "Jebediah and I laughed about it together. It was one of my last happy memories of him. He told me, Dex, that you made something that was there appear not to be. The Remington statue in the Dean's office, if I recall correctly. Jebediah was so proud of you."

I smiled. "Thank you, Patricio. This hole isn't the well. The well is under here," I said, pointing to the pile of rubble beside it.

Bones and Felix stared at each other incredulously. Then all hell broke loose.

"Felix – you and the others start digging," Bones hollered. "I'll get the rum."

It only took twenty minutes or so before they'd cleared the rubble down to eight feet below the surface and came across a rusted, steel container. The container held my father's journals, complete and intact, and below it were the gold cobs. As it turned out later, just over five thousand of them.

II

Nina left three days later. Colombia was calling her home and I, of all people, understood that call.

I made my way up the path to my parents' graves and sat between them, watching the sunset out over the Caribbean. I was at peace and I knew my mother and father were, too.

The gold cobs were safe and where they should be, the only place they belonged - in the Jebediah Snell Endowment Fund along with the million dollars Nina had collected from Cardeli for the fake cocaine. More deserving children in the Caribbean would be able to go to school now, and many more would be able to explore the Caribbean aboard the *Pelican* with Felix. I no longer needed monetary wealth. I had something more important.

The *Estrela / Sol* floated gently at anchor below me and somewhere to the south the Caribbean lapped up against the shores of Colombia and connected me to Nina. Thanks to my father I would never feel alone again.

I had friends in every port

ABOUT THE AUTHOR

J P Roszell is a Canadian, and a first-time novelist. In addition to a degree in political science and an MBA, he has traveled extensively throughout the world, particularly to third world countries and regions like those in this book. Among many 'careers', he has been a senior executive with a number of multinational corporations, a yacht dealer and an entrepreneur. He has had occasion to rub elbows with the elite as well as those who make their living along the shadowy edges of society. *He knows of what he writes.*

His website is *www.roszell.ca*

NATIONAL

EXPOSURE

J P Roszell

available early 2011

turn the page for a preview of
NATIONAL EXPOSURE

1. Miami. 2005 February

"So it all comes down to this?"

The lawyer played with a paperclip, straightening it then bending it in half again before answering. "I'm afraid so, Wade."

I rattled the ice in the cut crystal rocks glass, watching the single malt scotch swirl around the cubes. The reflected lights from the nightlife on South Beach reminded me there was a whole world out there that didn't give a shit. A world populated with people who didn't give a damn about anything more than what was happening right now, or perhaps what might happen – or not happen – in the next few hours, depending on whether or not they hooked up with somebody for the night. A world that lives on a headline, a sound bite or a picture that catches their attention for a fleeting second before they dash off to the next source of instant gratification, amusement or entertainment. A world whose mindless, amoral need to elevate their heroes to pedestals so that they could derive some crude satisfaction from watching them fall had made me rich.

"And there's no other way to stop them?" I asked.

"Wade, let's get this clear. I've already stopped them. I've stopped every son-of-a-bitch who's ever dared to take us on. The laws in this country were written for people like us, and I win every time. The ridiculous part is that the publicity we get just drives our circulation higher."

He was right about that. I'd made a fortune giving the public exactly what they wanted. Scandalous, juicy bits of outrageous gossip that titillates some portion of my readers' brains that otherwise go to sleep when their hands touch my paper. Ridiculous pieces of 'news' that feed the public's desire to see their heroes torn from the very heights to which they raise them. Pieces of trash that in any other context the thinking, reasoning portion of their cerebra would identify as garbage.

"I know you'll win in court tomorrow, but that's not what I want."

"Then what the hell is it, Wade? What else is there?"

I spun around and slammed the glass on the boardroom table, smashing it. Pieces of glass and ice flew across the room as the scotch puddled on the highly polished surface of the rare wood.

"I want this fucking thing settled out of court, that's what I want. Why can't you get that through that thick legal skull of yours? Is it so difficult? Settle it, you asshole!"

The smashing of the glass shocked the lawyer but not nearly as much so as my tirade. He made a show of wiping the scotch from his custom-tailored suit jacket and cleaning his splattered glasses while he regrouped.

"They won't settle, Wade. I've told you that."

I glared at the lawyer, who I knew from experience would visibly shrink. Predictably, and to my pleasure, he quickly averted his eyes while pretending to pick the glass out of his clothes.

"You call their ambulance-chaser and get this arranged. I want those papers on my desk by 7:00 a.m. tomorrow morning."

"That's what I'm trying to tell you, Wade. They won't settle for anything less than an amount that will cripple us. I've made all kinds of offers, and they won't budge. I tell you it's just stupid. It's them, not me. Their own counsel warned them they can't win, and they still won't budge. He's frantic. He's working on contingency, so he's got a stake in this, too. "

I leaned over the table, balancing on my knuckles, elbows out. "I don't care what it is they want. Get the best deal you can. Get it on paper and on my desk by 7:00 tomorrow morning or you're fired."

The lawyer was like a rat caught in a corner. A rat desperate not just because he was trapped but because he was in danger of being separated from his cheese. "The board won't approve this," he warned.

I resisted the impulse to spit. "The board has never approved any settlement in advance. I've never even gone to them before."

"This is different. It's never cost us this much before."

"Are you threatening to call the board?" I asked.

It amused me that the lawyer had the balls to glare back at me eyeball to eyeball, but it only lasted for three seconds before he blinked rapidly twice and tried another tack. "It just doesn't make sense, Wade."

"Cut the bullshit, Joel. I know you too damn well – the way your mind works. I don't have time for your fucking games."

"Wade..."

"Shut up and listen. And listen carefully. Don't even think about an end run around me to the board or any of your other slimy tricks. I want every damned bit of your creative energy focused on getting the best deal possible. I want a deal that nobody else can get. And I want it before the verdict. Do you understand that?"

"But we're going to win, Wade. The judge is going to decide in our favor. I'll stake my life on it."

I felt the color shoot up my neck, turning my face into a cruel mask. "Perfect choice of words, Joel. If you're thinking about taking the easy way out by simply showing up for the verdict tomorrow, it *will* cost you your life."

Joel laughed nervously. "Surely you're not threatening to kill me, Wade."

I left his words hanging between us for what seemed to be an eternity, and then, subconsciously, felt the hint of a smile touching the corners of my mouth.

"Do you remember that cute little actress?" I asked. "You know – the one who died from the overdose two years ago?" I turned my back on him and pretended to look out the window to let him think about what I'd just said.

"Christ, Wade. What are you suggesting? That I had something to do with that?"

As I turned back to deliver my last threat, I knew I had him.

"I have some interesting pictures, Joel. I'm sure your wife would like to see them. I know your father-in-law would."

The color drained from Joel's face.

I was already congratulating myself and wondering what kind of settlement Joel would reach when my world crashed in. It hit me in the lower back like a wrecking ball and flung me to the floor in a twisted heap, little slivers of tempered glass from the shattered floor-to-ceiling window peppering my hair and clothing. I remember suddenly hearing the noise from the street below and smelling the ocean breeze as Joel leaned over me, panic written across his face. Heather ran in from the suite next door, screaming for security even as she was dialing 911. I couldn't feel my legs, and Joel's face was fading in and out. I managed to spit out a few words and he leaned closer to hear me.

"You'd better hope I die you son of a bitch, or that you get that settlement."

And then everything went black.

To email the author, or visit his website, go to

<u>www.roszell.ca</u>

Made in the USA
Lexington, KY
18 October 2010